ROUGH JUSTICE

Set in 1936, *Rough Justice* is the first in a dramatic new series about the lives, loves and losses of the families who live and work in and around the Turnbury Buildings.

The Flanagans, the Tanners and the Lovells all live on the top floor of the Turnbury Buildings—a crumbling Victorian tenement in the heart of London's East End. Hardworking Nell is married to Stephen. She has hidden the abuse she has suffered at his hands from her children, although most of the neighbours realise what's going on. The Tanners, an older couple in Number 56, think she must be asking for it, but nineteen-year-old Martin, eldest son of the Lovells at Number 57, has always admired Nell. When he sees Stephen attacking Nell, he can stand back no longer, but his actions have repercussions for all the families...

ROUGH JUSTICE

Gilda O'Neill

WINDSOR
PARAGON

First published 2007
by
Arrow Books
This Large Print edition published 2007
by
BBC Audiobooks Ltd by arrangement with
Random House Group Ltd

Hardcover ISBN: 978 1 405 61555 6
Softcover   ISBN: 978 1 405 61556 3

British Library Cataloguing in Publication Data available

Printed and bound in Great Britain by
Antony Rowe Ltd., Chippenham, Wiltshire

For everyone at Random House, people who have been kinder to me this year than they will ever realise

ACKNOWLEDGEMENTS

With my thanks as always to Chris Lloyd and Malcolm Barr-Hamilton of the wonderful Tower Hamlets Local History Library and Archives for their skill, generosity and patience.

My thanks also to Helen Kent of London's Transport Museum.

Although this is the story of one young woman's love for and struggle against a violent man, it is the story of many. Today, in the UK, two women die each week as a result of domestic violence. Further information can be found at womensaid.org.uk

There is also a domestic violence helpline: 0808 2000 247

PROLOGUE

The woman, so weak and so very tired, sat on the almost completely flattened ticking-covered mattress, with a tiny scrap of a child huddled beside her to keep warm. There was no bedstead—that had been sold long ago, well before the poor creature would ever have believed that one day she and her husband and daughter would be living somewhere so sordid.

Apart from the mattress, with its one thin blanket, and the ragged coat used in place of a counterpane, there was no other furniture in the room save for a rickety kitchen chair, with the just visible remains of pale green paint on one of its legs, and a rough, splintered orange box—discarded by a market trader as too damaged to be of any further use—that had been set on its side to serve as a cupboard.

The meagre light that barely illuminated the room came from an oil lamp hanging off a nail banged into a rotting rafter above their heads. The lamp swung back and forth in the wind moaning in from around the ill-fitting door that was just about held in place by its rusting hinges, and through the ragged hopsacking that had been nailed over what remained of the glass in the single window.

'Never forget, my little angel,' the woman said, her voice as frail as her bony body. 'This is going to be yours one day.'

She was showing the child a pearl and gold

brooch fashioned in the shape of a curling capital letter N. She twisted it in the light so the little one could see it better, its prettiness incongruous in the squalid surroundings. She smiled and stroked the child's cheek, and then struggled to her feet and stumbled over to the window, where she took her time concealing and pinning the brooch in the folds of the hessian sacking.

'And no one must ever take it from you. Always remember that, my little angel. It's yours. My gift to you, something to remember me by when you're all grown up.'

She smiled again at the child before going over to the makeshift orange-box cupboard. She took out a chipped thick china bowl half-filled with stale bread that had been steeped in cold tea, and gave it to the little girl.

'Now you eat that up and make yourself big and strong. You don't want to grow up and be all scraggy like your daft old mum, now do you eh?'

She put her lips to her child's soft fair curls and then sighed loudly. 'Mummy won't be long; I've just got to go and see some friends to get us some money.'

The child put down the bowl, reached out to her mother and whimpered.

'Ssshh, don't fret, this is our home now, so you stay here, all nice and safe, and don't you open that door to anyone.'

She paused, and then went over to the window again, adjusting the sacking one more time.

'We don't want to risk losing that pretty brooch, now do we, little one? There are bad people out there, bad people who'd take it off you, just like that. So we'll have to keep it nice and safe, because it's going to be yours, and it'll be our secret where we keep it, you remember that, my little angel, our special secret.'

New Year's Eve
1913

CHAPTER 1

Tears ran down the creases of Henry Tolliver's weather-beaten face, leaving salty white rivulets on his filth-ingrained cheeks. His body was shaking as violently as the battered oil lamp hanging above his head. It was rattling and swinging around after he had crashed into it during the brutal struggle that had just reached its horrific climax in the sordid little Thames-side shack. The wild swaying of the lantern threw hellish shadows up against the walls of the stinking lean-to, making it seem even more forbidding and ugly than it really was.

Henry gnawed on his dry, cracked lips. 'How could this have happened to us, Lottie?' he cried. 'How?'

His wailing sounded more animal than human, like the moans that came from the damaged creatures who somehow managed to survive in the unseen depths of the surrounding riverside slums, as they keened over the tragedy of their unspeakable lives.

'Why did you have to make me do this to you? Why?' He smacked the flimsy door frame with the flat of his hand, not even noticing as one whole side of the jamb dislodged.

'How could you? My beautiful Lottie, nothing better than a whore, going with men for money. Shaming me.' He swiped roughly at the snot dripping from his nose. 'Making me do this to you. How could you? How could you?'

Henry threw back his head and howled, wondering at the injustice of it all, and the why of it all, but deep in his heart he knew the answer only too well.

He'd come to the East End of London from the depths of the Essex marshes, a proud and fit young man, with his heart full of hope and his head full of ideas. Anything had seemed possible in those days. But gradually, like too many others who had come to depend on the vagaries of the docks and the river for their daily bread, when times had grown hard he had been seduced—at first, only now and then—by the lure of the taverns and the alehouses. He soon discovered that he liked the drink, it made him forget the futility of all those hopes and dreams he had once had, and the fact that he'd condemned his wife and child to living in nothing more than beast-like squalor. But as he became ever more inclined to spend his time—and what little money he had in his pocket—in the pubs and gin palaces on cheap booze, rather than in queuing on the stones at the dock gate waiting to be called for a day's casual labour, things began to go very wrong for Henry Tolliver. Now, on the increasingly rare occasions when he actually bothered to turn up to look for work, he found himself less and less likely to be picked. His place on the stones had been taken by healthier, younger, more sober men, just as surely as his place in his wife's arms had been taken by the sailors she had demeaned herself with by picking them up at the dock gates.

He dropped his chin to his chest. He felt sick at the very thought of what she had been doing, just as he felt sick at himself for having let down the beautiful girl he had once sworn to love for ever, because he knew she was only doing what she had to.

4

Slowly, Henry raised his red-rimmed eyes from the rotten, bare floorboards, let out a whiskey-fuelled belch, and swallowed back the bile that rose in his throat. He forced himself to stare into the gloomy corner of the foul-smelling hovel that had been their so-called home for these past six months. Eventually he managed to focus on the pile of ragged bedding and on the lifeless body of what had once been his beloved wife, but was now a broken, tarnished, grotesque puppet.

He unhooked the oil lamp from the nail jutting from the low beam above his head, and, scrubbing the back of his hand across his nose again, he turned his back on the desolation, knowing himself to be the cause of the misery he was about to leave behind him.

And knowing himself to be a murderer.

He hadn't meant to strike her. But when she had told him she was carrying another child, the thought that it might not belong to him was more than Henry could bear. He had known for months—since they had come to this place—what she'd been doing, and that she had only done it to put food on their table and to give him, Henry Tolliver, money to throw away on drink. Up until tonight he had put away that knowledge somewhere in the back of his mind, and had chosen to ignore the taunts and rumours and the gossip he heard about her in the pubs. He would do anything to buy the drink to make him forget the horror of their lives. But then when he'd come into the room just now and she had been waiting there bold as brass to tell him about the child she was carrying, all sense and reason had abandoned him, and in a moment of madness he had snapped.

It had taken no more than a few minutes, a few vile, unthinking moments, and she was dead. With a self-pitying sob, Henry stood in the doorway with his back turned on the room, and on the wife who was no longer his.

He was about to dash the lantern to the floor, to burn the wretched place to the ground—and the evidence of his terrible shame along with it—when he remembered the brooch. It would surely fetch enough for at least a couple of nights' cheap lodgings somewhere, a bit of food to fill his empty belly, and, most importantly, leave something over for enough drink to numb the pain of what he had done. Of what he, Henry Tolliver, had become. He would never have sold it when she was alive, but what did it matter now?

He rubbed the heel of his hand into his temple, trying to clear his aching, drink-fuddled head. The brooch. Would she be wearing it? Would it be pinned somewhere amongst her layers of musty old skirts and petticoats?

No, she was far too wary for that; she'd said she'd only just come home, and she'd have been too scared of being robbed while she'd been out 'working' that night to have it with her. It had to be hidden somewhere in the room.

It didn't take him long to search the few places where Lottie might have secreted the little gold and pearl brooch—the whole room, their family home, was not as big as the ramshackle sculleries tacked onto the back of the meanest of terraced, jerry-built houses—before coming to the conclusion that she must have pawned it.

But how could she have done that? When he had given it to Lottie on their wedding day, and he had told her that the brooch had belonged to his mother, his lovely young bride had taken an oath with him that she would never ever pledge it for cash. They had both sworn they would never do that, no matter what, even when times got hard; it was the bond between them, their only treasure. And, up until now, she had kept her word. Not even when they had nothing save for a few crusts of stale bread for the child. Not even when she had been reduced to going to the dock gates to pick up lonely seamen and had given them her once plump and beautiful body for money.

He had dragged them down to this: to her parting with the only token he had ever given her, the token that had signified their once pure, but now forever corrupted love, and—*how had it happened?*—to him beating the very life out of her.

With a roar, coming now from frustrated resignation rather than despair, Henry dashed the lamp to the floor, where it smashed onto the bare boards, spilling sparks, oil and its cleansing force of destruction.

As the flames took hold, eating their way greedily into the rotten wood, he was out of the door and was on the brink of making his escape along the dark alley, when a terrified whimpering froze him to the spot.

It couldn't be. Lottie was dead.

But there it was again.

He hesitated in the doorway, considering, for a long, reprehensible moment, what do to, before diving back into the room with his arm shielding his face from the heat.

Grabbing at his wife's shabby clothing, he pulled and tugged her from the tangle of bedding.

As her cold, clammy body flopped forward, what Henry saw made him start back in horror. What had he nearly done, God help him? How much worse could this nightmare become?

There, on the flattened, straw-filled mattress was the cowering form of a skinny, snivelling child.

He had nearly burned his own daughter to death.

But what was she doing here? When he'd come home, his lying trollop of a wife had sworn she'd sent the child over to the Old Dog with the other street urchins, to scrounge ha'pennies from the seamen made sentimental by the booze. She'd sent her out, she said, so she could tell him about the baby in her belly without their daughter hearing. But she'd been taking him for a fool; she had had the brat hidden away in the bedding all along.

If Lottie hadn't already been dead, Henry would have killed her there and then. He knew exactly what she'd been thinking when she'd lied to him about the child being over the road: she'd been protecting her from him, Henry Tolliver—her own father. And he knew why. She would have been scared, quite rightly, about how he would react when she told him about the thing she was carrying inside her.

The scrawny scrap of a girl stared up at him. Her pale grey eyes—made huge by terror and the thinness of her pinched little face—prickled and stung with unspilled tears. But, young as she was, she knew she mustn't cry. Her mother had taught her that crying made him angry, even angrier than usual, especially when there was that stink about him, the stink that meant he had been in the pub. And she had to be careful to keep her mouth closed tight like Mummy had told her, when she had warned her how upset he was going to be tonight.

Despite the heat, Henry did nothing at first, but then, with a self-admonishing *I don't know why the hell I should care what happens to that whore's bastard,* he snatched the child from the mattress and dragged her from the room. She couldn't help it, she whimpered again in fear, partly of the flames that were now licking their way up the hopsacking nailed to the broken windowpanes, but mostly because of her dread of her father, the man she had just seen batter her mother to death with the leg of the only chair they possessed.

Henry Tolliver dumped the child down on the icy slush in the alley, apparently oblivious of the fire that was taking hold behind them.

'What did you see back there? Tell me. What?'

The child said nothing; she just kept her mouth shut and stared up at him.

'Wait there, damn you,' he hissed through his teeth. 'Don't you dare move.' Then, taking a big gulp of air, he scrambled back through the now smoke-filled room to the lifeless form of Lottie Tolliver.

With his lungs almost bursting, he grabbed his dead wife's hand and wrenched the narrow wedding band from her emaciated finger.

Like the finger, the ring was thin and worn, but it was made of gold, so it had to be worth something. Why hadn't she pawned that instead of his mother's brooch?

Because she was a spiteful bitch, that's why.

CHAPTER 2

With his traumatised child now wrapped in the folds of his shabby black overcoat, Henry shoved his way through the crowds of revellers as they laughed and sang in their drunken huddles in the freezing, fog-shrouded riverside byways, courts and alleys. For once, he wanted nothing to do with such things; he just wanted to stick close to the high, blind walls of the massive bonded warehouses, to seek the anonymity of their shadows and the shelter they offered from the bitter wind that was slicing through his threadbare clothes as it gusted in off the Thames.

Now almost completely sobered by a combination of the realisation of the enormity of what he had done and the perishing bite of the night air, Henry came to a halt by a crumbling terrace in Old Gravel Lane in Wapping. It looked, even by a slum-dweller's standards, as if it should have been abandoned or even demolished a long time ago.

After swallowing hard and taking a deep breath, he banged on the front door with the side of his fist.

What seemed like an age passed, and then a downstairs window was thrown up with a crack of splintering wood and a muttered oath. A wild-haired woman stuck her head out into the street.

'Blast your eyes, whoever you are. What do you want, disturbing me at this time of night?'

'They say you take in young ones.'

'Who does?'

'A girl who works in the Dolphin and Crown. That pub, the one up on the crossroads.'

Henry knew what he said was true, he'd heard the barmaid talking about the woman only the other day; he'd gone in there as part of a pub crawl when the landlord in the Old Dog had refused to let him have any more drinks on the slate. The girl had been telling another barmaid where she could find someone to look after her newborn baby. Henry Tolliver now conveniently chose to forget the fact that the new mother hadn't seemed very impressed with what she'd been told the woman had to offer by way of caring for youngsters. But then maybe she'd had more choices than he did.

There was a brief silence while the woman considered this piece of information, weighing it up for reliability. She did recall a dark-haired girl, a silly daft tart who was always singing to herself like she had something to be happy about. She remembered minding her kid for a good few months—till it was carried off with the whooping cough. She knew that girl had sometimes done a bit of work in a pub over that way.

The woman decided to tolerate this intruder into her sleep for a few moments longer—maybe he had some business to put her way, and she never said no to a few bob extra.

'And what if I do take people's chavvies in?' she ventured cautiously, not wanting to seem keen, or he might try to get her to lower the price.

'I'll pay you.'

The woman let out a loud, scornful grunting sound that might have been a derisive laugh, but could just as easily have been the start of a fit of repulsively bronchial coughing.

'Will you now?' Her head disappeared back into the room, and Henry listened as she first cleared her throat and then spat noisily.

'You don't think I look after the little bleeders out of the goodness of me own heart, now do you?' he heard her rasp.

Henry closed his eyes, feeling the bony featherweight child against his chest, as sleety rain began to drive through his coat, chilling them both. 'Let me in. Please. I've got a proposition for you.'

The woman smiled horribly to herself as she unbolted the street door. She could smell someone's desperation as surely as she could sniff out a stinking fish washed up on the mud at low tide.

*　　　*　　　*

Eliza Watts, the brown-toothed old hag of a baby farmer, tied her grey, greasy wrapper more tightly around her middle—as though she had anything desirable to hide from a man—and then peered at the pitifully narrow wedding band that Henry had handed her. He had also tried to hand her the now urine-soaked child that he had produced from under his coat, but when Eliza brushed his efforts aside he had set the little one down on the cold flags of her scullery floor.

The woman curled her lip at the wafer-thin gold of the ring; she'd got this one completely wrong. Admittedly he looked a bit manky, but she really hadn't thought he'd be this mean. Guilt usually had even the poorest of them nicking something better than this as a down payment for her services. Blast him; she'd gone and let him in for

12

nothing.

'This won't pay for much,' she said, making a final effort to see if he had anything hidden away that he might just be willing to part with. 'Young as they are, these nippers have bellies to fill. So I'll be needing the next instalment sooner rather than later, or I won't be held accountable for what happens to the poor little thing. Worst comes to the worst, and it'll have to be a foundlings' home for her. You do know that, don't you?'

He nodded, a picture of self-pitying misery. 'I know.' He also knew that as sure as his soul was cursed to damnation for what he had just done to his wife, and for what he was about to do to his daughter, he had nothing more to give her. Nothing. He could have lied to himself, could have made plans that he would find work, pay this woman to care for his daughter until he could afford a decent home where he could make a life for them that would be worth living. But why bother to lie? He knew that a foundlings' home would be his child's sad lot in life. At least he wouldn't be soiling his hands any further by being the one who took her there.

Even if he could find the strength to take her to such a place himself, they'd be sure to guess he was her father and refuse to accept her. There were too many calls on the orphanages, settlements and churches around those benighted parts for them to be anything other than discerning about whom they chose to help. It would have been laughable if it wasn't so heartbreaking, but having a parent, any parent—even one as useless as him—put the child, as far as the already overpressed charities were concerned, in too fortunate a category to warrant

13

their attention.

The Lord alone knew what might happen to her if even the sanctuary of the orphanage was denied her.

'You'll have your money by the end of the week. I swear on my life.'

The baby farmer scratched herself, absorbed for the moment in something lodged in the recess of her armpit. Then she looked Henry directly in the eye. 'What's your trade?'

'I'm in the docks.'

'What? Stevedore, are you?'

He bowed his head. 'No. I'm a casual.'

With those words, Henry had sealed his child's fate.

He couldn't bring himself to look at his daughter. 'Her name's Nell,' he said, his voice cracking with emotion. 'After her grandmother. My mother.' He turned his head to hide his tears. 'May God take care of her soul.'

Eliza Watts wasn't sure whether he was talking about God taking care of his mother or of his child.

And nor was he.

*   *   *

As Henry made his way back through the crowds down towards the river in search of a ship that might prove to be his salvation—if he would ever deserve such a thing after what he had done—the bells of nearby St George's began ringing out their joyous message of welcome to the new year.

The crowds erupted into yet more ebullient shouts, laughs and cheers, and he was surrounded by roaring, drunken women trying to kiss him and hug him, even to dance with him. He pushed them all away.

What could he possibly ever have to celebrate again? All he could do was pray that 1914 would bring him some sort of peace and forgiveness, that his dead wife would find some sort of rest at last, and that their child might be granted some sort of a life—if there was a god who would even begin to listen to the prayers of a man as wicked as Henry Tolliver.

*   *   *

Eliza Watts tossed Lottie Tolliver's sad little wedding band into a cracked blue and white jug that stood on the dust-laden overmantel above the blazing fire in her front parlour, the room where she slept on a battered, old-fashioned couch. It was the only room in the house that she ever heated, and she was the only person who was ever allowed to go into it. Being suspicious of anyone and everyone, Eliza was a woman who preferred to keep her own company and her own counsel. Nell, chilled to the bone, still silent, and soaked in urine, had been dumped on a foul-smelling palliasse in one of the two upstairs rooms that were packed with all the rest of the young charges in Eliza's supposed care.

'Some chance of getting any more dough out of that one.' Eliza Watts spoke out loud even though she was the only one in the room. 'In fact, there's as much chance of that bloke turning up again with money to pay for the upkeep of his little bastard, as there is of them posh tarts getting anywhere with all their old votes for women nonsense. Votes?

15

What good's votes to anyone? Money, that's the only thing of any use.'

She spat into the fire and sniffed inelegantly, staring at the flames as she worked out her plan of action.

'I'll wait till it gets light. That's what I'll do. Then them fools out celebrating the new year'— she said *celebrating* as if it were a curse—'will have either collapsed unconscious in the street, or they'll have found their drunken way home. Then I can offload that louse-infected little mare in a bit of privacy.'

She laughed coarsely. 'Can't have me reputation for looking after all the dear little kiddie-winkies being ruined, now can I? Aw no, that wouldn't do at all.'

Poking thoughtfully at the roaring coals, Eliza Watts considered the options. 'Now let's see— Whitechapel. That should be far enough away. I mean, I don't want no one checking up on me, now do I? Bleed'n' welfare ladies. I'd never hear the end of it. Never see the back of the buggers.'

Eliza Watts had no place in her home—or her heart—for nosy parkers, or for sentimentality, or, least of all, for unprofitable children.

CHAPTER 3

The matron tapped the end of her pen on a heavy, leather-bound ledger that took pride of place on the immaculately polished desk in her office—a tiny cubbyhole of a space that smelled of a combination of boiled cabbage, coal tar soap and wet laundry. She studied Eliza Watts through her wire-rimmed spectacles, her eyes small in her chubby face, despite the magnifying thickness of the lenses. Eliza was sitting on a straight-backed chair, sniffing pitifully as she twisted a grubby-looking handkerchief through her fingers in a dramatic gesture of inconsolable anguish.

'So,' said the matron, 'she was left on your doorstep last night, Mrs Jenkins. In weather as cold as we've been having?'

Eliza Watts adjusted her features into what she believed was an even more distraught expression, but which actually contorted her face into a rictus-like grimace that was more likely to provoke horror than sympathy.

'That's right.' She shook her head in disbelief. 'Who'd warrant such cruelty, eh? It's terrible, that's what it is. Proper shocking. I tried to get her to talk to me, to try and find out where she'd come from, but I've not been able to get a peep out of her. So my hands were tied. What else could I do but find somewhere respectable for her to stay? Trouble is, see, everyone knows how I look after people's dear little ones, and so the chancers out there, well they just take advantage of me. It's my kind heart, see. It's made me a fool to myself over the years.'

The matron lifted her chin and looked along her nose at the increasingly aggravating woman. 'So you said.'

'It's a real service I provide. But I still have to pay my way.' She dabbed at an imaginary tear. 'I have to put a little bit of grub in my belly.'

'Of course, Mrs Jenkins,' said the matron, her disgust at the woman's coarse language obvious in her tone. 'As do we all.'

'Well, when I woke up this morning and found the little mite sitting out there all by herself, well . . .' Eliza Watts could only hope that the child continued to keep her mouth shut—at least until she'd made her way safely back to the anonymity of Wapping, when there'd be no chance of them tracing the non-existent Mrs Jenkins.

'My heart, it went out to her. But what could I do? I knew I couldn't afford to keep her with me, much as I'd have loved to.' She sighed histrionically. 'And her such a pretty little thing and all. So I asked around and everyone, every single soul, spoke so highly of your establishment here that I knew this was the right place to come to, to ask for help for her.'

'You asked around did you, Mrs Jenkins? And these people knew about the home. So that means you're local then.'

Eliza Watts stood up; this wasn't as easy as she'd hoped. The last thing she wanted was to be questioned by this old bag. She should have taken the little brat round to the railway arches and left her there—someone might have found her before she froze to death. Why had she been so soft-hearted?

'Look, I'm very sorry Matron but much as I'd like to stay and have a chat, I do have my own charges to get back to.'

'You've not left them alone, surely, Mrs Jenkins?' The matron intended to keep very much on the high ground in this discussion.

Eliza Watts looked suitably scandalised at the very idea. 'Of course not,' she said, crossing her fingers behind her back to excuse the lie.

She might have been a hard woman, and even a wicked old liar, but she was as superstitious as the next slum-dweller. When you had little but your wits to depend on for survival, it never hurt to shorten the odds a bit, maybe by repeating a special rhyme when you passed the fever hospital, or by touching a sailor's collar for a bit of good luck. Mind you, fat chance there was of any of that coming her way, when all she wound up with as payment for her trouble and her generosity was a cheap wedding ring—and that was probably made out of brass.

'Well that's me then.' Eliza Watts backed towards the door. 'Aw, and a happy and a prosperous new year to you and yours, Matron.'

*   *   *

Five minutes later, and without the cup of tea she had vainly supposed she'd have at least been offered—not that she would have fancied hanging around to drink it—Eliza Watts was standing in the corridor outside the matron's office. She hadn't been quick enough on her feet and the matron had followed her out and caught up with her. They were now staring down at Nell, who was sitting on a miniature Windsor chair. The tiny child hadn't shifted so much as an inch since Eliza had told her to wait there while she went and talked to the lady in the starched white cap and apron.

Now even more keen to get away—before the child opened her mouth and more awkward questions were asked—Eliza Watts replaced her sad look with a sickly smile.

She touched the matron on the arm, cocked her

19

head to one side and said, with a grateful smack of her lips, 'I know you'll take good care of the poor orphaned little dear.' Then added with what she thought was a kind touch to win the old cow over, but immediately realised was a mistake, 'Nell, her name is. Bless her little heart.'

'How do you know her name, Mrs Jenkins?' said the matron, staring icily at Eliza's grubby hand on her clean white sleeve. 'You said earlier that she hadn't said anything to you.'

'Pinned to her front on a bit of old paper,' she blurted out, and with that she marched briskly off towards the big double doors without so much as a glance over her shoulder, or even the slightest glimmer of pity in her eyes.

The matron, well aware that she would be wasting her time trying to get any further information—never mind the truth—out of such a malodorous harridan, let her go. From her long experience it was obvious that the woman was a baby farmer, who no doubt had been welched on by some slum Jezebel or other, and there were plenty of those to choose from. Anyway, it probably wouldn't hurt to keep the child. When the charitable ladies came on their visits to the home, the sight of the smaller ones—especially those with blonde curls and big grey eyes like this one had—always had them sniffling into their handkerchiefs and then digging into their husband's bank accounts to make some very generous donations.

'So . . . Nell,' she said, shooshing her stiff white elasticated cuffs up her arms. 'Up you get. You're going to have a bath, child.'

CHAPTER 4

Clara Sully, the thin-lipped, wobbling mound of a matron of the St Lawrence's Whitechapel Foundlings' and Orphans' Home, didn't think of herself as unkind, but rather as a pragmatic type of woman—and she considered practicality to be the most important trait in a matron. Why waste time on sentiment when there were ledgers to be filled, lists to be made, orders to be issued, and jobs—no matter how unpleasant—to be completed?

And the job before her—bathing this very damp and smelly child—was certainly unpleasant. One she could definitely have done without at this time of the morning, or at any time of the day for that matter.

It was all a case of bad luck. On any normal morning Matron Clara Sully would have had any number of girls on call to do it for her, as some of the older orphans and foundlings—because they were either too stupid or too disagreeable-looking to find alternative employment—stayed on as ill-paid employees of the home, despite having reached fourteen years of age. But, for some reason that Matron Sully preferred not to think about too much, Walter Thanet—the senior governor of the home's board, with authority over the entire staff in the establishment—had chosen to give them all the day off to mark the opening of the new year. He had added that so long as the cook left sufficient provisions for the day, he would take care of the younger children himself. It was only the outbreak of a spate of vomiting, and the subsequent admission of four of the children to the hospital ward, which had caused Mr Thanet, somewhat reluctantly, to request that the matron should come down from her top-floor quarters and then remain on duty with him.

Clara Sully had agreed to do so with a mixture of anger and relief: anger at missing the opportunity to visit her brother and his wife in their neat little home in Bow, but relief that the children would have her there on the premises should they need any sort of . . . well, *help* or *protection*. Not that there would be any circumstance or even any likelihood that they would need her for either of those, of course, she added to herself in the mental note that had become automatic over the years of her employment by Mr Thanet. This thought process allowed her to carry on in the self-deluding pretence that nothing wayward had ever occurred in the home. And neither would it ever occur in the future.

Anyway, it was lucky she had been there; efficient as Walter Thanet might have been when it came to fund-raising, and the eliciting of public support for the good works of the establishment, Clara was thankful that his skills in bathing vomit from little girls' naked flesh would not be called upon. It wasn't that she thought that the youngsters would suffer: even if, perish the ridiculous thought, something should occur, from what she had read and had heard they were from a class where such things were seen as normal and had no effect on them whatsoever. But all that was of no matter—what was most important was that nothing should happen that might arouse the interest of any do-gooding busybodies, resulting in a scandal and the place being brought to the attention of the authorities. It was, after all, not only the children's home, it was her home too, the place where she had lived for so many years. If it were to be closed down because of Mr Thanet's indiscretions—that didn't even happen, of course—where on earth would she go? She had every intention of making this place her home until they carried her out in all her glory, and, if she had anything to do with it, nothing was going to prevent that from happening.

*   *   *

Accustomed as she had become to children being quite filthy when they were admitted to the home, Clara Sully still could not prevent herself from gagging as she stripped off Nell's clothes in preparation for immersing her in the tin tub that she had filled with hot water and a good grating of carbolic. Dirt and disorder disgusted her. It was one of the reasons—along, of course, with the accommodation, the excellent regular meals, the free laundry and the succession of girls to clean her rooms—that she had taken to this work in the first place. It had become Matron Clara Sully's mission to introduce a little decency into the lives of those less fortunate than her. It didn't stop her feelings of revulsion, though, and not only at the dirt. The matron would also never cease to be appalled by the women who led the sorts of lives that resulted in them having children, which were then discarded.

Despite all those many years of experience,

23

when Clara Sully peeled off the child's final petticoat, she was shocked at just how thin the little girl actually was. Obviously, this tiny scrap of undernourished childhood was the unwanted offspring of some wanton creature who had neither the means nor the intention of caring for her, so why hadn't she bothered to dispose of the child earlier? The matron knew the answer. It was obvious. Those idle wretches were too lazy even to do that. She'd like to meet some of those women face to face, and give them a good talking-to, teach them some firm lessons about keeping themselves to themselves. She would make sure she instructed them in how to avoid any kind of unpleasantness with men, and so stop them breeding more of their type. It was the only answer. If she could have caught them early enough, that was what she would have done—drilled into them the unquestionable necessity of keeping themselves pure and, as she liked to think of it, unopened.

Just as she herself had done.

*   *   *

Although the child weighed barely more than a basket of vegetables, Clara puffed from the effort of lifting the still silent Nell into the bath. From the expression on the little girl's face, it was probably the first time she had ever been immersed in hot water. She looked terrified.

'I'm Matron, Matron Sully.' Clara filled an enamel jug full of bathwater, ready to pour over the child's hair. 'Now, are you going to tell me your name? You'll be living here with us now, and I have to know what to call you. The,' she hesitated over the next word, *'lady* who brought you here said you were called Nell. Is that correct?'

Nell said nothing; she just nodded, kept her eyes wide open and her mouth tightly closed.

'Is your tongue sore? Or your teeth?'

The matron was beginning to feel that she might come to regret accepting the child into the home, because it looked as if she might have some sort of deformity of the mouth, and that wouldn't go down well with the charitable ladies, they liked their orphans to be pretty and presentable. It certainly wouldn't be unusual for an unwanted child to have a defect. But she had to look on the bright side, maybe she hadn't learned to speak yet. As she was so scrawny, it was difficult to judge just how old she was. She could be anything from perhaps as young as eighteen months to as much as four years old.

Clara pulled an elbow-length gauntlet onto her hand and up her bulging forearm. 'Let's have a look in there, shall we?'

She poked a thick rubber-clad finger at the child's mouth.

Nell shook her head.

Clara wasn't impressed. She was showing the child kindness and concern and how was she being repaid? With blatant disobedience, that's how.

She shoved her glasses up to the bridge of her nose with the back of her hand. 'Come on, open up you little madam. Let me see if there's anything nasty or catching in there, or I'll have to tan your hide for you.'

The matron had no actual interest in anything the child might have to say for herself, or even if she had the ability to speak, but she had to exert her authority over her. She had seen children—especially the pretty ones—probably even younger than Nell, running rings around less disciplined members of staff.

Following a surprisingly difficult struggle, Clara got her finger into Nell's mouth, but, astonished, she immediately pulled it out again.

'Did you try to bite me?'

Clara pulled off the glove; on her finger was a single ruby bead of blood. She frowned. It was like a pinprick.

'Show me, child. What have you got in there?'

The matron was going to get to the bottom of this. With her determination sharpened by anger, she forced open Nell's mouth.

Clara let out a little laugh of surprise as she hooked out a gold and pearl brooch fashioned in the shape of a capital N.

'So that's why you've had nothing to say for yourself. You were hiding this.' Clara Sully shook her head. 'So, you're a little thief as well as being someone's unwanted brat then, are you? I'll never cease to be amazed by the ways of you gutter-prowlers from the slums.'

Nell struggled to get to her feet in the slippery bath. 'Mine,' she pleaded. 'Mine. Mummy said.'

'Mummy?' The matron's piggy eyes narrowed until they were little more than slits. Surely that Jenkins woman was too old to be her mother, and anyway it was hardly likely that her sort would have something as fine as a pearl brooch—or let it out of her sight if she did. She was beginning to feel as if she had been more than taken advantage of—she had been thoroughly duped. It was a feeling she definitely did not care for.

'Your mummy, where is she?'

Nell shook her head and, she couldn't help it, the tears started to flow. 'Mummy gone,' she snivelled. 'The chair. Hurt.' She could barely speak through her sobs. 'Fire. Hot.'

The matron tutted crossly. For goodness' sake, she didn't have time to figure out all this nonsense; she had a child to bathe and dress, and, more importantly, forms to fill in and details to enter into ledgers. She pinned the brooch to her apron bib, and patted it. It was surprisingly lovely. Feminine. Delicate.

Clara Sully had never owned a piece of jewellery before. But now that she did, it made her lips twitch into what was almost a smile of pleasure.

Why should only those bold women with powdered cheeks and rouged lips have nice things? Things that men gave them as gifts for their unspeakable—she shuddered at the thought—attentions. Women that they called *pretty*, something they had never called her. But what did she care?

Clara patted the brooch again, and told herself that by wearing it she was striking a blow against all those men who chose to ignore women like her—women who didn't have bouncing blonde curls, or big bold eyes, and who had no interest in being drawn in by men's wicked ways. She was a proud and brave pioneer against such evil.

Yes, that's what she was, no matter that the look on the child's face said otherwise. She was a pioneer.

October
1927

CHAPTER 5

Matron Clara Sully stood in the doorway of her office peering round Mr Thanet, the senior governor, as if she was hiding from someone she was secretly spying on—which she thought she was. Both she and Mr Thanet were watching Nell. Tall, grown-up, beautiful Nell. She was smiling sweetly as she squatted down in front of a little boy, fully aware that the matron was there.

Nell was whispering to the boy, so quietly that Matron Sully couldn't hear what she was saying, but the matron knew it would be something that would have got the girl into trouble if she had been able to hear her words. She thought she was so clever, sweedling up to Mr Thanet—*can I do this for you, Mr Thanet? Can I do that? Is that quick enough for you, sir?*—all the while acting as if butter wouldn't melt in her devious mouth. But she couldn't fool Matron Sully, she was always one up on her, and could always see through her and her crafty ways. She knew what the girl was up to. She wanted to steal her job.

'There you are, Sam,' Nell said softly. 'You do it like that and you won't keep tripping over them. I thought you were going to come a right cropper when you were getting down from the breakfast table just now.'

She leaned closer. 'And keep them neat in a double bow like that and you won't keep annoying Matron, and she won't keep getting so cross with you. Now wipe the dripping off your chin, stand up straight, and get yourself off to the schoolroom, before you get yourself another caning for being late.'

The little boy threw his arms around Nell's neck and kissed her, hugging her to him.

Nell ruffled his hair as she looked into his serious little face. It saddened her when the younger children, or the less clever older ones got into trouble with Matron, she could be so spiteful to them. If she could have, she would have folded them all in her arms and cared for every one of them just like the lady she remembered from long ago had cared for her. But Nell knew she couldn't take the blame for everything in her efforts to protect them from Matron's temper. Unfortunately for Sam, tripping over right in front of Matron wasn't one of the things for which she could claim responsibility.

'What a delightful girl Nell has grown up to be,' Walter Thanet said, smiling down at the scene before him. 'Always so willing and helpful, no matter what the task before her. Such an asset to the home.'

Nell turned round and returned his smile, pleased to be rewarded with such kind words. 'Thank you, sir.'

Matron Sully pressed together her already thin lips, her jowly face quivering from the strain of controlling her displeasure. She was fed up with hearing from the governor what a treasure the girl had become, and being told by the charitable ladies how patient she was, and how pretty, with her soft blonde curls, her wide, pale grey eyes, and her no longer scrawny body. Well, the very sight of her made Clara Sully feel queasy, filling her with what had become over the years a poisonous combination of resentment and, much as she hated to admit it, guilt. Not that the guilt was warranted, of course, it was just another of the girl's vile tricks that she used to upset her, Matron Sully, the person who had been kindest to her.

The matron put her hand to her chest, covering the pearl and gold pin. She knew full well that the girl had only wheedled her way into Mr Thanet's good books to make her look bad, and all because she had never forgiven her for taking the brooch off her on the day when that Jenkins woman had brought her to the home. Yet she was so sly she had never so much as mentioned the incident. Not once. Oh no, she had been far craftier than that, and had chosen instead to cast sidelong glances at the bib of the matron's starched white apron, where the jewel was pinned.

But Clara Sully had never stopped wearing the brooch, because it would be a bad day all round when she let a mere girl get the better of her. Especially a girl who would do better to be grateful that she had been taken in at all, what with her coming from a baby farmer and not being a true foundling, instead of acting with such impertinence to the one who had rescued her. But that was the trouble with young women today—no gratitude. Any right-minded person would be able to see immediately how kind she had been to the nasty little wretch, and that her generosity alone—never mind all the time she had taken to instruct her in the ways and the manners of decent people—made Matron Sully fully entitled to wear the brooch whenever she wished. Yes, it would be obvious to anybody, but not to Nell.

The matron nibbled at the inside of her cheek,

still staring at the girl as she fussed over the little boy, hitching up his socks.

How had that pathetic, scraggy toddler blossomed into such a scheming, irritating beauty? And why did she have to pretend to be so cheerful all the time? That girl should have just a tenth of the worries that the matron had, and maybe then she'd stop this phoney grinning like a fool. What with all the talk of adoption societies going on all over the place, if the board didn't watch out, the home would be a thing of the past, and then what would Clara Sully do? She had given her life to caring for these selfish, unappreciative little monsters, and how did they repay her? Insolence and begrudging her any little thing for herself, that's how. Why shouldn't she have a modest token by way of payment?

It wasn't bloody fair. It wasn't bloody fair at all.

The matron turned away hurriedly so that Nell wouldn't be able to glimpse her burning red cheeks, alarmed that such a profanity had slipped into her mind.

What if it had actually slipped from her mouth, and Mr Thanet had heard her?

That was the effect the spoiled little madam had on her. She was worse than a witch.

She spun back round, surprisingly quickly for such a big woman. 'Have you nothing better to do than play with that child?' she snapped over Mr Thanet's shoulder, the words fired at Nell like bullets.

Nell winked at the little boy, stroked his cheek and lifted her chin in the direction of the schoolroom. 'Go on. Hurry up. But don't run.'

For once, young Sam was only too pleased to be

off to his lessons. The matron scared the wits out of him at the best of times, but when she was in a mood like this she completely terrified him. He didn't even need to feel the welts on his backside to remind him of what she could do when roused.

Nell rose to her feet, being careful not to lift herself to her full height as she was now considerably taller than the matron, and Nell knew that for some reason this infuriated the older woman.

'Good morning, Mr Thanet, Matron Sully,' she said politely. 'What would you like me to do today?'

'I'll deal with this, Mr Thanet,' said the matron, before the governor could speak. 'I know how busy you are.'

'Well, I am rather, Matron Sully,' said Mr Thanet with a pleasant nod, only too glad of the opportunity to slip away for a post-breakfast browse of the newspaper followed maybe by a short nap before luncheon.

'If there's anything I can do to help, sir?' Nell kept her gaze lowered, wary of annoying the matron any more than necessary.

'That won't be necessary, my dear,' said Mr Thanet, not wanting his morning spoiled by having to do anything that resembled actual work. 'But, as always, thank you for your kindness.'

Clara Sully barely managed to keep her lip buttoned as she waited until the governor was out of earshot; she then stepped out into the corridor.

'Right, bedding; first floor,' she barked, knowing it to be the worst of all the jobs in the home— stripping and then laundering the almost invariably soiled sheets from the cribs and cots of the younger inmates. It was even worse than cleaning the lavatories, especially in such cold weather, because the steamy heat of the laundry made the chilblains of those unfortunate enough to be selected for the task tingle, irritating them so badly that without self-discipline they would scratch them until they bled.

'Right away, Matron,' said Nell courteously, annoying Clara Sully so much that the woman had to stop herself from slapping the girl around her simpering, smiling face—the privacy of the office, not the corridor, was the place for that.

The matron had intended to pick out a couple of other troublesome girls to help her in the laundry, but after that behaviour, why should she? *Anything I can do to help, sir?* Let the ungrateful wretch do it all by herself for trying to make her look inadequate in front of the governor, for showing her such contempt.

She watched Nell walking away, so briskly, so artificially keenly that she felt like running after her to give her a good shake.

This time, the girl really might have pushed her too far.

CHAPTER 6

A dense, wintry darkness had fallen outside the tall narrow windows before Nell had at last finished her work in the laundry—a grim, double-height corridor-like space that ran along the length of the whole of the back of the home. Her hands were red raw from scrubbing and wringing and mangling, and her arms and back ached from draping the piles of wet linen over the drying racks, and from tugging the ropes through the pulleys to lift the racks high into the air. Her clothes and hair were damp through from the steam and the constant dripping down from the sheets above her head. She was doing her best not to think about her chilblains, but she couldn't deny that she was worn out. Despite her tiredness, she knew that rather than retreating to the dormitory, falling onto her bed and giving in to the deep sleep she so craved, she would have to go into supper or risk inflaming the increasingly bad-tempered Matron Sully to the point where she resorted again to physical punishment. Nell ached enough without being beaten with the cane across the back of her thighs into the bargain.

She walked slowly along the ill-lit passageway that led from the laundry back into the main building, with the gas mantles popping and fizzing and her footsteps ringing on the flagstones. She paused for a moment to glance at her reflection in the glass-panelled door at the end of the passage, patting at her hair, trying to make herself look at least reasonably tidy—as if she could ever reach the standards Matron Sully expected of her. And then she heard it: the supper bell sounding the first of its six chimes calling the children to eat. She'd had no idea it was that late. She had to move—fast—or she'd be in bother yet again.

She took the short cut, haring through the narrow walkways that led off to the kitchen and the washrooms, and skidded into the chilly refectory, managing to slow to a more dignified pace just as the final strike rang out. With chin lowered, she walked over to her usual place at one of the long, bare trestle tables, sat down, put her hands together and began to speak the familiar words of the grace. Even with her eyes closed, she could feel the glare of Matron Sully burning into her, knowing she would be thinking what a sight she looked with her wet hair stuck to her head and her grey serge uniform dress clinging in sodden folds to her legs.

The matron was sitting alongside Walter Thanet on a dais at the far end of the room at the high table, which, as always, had been draped in freshly laundered, crisp white napery. But knowing that even a quick peek in their direction while they were eating could provoke rage in the matron, Nell knew better than to return the woman's stare. She really didn't know why, but no matter how hard she worked, punishments came too easily these days for her to risk doing anything that could be construed by Matron as showing even the slightest hint of insolence. So, instead, just as all the older children did each evening, Nell lifted the lid off the earthenware pot that had been set out earlier by the cook, and began ladling out the thin, watery stew for the younger children seated at her table, only serving herself when everyone else had a full bowl.

As the children ate their supper—mopping up every last morsel of gristle and pearl barley with the slab of dry, greyish bread they had each been given—and as the matron and governor savoured their mutton chops, parsnips and crisply roasted potatoes smothered in thick gravy, a girl stood at a lectern and read out improving verses from the Bible. Nobody else in the cold, draughty room spoke except for the two adults at the high table, who were engaged in what sounded to Nell's ears almost like an argument.

'Oh no, Matron Sully,' said the governor firmly, with a rather superior look on his face. 'I really don't think it would be sensible to allow that.'

'So you said, Mr Thanet.' The matron paused, building up to her trump card. 'But we can't keep young people here against their will once they have reached a certain age, now can we? How would that appear should the board come to hear of it? People might start making enquiries into the way the place is run.'

Walter Thanet put down his knife and fork, dabbed his lips with his napkin, and sipped from his glass of water.

*   *   *

With the youngsters' meagre meal over, and the tables cleared, Nell walked towards the door, looking forward to the blessed relief of being able to sleep at last.

Just as she was about to enter the dormitory, already unbuttoning the cuffs of her dress, she felt a tap on her shoulder. She half turned to see Matron Sully standing behind her, grease from her rich meal still glistening on her lips.

'I want to see you in the office. Now. So don't just stand there staring at me, girl, come along. And dress yourself properly. Do up those cuffs.' She looked Nell up and down. 'I really fail to understand how, after all my hard work, you have learned nothing about the manners and the behaviour of decent people.' She sighed disapprovingly. 'I suppose it was always too much to ask, turning a child from the gutter into a person of propriety.'

The matron thumped away along the corridor with Nell following at a respectful distance; she could only wonder what she was supposed to have done wrong this time. She was sure she had done the laundry as well as humanly possible, especially considering that she had had to do it all alone, and there was nothing else she could think of that might warrant a punishment. She hadn't even been late for supper.

*   *   *

As Nell entered the little room, Matron Sully was already sitting at her desk with her back to the door. 'Mr Thanet and I have decided,' she said, flicking through a pile of papers, 'that the time has come for you to leave.'

Nell didn't know what to say. She couldn't have been more shocked if the matron had reached out and hugged her to her bosom. And although she couldn't see the woman's face, and it was hardly in the matron's nature, Nell could only think that she was playing a trick on her, that she was teasing her for some reason. There was no other explanation.

'The usual firms will be contacted, and enquiries made regarding opportunities for employment, although I can't think of many positions you'd be fit for, not with your attitude.'

'I'm very sorry, Matron Sully, but I don't understand.'

'Don't play the fool with me, girl. You heard what I said—the time has come for you to leave.'

'Leave? Leave where? Not here? I can't. I'm not old enough.'

'Of course you are, you ridiculous girl.'

'But I'm not, I'm—'

'Fifteen,' the matron interrupted her. 'Almost sixteen, in fact. So rather than argue with me, you should be grateful you weren't asked to leave some time ago. Although even that's too much to expect from the likes of you, I suppose.'

Nell wasn't listening to her any longer. 'How do you know how old I am? I don't even know that.'

She had never dared speak to the matron in such a way before, but fear and confusion were making her reckless.

Matron Sully inhaled deeply and noisily through her nostrils, more a whinny than a breath. 'Because I know everything about every child in this place.'

'No.'

'Oh yes.' She stabbed a dimpled finger at the rows of leather-bound ledgers stacked neatly on the shelves above her desk. 'And that's how. From those books. Those books that cannot lie because I wrote every one of the words within them. Not that it's anything to do with you, of course. And from the way you've begrudged doing every little task ever asked of you, I'd have thought you'd be glad to leave here. You are a stupid, ungrateful girl. You've been fed, sheltered, and educated—even taught how to use a typewriting machine.'

'Only so that I can do your and Mr Thanet's chores in the office.'

That had the matron turning around all right.

Nell took a step backwards, terrified by what she had just done, but knowing she had to carry on. 'I want to speak to him, to Mr Thanet.'

41

The matron smiled unpleasantly. 'Think you can get round him do you, you with your pretty face? Well, that's where you're wrong. You're far too old to hold any appeal for the governor. And, while we're on the subject, when you were younger it was only because I protected you from him that you were left alone. I thought that that in itself might warrant some gratitude.'

Nell frowned. 'I don't understand what you mean by that either, but if you ever protected me from anything, then I know why. It was because of that.'

She pointed at the gold and pearl N pinned on the bib of the woman's apron, struggling, as she always did when she dared to snatch a look at it, to catch the memory that flitted around in the shadows of her mind. The memory was of someone so kind and beautiful she was more like an angel from the books that they let her read at Sunday school than an ordinary woman. And she was sure that the woman had cared about her, maybe had even loved her; but then there was something else, something about a fire, and a man who had hurt the lovely woman. But it was a memory she could never quite grasp.

Nell dropped her head and stared down at the floor, feeling the familiar confusion of loving warmth and fear. She then lifted her chin slowly and stared directly at the woman. 'My brooch,' she said quietly. 'And because I work harder than anyone in here—Mr Thanet always says so. And I don't know why but that seems to make you angry with me.'

'Oh he's always telling you that, is he? That he thinks you're such a hard worker.' Her voice was low, menacing. 'How charming. So I suppose you're planning to steal my job from me, are you?' She rose to her feet and took a step towards Nell. 'And that's why you're so keen to stay.' She poked Nell hard in the chest. *'You want my job.'*

'Matron Sully, I promise you, I don't want to cause any trouble for you. I just want to ask Mr Thanet if I can stay here. Ask him to go to the board and see if they can find me a proper job in the home so I can stay. Not your job, of course. Truly, not yours. I would never be able to do what you do. But whatever job I'm given, I'll do it however you tell me to, honestly I will. And I'll do anything. Please. I've nowhere else to go.'

The thought of having Nell hanging around the place, continuing to cast her furtive little glances at the brooch, had been almost too much for Matron Clara Sully. Now that she had been so insolently open about it, actually talking about the thing, well, the situation had become intolerable. Worse, if Mr Thanet really did think that the girl was capable of doing her job, what would that mean for her, a woman who had given her life to the home? Employing someone like this troublemaker would certainly be cheaper for the board, and as the girl had no idea about the governor's 'special interests' in the younger ones he'd probably be doubly keen for her to take over.

It all made her resolve even firmer. She'd been right all along, she had no option; she had to get rid of her, and now she knew it had to be without delay. It was that little witch or her.

'Matron Sully, about the brooch—' Nell was about to say that she could keep it if it meant so much to her, and if she could stay in the home, stay there with the other children who were her only family, then she would do anything. But the matron didn't let her finish, wouldn't even listen.

'For God's sake girl, if it's so important to you, just take the damned thing will you.' She fumbled around unpinning the brooch, not even noticing that she had taken the Lord's name in vain. 'This thing has caused me nothing but misery from the day I set eyes on it. Just like you and your conniving ways. Well, let me tell you, you won't get the better of me.'

She thrust the brooch at the now totally amazed Nell, who, without thought, immediately put it deep into her pocket, her fingers outlining the unfamiliar feel of the bumps of the pearls, the curling shape of the gold N, the sharpness of the pin.

'Now get out of my sight. You will leave here first thing in the morning, before breakfast, and I'll hear no more about it.'

She would have sent her away there and then, but she had to be careful: if she did so and Mr Thanet were to hear about it, she'd have some explaining to do. It was going to be tricky as it was. He'd already taken some persuading on the matter when the matron had told him over supper that it was Nell who had asked to leave the home. He'd actually come close to accusing her of lying, had even raised his voice to her. So, for her own peace of mind—and for her reputation—Matron Sully had to put a stop to all this nonsense right now. Just in time, before things got out of hand, and her position was jeopardised any further.

'But, Matron, please.'

'Get out' were the final words that Nell would

ever hear the matron speak.

CHAPTER 7

When Nell heard the sounds of the children assigned to early morning cleaning duty sweeping and polishing in the corridor outside the dormitory, she was already sitting fully dressed on the edge of her neatly made bed, having barely slept all night. She had been scared to leave any earlier, but was even more scared to wait any longer. Obeying Matron Sully had become too much of a habit to shake easily.

She stood up, her legs feeling unsteady, and went downstairs to the older girls' washroom to get ready to leave the only home she could ever remember.

As she stood at the sink and washed her hands and face, Nell wondered if she would ever see young Sam again. How would he ever manage without her looking out for him? How would any of the little ones manage?

She sniffed quietly, dried her face and her tears on the rough towel that hung from the peg behind the door, and put on her coat.

*   *   *

Nell left the building by the side door where the tradesmen delivered their goods, so avoiding going past the matron's office—not that she'd be out of bed at this early hour—and stepped out into the cold and misty morning. She gripped the brooch tightly—her one and only possession—and pushed it deep down in her coat pocket. She had somehow always known it was hers, this brooch that was in the shape of the letter that began her name—N for Nell.

*   *   *

Before that day, Nell had only ever left the home on Sundays, and then only to go just around the corner to the meeting hall to attend the religious services that were held in the mornings, and back again in the afternoon for Sunday school. And so she certainly wasn't prepared for the crush, noise and bustle of weekdays in Whitechapel High Street. It wasn't quite eight o'clock and yet the place was already heaving, crowded with people who all seemed to be hurrying somewhere—unlike Nell, who had nowhere to go and who had just been wandering aimlessly through the maze of unfamiliar back streets, until she had stepped out into this bedlam.

There were horses pulling carts stacked high with hay, market stalls being set out with displays of shiny fruit and colourful vegetables that looked far nicer than any she had ever seen the cook cutting up in the kitchen, and motor buses packed with passengers. Trying to walk along the pavement felt just like the dream she sometimes had about being a tiny child carried by a huge man. In the dream she was cold and wet, and there were crowds and crowds of people, and whoever was holding her couldn't force his way past them and it made him angry. She didn't like the dream, but at least it wasn't noisy. Out here on the street, it was

46

the noise that alarmed her most of all. After being in the home where Matron had insisted that all conversations should be conducted at little more than a whisper, and where everyone had been ordered to walk through the dun-coloured corridors at a 'decent' speed, it was like being in a madhouse.

Everyone seemed to be shouting, calling out to one another, issuing instructions, laughing as though they would never stop. Horses whinnied and motor vehicles roared, horns were sounded and wagon drivers hollered.

Nell, with her chin down, eyes lowered and shoulders hunched against the already wintry October weather, walked along the pavement keeping close to the wall, not wanting to be seen, and definitely not wanting to cause a fuss. She had learned from her life in the home that silent invisibility was always the safest option—as had been proved last night when she had been foolish enough to answer back to the matron.

She was shivering; her dress hadn't dried out properly from working in the laundry the day before, and the thin serge of her overcoat did little to keep out the piercing wind. She was used to never being really warm in the home, but this was different. If she didn't find somewhere to dry off, she thought she might die from the cold. Nell was beginning to panic: what if she couldn't find anywhere? What would become of her then?

As a feeling of sickness rose in her empty belly a man absorbed in reading his morning newspaper walked straight into her, sending her stumbling backwards.

'Watch where you're going, will you?' he barked,

47

striding off without even offering to help her.

Nell tried to save herself, but the thin soles of her shoes slipped on the damp paving stones and she lost her footing, finishing up almost sitting on top of a petite, red-haired young woman who was kneeling on a coconut mat, scrubbing the front step of a pub.

'Oi! Look out you dozy ha'p'orth,' she yelled. 'You've knocked my bloody hat right off my flipping head, and soaked my sleeve all the way up to my blooming elbow.'

'I'm very sorry, miss.' Nell was now round-eyed with fear. Would the woman attack her? 'I didn't mean to. Honestly I didn't.'

She bent down to right the woman's bucket, but her frozen fingers had no grip and the pail went crashing to the pavement, sending what water there was left all over Nell's already chilled bare legs. She burst into tears of miserable self-pity.

Getting to her feet, the red-haired young woman sighed loudly. 'All right, don't make such a bloody fuss. It's only a drop of water. And it was your own fault. I didn't chuck it at you. Not like you chucked it over me.'

She put her arm around Nell's shoulders. 'I'm probably going to regret ever doing this, cos you might be a mad axe-murderer for all I know, but look at you, I can't leave you out here, you're trembling. Come on, come inside and we'll get you all dried off.'

Nell resisted for a brief moment—she had never seen anyone with so much powder and lipstick plastered on her face—but not knowing what else to do, she gave in and let the woman usher her inside the pub.

48

As she pushed her way past the folds of a heavy red velvet curtain that hung the full length of the doorway, Nell gasped. She had never seen anything like it.

The place was glittering with ornate bevelled mirrors and burnished brass rails and gasoliers. There were rows of variously sized and coloured bottles on glass shelves, polished wood and ceramic pumps on a curving mahogany bar that was divided up by etched-glass snob screens.

Nell thought it must be one of the most beautiful places in the world.

And it was so warm. The heat was coming from what looked like a freshly set fire that was blazing away in a tiled and blackleaded grate, and the air was thick with heavy scents that she couldn't recognise or name, but which reminded her of Mr Thanet.

'So, what do they call you then, sweetheart?' said the young woman, peeling Nell's coat from her drooping shoulders. 'They call me Sylvia.'

'Nell, miss,' she said, making sure her brooch was safely tucked into her fist, a memory flashing into her mind of being told to keep it safe in her mouth before the man came.

'That's a nice name; I had a friend called Nell once.' Sylvia pulled a chair close to the fire and draped the coat over it to dry. 'But she got married and moved over to south London. Gawd knows why she did that.' She turned back to face Nell. 'And I'm not *Miss*, I'm . . . Here, hang on a minute. Your dress. Isn't that one of them they wear in that home that's off the back of the high street?'

Nell nodded. 'Yes, miss.'

'You've not gone and pinched it off their line or

49

nothing, have you?'

'No, it's mine.' Nell's head had started aching and her fingers and heels were tingling as the heat warmed her skin.

'So what were you doing out in the street then?'

'I left this morning,' she said, then added hurriedly, 'because I'm sixteen.'

Sylvia frowned; there was something funny going on here. 'I thought they were meant to get you girls work once you turned fourteen. Yeah, that's right they do, they get all the girls from that place jobs in the schmutter trade. I've got customers who've taken them on as finishers and pressers.'

She paused, looking Nell up and down, taking in the girl's bare legs and her damp dress. She knew the home had a bit of a reputation for being strict and for not exactly overflowing with the milk of human kindness, but surely even they wouldn't send a kid out dressed like that, not in this weather. Sylvia was wearing a good thick coat and warm stockings, and she felt bloody cold enough.

'Here, you haven't run away have you? Cos if you have, then I don't want you here, because I'm not having you bringing any trouble to my door; this is a respectable house.'

'No. It was Matron, she told me I had to leave.'

'Well where are your things then?'

'I haven't got any.'

'So you're saying they kept you on longer than they should have, but then they just chucked you out with nothing? Are you telling me the truth?'

Nell shrugged, embarrassed, but not daring to mention the row over the brooch. 'Matron let me stay until now because I was doing all her office work.'

She pressed her lips together, determined not to cry again. 'I can do typewriting, you see. And I did loads of laundry and cleaning, and looked after the little ones, taught them their letters if they were finding it hard. But for some reason she got all upset with me, and said I had to go.'

'Did you steal something? Is that why she got upset with you?'

'No.' Nell closed her hand tighter round the brooch. 'I never took anything, not all the time I was there. I never even stole the vegetable peelings from outside the back of the kitchen, not even when I was really hungry, even though some of the others did. I don't know why she was always so cross with me. I always worked as hard as I could. And Mr Thanet, he said I was the hardest worker in the home. Best he'd ever had.'

Sylvia's face softened. 'You say you did laundry and cleaning, eh? So where are you working now then, Nell?'

'Nowhere.' Nell's bottom lip started to wobble. 'I don't really know how to get a job.'

'Right.' Sylvia fussed about with Nell's coat, turning it over and moving the chair nearer the fire. 'Tell you what, you wait there for me a minute, sweetheart, and I'll be right back.'

As Sylvia disappeared through a door at the side of the bar, Nell could hear her calling, 'Bernie, come down here will you, darling, there's someone I want you to meet.'

'Aw, Sylv, do I have to?'

'Come on, Bern, do us a favour. It won't take long. It's important.'

There was a sound of floorboards creaking and

51

of a chair dragging heavily across a floor from somewhere above Nell's head, followed by footsteps coming down a flight of stairs. Then Sylvia reappeared with a man behind her, his huge frame making the diminutive woman look even tinier. He was completely bald with a big, round, friendly face.

'Bernie, this is Nell. Nell, this is my husband who runs the pub with me.'

Bernie Woods nodded and smiled.

Nell did her best to smile back, but hearing that this man who looked to be about Mr Thanet's age—at least fifty—was married to Sylvia, who couldn't have been more than in her late twenties, was something of a shock. He was old enough to be her dad. But perhaps that was how things worked in the world outside the home and outside the books at Sunday school. She felt bewildered. She was beginning to think she didn't know much about anything at all.

'And, do you know what?' Sylvia continued. 'We've been looking for a good, hard-working girl for a while now, not a lazy, dozy mare like the ones we've had working here lately.' She looked at Bernie and rolled her eyes. 'Right Bern?'

'Right Sylv.'

'So, how d'you fancy doing a bit of cleaning work for us?'

Before Nell could answer, Bernie had cut in. 'You can give her more than a bit of cleaning, Sylv. With her looks we'll have the blokes flocking in if we stick her behind the bar.'

'I think you could be right.' Sylvia eyed Nell closely, not as she had done before, but this time taking in her trim figure, her wide grey eyes, and

52

her badly cut yet still pretty blonde curls.

She thought for only a few moments. 'Here, I'll tell you what, Nell, you can do the cleaning down here, help me upstairs with a few jobs, maybe a bit of laundry and that, and then you can have a couple of hours behind the bar. How does that sound?'

'Thank you, miss.' Nell could hardly say the words, not because she was still shocked at her being married to Bernie—that was all forgotten in this fast-moving, strange world—but because she was so excited; her mouth had gone dry and she felt as if her tongue was going to stick to the roof of her mouth.

Then cold reality struck her like a slap in the face from Matron Sully. 'But first I have to find somewhere to stay.'

Sylvia shrugged. 'Don't worry about that, you can live in if you like. How'd that suit you?'

Nell stared down at the ground, feeling stupid, just like she did whenever Matron had scolded her for getting something wrong. 'Live in? I don't know what that means.'

'It means I'll sort out a room for you here, Nell.' She nodded towards the door by the bar. 'Upstairs. We've got loads of space. Rooms we don't even go in, let alone use. And you can have your meals chucked in and all, and we'll get you a couple of frocks, a sight better than that one, and, let's say what, five bob? No, don't let's get into an argument over it, seven and six a week?'

Nell nodded, her face glowing with the gratitude that she felt towards this wonderful woman.

It was now Sylvia who couldn't believe her luck: a general dogsbody for seven and six a week, a couple of frocks off the market, and a bit of grub. She could already imagine having a lovely long lie-in of a morning before sitting down with a nice cup of tea. Living exactly the life she'd expected she was going to have the day she'd agreed to marry Bernie, when she'd been working for him as a barmaid.

Bernie patted Nell on the head. 'Good girl,' he said, and made his way back towards the door by the bar.

'I'll leave you two girls to sort out the details,' he said, puffing as he started to climb the stairs. 'I'm back up to the kitchen to finish off my breakfast. And from the sound of that girl's rumbling belly, I reckon she could do with a bit of something and all, Sylv.'

'I'll make her a couple of rounds of toast,' said Sylvia, following him through the doorway. 'You warm yourself by the fire, Nell, while I go and get the bread. And give that coat a turn or it'll scorch.'

*　　　*　　　*

Nell watched in amazement as Sylvia sat next to her by the fire and first toasted the thickly sliced, really white, fluffy-looking bread on a long metal fork, and then spread it with bright yellow butter—something she'd only ever seen when taking Matron in her afternoon crumpets, certainly something she'd never eaten. Sylvia then put big dollops of glistening deep red jam on top.

Nell ate three of the thick slices and drank two cups of tea with sugar and milk, out of the prettiest cup and saucer—even better than Matron's—she'd ever seen. It was as if the angels in those books at

Sunday school had lifted her up.

'Better?' asked Sylvia.

'Yes, thank you very much, miss.' Nell shifted slightly on her chair so that she wasn't looking Sylvia in the face. 'There is one thing, though.'

Here we go, thought Sylvia. She should have known it was too good to be true. 'And that one thing, what would that be then?'

'What your husband said, about blokes flocking in. I didn't really know what he meant. What do I have to do?'

Sylvia covered her spluttering laughter with a hurried coughing fit.

'You don't have to do anything, darling,' she finally managed to spit out. 'When you're a young girl with looks like yours, men will take a proper shine to you. They're only interested in one thing about a girl, see, the whole bloody lot of them. You know what men are like.'

'No, not really, I don't think I do.' Nell was slowly shaking her head. 'I've only ever really known one man, and that's Mr Thanet. He's the governor at the home, and Matron said I was too old for him to be interested in me.'

This time, Sylvia's coughing fit didn't have to be put on.

CHAPTER 8

'Well, I must say, Nell, you've picked this up in no time, darling.'

Nell smiled across at Sylvia, as she gave the brass rings around the beer pumps a final polish.

'It's all so beautiful, I feel lucky that you let me do it.'

'I have to admit I hadn't been seeing the Hope and Anchor in that sort of a light lately. It's been more like a bloody millstone round me flaming neck than a thing of beauty—what with all the cleaning and scrubbing involved. It was all too much for one person to cope with. You've brought a proper breath of fresh air to the place. It's been like having a special friend living here with me, or even the daughter I might have had.'

'Why haven't you had children, Sylvia, you'd be a smashing mum?'

Sylvia suddenly found herself preoccupied with a smudge on the front of her dress. 'Didn't happen, that's all. After I had a bit of trouble. Anyway, I'm happy enough. And I've got you now, haven't I?'

She looked at Nell, studying her shining hair, and her soft, unblemished skin. How old *was* she?

Nell was apparently concentrating on folding the rag she'd been using as a duster into a neat square, flattening it firmly on the bar with slow sweeps of her hand. 'I don't remember my own mum, Sylv. Like I said, all I do know is there's someone I think I remember, a kind, beautiful lady, but then there was a fire and then I was in the home, and . . .' She ran a finger round the outline of the brooch she now never failed to pin onto whatever she was wearing. 'For some reason I always knew this was mine, mine by rights; something to do with remembering someone, and the fire.'

Nell lifted her chin and looked at Sylvia. 'But I hope she was like you, Sylv, however old I am. Though I reckon we're more like sisters, you and me.'

Sylvia bit down on her scarlet-stained bottom lip and held out her arms. 'Come over here and give me a cuddle, you silly great ha'p'orth.'

Nell hugged her tightly. 'I can't remember ever being this happy. Not ever.'

She had had more loving attention in the time she'd been at the Hope and Anchor than she had experienced in her whole life before she had bumped into Sylvia, on that day when the man had knocked her over. Now Christmas was coming, and Sylvia was promising to put on what she called 'a really good do'. And then there was Stephen Flanagan.

Could her life get any better?

Nell suddenly pulled away from Sylvia, went behind the bar and gave the pumps another unnecessary rub with the rag. 'I'd better get on.'

Nell knew Stephen Flanagan was a bit of a sore point with Sylvia for some reason—although she always said she could never explain why—and, she didn't know how, but Sylvia seemed to be able to read her mind whenever she was thinking about him.

'Nell, you do know how old that man is, don't you?'

Nell laughed—not very convincingly. She knew Sylvia was serious about this, and had become even more so over the past few weeks as Nell had grown closer to Stephen. 'Sylv, I told you, I haven't even got any idea how old I am, let alone how old anyone else is.'

Sylvia moved closer to Nell, reached up and brushed her soft fair hair from her forehead. 'Look at you, however old you are, you're flipping lovely,

Nell. Any man would be proud to have you on his arm, so why bother with an old bloke like Stephen Flanagan?'

'But you're younger than Bernie.'

Sylvia shrugged dismissively. 'But I'm not a kid, am I? You told me you reckon you're sixteen, and I know I told Bernie you're eighteen, but me, I truthfully wouldn't put you at more than fourteen, fifteen at most. And as for Stephen, the man's got to be at least forty-bloody-five years old, and that's not including the year he had measles.'

'He's nice to me, Sylv. He's kind. And he says such nice things to me.'

'I know, but there's something about him, Nell.'

'Please, Sylvia, don't let's get stuck on this again. We're opening up soon, and I've not even polished the glasses yet.'

Sylvia leaned her back against the bar, taking in the sparkling bottles on the spotless glass shelves, the glow of buffed wood, and the glint of firelight sparking off the brass. Nell was more than a breath of fresh air; she was a bloody force of nature. Sylvia had never seen the place looking so good or anyone work so hard in all her life. The home might have had a rotten reputation for the way it treated the kids it was supposed to be caring for, but it knew how to train them to graft for a living all right. A few more girls like Nell working for her, and Sylvia would have been able to open a whole chain of pubs, and just sit on her arse all day watching them earning her money. But now Stephen—'just one more pint'—flaming Flanagan had his eye on her. He might have been a big drinker—in fact he was in the pub just about every day—but he wasn't a stupid man. Far from it.

58

Sylvia always tried to give people the benefit of the doubt, but he made her suspicious for some reason. From what she'd heard he'd had some sort of a turn since his wife had gone amongst the missing. Mind you, who could blame her for doing a runner from him and those horrible twins of his? Good on the woman, whoever she was, was Sylvia's opinion.

She closed her eyes and let out a long slow breath. If Nell decided she was going to go off with the old bugger, she'd be like flipping Cinderella, but without the benefit of a fairy godmother. But was she just being selfish, not wanting to lose her?

Sylvia plastered on a smile. 'Darling, you do know—and you mustn't mind me saying this—that all I want is for you to be happy, don't you? But to be honest with you, love, wouldn't you miss all this? We have a good laugh working here together, don't we? And going shopping down the market. Having our cup of tea and toast together. You always love that. You would miss it, I know you would.'

Nell blinked back the tears that were threatening to show her up in front of Sylvia. 'Course I'd miss it. All of it. Keeping everything looking nice, having you to talk to.'

She couldn't control the urge to cry any longer. What was wrong with her? She'd never been so happy, but she'd never cried so much in all her young life either. 'And having you as my friend,' she sobbed. 'Everything.'

Sylvia reached across the bar and took Nell's face in her hands. 'I've always said it: you're a daft great ha'p'orth. And I'll never stop being your friend, but I won't stop worrying about you either.

Please, Nell, please think about it.'

'He only wants me to go down the Lane for a wander.'

'Yeah, and—' Sylvia paused, searching for an explanation that Nell would understand. Not easy, when she didn't really know what she meant herself. 'And the snake only wanted Eve to have a little nibble of his apple, if you get my meaning. You've been to Sunday school, you know what happened next.'

CHAPTER 9

As usual, Stephen Flanagan came into the Hope and Anchor at half past seven, and, as had happened for the past two months, Nell pulled him his pint of mild and bitter before he even had a chance to ask for it.

Sylvia watched, skunk-eyed, as the man brushed his fingers along Nell's forearm.

'All right there?' she snapped, making Stephen pull his hand away, as if she'd just caught him rifling through the till. 'Over here, Nell, there's people want serving.'

While a blushing Nell took orders from a group of animated young doctors from the nearby hospital, Sylvia marched over to Bernie to bend his ear.

'I'm telling you, Bernie, I don't like the way that that Stephen Flanagan looks at her. And I ask you, did you see him touch her just now? It's disgusting, enough to make you feel sick. Man of his age. He's old enough to be her father. No, I'll change me

60

mind over that one, he's old enough to be her bloody grandfather.'

'Don't keep leading off, Sylv, he's only doing what any other red-blooded man'd do if he was brave enough.'

Sylvia blinked very slowly. 'I beg your pardon, Bernard?'

''Cept me, of course, my little beloved. But while we're at it, we're not exactly the same age, now are we?'

'You sound like Nell, but like I said to her: at least I'm a grown woman with a bit of understanding about the ways of the world. She's so bloody innocent.' Sylvia shook her head. 'I just don't like it. He's got them two kids that are older than her, and a vacancy for a bloody skivvy to look after the three of them if you ask me.'

'You worry too much, Sylv. You can see in the bloke's face how taken he is with her. Leave 'em to it and it'll all work out—it always does. And now,' he said, pushing back his chair and standing up, 'if you'll excuse me, my little firecracker, I am off to have a word with the man himself.'

Sylvia fussed around, straightening her husband's already straight braces. 'Bernie, you know I love you, you great big lump, but why, where that man's concerned, do I get the feeling that there's something you'd rather I didn't know about him?'

*   *   *

Having finished sorting out the drinks for the young medics—the who was going to pay for what, and the dealing politely and blushingly with their

61

cheeky suggestions—Nell found herself urgently needing to wipe down the table where Stephen was now sitting with Bernie.

'You were saying earlier?' Nell said, without making eye contact with either of the men, her heart racing and her cheeks burning red.

Stephen brushed the drips from his beery, salt and pepper moustache and stood up. ' 'Scuse me a minute, Bern.'

He gestured for Nell to follow him to the other end of the bar, well away from where Sylvia was serving.

'What I was saying was,' he said, 'was I wondered if you'd thought about what I asked you. You know, if you'd like to come and have a walk with me over Petticoat Lane next Sunday morning. I never mentioned it before, but there's a bloke who's got a greengrocer's pitch for sale and I thought I might go and see how the stall's doing. See, since I stopped going to Mass—you know, after my Violet upped and left—I never really saw the point about not working on a Sunday. So I might as well be earning as sitting indoors by myself all miserable, eh? Especially now there's nothing doing down the docks for anyone again. And if it takes off, I might try my luck down the Mile End Waste with a weekday pitch and all. People always have to eat, so there should be a good couple of bob to be earned.'

He glanced away from her, as if he didn't want her to see his pain. 'It'll be good for me, take my mind off all the misery in my life.'

Nell could feel her eyes prickling again. The poor man, how he must have suffered—must still be suffering.

'What about your children?' she said. 'Couldn't you spend a bit more time with them during the week?' She knew that was what she'd have wanted if she'd had a mum or dad of her own.

He looked into her eyes. 'The twins don't need me no more, not in that way they don't. They're nineteen now.'

'Nineteen?' Nell was completely taken aback. She had imagined the twins to be little ones, like Sam, her favourite young boy back at the home. It hadn't occurred to her that they might be even older than she was.

Stephen caught the change in her tone. 'I never see my other kids; they'd got lives of their own, or so they told me when they took off. The twins are my last two at home, but they'll be leaving and all before I know it. So they won't be putting their money on the table for much longer.'

His expression clouded. 'So I've got to find myself some work. And not just to occupy me.' He drained his glass and slammed it on the bar. 'Someone's got to pay the bills and buy the food, and this stall might be the answer. But most important, it'll give me something to do, help me forget my worries. So what d'you think? Will you come and have a look with me? I'd appreciate your opinion.'

Stephen kept looking at her steadily, directly. She was a beauty all right, a real little Christmas fairy, fit to put right on top of the tree. But had he persuaded her? Would she go with him?

Nell gulped, feeling herself welling up again. What on earth was wrong with her? She could count on one hand the number of times she'd cried when she was in the home, and now she'd turned into a proper waterworks.

'Of course I'll come with you, Stephen. It would be my pleasure.'

'Good. Now I need to get back to Bernie.'

He put his hand on her shoulder, making her sort of shiver inside. She didn't know how she'd be able to wait until Sunday.

*   *   *

'Nell, darling.' Sylvia did her best to sound casual as she flicked a feather duster over the already clean bar. 'Before you go up to bed can we have a word?'

Nell looked dismayed. 'What have I done? I'm ever so sorry.'

Sylvia put her arm around the girl's shoulders. 'Nell, I keep telling you: you are not in that bloody place any more. No one's going to punish you or hurt you. I just wanted to say that I'm worried— and you know what I'm going to say—about the attention Stephen Flanagan was paying you again tonight.'

Nell didn't like Sylvia hugging her when she spoke like that. It made her feel guilty, as if she didn't deserve it. 'It's nothing. You mustn't worry about me.'

'How can I help it? I heard him asking you out on Sunday morning. Again.'

Nell blushed. 'He's thinking about buying a stall.'

'You've said yes, haven't you? You're going with him.'

Nell nodded.

'Bloody hell, Nelly. I can't believe what you see

64

in an old feller like him,' said Sylvia, thinking, but not daring to add out loud: *Don't you think there's something stupid about Stephen bloody Flanagan— that he doesn't even try to hide whatever it is he's up to?*

Instead she said, 'I don't suppose you ever had a chance to have a boyfriend in that place, did you, let alone go with a man?'

Nell didn't answer.

'Here, you haven't, have you? You haven't ever been with a bloke?'

Please God, she hadn't been with Stephen Flanagan. If she went and got herself knocked up by him, that'd be it. No, it was too horrible to even think about.

'How do you mean, have I ever been with a bloke?'

Sylvia stepped away from her, rested her elbows on the bar and covered her face with her hands. Did they teach them nothing about the world in that place?

She dropped her hands, puffed out her cheeks and looked up at the ceiling. 'This is flaming worse than I thought.'

*   *   *

Half an hour later, a shocked, yet still rather sceptical Nell swallowed the last of the medicinal port and lemon that Sylvia had insisted she drink, while she continued to listen to the description of what the landlady called, as delicately as she could, 'having ladies and gentlemen'.

At least it explained the monthly bleeding in terms other than the matron's 'curse of

65

womankind' that had so frightened her—and the feelings she had had when Stephen Flanagan had stroked her arm.

CHAPTER 10

Stephen Flanagan looked so different in his Sunday-best clothes. He had shaved his chin, oiled his hair to a flat, shiny grey cap and, from the glimpse of white peeping out from the neck of his heavy overcoat, Nell could see he had even put a collar on his shirt.

He handed her a brown paper bag.

'It's an orange,' he said. 'All the way from Spain. I'm partial to oranges. Bought a few last week, and that one was left over. Thought you might like it.'

Nell took the bag and looked inside. 'I've never had an orange before,' she said. 'I've seen them though. Matron used to have them. In the home. Sylvia, she prefers apples, so we have them sometimes. They're nice. Do you like apples?'

'They're all right.'

He didn't sound that interested, and Nell wished so hard that she could have said something funny or clever instead of making herself sound like an idiot.

'Shall we go then?' he said, looking around. 'Time's getting on and I've got things to do, and this bloke to meet.'

'I'll just run this up to my room.'

*　　　*　　　*

66

When she came back downstairs, Nell felt her stomach churn—there was no sign of Stephen Flanagan. But Sylvia was there, standing behind the bar fussing about with a crate of quart bottles of pale ale.

'He's waiting outside,' said Sylvia coolly. 'I don't think he fancied the thought of a little chat with me.' She let the crate drop with a loud crash. 'Cos he knows I don't approve.'

Nell nodded, not knowing what to say, and started towards the door, but before she reached it Sylvia had skipped around from behind the bar and dodged in front of her, blocking her way.

'You will keep your wits about you, won't you, darling?'

'Course I will, I promise I'll be back before opening time.'

'I didn't mean that,' Sylvia said, flashing a look over her shoulder at Stephen, who was standing outside on the frosty pavement with his hands in his pockets and his chin in the air. He looked, to Sylvia's eyes, as if he thought he owned the place.

'How exactly do you think he's going to pay for this pitch he's going after in the market?'

'I don't believe it's my place to think about it, Sylvia. I'm sorry, but I've got to go, Stephen's waiting.'

Feeling helpless, Sylvia could only watch as Nell walked off along the street with Stephen Flanagan. OK, the man seemed really taken with Nell, but as Bernie said, what man wouldn't be? But why didn't the girl wonder where someone like him, a washed-up casual from the docks, could find the money for the pitch? Since he'd started making a play for Nell, Sylvia had wondered constantly about where

67

the cash could possibly have come from, and now she had more than a good idea. And she didn't much like it.

*   *   *

Nell had been to the Petticoat Lane market on Sunday mornings before, she'd gone with Sylvia on clothes-hunting expeditions, and she had loved every brightly coloured, overexcited minute of the whole experience. But never had the market seemed as wonderful as it did today. With only a few weeks left until Christmas, the streets were heaving, and alongside all the regular stallholders and the pavement traders selling their herrings, beigels and cucumbers from wooden barrels and baskets, there were stalls stacked high with festive decorations, brightly painted tin toys and glowing, foil-wrapped sweetmeats and fruits. They were perfect for filling Christmas stockings like the ones Nell had seen in books, and, making it all seem even more magical, the gloomy December morning light had been banished by the naphtha lamps that lit up the market with a soft warm glow. She was so looking forward to having what Sylvia called a 'real Christmas' for once—something she had never experienced before.

And she was with Stephen Flanagan.

It was so exciting, nearly all the stallholders seemed to know him, and they acknowledged him as he walked by with a nod of the head, a lift of the chin or a call of: 'All right, Steve-o?'

He replied in turn with a slight lift of his eyebrows or a flash of a thumbs up—no words, simply gestures.

Then there were the winks and looks directed at Nell, and the saucy observations about the old so-and-so Stephen Flanagan finding such a looker for himself, and how it must all be down to the luck of the Irish.

Nell felt as if she were walking along the street with a film star—a glamorous man just like the ones Sylvia had taken her to see on the newsreels. And, although she couldn't understand why, that glamour was somehow rubbing off on her.

Then, when they came to a greengrocer's stall that was close to the corner of where Wentworth Street met Middlesex Street, Stephen suddenly stopped.

'You wait here,' he said to Nell, indicating that she should stand by the corner of the stall, then he went round the back where a stooped elderly man was serving alongside a young lad.

'Solly, you look frozen, old mate,' said Stephen, holding out his hand to the older man, whose gnarled arthritic fingers were sticking out from the fraying ends of knitted fingerless gloves.

Stephen flexed his shoulders. 'Got time to discuss that bit of business we talked about?'

Solly nodded and indicated that Stephen should join him further back on the pavement. Nell, left to her own devices, could only stand there and stare at Solly's miserable-looking young assistant as he selected, weighed and bagged customers' orders from the mounds of fruit and vegetables.

Solly beckoned for Stephen to come closer until they were standing almost nose to nose.

'We discussed the price, but you do know you have to pay the premium to the—' He paused, looking about him. '*Special fund* when you take

69

over the pitch, don't you, Steve-o?'

'Course I do.'

'And you do know who the enforcer is, don't you? The one who'll be expecting the payment and who'll turn very nasty if you ever forget?'

'Would I be right in thinking that it might be a Mr Jack Spot?'

'Keep your voice down, will you?' Solly could only imagine that the man didn't believe what everyone had heard about Jack Spot. 'Listen Steve-o, that bloke's used to dealing with us nice placid Jewish fellers and girls in the market. He won't be very happy if some big-mouthed lump of an Irishman starts broadcasting his private arrangements out loud to any passing schmuck.'

'I'm not a fool, Solly.' Stephen winked and lifted his chin towards Nell. 'I wouldn't have that one in tow if I was, now would I?'

'But you watch out all the same. Spot's not the sort to give a person a second chance. And, you have to believe me, the stories you've heard about him are all true.' He held up a finger to Stephen's face. 'And this is our debt cancelled.'

'It is.'

'All of it? Every last penny?'

'All of it.'

Stephen spat on his palm and held out his hand to Solly, and that was it, it was over. Stephen was being patted on the back, and being shaken firmly by the hand by Solly. The assistant sniffed in bored response, apparently not realising or not caring that his job might soon be gone and he would be joining all the other unemployed cockneys who were pointlessly seeking work in what was supposed to be the greatest capital city in the whole world.

Nell knew it was nothing to do with her, but Sylvia had put ideas into her head and she couldn't help but wonder why this man would let Stephen buy his pitch. She knew from talk in the pub and from listening to the wireless how hard it was for people to get work.

She watched as Stephen started talking again, but from where she was standing she wasn't able to make out what he was saying. She would have been even more puzzled if she had heard his words.

'Solly, you have my word on it, old son. And although you're settling a debt here, I am still going to make sure you get a nice little drink out of this, cos you have no idea how much I appreciate it.'

Nell saw Solly smiling, but he looked more cynical than amused.

'Matter of fact, Steve-o, I think I have a very good idea. With nothing doing down the dock, I'll bet you've been scratching your head wondering how to cover up where the money's coming from.'

Stephen's grin looked far more convincing. 'How did a clever man like you wind up in so much debt?'

Solly shrugged. 'Gambling, it's a bok. You know what they say—better to be born lucky than to be born clever. But let's be happy today.' He took Stephen's face in his hands, his ratty gloves rough on the younger man's cheeks. 'You won't have no trouble now, Steve-o,' he whispered into Stephen's ear. 'Everyone knows there's no such thing as a poor market trader—except if you're a fool like me, of course. Trouble is, my friend, you're going to have to put in some very long hours. Or maybe you could get those twins of yours doing their bit for their father.'

Now Stephen's grin seemed forced. 'Them two? Our George wouldn't know a day's work if it bit him on the arse, and as for Lily I've never seen the girl out of bed before dinnertime, let alone work.'

'You're going to be in for a shock then, Steve-o, I'm telling you.'

'How hard can it be?'

Solly looked at his dour assistant, and waved a hand at Stephen. 'How long d'you give him before he learns how hard market trading really is?'

That actually had the miserable lad cracking a snaggle-toothed smile.

'Why don't you give them a shake then?'

'Never had any cause. Their mother left when they were kids, and they just got on with things in their own way.'

'Believe me, I understand you don't want your kids to suffer, but we're talking about them helping you earn a living here.'

'If I want advice on how to raise my family—'

'I spoke out of turn, and I apologise, Steve-o, but give it a few weeks and I guarantee you'll change your tune.'

Nell didn't know what was going on, but she was beginning to feel uncomfortable. How long was this going to take? She'd only just got used to all the noisy racket and banter in the pub, but at least in there she had Sylvie to protect her and—how did Sylvie put it?—to 'kid her along'. She wasn't used to all this row going on around her while she was left standing alone.

But then, before Nell knew what was happening, Stephen had let go of Solly's hand, and had taken her by the elbow—nothing too intimate, but sort of protective she thought—and now he was steering her towards the Ten Bells pub on the corner of Commercial and Fournier Street.

'Where are we going?' she said, skipping out of the path of a gruff-looking man with a handcart piled high with root vegetables.

'I think it's time to celebrate,' he said, pushing open the pub door.

'I'm sorry, Stephen,' Nell whispered, 'but I have to get back to the Hope. I didn't realise it was opening time. Sylv'll be expecting me and I'd hate to let her down after all she's done for me. I'm sorry, but I've got to go.'

'Surely even Sylvia wouldn't begrudge you a drink to toast your engagement?'

She stopped dead. 'My what?'

'Your engagement. You and me, Nell, we're getting engaged. I'm going to be right busy, what with having to sort out the new stall, so I thought we might as well get on with it. And sooner rather than later. Never saw any point in mucking around.'

He lifted his hand to the barmaid. 'Pint of mild and bitter and a lemonade over here, girl. Quick as you like, I'm spitting feathers.'

Stephen kept his eye on the barmaid as she poured the drinks, watching to make sure he got his full measure and not a quick top-up from the slops tray. He'd seen her cheating people on a Sunday morning before.

'The twins are bound to be off before long, so I thought you might as well move into Turnbury Buildings with me. Don't see any point in hanging about. Never have. It's not my way. And I'm sure you feel the same about me as I do about you. You're a pretty girl, Nell, a right pretty girl, and I've seen you working—you're a grafter and you've got a good head on your shoulders, I admire that. And I'm fed up with being lonely. You know what that's like, Nell, don't you, coming from the home and everything. So, how about it? Us getting engaged? Cos I know it's what I want.'

Nell put her hand to her mouth. Had she heard him right? 'Do you mean engaged, like engaged to be married?' she asked through her fingers.

'Sort of, yeah.' Stephen sniffed, considering his words. 'But there can't be no marriage, of course, because even though she might have run out on me and her own children, I'm still married to my Violet, remember. So you won't be able to go setting your heart on no wedding day or anything like that. But how about it? Me and you?'

Nell was astonished; this man actually wanted her. It would be just like having a family of her own, and she'd have her very own place to live and everything. And it wasn't as if he had any choice about getting married properly—not for now, at least. But who knew what might happen in the future?

She didn't know what to say, so she just nodded and took a sip of her lemonade.

CHAPTER 11

A week later, Sylvia stood grim-faced behind the bar of the Hope and Anchor, while Bernie made sure that everyone had a drink in their hand to celebrate Stephen and Nell's engagement—their 'happy day', as everyone except Sylvia seemed to be calling it. There was no denying it, Nell looked beautiful. She was wearing a simple ivory satin sheath dress and matching coat, adorned with the pearl and gold brooch, Sylvia's fox-fur stole that she'd loaned her for the day, and a little veiled hat that was just right—unlike this sham of an engagement that couldn't even lead to a marriage, and most definitely wasn't right in any way at all.

Since Nell had come bursting into the pub last Sunday with her supposedly good news, Sylvia had done everything she could think of to make her see sense, to persuade her that it was ridiculous even to contemplate getting engaged to Stephen rotten Flanagan. But in her usual sweet way Nell had told Sylvia not to worry about her, and that moving in with Stephen would be just like being given a ready-made family—perfect. Even God would forgive her, Nell went on, as he would understand that Stephen couldn't help it that his wife had run away from him and his poor children.

Sylvia thought, but didn't have the heart to say, that it wasn't God she was bloody worried about, and having two kids who were at least four years older than you—if not more—was hardly having a ready-made family.

'Come on, Sylv,' Bernie said, nudging his wife, as he pulled yet another pint. 'At least it'll give her a bit of security, and Stephen's right taken with her, anyone can see that. And, be fair, you couldn't expect the kid to stay here with us for the rest of her natural.'

'You said it, Bern—she's a kid. Just a kid. And he's a dirty old man. Our Nelly deserves better

75

than him. Much better.'

'Well, I think she should be thanking her lucky stars. For a start he's got that place in Turnbury Buildings. Little palaces everyone says they are. Even got their own lavs and a communal wash house.'

Sylvia looked at him as if he'd lost his mind. 'You've never even washed a rotten handkerchief, so what do you know about wash houses? Communal or bloody otherwise.'

He shrugged. 'I hear people talking. Cos people do talk in boozers, you know. And she won't have to go carting stuff down the public baths like she does for us no more.'

'No, but guess who'll be using the *communal wash house* morning, noon and night? My little Nelly, that's who. She'll be nothing more than a skivvy for the three of them, you just wait and see.'

'She's not much more than that here really, is she Sylv?' Bernie handed the foaming glass across the counter to a customer keen to get his share of this unexpected Sunday lunchtime bounty. 'The girl don't stop.'

'She's paid for what she does here. Full board and a fair wage, and I know you treat her well—and don't look at me like that, she told me, in case I expected her to pay it back out of what I give her. And I've bought her all them new clothes and got her hair cut all nice for her. You watch, she'll be ground down by him in no time. And them two lousy kids of his'll find a way to take advantage of her good nature, you can guarantee it. It's not right, Bernie, you've got to put a stop to it. He's not even bought her a bloody ring. Nell told me the tight sod hadn't had time.'

76

He looked across the crowded saloon bar—word had soon been passed around that there were free drinks to be had in the Hope and Anchor—and all he could see was a pink-cheeked, smiling beauty of a girl, who looked as if her every dream had come true.

Bernie turned to his wife. 'If you want her heart broken, Sylv, well then you do it. Cos me, I'm saying nothing.'

*   *   *

They all stood on the pavement outside the pub, while Bernie captured the moment on his box Brownie—with Nell smiling as if she'd never stop and Stephen becoming agitated by all the attention.

'How much longer is this gonna take, Bern?' he complained, grinding out his cigarette butt with his heel.

Bernie grinned. 'If I'm getting it in the neck from Sylvie about all this, then you can have some of it and all. So just one more for luck, eh?' He beckoned to his wife. 'Come on Sylv, let's have one of you and Nell. The two most beautiful girls in the world in one picture. Who could resist 'em?'

Sylvia softened, if only for the moment, and she found herself smiling warmly. She linked arms with Nell and they beamed into Bernie's camera lens.

Stephen lit another cigarette. 'Hurry it up, can't you? I'm bloody freezing standing here.'

The shutter clicked and Nell's smile slowly dissolved, like the slush melting in the gutter.

*   *   *

With a single glance back at Sylvia, Nell trotted along beside Stephen as he strode away from the pub in the direction of his 'little palace' in Turnbury Buildings, Wapping.

'You know you're both welcome over here with us for Christmas dinner,' Sylvia called after them, grudging the offer to Stephen but wanting—desperately—Nell to see what Christmas could be like.

'I don't think so, thanks all the same,' Stephen replied for both of them, flagging down a taxicab. 'We'll be fine indoors.'

It seemed that Nell wasn't going to spend Christmas with Sylvia after all. But the excitement of riding in a taxi for the very first time made it not matter—well, not quite as much.

Nell wasn't sure why she did it, but as Stephen leaned forward to speak to the driver she covered her brooch with her fingers, surreptitiously unclasped it from her collar and slipped it into her bag.

*   *   *

When the taxi drove through a curved archway and drew up at Turnbury Buildings, it wasn't exactly what Nell had been expecting. Rather than the collection of 'little palaces' that everyone had talked about, it looked more like a forbidding fortress with high brick blocks enclosing three sides of a tarmacked courtyard. Standing in a wasteland of demolished slums, bordered on the waterside by the wharves and warehouses, the Buildings resembled a giant tooth left in an otherwise gummy mouth.

Nell saw curtains twitch as curious residents craned their necks to see who would be making such an entrance, and a crowd of wild-looking children playing in the yard despite the cold rushed over to the cab. Unlike the older inhabitants of the Buildings, who stared anonymously from behind the shelter of their windows, the youngsters weren't nearly as shy. They stared openly at Nell as she stepped out of the cab and stood there shivering in her ivory satin outfit and smart hat, while Stephen paid the driver. She was glad she'd taken off the brooch earlier—any one of the children looked capable of snatching it from her.

'Chuck out your mouldies, Mr Flanagan,' said one of them hopefully, as Stephen counted out his change.

'Bugger off,' snapped Stephen, taking Nell by the arm and steering her towards the entrance to one of the blocks.

CHAPTER 12

Nell stood at the kitchen sink of Number 55 Turnbury Buildings, washing the dishes from Stephen's breakfast, now a familiar part of her daily routine. Apart from having to work out how to cook a capon on Christmas day, nothing else had proved too challenging, and the routine had soon become clear. Nell was responsible for everything indoors, and every day Stephen went to set up his stall—Monday to Saturday on the Mile End Waste and on Sundays 'down the Lane'—

always working until mid-afternoon. Twice a week he would leave home in the early hours to go to the wholesale market. Each day he would have a few drinks before coming home for his tea, and most evenings, after he'd eaten, he would go out again.

Stephen had explained to Nell that she had to get up fifteen minutes before him, so she could light a small fire in the front room—just big enough to last him until he was ready to leave—and boil some water on the stove for him to wash and shave in the kitchen. He never went down to the communal wash house in the basement where the baths and laundry were—she wasn't even sure if he realised they were down there under the ground-floor flats. He always had a 'wash down', as he called it, at the sink, but she wished he would go and use the baths occasionally. She'd been used to having a weekly bath when she'd been in the home, and when she'd lived with Sylvia and Bernie she and Sylvia had loved their weekly trip to the Gaulston Street Baths, Sylvia paying the extra so they could have a nice hot soak instead of a quick lukewarm dip. Nell couldn't understand why Stephen didn't take more pride in his appearance; he was a good-looking man for his age. Even the twins, George and Lily, managed a bath most weeks. Maybe he was just tired from all the work he was doing; not that the money he put on the table on a Friday night reflected all the hours he was supposed to be working.

Nell scrubbed the remains of scrambled egg from the pan and rinsed it under the tap, ashamed that she was even thinking such things. She had a home now, and a man and his children to take care of, something that a lot of women would have been only too happy with, especially if they had come from a foundlings' home and had nothing but a brooch to call their own. This was the real world and she should be grateful to be part of it— especially as Stephen worked so hard. That was why she couldn't blame him for going off to one of the market pubs to have a few pints so he could relax a bit before he was ready to come home for his dinner. The trouble was, he must have been drinking gallons of the stuff to use up so much of the money he was making, unless the stalls weren't working out as well as he'd hoped. But, whatever was happening, Nell was struggling to manage on the money he was giving her. She had tried— once—asking Stephen for a little more, but he wouldn't even discuss it with her. In fact, it had soon become obvious that the only time he wanted to have anything to do with her was at night. Then he couldn't have been more attentive, although whether Nell welcomed that attention didn't seem to come into question.

The first night when he had taken her into his bed she had been little short of terrified, despite the talk that Sylvia had given her, and it proved to be just as bad as she had feared. Nell really didn't enjoy what Stephen did to her as she lay there waiting for him to finish, but she understood that it was her duty—she was living under his roof. He was as good as her husband.

Although it was far less harrowing than Stephen touching her in that way, Nell also hated being expected to eat early with the twins. She dreaded sitting at the table with them. But that was what Stephen wanted her to do, so she did it. Stephen always ate later, on his own. It wasn't that he was being unkind to her, she reassured herself, it was just that he was tired after work and didn't like to talk while he had his meal. He preferred to study the sports pages of the evening paper that he would spread out on the kitchen table in front of him. Nell understood that, of course she did. This was her life now, and even though Lily and George treated her with open contempt, behaving as if she were little more than their unpaid servant, and flatly ignoring any effort on her part to be agreeable, at least she had the neighbours from the Buildings. If it hadn't been for them, for Sarah Meckel in the corner shop, and the weekly visit she had from Sylvia, life for her in 55 Turnbury Buildings would have been very lonely.

She tipped the dirty washing-up water down the sink and started drying, still amazed, regardless of her reservations about some aspects of life in Turnbury Buildings, that she was actually in her own little kitchen. After spending so much time in the home, she did her best to remind herself each day that she should count her blessings. And there were lots of good things about living in the Buildings, including those neighbours.

There was one family she really liked—the Lovells, Mary and Joe and their son Martin, who lived just across the landing in Number 57. Despite times being hard for them since Joe had lost his job, Mary remained a kind, motherly woman. Nell thought that Martin seemed a nice boy, he was always smiling whenever she saw him on his way to work, but he was too shy to speak, blushing and never saying much more than a mumbled good morning. For Nell, though, that was charming, especially compared to the boisterous behaviour of some of the young men that she'd experienced when she'd been working in the Hope.

Martin's mum, Mary Lovell, was far more outgoing, and had taken Nell under her wing. She'd only been there a couple of days before Mary had made sure she knew how to wrap the rubbish in newspaper before launching it down the chute that ran from each floor to the massive bins in the rubbish sheds. On the first Monday, Mary had taken her down to the basement laundry and had shown her how to use the water heaters and drying racks. She'd seen to it that Nell met the other women from the Buildings as they busied themselves with their weekly wash, and she made a particular point of warning Nell about one or two of them whom she should be careful of, as they could be what she called 'a bit tricky'. One particular individual that she singled out was Ada Tanner, a sour-faced elderly woman from Number 56, the third and final flat on the top landing, where she lived with her equally difficult husband, Albert.

Mary had then introduced Nell to Sarah in the corner shop, where Mary worked part-time. But, friendly as she was, Mary didn't impose, and when Sylvia paid Nell her weekly morning visit she would never accept the invitation to come in and join them for a cup of tea—although Nell wondered if that was as much to do with Mary worrying that the twins might get up out of their beds and start their complaining, as it was about her not wanting to intrude.

Apart from Mary Lovell, Sarah Meckel was definitely Nell's favourite from the neighbourhood, and she would have liked to have popped into the corner shop for a chat every day, as Sarah could always make her smile. Like Mary, she was a good woman, always willing to help anyone, despite the hardships she herself had to endure.

Nell didn't know the full story, Sarah was reluctant to talk about it, but what she gathered was that Sarah's parents had come to London from somewhere in Russia where there was a lot of trouble, and had started the shop. Then they had died in the great flu epidemic, leaving Sarah to run the shop alone. But she had had something to look forward to—her fiancé, David, was coming home from where he'd been fighting in Europe in the Great War. They would get married right away and he would help her and they'd have children and live happily ever after. David did return, and they did get married, but he was never able to help her as she'd dreamed. Now, as well as running the shop, Sarah looked after David, who, in Ada Tanner's words, 'hadn't been right in the head' since he'd come home. Ada had added, even more nastily, that it wasn't as if he'd been the only one who'd been in the trenches. But Sarah Meckel treasured the man, and never gave even the slightest hint that life might sometimes get her down.

Sarah said how much she enjoyed having Mary Lovell working in the shop with her, but according to Ada Tanner it was an act of 'stupid waste'—Nell thought of it as kindness—rather than a necessity. Sarah really didn't need more than a few hours' help here and there, especially with money being so short for everyone, but she knew that Mary Lovell needed the work. Joe Lovell, like too many others, hadn't been able to get a job no matter how hard he tried, and Martin, his son, was only bringing in a boy's wage. But Mary spoke proudly of the fact that he gave what he earned gladly to his family every Friday evening when he came home from his shift in the brewery.

Nell stacked the dry pans on the rack above the stove and turned her attention to drying the crockery.

She felt her cheeks begin to colour as she thought about how Sarah Meckel even allowed Florrie Talbot to lodge upstairs above the shop, despite her being what Ada Tanner described as a 'dockside tom'. Nell had been shocked when Sylvia explained to her what that meant, but then not a little torn when she thought of how she herself was living with Stephen without being married. She remembered the horrible moment when she had stood in the shop and flushed as red as a tomato when Ada had started leading off about Florrie again, and what she thought about the sort of person who would do such things without the benefit of having marriage lines tucked safely in her handbag.

Nell opened the glass door of the fitted dresser that ran the length of one wall and put away the crockery on top of the neat piles she had taken such pleasure in arranging during the first week she had moved in. Bringing order to the chaos that had reigned in the kitchen made her feel so much better, as did her recalling how Sarah had stood up for Florrie Talbot. Sarah had made it quite clear that Florrie's business was her own, and had asked Ada what right she had to slander the reputation of a woman who had made the ultimate sacrifice when she had lost her beloved fiancé in the war.

There was always something like that going on in the corner shop—things to learn and things to make Nell think. She only wished she could spend more time with Sarah, but Stephen didn't like Nell going there too often, he said she'd only go wasting money. Instead, he brought in most of what he thought they needed when he came home from the market—usually the overblown remains of his stock and some cheap cut of meat from one of the side-street butcher's shops.

Stephen also said he didn't like Sarah and David Meckel because they were Jews. Nell didn't understand why that should mean there was anything wrong with them, especially as he had seemed only too keen to do the business deal with Solly over the stall. Then, when Nell had asked Sylvia, she just shrugged and said, 'You know what some people are like, my dad was Jewish and my mum's family disowned her,' immediately bringing the matter to an end. And Nell wasn't about to ask Stephen. Her years in the home had taught her the warning signs of potentially aggressive behaviour, and she'd soon discovered that Stephen Flanagan was the type of man who lost his temper very easily. So she ignored her doubts and got on with doing what she had to do—just as she always had.

She dried her hands on her apron, and then gave the glass doors of the dresser a final polish with the tea towel, pleased with a job well done. It wasn't the hard work that Nell minded, she'd never minded that, and it made the days pass by more quickly, but, she couldn't help thinking about it, it was the nights she dreaded. She had begun to loathe even the idea of bedtime.

She filled the kettle without really thinking what she was doing.

When Sylvia had explained 'things' to her, she had made it sound almost nice, in a frightening sort of a way, but then she didn't have Stephen and his grunting and his boozy breath to put up with. Nell had tried making excuses for not going to bed—some job or other to finish, or things to prepare for the morning—but Stephen had told her she could just get up a bit earlier if there were chores still to be done. It was then that Nell truly wished she had listened to Sylvia, but she had done it now, she had committed herself to living under Stephen's roof and she had to make the best of it—and he wasn't so bad, he worked such long hours to provide for all of them.

Yet, as she looked about the kitchen on this dark, raw February morning, she had to admit that she was scared of what would become of her. Was this really what her life would be like until the day she died?

Nell went back into the bedroom, thinking that she might snatch maybe a quarter of an hour more in bed. The alarm clock ticked ominously, its mechanical rhythm moving it slightly, rocking the battered tin plate on which it stood, and swirling the handful of glass marbles noisily around its feet—Stephen's tricks to ensure that Nell wouldn't be able to oversleep. Was this her punishment, she wondered, for living with a man outside wedlock? Was God watching her like Matron Sully always claimed, watching to catch her out in a sin?

It was one of Stephen's wholesale days, and he had been gone for what must have been almost two hours now; as usual, before he'd left, he had made sure that Nell didn't forget how 'good' he was—getting up and going out so early just to bring in money so that she could have such an easy life—and now she actually felt guilty that she had crept back to bed for a while. Was her life really so bad? Why should she expect more? Why should she think that she was in any way special? She was sure that plenty of women would be flattered to be told by Stephen Flanagan that he wanted to have them move in and share his home.

She sat on the edge of the bed and looked at the clock again, and instead of climbing back under the bedclothes she returned to the kitchen and began to organise breakfast for the twins. Stephen had decided the night before that Solly had been right—market life was hard—and that it was time that Lily and George started doing their bit and contributing to the household. He had become quite angry with them, demanding why it should be him who was doing all the work, especially as they were still showing no signs of leaving home.

Why would they, thought Nell, as she stood at the kitchen sink washing her hands before slicing bread for the twins' toast, when they were living like a prince and princess?

She shivered against the chill—living with Sylvie and Bernie had made her soft.

CHAPTER 13

Kettle on and grill heated, Nell braced herself to rouse the twins. George's was the first door along the hall, so she might as well start with him.

At nineteen years of age, and the image of his father in bulk, height and temperament, George Flanagan towered over Nell in every way. He could easily be sharing the load with Stephen, but working on a fruit and vegetable stall apparently wasn't good enough for George. He didn't know what he did want to do, but he knew it didn't involve getting up while it was still dark. Nell would happily have left him stewing in his pit, but Stephen had been very firm, and her allegiance had to be to him rather than to his brutish son. If Stephen wanted his children up and out of bed at what he considered a decent hour, then that was what Nell would make sure happened.

She took a deep breath and knocked on George's door. 'It's gone six, George. Your dad's expecting you on the stall.'

No reply from him, but a loud groan came from Lily's room.

Lily was almost as coarse as her brother, and Nell could only imagine the perverse delight Matron Sully would have taken in instructing her in 'decent' ways. Their mother had left when the twins were just children, and in the subsequent years Lily had stored up enough resentment against the world to make her one of the most sullen, disagreeable people that Nell had ever met—even angrier with her lot in life than Matron had been. But Nell knew what it felt like to know she wasn't wanted, so she made every effort to get on with Lily—but it didn't seem to have much effect.

'You should try and be grateful for what your dad gives you,' Nell had said when she'd encountered Lily's brick wall of bitterness after she had first moved in. 'He works so hard, he's had to be like both your mum and your dad, and you've got this lovely flat and your own room. In the home we never had anything for ourselves.'

'Well, I'm not a stinking orphan am I? I've got a dad. Not like you.'

Nell tried a smile. 'And now you've got a mum as well.'

'You? Piss off, you're just a bloody kid. You're not even married. You're nothing more than a poxy lodger.' Lily looked her up and down, her expression one of raw derision. 'You're not even the first one he's brought home. He's had birds in and out of this place ever since that old tart buggered off and left us. You're just the only one who's stayed, that's all. Nowhere else to go I suppose, cos all the others cleared off in no time.'

Over a month later Nell still recalled the shock, almost as hard as a physical blow, at the cruelty of Lily's words.

She hadn't been the first.

How could she have been so naive? Nell had felt soiled. Used. And so upset that she had hardly registered that Lily had sworn at her. The customers in the Hope and Anchor had cursed a bit when they'd had a few too many, but it only took Sylvia to remind them that there were ladies present, and that 'outdoor language' wasn't acceptable, and they'd mumble their apologies and lower their voices—even though everyone accepted that a few choice words often slipped into Sylvia's own conversation. But all that was just a harmless use of language; Lily's had been so much more than that. Lily had really wanted to hurt her. And she had succeeded.

But then Lily and George were full of surprises and she could only wonder, as she tried to rouse them from their beds, if they had any more waiting for her this morning.

'Time to get up, you two,' she called, rapping her knuckles on George's door. 'Please, come on, I promised your dad.' It never failed to amaze her that they each had these lovely rooms of their own and yet still they complained. 'And the porridge I've made you will set like stone. And you know your dad wants you both down the market to start learning how to run the stall.'

Still no reply.

Nell took another deep breath, and straightened her apron. 'Please, George, will you get up?'

'What the hell's all that bloody noise about?' Lily shouted from her room.

'It's her going on again,' George shouted back.

'Well, shut her up, can't you? I'm just about sick to the back teeth of her and her moaning.'

George's door was suddenly flung open. He stood there in his green-striped pyjama bottoms and baggy vest, with his dark, greasy hair plastered to one side of his head, and his chin covered in dark stubble. It might not have been obvious to outsiders how such an almost pathetic presence could have been so terrifying, but Nell had seen that look of unconcealed fury before—not when his father had been there, of course—resulting in the smashed china and overturned table for which she had been blamed. So she was as good as expecting it when he lunged towards her, with his open hand raised high above his head ready to strike her across the face. Not being half asleep like George, Nell had the advantage, and she was

91

able to duck out of his reach and take off along the hallway to the front door. She had her hand on the latch a bare moment before he reached her.

Nell flung open the door and threw herself out onto the landing—right into the arms of Martin, Joe and Mary Lovell's son. He was just stepping out onto the landing from Number 57.

'Morning,' he said with a bashful grin, stepping back as he took his hands away from her. He raised them to his shoulders, making it clear that he'd not intended to touch her. 'What's the rush? Someone after you, are they? If they are I hope they're—'

It was the most that Martin had ever said to her, but he wasn't given the opportunity of saying anything more. George had launched himself across the landing and grabbed Martin by the collar of his overcoat. He started shaking him with the force of a muscular bull mastiff dispatching a wiry young terrier pup.

'You get away from her, you nasty little bastard,' George spat through clenched, morning-furred teeth. 'Right now. D'you hear me? Now.'

Martin waved his hands in mock surrender. 'Come on, George, nothing intended. She only run into me by mistake.' He nodded at Nell, and smiled. 'You're all right, aren't you, Nell?' Martin blushed as he said her name out loud for the first time—although he'd repeated it in his head enough times. 'You were going at about twenty miles an hour just now.'

He tried another grin. 'Sorry if I embarrassed you. I didn't mean anything.'

Nell didn't reply, she just stared down at her shoes.

'What's this then, a bloody tea party, all having a

nice little chit-chat are we?' George gripped Nell by the upper arm and started hauling her back to Number 55. 'Come on, move your bleed'n' self.'

Martin, now frowning, followed them. 'Here, George, aren't you being a bit rough with her? I mean, look at the size of you, mate.'

George had spun round and thrown himself on him before Martin even knew what was happening. George slammed him in the chest and threw him backwards, smacking him into the wall beside the open door of Number 57. Martin's head hit the lime-washed brick with a thud. But he didn't fall; instead he rocked forward and squared up in a boxer's stance, fists up in front of his chest.

'All right then, George, if you think you're so tough, let's have you. Or d'you only pick on girls?'

George looked at Martin, pausing to consider—could he, a whacking great nineteen-year-old, take on this smaller, much slighter lad of sixteen? Even one who went to a boxing club?

Course he could. He was twice his size.

As it happened, George was wrong, and when Martin's parents appeared in the doorway of their flat curious to see what all the commotion was about, they saw George stretched out on the floor, panting like a train, dabbing at his bloody nose with the back of his hand. Their son was straddling him, fists raised ready to lay him out again, daring him to move.

'Martin?' Joe Lovell said quietly. 'What's going on here, son?'

'He was hurting Nell, Dad.'

Mary Lovell, dressed to go out, took off her gloves as she stepped around her son and the still horizontal George. 'You get yourself off to work,

93

Martin, or you'll be late,' she said, drawing Nell close to her. 'And I'd better get myself down the shop soon or Sarah'll be wondering where I've got to. It's one of the mornings when I set up with her, see Nell.' She spoke evenly, as if everything was perfectly normal. 'But I've got enough time to make you a nice cup of tea before I go, love. You come indoors with me, eh?'

Mary knew she had to calm the situation; the last thing she wanted was a feud with the Flanagans. Stephen and George had the reputation of behaving like a pair of lunatics when they got going, and Lily wasn't a lot better. That was what happened when there was no mother to keep the pot from boiling over.

Nell shook her head. 'No thank you, Mrs Lovell.' She knew Stephen's views on women who wasted their time drinking tea with the neighbours; she didn't even let him know that Sylvia came by regularly.

'As you like, love, but I told you before, you're to call me Mary, all right?'

'Yes, thank you, Mary.'

George gave Martin a half-hearted shove in the chest and propped himself up on one elbow. 'Call me bleed'n' Mary? And a nice cup of tea? Is that all you've got to say for yourself? Your son's just split my nose open.'

Joe Lovell frowned and pulled his chin tight into his chest. 'What, our little sixteen-year-old lad did that to you? The one who's not even a fully grown man yet?'

'What does it matter how old he is? Look at the state of me.' George examined the blood on the back of his hand. 'Tell you what, I've got a mind to

94

call the law.'

Joe snorted. 'And make you and your family a laughing stock?'

The door to Number 56 opened—up until then the only closed door of the three on the landing—to reveal Ada Tanner in all her morning glory: hand-knitted cardigan over an ankle-length winceyette nightgown and her head bristling with the vicious-looking metal grips that she firmly believed coaxed her hair into film-star waves.

'Who's a laughing stock?' she demanded. Never knowingly pleasant, was Ada. 'What have I missed then?'

Mary Lovell closed her eyes. Ada Tanner, just what they needed to add too much salt to the stew. 'Nothing, Ada. Nothing at all. So why don't you go back inside in the warm? It's not even seven o'clock and it's freezing out here. You'll catch your death.'

'With a bit of luck,' mumbled George.

Ada wasn't drawn, being too busy looking from one face to another, trying to sort out the playing order of whatever it was that had occurred in her absence.

She paused on Nell. 'Well, I might have known she'd be involved in whatever it was.' She waggled a thumb at Number 55. 'I've not heard anything but shouting and hollering from in there these past two months. And you can't tell me it's a coincidence that it was then that he moved her in there with him. Trollop, look at her, not even a ring on her finger.'

Nell shrivelled back against the wall.

Joe nodded at his son. 'Go on, Martin. Do as your mother says, or you'll be late.'

95

'Yeah, you'd better get off to work like your mother tells you, Martin,' chipped in Ada, her voice dripping with sarcasm as she turned her attention away from Nell. 'And your mother had better not hang around too long either, or who'll bring in your father's beer money?'

'Take no notice of her, Joe,' said Mary, stretching over George so she could kiss her husband on the cheek. 'She thinks all men are like her Albert. Still in bed is he, Ada? Resting while he waits for your granddaughter to bring round the family "contribution"?'

George scrambled to his feet. 'Hang about, you lot. I don't give a shit about whose husband does what. Why's nobody worried about me? That scraggy little bastard just assaulted me.'

'Makes a change from the Flanagans using their fists,' said Martin, moving menacingly closer to George.

'Leave off, you two,' Mary said, concentrating on pulling her gloves back on. 'If you're sure you don't want a cup of tea, dear, me and Martin will be on our way.'

George stabbed a finger at Martin. 'You've done it now, Lovell. You just wait till I tell my dad what you've done.'

'Tell your dad?' Joe shook his head. 'How old are you, George?'

Mary tutted impatiently. 'Please, grow up all of you. And you, Nell,' she finished drawing down the last finger of her gloves, 'if you change your mind, Joe'll make you a nice cup of tea, won't you Joe?'

Ada threw up her hands. 'I don't know about Mary and Joe Lovell, you two are more like Mary and Mary Ann Lovell. A man making another

96

woman tea while his own wife's out at work? I ask you. What are things coming to?'

Joe stood up straight and proud, pulling back his shoulders as he stared Ada directly in the eye. 'And I'll have the flat all shipshape and your tea on the table when you get home, Mary.'

'Thanks, love,' said Mary, but she was distracted, looking about her, frowning. 'Nell. Where is she?'

Only Martin had noticed Nell slipping away down the stairs. Why hadn't he had the guts to go after her?

CHAPTER 14

'Blimey, hold up out there, I'm going as fast as I can.' Sylvia tucked a stray lock of her bright auburn hair behind her ear and stretched up to slide back the brass bolt. 'We're not open for hours yet, so if you think you're getting a drink, you've got another—'

As she opened the pub door, Sylvia let the cleaning cloth she'd been holding drop to the floor. 'Nell, darling, whatever's up?' She took Nell by the hand and drew her inside, over to the fire. 'What the bloody hell do you think you're doing coming out without a hat and coat on? It's ready to snow again out there.'

Nell couldn't bring herself to look at her friend; she didn't want to lie to Sylvia, but she'd walked for over an hour without thinking and had found herself standing outside the pub, with no idea where else she might go. What was she supposed to do, wander the streets until she collapsed from the cold? Maybe that wouldn't have been such a bad idea, to have just fallen down in a heap and not to have woken up again.

'Nell, I asked you a question, darling.'

'I'm sorry, yeah. I just thought I'd pop round and see you. But I can tell you're busy. I'll come back later on.'

Nell tried to pull away, but Sylvia was having none of it.

'You'll do no such thing. You sit yourself down there and I'll make you a cup of tea with a little something extra in it to warm up your insides for you.' Sylvia pushed her none too gently onto a chair by the fireside. 'You had your breakfast yet?'

Nell shook her head.

'Somehow I thought that's what you'd say.'

Bernie poked his head around the door beside the bar. 'I thought I heard voices.' He didn't look impressed to see Nell there. 'Everything all right?'

'Yes thank you, Bernie,' said Sylvia pointedly.

'There is work to be done, you know, Sylv.'

'I do know, thank you, Bernie.'

'Just so long as you do.' He looked at Nell. 'Give my regards to Stephen.'

'Why would she bother to do that?' snapped Sylvia. 'He's in here every bloody night yakking away to you, I'm surprised you've not offered him a sodding room.'

Sylvia and Bernie were too busy glaring at one another to notice the deflated look on Nell's face as she took in Sylvia's words—Stephen was in the Hope every night. Now Nell knew she really did have nowhere to go.

'So, you say you've missed me.' Sylvia was looking at Nell with her head cocked on one side, trying to figure out what was going on as she watched her friend hardly touch the thickly buttered hot toast that she used to scoff down almost as fast as Sylvia could churn it out for her. 'And that's why you came out in the freezing cold with no hat and coat on, with your apron flapping and your hair all over the place?'

'That's right.'

'Well, like I said, Nell, it's always lovely to see you, sweetheart, but if there's anything wrong, anything you want to tell me—say, how things are indoors maybe—well, you know me, I'm a good listener.' She laughed without any hint of humour. 'And why wouldn't I be? I've had enough practice running this place. You wouldn't believe some of the things I've heard in here.'

There was a long moment of silence, then Nell said quietly, 'Things are fine indoors, thanks.'

Sylvia patted her knee. 'Good. I'm glad.' So that approach wasn't going to work. 'I'm very glad to hear it, but if you ever do have anything you want to talk about, you know I'll always be here, ready to listen, don't you, Nell?'

Nell said nothing.

'All right? Nell?'

'Yes. Thank you.' Her voice was lifeless, crushed.

As she sipped her tea, Sylvia watched Nell over the edge of her cup. Whatever it was that was wrong with the poor kid, she knew she wasn't going to get it out of her by going on and on about it. It really wasn't easy for someone of Sylvia's temperament, but she'd just have to let Nell take her own good time. But whatever the details were, it didn't need a genius to figure out the gist of it.

Sylvia could have cheerfully skinned that bloody Stephen Flanagan, and his two horrible kids, no matter what Bernie would have to say about her getting involved. She couldn't stand seeing her lovely little Nell looking like this. She'd have to come up with something or other to sort this mess out, even if it did mean that Bernie had to stop being bloody mates with Stephen Flanagan.

*   *   *

While Sylvia sat across from the still determinedly uncommunicative Nell—vainly trying to tempt her with soft-boiled eggs, a crispy bacon sandwich or anything else she fancied for that matter—Mary Lovell was hanging up her hat and coat, ready to start helping Sarah Meckel set up the corner shop for the day's trading.

'Sorry I'm late, Sarah.'

'Don't be silly, Mary,' Sarah said, arranging big stoneware jars of jam, treacle and mustard pickles at one end of the scrubbed wooden counter; she untied the muslin covers, and stuck a long-handled serving spoon into each one. 'What's a couple of minutes between friends? I was just worried that there was something wrong.'

'Well, there was a bit of a turnout across the landing,' Mary said, dragging a sackful of bundles of kindling wood from the store room. She began stacking the bundles in a tidy pile close to the door, where customers could collect them on their way out. 'A right old business it was.'

'Don't tell me—Ada was giving her poor old Albert a hard time again.'

'Funnily enough, it wasn't them two at it for once, but she made sure she was in the audience, and she loved every minute of it.'

'Typical,' Sarah said, from somewhere under the counter.

'This time,' said Mary, squinting with concentration as she opened a fresh sack of poultry meal using an old bone-handled knife, 'it was that waster George Flanagan causing all the trouble.'

'Having the Flanagans and the Tanners on your landing—you won the first prize there, Mary. Must have been your lucky day when they moved you out of the terrace.'

Mary laughed. 'I think I must have done something bad when I was a kid, something that I've wiped from my mind, but that I'm still being punished for.'

Now Sarah was laughing too.

'It's not funny really though, Sarah. He was upsetting that young Nell; he had hold of her, according to my Martin, and he was being right rough with the girl. And I don't suppose it's the last we've heard of it either, because Martin wasn't having that. He wound up punching the cocky so-and-so right on the nose.' Mary put down the sack and rolled her eyes at Sarah. 'Between George's old man and Ada Tanner I reckon this one's going to run and run. And I'm not saying I think it's right, Martin interfering like that, but George is twice that young girl's size. She was so scared she took off somewhere. No coat or anything. We looked for her for a bit—that's why I

101

was late—but we didn't find her.'

'If you ask me, Mary, it's only a pity someone's not punched that one a bit sooner. He's a nasty piece of work is that George, there's been something strange about him ever since he was a little kid.' Sarah shook her head as she unwrapped the greaseproof paper from a big block of cheese, set it on the marble slab at the other end of the counter from the jams and pickles and covered it with a dome-shaped food net.

'How did a nice young girl like that Nell ever get caught up with the Flanagans, eh Mary? I could understand some of the ones that he's had living up there with him in the past, the types who saw he had a few shillings in his pocket—and wherever he got that from before he started down the market I don't know—and were out for what they could get, but she seems different, innocent. A really sweet girl.'

'I think that's the problem, Sarah. That's what she is—sweet and innocent. I don't suppose she had the first idea what she was letting herself in for when she moved in with that lot. I reckon she just thought she was getting herself somewhere steady, you know coming from the kiddies' home and that, having no family. It must be hard being all by yourself with no one to love or to love you.'

'How old is she?'

'Don't know, Sarah, but I'd put money on her being younger than them twins.'

'A girl of that age should be the one being looked after. She shouldn't be spending her time running around after them three.'

'There is a pleasant young woman—a few years older than Nell—Sylvia I think she said her name

102

is, who comes to see her once a week, but apart from that there's no one, not a single soul to stick up for her. Just imagine, being orphaned and then getting hiked up with the likes of the Flanagans. Life's not fair sometimes, is it, Sarah? That girl deserves better.'

'From your lips to God's ears, Mary.'

Sarah went through to the back room of the shop and reappeared with a blackened metal baking tray packed with spice-fragrant bread pudding hot and fresh from the oven, just as the bell over the door rang to announce the first customer of the morning.

'Hello, Ada,' said Mary, turning to wink over her shoulder at Sarah. 'Thought you might be popping in.'

*   *   *

Nell ran the clothes brush over the coat that Sylvia had made her wear for her journey home—despite it being far too small—and hung it in the back of the wardrobe. She didn't intend to wait to find out whether it would infuriate Stephen if he saw it, she just knew it would; most things Nell did now seemed to drive him into a fury for some reason. It was all so different from the first few weeks that they had been together, everything had seemed possible then—even, she had secretly believed, that they might somehow get married one day. But now all that seemed like so much nonsense; this was to be her lot from now on, and she'd just have to make the best of it. It wasn't something she wanted to admit even to herself, or even think about, but she knew it was true—this was her life.

103

After all, who else would ever be interested in her now, someone who'd been living in sin with a man? This was her punishment.

She closed the wardrobe door, stroking the walnut veneer she polished so carefully, and then went through to the kitchen to clear up what mess George and Lily had left, and to see what food there was that she could stretch to the meal that they and Stephen would be expecting later.

There was no sign of George; maybe he'd gone back to bed or gone out somewhere—she doubted very much that he'd actually gone to the market—but Lily was sitting at the table, flicking through a magazine. Her hair was in curlers and she was wearing her dressing gown, even though it was now past noon.

'Where have you been?' Lily said, without looking up. 'Dad'll want to know what you've been up to. Especially after what happened with him,' she jerked her head towards the door. 'That one across the landing. I saw the way that that Martin was looking at you. Dirty little sod. He's never looked at me that way, and I'm not even living over the brush with someone—not like you.'

Nell felt dizzy with fear—Lily was so spiteful, she was capable of anything. At least with the matron there had been rules that everyone had understood, even if they hadn't always liked them. She steadied her breathing and went over to the dresser, opened one of the drawers and took out a clean apron. She put it on and then shook out her wet apron from the paper carrier bag that Sylvia had given her, and hooked it onto the nail on the back of the kitchen door to dry.

Nell jumped when Lily shouted at her. 'Have

104

you gone deaf? I asked you where you've bloody well been.'

She jumped again as Lily slapped her magazine down on the table.

'Well? What have you got to say for yourself?'

'Nowhere. I've been nowhere. Where would I have to go?'

'You wait. You just wait till Dad gets home. He'll give you nowhere.'

CHAPTER 15

Nell stood at the sink scouring the pots while Stephen sat at the table noisily scoffing down the neck of lamb stew she had had waiting ready for him. George had come home with his father, and had sat next to him at the kitchen table, glaring at Nell's back, but refusing to touch the food she'd kept warm for him because his face was 'too painful to be able to eat'. Lily had had no such qualms when, earlier, Nell had given her her food, and she had even eaten another plateful when Nell's appetite had deserted her as she waited—so nervously—to see what would happen when Stephen came home.

Nell flinched as she heard him throw down his spoon and fork and skid his bowl across the table away from him.

'You, out.' Stephen's voice was low, frightening.

Nell wiped her hands on her apron and started for the door.

'Not you, you silly whore.'

She stopped dead in her tracks.

'Him.'

George was up and out of the room before Nell had dared move, and even if Stephen had crept across the kitchen in his bare feet rather than in his heavy, clumping boots, she would still have known he was looming right there behind her.

'Well?'

Nell gulped down a breath that threatened to choke her. How could he expect her to speak?

She felt him grab her by the hair, and then her head was being jerked back and he was dragging her sideways over to the table.

'George saw you messing around with that little bastard across the landing. It's a man you want, not a fucking kid.'

'Please, Stephen, leave me alone. Please.'

Stephen smacked her hard across the face with the flat of his hand, wrenched her body round and slammed her face down onto the table, sending the bowl, spoon and fork and the remains of his supper crashing to the floor.

There was nothing she could do except squeeze her eyes tight to hold back the tears as he tore down her knickers and thrust himself into her.

Soon sated, Stephen wiped himself dry on the tea towel and set about buttoning up his fly. 'Don't you ever show me up like that again.'

He calmly looked towards the open door where George was standing watching them, his swollen penis gripped in his hand.

'You won't get that back in your trousers when it's like that,' he said matter-of-factly to George. 'And if you don't want another bloody nose tomorrow, you can get yourself and your lazy-arsed sister down that market in the morning. I've got better things to do than run a stall. And don't you think I'm kidding, boy. Cos I'm not. I am a busy man, and you and her are taking over that stall or you'll pay what for, you have my word on that.'

Nell wouldn't have understood what Stephen was talking about when he claimed he had better things to do with his time—even if she hadn't been preoccupied with vomiting into the sink.

Stephen pushed past her. 'And make sure you clean up this kitchen before you come to bed.'

She didn't even register George's agonised gasp as his father punched him squarely in the solar plexus.

'Have that as a little reminder for you not to let me down in the morning, Georgie boy, or you really will have something to complain about.'

Across the landing Martin was standing in the open doorway of number 57, fists up, flexing his shoulders, his chest visibly rising and falling.

'What do you think you're doing out here?' It was Mary Lovell, standing behind her son, looking over his shoulder at the empty landing.

'Can't you hear the noise from the Flanagans, Mum? I'll bet that bully's knocking her about because I punched him this morning. I'm going over to see what's going on.'

'Aw no you're not. It was different earlier, you were all out on the landing, but you've been brought up better than to interfere in what goes on behind people's closed doors. Now get back in here before there's any more trouble.'

'But Mum, I heard her shouting for him to leave her alone. That George makes me sick, treating her like that. I'm going to have him. Teach him how to behave. Someone's got to.'

'Do I have to call your father?'

'I'm not a kid, Mum.'

'No?'

'No, I'm not. I bring money into this house, remember.'

Mary blinked slowly. 'I do know, son. Of course I do.'

Martin threw up his hands, furious with his big mouth. 'I'm really sorry, Mum, that wasn't fair. Course I bring money in, and I'm really glad that I do. This is my family and we all pull together. We do what has to be done. Dad looked after me when I was little, and now I can make some sort of repayment for all the things you both did for me. Please, Mum, don't be upset. I know I sounded like I begrudge it, but course I don't. You know that. I'll stay here for as long as you both need me. I promise you.'

Mary dug up a smile from somewhere and stroked her son gently on the cheek. 'Like when you were a little boy and you used to promise me you'd take me to the seaside one day?'

Martin shrugged. 'Yeah. One day, eh Mum?'

'Yeah, one day, son.'

CHAPTER 16

Nell's hands were shaking as she buttoned her coat. For once, Stephen had insisted that she should go to the corner shop to buy some corned beef—he said he fancied hash for his supper. They both knew full well he would usually bring some home, but he'd made it quite clear that today at least he was only going to stay at the market long enough to show Lily and George how to run the stall, and then he was off somewhere. Apparently this meant going to some place where he couldn't buy corned beef.

As Stephen had issued his instructions about her going to the shop, Nell had watched him mopping up the last of the egg yolk with a slice of toast—all that was left of the plateful of fried breakfast she had made for him. And she had really wondered for one almost happy moment if it was his way of apologising for what he'd done to her the night before, his clumsy way of saying sorry. But she had rapidly returned to reality—Stephen wasn't a man who said sorry. Yet still she knew she had to struggle to pull herself together, make up her mind to find some good even in a morning like this, or else she would sink as surely as a bag of rubbish that had been tossed in the river. She had to find some strength from somewhere.

She closed her eyes. Right. For a start, George and Lily, in an unusually quiet and compliant mood, had left the Buildings with their father. That had to be good. There, that was something to start with. And, if she were lucky, they wouldn't be home until late afternoon.

Blissful peace for hours . . .

Maybe she should try looking on the bright side a bit more often. It had to be better than feeling miserable and alone all the time.

She couldn't help but think about Sarah Meckel from the corner shop, and how she always tried to make the best of everything despite the hardships and disappointments she'd suffered. When people asked her about her husband, David, she always said the same thing—that he was fine, and how it was important that you realised that you had to work at a marriage to make it last, and that everyone went through their little bad patches. If that was true for Sarah and David then maybe it could be true for her and Stephen, and while they weren't officially man and wife like the Meckels, they were as good as married. Maybe if she tried a bit harder life would be easier, better.

Nell took a comb from her handbag and turned to the mirror above the kitchen sink, preparing to go round to the corner shop.

As soon as she saw herself, her mood darkened immediately. The left side of her face was covered in a livid purple-brown bruise.

Now she understood what Stephen was doing— he was sending her to the shop so that everyone could see her—it was more punishment. Stephen was going to make sure that everyone saw what he had done to her, to show the power he had over her and what he could do if she displeased him. But she had made the decision to live with a man without being his wife—and with everyone knowing it—so how could she think it was unfair? Even if she had only run away from George to protect herself, maybe she deserved to be punished and humiliated.

*   *   *

As Nell went into the shop, her head held down and her chin tilted away from them, Sarah Meckel and Mary Lovell exchanged glances.

'Morning, Nell,' said Mary brightly.

'Yeah, morning, Nell,' chimed in Sarah. 'What

can we get for you today? Some washing soda? A slab of soap maybe?'

'No thanks,' said Nell, barely audibly. 'I'd like six ounces of corned beef, please.'

That had Sarah and Mary flashing another look at each other along the counter.

'Corned beef? Not like you, coming in for something like that.' Sarah lifted the rectangular slab of red, fat-marbled meat off the white porcelain stand and onto the bacon slicer. 'I thought Stephen always fetched in the food. Thought we were only good enough for household bits and pieces.'

Nell shrank down into her coat. 'I'm sorry if I've offended you, Sarah. If you'd rather I went somewhere else.'

Both of the women heard the sob in her voice.

'Don't be silly, Nell,' said Sarah. 'I was only playing. Now, let's see, six ounces was it?'

'Yes, please.'

'Funny old weather we're having,' Mary said, sorting through the biscuits in the big glass-lidded tins and putting any broken ones in the mixed bargain barrel. 'One minute you think spring's here, then it starts getting all gloomy again.'

Sarah turned the chrome handle of the slicer, activating the blade that carved through the meat, and caught the slices on a sheet of greaseproof paper. 'Me and Mary, we were going to have a cup of tea in a minute. Stay and have one with us if you like.' Another quick look at Mary. 'We can have a nice little chat. Just the three of us. Tell you what, we'll put the closed sign up on the door and have a real good natter.'

'I can't, I've got to get back.'

Sarah put the meat on the scale and watched the arrow move across. 'Just under. Want another slice?'

'No, that'll do. Thank you. I've got to go.'

'If you're sure.'

'Stephen said to put it on the slate, please.' Nell's voice was now quavering, and she snatched up the greaseproof paper before Sarah could parcel it up. That was a mistake. The slices of meat fell all over the scrubbed wooden counter and Nell burst into tears.

'Right, that's it.' Sarah went over to the door, bolted it tight and turned the sign round to read CLOSED. 'We're going to get to the bottom of this.'

'Sarah,' said Mary, pulling a *please shut up* face. 'The girl said she's got to go home.'

'Too bad, now go and put the kettle on.'

'I don't want any tea,' sniffed Nell. 'I feel sick.' She dropped down onto the customer's chair that stood by the counter.

'You don't have to stay with him, you know,' said Sarah, patting her shoulder. 'It's not as if you're, you know, married to the man.'

Nell didn't even bother to try and hide her tears. 'You don't understand. No one does. I've got to stay with him. I've got no choice. I've just got to.'

'No you haven't. A beautiful young girl like you, there are so many boys out there—boys your own age, boys who'd love the chance to be with someone like you.' Sarah stroked Nell's hair. 'You've got your whole life in front of you. Course you haven't got to stay with him.'

'Yes I do have to.'

'But darling, why?'

Nell pulled her handkerchief from her bag, and

112

although she held it up to her mouth, what she said next was horribly clear to Sarah and Mary. 'Cos not only have I been living in sin like some cheap tart, but I think I'm expecting. I keep being sick and I've not seen my, you know, my—' She dropped her voice. 'My period. Again. That's two I've missed. Two.'

Sarah said something in a language that neither Nell nor Mary understood, while 'Blimmin' hell,' was as much as Mary could manage by way of response.

Sarah squatted down next to the chair. 'There are things you can do, you know.'

Nell sniffed and wiped her nose.

'I mean, you don't have to have it.'

Mary tutted loudly, concerned but exasperated. 'Have you got any idea what Sarah's talking about, love? Cos I don't suppose they told you about these things in the home, now did they?'

'They didn't tell us anything much in the home, but I do know what she means. My friend Sylvia, she explained all sorts of things to me when I lived at the pub. But I couldn't do what you're talking about. I just couldn't. I wasn't wanted when I was little and I know what that feels like, having no one wanting you.' She put her hand on her stomach and let out a little huff of mirthless laughter. 'I might have been wrong when I thought that Stephen Flanagan actually wanted me because he loved me—me, daft little Nelly—but I know I want my baby.'

'Where will you go, sweetheart?'

'Nowhere. There's nowhere for me to go.'

'How about the pub? The Hope with that Sylvia Woods? You used to live there all right, didn't you?'

'That was before. It's different now. Stephen's a good friend of the owner, he's in there all the time, so I'd hardly be welcome there if I went and left him.'

'But that'll mean you being stuck with the Flanagans.'

'If that's what I have to do, then that's what I have to do.'

Tenderly, Sarah touched the bruise on the side of Nell's face. 'Tell me, darling, how did that happen?'

'I left the cupboard door open, and forgot.'

'And in a minute my David's going to walk down them back stairs, tell me to put my feet up and start running the shop for me.'

Mary took herself back behind the counter and began to wrap the scattered slices of corned beef. 'The girl doesn't want to talk about it, Sarah.'

Sarah stood up. 'And that's exactly how men like him get away with it.'

CHAPTER 17

'Go on Steve-o, let's have a bit of credit, mate. Just a couple of bob each way. I'll pay you back in a few days, I give you my solemn word on it. In fact, I swear on my old woman's life. I'll repay you every penny. You can trust me, Steve-o, you know that.'

Stephen was leaning against the wall outside a tobacconist's shop in Brick Lane. He had his cap pulled down hard over his well-oiled hair, and a white silky muffler knotted around his neck. He took a leisurely drag of his roll-up before bothering to answer.

'Pay me back in a couple of days, now will you?'

'Sure I will.'

'You can't be that confident of winning then, feller, now can you, or you'd be promising to pay me back right after this afternoon's race—straight after you've won. So do us all a favour and piss off, I've got these genuine customers waiting here, men with money in their pockets waiting to lay real bets.'

The shabbily dressed man, hands deep in his trouser pockets, slunk away, with Stephen's mocking laughter ringing after him.

'Reckon he thinks I'm straight off the boat, that one.' Stephen flicked the butt of his roll-up into the gutter. 'Right, who's for any more? And I am talking about the exchange of actual money here remember, gentlemen. So please don't ask for tick, cos a punch in the gob often offends. If it's credit you want you have definitely come to the wrong man.'

*　　　*　　　*

Stephen walked into the Hope and Anchor, completely ignoring Sylvia who was busy serving the lunchtime rush, and made his way to the back of the pub where Bernie was leaning, studying the newspaper he had spread out on the bar in front of him.

'All right, Bernard?'

'Not so shabby.' Bernie winked at Stephen, closed his newspaper and nodded towards the corner table, which the regulars knew was for the

115

landlord's exclusive use. 'Stephen, would you care to join me in my office?'

Sylvia watched as they sat down, and Stephen, with his back carefully set towards her, handed a canvas bag to her husband, which Bernie then secreted in the folds of his newspaper. They exchanged a few words and Bernie turned his head towards the bar. Sylvia hurriedly looked away.

'Couple of light and bitters over here, Sylv,' Bernie called across to her.

Sylvia filled the glasses and took them over to the corner table.

'Hello Stephen, how're things doing down the market?'

'Good.'

'Glad to hear it. And how about Nell, how's she?'

Stephen took a sip of his drink, giving himself a moment to think. The last thing he wanted was this nosy cow sticking her beak in and threatening to cause any friction or unpleasantness between him and Bernie. 'Not too well as it happens. But thanks for asking.'

Sylvia frowned. 'What's wrong with her?'

'Just a bit under the weather. I told her to go back to bed,' he lied.

'Give her my love, won't you,' said Sylvia, glancing at the bulging newspaper. 'And tell her to pop in and see me when she's feeling better.'

'Course I will.'

Bernie jerked his thumb towards the bar. 'There's people waiting to be served over there, Sylv.'

'Yes, sir,' she said with a mocking curtsey, and planted a lipsticky kiss on his bald head.

116

Surely Bernie must have realised by now that she'd known what he was up to practically from the day she'd started working in the pub as a barmaid—never mind the things she'd found out about him since they'd been married—and lately Stephen's involvement in matters had become too obvious to ignore. That's why Bernie was so irritable whenever Nell was around. He knew she wasn't like Sylvia. She was so naive Bernie was scared she would open her mouth all innocently and ruin everything.

It was a good job Sylvia loved the daft old sod— and, she had to admit, all the fancy trimmings his dodgy dealings brought her—or who knows what mischief she could have caused him. She smiled at the line of customers.

'Right chaps, who's next then?'

As she looked at the men standing before her, she wondered what sort of secrets they were hiding from their wives—everyone said women were the last to know what their husbands were up to. But Sylvia wasn't like most women, and neither did she have any qualms about sticking up for a friend if she thought she was in trouble. Maybe this afternoon, once they'd closed, she might cheer up Nell by taking her one of the sugary doughnuts from the baker's next door to the pub. She used to love them, especially when the jam squelched out from the doughy middle. She smiled to herself as she remembered the two of them laughing until their sides ached when they had competitions to see who could eat a whole one of the sugar-covered things without licking their lips.

Now barely smiling, Sylvia's eyes stung as she blinked back the tears, missing Nell, missing her so very much, and feeling so very sorry that she had let her friend get involved with Stephen Flanagan.

*   *   *

Sylvia had hardly an ounce of spare flesh on her tiny frame, but she wasn't used to climbing so many stairs on a regular basis, and by the time she'd got to the Flanagans' flat on the top floor of Turnbury Buildings she was puffing like a steam train.

She took a moment to catch her breath, hand leaning against the wall, head bowed, before she knocked on the door, but she'd wasted her time. No one answered.

'Bugger, Nell must be asleep. Have I really done all them rotten stairs for flipping nothing?'

'What did you say?'

Sylvia turned round to see Ada Tanner, arms folded, looking her up and down as if she'd never seen the like before.

'Nothing to concern you; just talking to myself.'

Ada pointed at the paper baker's bag in Sylvia's hand. 'So what you got in there then?'

'A tube of nose ointment.' Sylvia held out the bag. 'Here, do you want a dab? Cos that nose of yours must be right sore from sticking it in other people's business all the time.'

'That's a nice way to talk to a woman old enough to be your mother.'

'Grandmother more like,' muttered Sylvia.

'What did you say?'

Sylvia mocked up a smile. 'I said—have you got a pencil I can borrow, please?'

'What for?'

118

Sylvia was about to say *To stick up your arse, you nosy old cow*, but she needed a pencil. 'I thought I'd leave a note for Nell. Let her know I came round to see her.'

Ada narrowed her eyes. 'You wait there and I'll fetch the one my Albert uses.' She hesitated. 'I said wait. Get me?'

'Thank you,' said Sylvia, who had absolutely no intention of going anywhere near the horrible old woman's front room. It was probably full of broomsticks and black cats, and her Albert probably used the pencil to write down her spells for her.

*   *   *

Sylvia tore off a bit of the baker's bag and just stopped herself from licking the end of the pencil—goodness only knew where it had been or what it had really been used for—and then she wrote:

Dear Nell, sorry I missed seeing you, darling. Hope you had a good sleep and that you'll be feeling better soon. Come and see me when you do. Love from your friend, Sylvia.

She put the note in the bag, rolled the top over and set about shoving it through the letter box. It took a bit of squashing, but she managed.

'That'll be nice for her to come home to,' said Ada, taking back the pencil.

Sylvia's pleasantly surprised smile at what she first thought were Ada's kind words didn't last long when it quickly dawned on her what the woman actually meant—she was saying that Nell wasn't at home. But she had to be wrong; Nell was poorly—

in bed asleep, getting better.

While Sylvia's mind churned over these confusing thoughts, Ada was warming to her subject.

'You know what'll happen, don't you? She'll be bound to step on it and then she'll get jam all over the hall runner, and then she'll have to get down on her hands and knees and scrub off all the mess.'

'I think you're wrong there, because if you must know, the poor girl's in there in bed. She's not well.'

'If you say so, but I reckon I know better. I'm telling you, that girl was in the shop.' Ada didn't give Sylvia the chance to reply, she just shut the door firmly in her face.

Sylvia didn't know what to think any more, and as she made her way down the stairs—so much easier than climbing the buggers—she was even more concerned for her friend.

It was only a pity that she didn't notice Nell, with her hand covering her bruised and swollen face, as she pressed herself flat against the wall in the shadows by the rubbish chute, the place where she'd been hiding ever since she'd heard Sylvia's voice and had been too ashamed to show herself. Not only ashamed, but too scared to show herself to her dearest friend in the whole world for fear of what she might do.

As she heard Sylvia's footsteps echoing and fading away down the stairs, Nell thought about her precious brooch hidden under the pile of handkerchiefs in the bedside cabinet, and wondered how she could make sure that if something really bad happened to her it would become Sylvia's. Because, the way she felt now,

Nell honestly wasn't sure how much longer she was going to be able to last in this world.

1936

CHAPTER 18

'Get that boy away from me, or you'll both be sorry.' Stephen was threatening Nell but concentrating on his food.

'But I only want the leftover bits.'

Nell raised her eyebrows and shook her head urgently at her now almost eight-year-old Tommy as he hovered around the table, staring at the thick glossy brown rind that Stephen had cut off a fat slice of gammon, which almost filled his plate.

Tommy's mouth watered as he twiddled his thick dark fringe around his finger. He *loved* the smell of fried bacon.

'Tommy, don't bother your dad while he's having his tea, there's a good boy. I know, why don't you go down and play in the courtyard? Go on. And why don't you take Dolly down there with you?'

Dolly—Nell and Stephen's six-year-old, the blonde curly-haired image of her mother—was hanging on Nell's apron as Nell stood at the sink washing up the pots and pans. Dolly stared at her father's back, her thumb plugged in her mouth.

Nell turned to look out of the window. 'It's lovely out there. I bet the kids'll all be playing Olympics again. Go on. Go and join in.'

'That was last week,' said Tommy, taking a last lingering look at his father's bacon, but, as usual, he did as his mother told him, judging—correctly—from the tone of her voice that she wasn't actually asking him if he fancied going down to play, she was most definitely telling him to make himself scarce.

'Well, whatever they're up to, they'll all be out in this lovely sunshine.' Nell ruffled her children's hair, and shooed them out of the door with a smile. 'And Tommy, make sure you keep hold of Dolly's hand when you're going down the stairs,' she called. 'You know how steep they are for her.'

She turned her attention back to the sink. Cooking and clearing up after everyone took more hours than there seemed to be in the day lately. It wouldn't be so bad if Lily and George would just wait an hour or so to eat until the little ones came in for their tea. But that would be too easy, too kind for those two even to think of doing. Oh no, they had to have their meal waiting for them ready to be put on the table as soon as they got back from the market, and if that was just after three, then it was Nell's bad luck.

The twins might have reached twenty-eight years of age but they were still showing no sign of leaving home, or of even going out with anyone on any sort of regular basis. Whether there would ever be anyone stupid enough to have a long-term interest in either of the spiteful pair was anybody's guess. Nell certainly couldn't think of anyone. There had been one or two that she had found out about over the years—involving maybe a couple of evening trips to the pictures, or a few visits to the pub—with various young women and young men whom the twins had met down the market, but nothing had ever come to much, or had ever lasted beyond that. But why would it? No one in their right mind would be prepared to put up with their tempers or their selfishness. No one but Nell, and

126

that was only because she had little choice in the matter, especially now she had her beloved children and wouldn't jeopardise their security by upsetting the twins—this, however much she hated it, was Tommy and Dolly's home. She would just have to put up with Lily and George, and Stephen. She thought, as she often did, about Joe and Martin Lovell, and how they did so many little things for Mary—carrying her bags up the stairs, taking the rubbish out to the chute, calling out to her over the balcony to make sure she was OK when she was down in the courtyard. And, as usual, she felt ashamed that she was jealous of a woman just because she had the good fortune to be living with two such kind men.

But at least Nell didn't have to eat with the twins as she had been forced to when she had first moved into Turnbury Buildings. Since having the children, she had sat down at the table each afternoon to have her tea with Tommy and Dolly, who, so long as Lily and George weren't hanging around in the kitchen, would chatter away happily, telling their mum about all the things they'd done while they'd been out playing or at school that day. Nell was so proud that she could help them with their numbers and letters—the home had given her those skills and a roof over her head, if not very much else.

Then Stephen would arrive home expecting his meal, and sit and eat in silence just as he was doing now. It was the time of day she had learned to fear in a way that she would never have thought possible before the children had come along, as anything they did or said was capable of incensing him.

127

She flinched as Stephen took a loud slurp of tea and then belched loudly without so much as an excuse me, the sounds jolting her back to the present and the dirty pan in her hands. She could only imagine what Matron Sully would have thought of him and his crude ways, but, more importantly, she wondered how long he would be hanging around the kitchen.

Nell no longer bothered herself with the mystery of what Stephen got up to all day while the twins were running the stalls, or that he spent most evenings at the Hope, she was just glad when he wasn't there. In the meantime, she carried on keeping the flat looking nice, cooking, cleaning, and being his and the twins' skivvy; and—except when he had more drink in him than usual—he seemed, thank goodness, to have lost interest in her. Maybe he'd found someone else who was willing to put up with him, and that was where he spent his days. Wherever he went, Nell just wished he'd spend even more time there, because what else had changed over the years was that she had become increasingly frightened of him losing his temper. She wasn't scared for herself—she had learned to put up with that; being attacked by Stephen and abused by the twins had become her way of life, just as it had been in the home with the matron. What really terrified her was that Stephen might one day direct his anger at her children.

Nell snatched a quick look at him as he sprinkled more vinegar over the last of his bacon.

OK, for now he kept his beatings for her, but she had to be so careful with the little ones, making sure that they didn't upset him and start him off on one of his rages. But if he did one day decide to

128

turn on them, if he laid just one finger on either of them, then she'd . . .

What? What would she do? She could never think beyond the horror of them being hurt.

His power over her was a weapon that hung in the air between them, one that Stephen used as a silent, forbidding threat if Nell didn't do exactly as he wanted, and she couldn't help but wonder what he might actually be capable of, what he might do to the children. Yet in spite of her fears for Tommy and Dolly, she still felt herself completely blessed to have them. The children were the loves of her life, her very own family. When the nurse had first put Tommy into her arms in the lying-in hospital she had been overwhelmed—it had been the first time she had ever knowingly held someone who shared her own blood. If she could only find a way for them to have a home of their own, just the three of them, with a little bedroom each instead of the children having to sleep in the front room, she would have had perfect happiness. But she knew she shouldn't be greedy. She was so lucky in other ways. She hadn't realised until she had the children what it was to feel such total love for another human being.

'Anything else?' she asked Stephen as she took his plate, keeping her voice light even though the rind that Tommy would have loved to have eaten wrapped in a slice of bread was staring up at her, mocking her powerlessness.

'No.' He got up and took his jacket from the back of his chair.

If she hadn't learnt that it would infuriate him, Nell could have burst into song: not only had the twins gone out, but now it looked as if he was going out too. That meant she could go down and watch the children enjoying themselves in the courtyard, the space bounded by the three five-floor tenements that served variously as a sports field and playground, a general meeting place, a parking area for babies sleeping in prams, and a sometime battlefield for warring neighbours. It was also a totally forbidden laundry-drying space, still used, of course, weather permitting. Sheets and pillowcases would flap from the illicit washing lines that the women from the Buildings would string between the blocks, and stretch high and taut with the tall wooden clothes props that would appear from their hiding places down in the basement. The pleasure of being able to dry your laundry in the open air was far too great for the women to worry themselves about following such mean-spirited rules.

CHAPTER 19

'Hello, Nell, come and sit here with me. The sunshine's still lovely and warm.' Mary Lovell was perched on the bottom of the stone steps that led down from their block into the courtyard. She had her crossover apron pulled modestly over her knees and a saucepan in her lap into which she was slicing runner beans.

She shuffled sideways on her bottom to make room so that Nell could join her. 'I've been watching your two little ones bouncing around, just like the jack rabbits you see when you go down hop picking they are. Just look at the pair of them.

Wish I had half their energy. Getting the tea ready is enough of an effort for me after a day's work.'

'You and me, Mary.' Nell shaded her eyes, checking where her children were, and that they were safe. 'I'm glad I've had a chance to see you alone. I wanted to ask you how Sarah's David is doing.' She asked the question in a quiet, almost matter-of-fact way, not wanting to seem to be prying, but genuinely concerned. 'I could hear from her voice this morning that she's been worried about something, and I just thought it might be David. Nothing else ever seems to get her down.'

Mary looked unseeingly at the heap of unsliced beans. 'You know me, Nell, I'm never one to gossip, but Sarah wouldn't mind me telling you. Like she always says: there's no shame in what's wrong with David—he's the way he is because he was such a brave young man, but I don't think he's too good at the minute, to be honest. He's, a bit, you know, worse than usual. Sarah said it was that thunderstorm the other night; it really gave him a bad turn. It was all the banging and crashing and the lightning. And when he eventually managed to get off to sleep, she said he had these terrible nightmares. Calling out, sweating and thrashing around she said he was. Must have been horrible for the pair of them. Sarah said she didn't know what to do—whether she should wake him up or leave him. I mean, you do hear these stories, don't you? People having heart attacks and suchlike if you wake them up suddenly. I suppose she's only lucky she lives over the shop and not here in the Buildings or she'd have her next door to me banging on the wall, complaining about the noise. I

131

can't stir my tea and put the spoon down in my saucer without her leading off. She drives me potty at times.'

'No one takes any notice of Ada, Mary. You mustn't let her get you down.'

'It's not her really, Nell, I know she's just a whining old bat, I just wish I could help Sarah and David. Things are so hard for that poor girl at times.'

'And she's such a kind person.'

'I know, and as for David, I just wish you'd known him when he was a young man, known him the way he used to be. He was such a good bloke. When you think, he came over here with his parents when he was a little boy, but he was one of the first to volunteer to fight for this country. So brave, and not much more than a kid really. Now he's stuck up there above the shop, fretting that he's not doing his best for Sarah, and not able to do anything about it. They both deserve better than that, Nell.'

'Things'll turn out, Mary, you see if they don't. Just like they will for you and Joe.'

'I do hope so, love. But for the life of me I can't think how. Things are really getting Joe down lately. I don't know what him and me are gonna do when Martin goes. We've already got used to the extra he's been bringing in since he got his promotion.'

Nell turned away, apparently suddenly fascinated by Dolly, who was clapping as Tommy cavorted about, springing handstands up against the wall, and turning cartwheels like a circus acrobat. 'So, Martin's met someone special, has he? Will he be leaving the Buildings very soon?'

'No, not yet, but you know him, always got girls chasing after him. But I shouldn't be surprised, should I? I know he's my boy, but he's a handsome young so-and-so.'

'Wish I could say the same about Lily and George,' said Nell lightly. 'That pair are so sour-faced and angry-looking all the time. The way things are going, I'll bet I'll be stuck with them living up in fifty-five for ever.'

Mary, knowing where lines were drawn, said nothing more.

Nell watched as all the children in the courtyard unexpectedly ran to one of the walls and gathered in a huddle, as if some signal, undetectable to adults' ears, had been sounded.

'So Martin's not got anyone special then, you say?' Her tone was casual, as if she was barely interested.

'No, like I say, not yet.' Mary tossed the top and tail of another bean onto the pile that had been growing on the sheet of newspaper by her feet. She stopped suddenly, the cutter in one hand, bean in the other. 'Not unless he's mentioned something about anyone to you, Nell.'

'Me? No.' Nell was nearly choking on the words. 'Why would he say anything to me?'

'That's a relief, because when he does decide it's time for him to go I wouldn't dream of stopping him, course I wouldn't. But for now we are so grateful that he got his promotion and that new job at the brewery. First office worker in the family he is, on both sides. I can't tell you how proud I am of him. But mainly, of course, it's the extra money that he's bringing in that's so handy.'

Mary tossed the bean slicer into the saucepan.

133

'Do you know, Nell, my Joe's tried everywhere. Everywhere. But there's nothing. I shouldn't complain though, Sarah gives me what hours she can in the shop, which is more than most people have. But I could work there morning, noon and night and it still wouldn't be enough to manage on, not without Martin's money coming in. And as for what would happen if we had to go to the Assistance, I don't even want to think what having to go through this new means test they've brought in would do to my Joe. It's a wicked thing to do to a decent, willing man.'

Nell patted Mary's hand, feeling guilty that although she and the children never derived much benefit from the good fortune that Stephen and the twins seemed to enjoy, they were hardly desperate.

'Did you hear about all them people marching to Trafalgar Square last week to protest about it?' Mary went on. 'Fifteen thousand people, Joe said the paper reckoned there were. Fifteen thousand desperate people. It's not right, is it, Nell?'

'I'm sorry things are so hard for you and Joe, Mary.'

'I don't even know if I'm going to bother going down hopping this year. I'd like to try and get a few extra bob for Christmas so I can at least treat Joe and Martin, but from what Martin's heard at the brewery they're probably going to cut the rates again this year. It'll be all strikes and rows and no work for days. Hardly worth it. Mind you, not that there's going to be much to celebrate the way things are, Christmas or no Christmas.'

'I'd love to take the kids down hopping,' said Nell. 'From what you've told me it sounds wonderful, all that green everywhere, and the animals, and the lovely fresh eggs and butter.'

'We'll all have to go together one year—you, me and the kids.'

It went unsaid between them that Stephen would never allow such a thing—what would he do without Nell there to run around after him and the twins?

'Still, at least we've got the courtyard to sit in, eh Mary?'

Mary nodded. 'Yeah, we're a lot luckier than most, I suppose.'

'And let's hope this weather holds until Monday, cos we'll have the washing dry in no time.'

'Washing day coming round again. Unbelievable.' Mary went back to slicing her beans. 'It's funny you know, I've no idea where the weeks or even the months go, but when I get home from doing my hours in the shop and go indoors the hours just drag by. Joe's sitting there, reading his paper, and I'm thinking how soon I can start the tea. It's like I'm trying to use up the minutes, waiting till bedtime, so I can pull the covers over myself, close my eyes and just forget about everything.'

'It'll all sort itself out, Mary. It always does.'

'I hope so, Nell, I really do.'

'Mum, Mum, look at me.'

Nell's attention was caught by Tommy as he shouted to her from across the yard. He was holding a makeshift cricket bat. It had been fashioned out of a cut-down plank of wood, with rough hairy string bound round one shaved-off end to serve as the handle. He was standing sideways on from a wicket that an older boy had chalked on

135

the wall of one of the far blocks.

Tommy flexed his skinny little eight-year-old shoulders. 'I'm gonna really whack this one.'

A freckled, ginger-haired boy of about ten took a fast skipping run across the tarmac and hurled a grubby, grey, almost hairless tennis ball with all his force right at Tommy's head.

'Oi! Watch it!' Tommy ducked, the ball hit the wall and went ricocheting across the yard. 'You bloody rotten cheat, Danny Leary. Who do you think I am—Don Bradman?'

'I heard that, Tommy Flanagan,' shouted Nell. She was doing her best not to look amused, and was rather more successful than Mary, who was sniggering into the back of her hand.

'Love him,' Mary spluttered. 'At least he's managed to make me laugh.'

'*Mummy.*' It was Dolly. She was sprinting across the yard to the steps as fast as her little legs could carry her. 'Did you hear what Tommy said? He said bloody and rotten, and we're not allowed to say those words. They're naughty. And only Auntie Sylvia can say them, because that's different.'

Nell reached out and scooped her daughter up onto her lap. 'He didn't mean it,' she said, wishing that everything could be as easy to deal with as children saying the odd bad word.

Mary couldn't hold back the laughter, it was as if something had been released from inside her. 'And how does a little one like you know about Don Bradman?' she snorted.

'Your Martin told me all about him,' Tommy called back, his eye firmly on Danny Leary as he shaped up to bowl again. 'They chucked the ball right at him. The rotten . . . I mean the flipping . . .

136

No, I mean the horrible cheats.'

Mary now had a pleased grin on her face. 'He's always had a nice way with kids has my Martin, God love him. He'll make a right good dad one day.'

'What are you lot up to then?' Nell looked up, surprised to see Martin himself walking towards them, the bright sunlight turning him into a dark silhouette. She couldn't make out his expression, but he was smiling broadly. 'I don't really care what it is, but I do know it's the first time I've seen Mum laughing like that for ages. All right if I join you girls for a bit, enjoy the last of this lovely sunshine?'

He didn't wait for an answer; he just plonked himself down on the step next to Nell, loosened his tie and took out the studs from his collar.

Nell's cheeks flushed red as his thigh brushed hers. 'I'd better be getting upstairs soon.'

'You're not leaving on my account are you, Nell?'

'Course I'm not.'

'Good.' Martin nodded, clearly pleased. 'Tell you what, Mum, why don't I pop over the road and get a jug of shandy for you two girls from the four-ale bar, and then you can sit here and have a nice cold drink.' He winked at Nell. 'Reckon you deserve it, cheering up Mum like that.'

Nell jumped to her feet as if she'd been doused in scalding water. 'I can't, I've got, I've got . . . polishing to do. That's what I've got. Polishing.'

She started off up the stone stairway. 'Would you tell Tommy and Dolly to come up when it starts getting dark, for me?' she called as she disappeared into the gloom.

CHAPTER 20

Stephen Flanagan was also about to disappear up a flight of stairs, but these were in the Hope and Anchor in Whitechapel.

'What d'you think then, Steve-o? Ready to go up, are we?' Bernie drained his glass. 'We might as well go and get set up, cos the others'll be here soon enough.'

Stephen finished his pint and stood up. 'Might as well.'

He was about to follow Bernie through the door at the side of the Hope's main bar when he heard a familiar voice calling him.

'Dad. Dad, hang on. Wait a minute.'

Stephen's frame stiffened. He closed his eyes and dropped his chin, summoning all his self-control. It was bloody George, what the hell did he want?

He turned round slowly, opening his eyes. For Christ's sake, it wasn't just George, it was the twins—the sodding pair of the buggers. What the hell did they want? 'What are you two doing here?'

Lily waggled her head angrily as if she were trying to shake off a persistent wasp. 'I don't know why you even have to ask that, Dad. It's not right. We keep trying to talk to you indoors, but you've never got any time for us any more. All you think about is her and those snotty-nosed rotten kids. They're always hanging around and listening, pair of little sneaks. We never get a chance to talk to you in private, so when we were having a couple of drinks up the road just now we decided we'd had

138

enough of it, and we came to find you.'

'You finished?'

Lily shrugged sullenly. 'I reckon I've only just begun.'

'Aw you do, do you?' Stephen ran his fingers through his hair. 'Now tell me, because I'm really interested, you've had enough of what exactly? And what is so important that you've got to show me up, following me about?'

George jumped in before Lily made it any worse. 'Her. It's her we want to talk about, Dad. Bloody butter-wouldn't-melt-in-her-mouth Nell. Like Lil said, we've had just about enough of it. Both of us have.'

'That's right,' chipped in Lily, glaring at her brother—they'd agreed that *she* would do the talking. 'We think she should be pulling her weight more. I mean, both of those kids of hers are going to be back at school in a few weeks, so what's she going to do with herself all day? She could easily do a few turns down the market. It wouldn't kill the idle bitch.'

'Lil's right. It's not fair, us having to do everything. We're working every hour there is. And what does she do? Nothing I can think of, the lazy cow.'

Stephen stepped closer to the twins, ignoring Lily but poking his finger in George's face. 'If this is a way of you two having a pop at me for not controlling her right, you do know I won't be very happy, don't you?'

George had to think fast—something he didn't excel at—because this wasn't going well. 'Course it's not, Dad. We know how busy you are with . . .' He paused for a moment. Bloody hell, he might have been better off approaching this when he was sober, or leaving it to Lil after all. 'Er . . . Other things.'

'I'm glad to hear it. Now if you don't mind, like you say, I'm busy. You want her to do something? Then you sort it out yourselves. You ain't bloody kids any more, you're adults—or you're meant to be—so start acting like it.'

'But Dad—'

Stephen shook his head. 'Leave it, George, and stop fucking moaning. Before I lose my temper.'

He went through the door and closed it behind him, leaving Lily and George standing there. They heard him trotting up the stairs to catch up with Bernie Woods.

All the while, Sylvia had been watching and listening. What on earth did they expect of that poor girl? They might as well tie a brush to her arse so she didn't waste any time not working when she was walking about the place. Sylvia wasn't having this. She wasn't going to see this lot taking liberties with her friend any more. No, she wasn't. She'd stood back for far too long. She was going to sort this out once and for all, and if she had anything to do with it Stephen Flanagan was going to get what was coming to him. It was about bloody time, and Sylvia was going to love every single minute of it.

CHAPTER 21

'No, Joe, I am not having you doing the washing. You do enough as it is—cooking for us all three nights a week, clearing up, changing the beds—no, and I mean no.' Mary poured herself another cup of tea. 'Anyway, I've got plenty of time to do it myself.'

'What you really mean is that you don't want me showing you up, because you don't fancy all the old birds in the Buildings seeing me down there in the laundry.'

Mary put her cup down so hard that the tea splashed over the side into the saucer. 'Joe, please love; don't start all this again. You know Sarah doesn't mind me going in a bit late of a Monday. The shop's nearly empty then, cos everyone's always busy of a Monday morning.'

'Yeah, everyone except me.'

'Don't Joe, don't do this to yourself. I know how it's getting to you, but don't get bitter, love.'

'Why shouldn't I be bitter? It's not fair. It's not bloody fair. No matter how hard I try I can't find anything or anyone even interested in taking me on. I'm not fussy, I'll do anything. What's going on in this world when a man can't earn the money to put food on his own table? Tell me that if you can. If you read the papers, they're saying how people are buying cars, even their own houses, spending like there's no tomorrow. But not the likes of me, aw no, not Joe Lovell. That'll be the future for the likes of Martin with his fancy new office job, him with his trilby hat instead of a cap. Me, I'm only fit for the rubbish heap. Do you know Mary, I really do not know what to think about this world any more. I've just about had a bellyful of it.'

Mary frowned as she noticed the light catch the grey in the stubble on his chin. 'You haven't shaved yet, love.'

141

'What's the point of wasting shaving soap? I'm not going anywhere important, am I?' Joe buried his face in his hands. 'I'm not going anywhere.'

'Morning, Mum, Dad.' Martin sat down at the kitchen table. He'd heard what his father had been saying and had waited outside in the hall, rather than go into the kitchen and risk making matters worse. He hated seeing his father suffering like this. He was a decent bloke who deserved better, as did the thousands of others like him who were being treated as if they were worthless, useless, fit for nothing. 'That last bit of toast going spare?'

'Yeah, there you are, love.' Mary pushed the plate towards him and handed him a little jug full of strawberry jam—at least they'd never go short of something to spread on their bread while Sarah owned the corner shop.

'Sure you don't want it, Dad?'

'No, you have it. Keep the food for those who have work to do. Don't waste it on work-shy bastards like me.'

'Joe!'

He ignored his wife and stood up, shoving his chair away. 'I've had enough of all this. I'm off out, and don't expect me back in for tea either.'

'Where you off to then, love?' she asked softly.

'If you must know, I'm going for a walk to help me waste the day, pop in the library to read the papers, and then tonight I've decided I'm going to a meeting over in Stepney.'

Martin tried a tight-lipped smile, hoping, silently praying that he had misunderstood. 'What, that Unemployed Union thing, Dad? I'll go along with you tonight if you like. More and more people are getting involved with them; they make a lot of sense getting like-minded people together. They could do a lot of good if they get the support.'

'No, I'm not going to that one, I'm going to another one.'

'Please tell me you're not going to listen to that Blackshirt nonsense again? Wasn't the once enough for you? I know it was enough for me. In fact they disgusted me.'

'Well you're not me, are you?' Joe kicked his chair back under the table and walked towards the kitchen door. 'So why should you care about what they've got to say? You're one of the bloody lucky ones. The ones with jobs and a bit of self-respect.'

He might not have waited to hear his son's answer, but Martin and Mary both heard him cursing loudly as he slammed the front door behind him.

Mary shook her head, crushed by the weight of what the world was doing to her husband. 'Martin, he hasn't even shaved.'

She turned away as tears began to spill down her cheeks. 'He's not a bad man, you mustn't get annoyed with him.'

Martin dropped the toast back on the plate. 'I know, Mum. I know.'

CHAPTER 22

With her sleeves rolled up above her elbows, and her hair tied back in a scarf, Nell dragged the steaming sheets out of one of the big boilers with a wooden copper stick and sloshed them into a two-handled enamel basin. The damp heat billowed off them into her face, adding to the already dripping atmosphere of the basement laundry. She heaved the basin up off the floor and carried it over to the bank of deep butler sinks that ran along one wall. Tipping the soapy washing into the sink, she turned on the cold tap and kneaded and pounded the linen, rinsing off the suds.

'Least the weather held, eh Mary?' she said, wiping the sweat from her forehead with the back of her hand. 'We'll have all this pegged out and dry in no time. I love it when we don't have to use the inside racks. In the home we never had anywhere like the courtyard.'

'I don't know how you stay so cheerful,' Mary answered, as she arranged the sleeve of one of Martin's shirts on the scrubbing board that she'd propped up in the sink next to the one Nell was using. Mary, despite the heat, was determined to have a good go at the cuffs; she took pride in bringing her whites up until they gleamed as if they were brand new. 'It's like a flipping furnace down here.'

'Could be worse,' said Nell, always happy to be occupied doing a good day's work; being busy meant not having to dwell on other things. 'Stephen and the twins could be at home getting under my feet. I love that feeling when they're all out and I can just get on with my jobs with no one in my way.'

'That's a nice way to talk, I don't think.'

It was Ada Tanner, standing behind Nell with Myrtle, a new tenant from the block opposite. Ada had recently befriended her after finding her as willing as she was to gossip, rumour-monger and be generally unpleasant about the neighbours.

144

'*Get on with my jobs with no one in the way*,' Ada mimicked. 'Anyone would think she was some sort of lady or something, the way she carries on. But do you know what? She's from out of a kids' home. Truth. I'm telling you. And now she lives over the brush with that Stephen Flanagan; I wouldn't mind, but she's years younger even than his children. Twins they are. And the pair of them work all hours in the market, while both her young ones are out playing all day when it's not schooltime, and her old man goes out at about half nine of a morning—Gawd alone knows where to or what he gets up to, though I've heard plenty of stories, I can tell you.'

Despite her claims, Ada didn't choose to pursue that particular line. Even she was sensible enough not to cross Stephen Flanagan.

'So what does she do all day?' she went on, lifting her chin at Nell. 'I'll tell you, she sits around on her arse, drinking tea and stuffing herself. All right for some, eh? They don't know they're flaming born.'

'You don't say, Ada,' said Myrtle, sounding suitably appalled and acting as if it was all news to her, even though she and Ada had already discussed the life history of just about everyone in the Buildings. Their conversation was solely for the purpose of being heard by Nell and anyone else within earshot. Being a Monday morning the place was full, and surreptitious glances were cast towards the potential source of a scrap—always a popular entertainment in Turnbury Buildings. And as Nell was well known for keeping herself to herself—and so a bit of a snob, some claimed—she didn't have too many advocates jumping to her

145

defence.

'I'm telling you, it's a fact; and another thing, you hardly ever see her without a black eye or a fat lip. The Lord alone knows what she gets up to, to drive a man to doing that to her. A right aggravating witch she must be.'

'That's it.' Mary Lovell threw her scrubbing brush into the sink of soapy water and started towards her neighbour. 'Why don't you just keep that mouth of yours shut for once, Ada Tanner?' She jabbed a wet finger at Myrtle. 'And as for her, she's just as bad. And you, you old cow, you encourage her.'

Nell grabbed her friend by the back of her crossover apron. 'Don't, Mary. Please. She doesn't bother me.'

'Well, I'm telling you, she bothers me.'

Ada folded her arms and looked Mary up and down. 'And I'm telling you, I know what's up with you and all.' She turned to Myrtle. 'They've had murders, her and her old man. That Joe went smashing out of their flat first thing this morning. Like a lunatic he was. Bloody commotion, he was making. And the language he was using. You should have heard him. Like a dog with a banger tied to its tail. Mind you, Myrt, who can blame him? He must be fed up to here with her treating him like he's a flaming woman. A man doing housework, if you don't mind. I ask you. No wonder I've got bad nerves having to live next door to the likes of them with all their hollering and hooting.'

Now all eyes were on Mary as she pulled herself free from Nell and cannoned across the duckboarded floor towards Ada.

146

Ada might have been a hefty type of a woman, but she had a very strong sense of self-preservation. She dodged out of Mary's grasp and shifted herself out of the laundry before Mary could reach her—although the fact that Nell had once more latched onto Mary's apron had slowed down her pursuer considerably.

'Why don't you let me finish your washing off for you, Mary? Then you can go get yourself into work. I can sort out Ada if she comes back down here.'

'Thanks, Nell, that's very kind of you, but I wouldn't give her the satisfaction of thinking she can drive me out of here.'

'Well, at least let me bring your washing in for you once it's dry. So you don't have to rush home. Maybe you could stay and have a cup of tea with Sarah after you finish work. You always say how she appreciates having company and a little chat before she goes upstairs for the evening.'

What Nell didn't say was that Mary should take a bit of time to calm down—what she had in her marriage to Joe was something to be envied, and she shouldn't let it be spoiled by the likes of Ada Tanner stirring up more bad feelings between the two of them.

'Thanks Nell, but I'm fine.'

But even after Mary had finished her weekly wash, had then pegged it all out, had gone back down to the laundry and cleaned up the area around the draining board and the sink she'd been using, and had then walked to the shop, she still hadn't had enough time to calm down. All she could hear were Joe's words going round and round in her head: *it's not fair; it's not bloody fair.*

147

And it wasn't, it really bloody wasn't fair at all.

But, no matter how much she loved him and sympathised with him, Mary still couldn't help secretly agreeing with her son, and feeling ashamed of the fact that her husband was listening to those bullies and thugs who were blaming the troubles of the world on other decent, innocent people who were suffering just as much as he was.

*   *   *

Sarah Meckel weighed out two ounces of tea—not even a quarter. Everyone seemed to be buying smaller and smaller portions these days, and sometimes it hardly seemed worth serving them. But Sarah was too kind to even dream of turning anyone away, plus there was the little matter of her needing all the custom she could get. She had to pay her suppliers and she couldn't face cutting Mary's hours, even with the reduced takings. Still, she and David were a lot better off than most round there. At least they made ends meet. The newspapers might have kept going on about how hard things were up in the north-east, and Sarah wouldn't deny that those poor folk were suffering, but she reckoned that the newspaper people should think about having a look at the East End— that'd give them something to write about. There were so many families who were struggling, and it was no good telling the rent man he'd have to wait for his money because you had to feed the kids, or you'd be out on your ear.

Sarah lifted the metal scoop off the scale and poured the tea into a twisted cone of stiff dark blue paper. 'There you are, Mrs Leigh. See you tomorrow, will we?'

'Yeah, thanks Sarah.' The elderly woman managed a feeble smile. 'If I've got anything left in my purse by then.'

'Your credit's always good here, Mrs Leigh, you know that.'

'Thank you, dear. I appreciate it. You're very kind.'

Sarah watched the elderly woman shuffle out of the shop, her second-hand boots slopping around her ankles, and her stockings more darn than lisle.

'Poor old girl,' she said quietly. 'Makes you want to cry to see what a hard time she's having.'

'And she's not the only one.' Mary ran past Sarah and into the stockroom behind the counter, where she burst into loud, sobbing tears.

Sarah rushed in after her. 'Whatever's wrong, Mary?' she said, hugging her. 'Do you want to tell me about it?'

Sarah felt like crying herself. Since she had opened up earlier that morning and had seen yet more filthy abuse chalked on the shop door about Jews and what should be done to them, she had been waiting for Mary to come in. She'd decided that rather than keep bottling it up, it was time to talk to someone about it. A problem shared and all that. But it just didn't seem the right time any more. Mary had been a good friend to her over the years, and if she needed a bit of comfort, then that was what she'd get. Sarah would just have to wait until another day to unburden herself of her worries.

'I know you're not one to tell people your problems, Mary, but if you want to chat about anything, I'm not going anywhere.'

149

Mary wiped her eyes on her apron. 'Take no notice of me, Sarah. I'm just feeling a bit cranky. Time of life, you know how it is.'

'Sure.'

Sarah looked at the defeated expression on Mary's face. How had things come to this?

CHAPTER 23

Nell was out in the courtyard, unpegging and folding her and Mary's laundry before it got too dry to iron. She smoothed Mary's sheets against her thigh and laid them in the basket, the pleasure in a job well done for once escaping her; if a marriage as strong as Mary and Joe's could have such problems, what hope was there for anyone else—particularly for the likes of her and Stephen—to ever find happiness?

Trying to banish her worries, Nell picked up the basket, closed her eyes and sniffed the sweet smell of linen dried in the open air in warm summer sunshine. The heated racks in the laundry were a blessing in bad weather, but being able to dry washing outside was so much nicer. It was something that had never been possible in the home, so Nell valued it especially, but it was hard to think of much else that she liked about the place.

'Penny for 'em, darling?'

She opened her eyes. It was Sylvia, her face as heavily made up as always, despite the scorching heat. She was wearing a floral print dress and a neat straw hat topped off with a little bunch of cherries that dangled saucily over one side.

'Well, are you going to tell your old mate what's going on in that pretty little head of yours or just stand there gawping?'

'I'm just enjoying this lovely weather.'

'Yeah, course you are.' Sylvia didn't sound convinced. 'Now, have you got time to make me a cup of tea before you start ironing that lot? Or I can just sit and watch while you get on with it if you like. You know me, Nell, I've never minded watching people work.'

'I'm a bit pushed this morning to be honest, Sylv.'

She'd have loved to have sat and had a chat with Sylvia, she could always cheer her up, but Nell couldn't be sure when Stephen might turn up, and what with everything else, she really didn't feel like risking another row.

'Go on, Nell.' Sylvia screwed up her nose and pinched Nell softly on the cheek. 'Only just a quick one. I have come all this way.'

Nell was torn. 'It'll have to be ever so quick. I've got so many jobs to do.'

I'll bet you have, thought Sylvia. She held up her shopping basket. 'And I hope you don't mind. I've bought a few bits round for the kids.'

'Thanks, Sylv, but you really shouldn't; you spoil them two.'

'Loving them's not spoiling them, Nell, you know that.'

*   *   *

With Sylvia settled down with her cup of tea, Nell took the presents she'd bought for the children—a

151

whole tin of lead soldiers for Tommy and a pink, fluffy rabbit for Dolly—and hid them away in the back of the wardrobe. She would find a way of letting the children play with them without Stephen and the twins finding out, otherwise they'd only accuse her of wasting money, and they'd call her a liar if she said Sylvia had bought them—such kindness wasn't within their understanding.

Nell came back into the kitchen, spread the ironing blanket on the kitchen table and set about working her way through the pile of laundry. 'I know I said you shouldn't, but Tommy and Dolly will love them, thanks Sylv. You're so good to them.'

'How many years have we been friends now, Nell? Must be what, getting on for nine years?'

'Must be.'

'Well, however long it is, you do know I feel like you and the kids are part of the family, don't you?'

Nell smiled at her. 'Course I know.'

'And you know you can always tell me anything, don't you?'

'Course I do.'

'Blimmin' heck, Nell, this is like pulling teeth here.'

'I don't know what you mean.'

'Listen to me, I know you're not happy living here. And you're grafting so hard, and you look—'

Nell stiffened. 'Hard work never did anyone any harm.' As if to demonstrate the point, she went at the sheet with even more vigour.

'Aw no? Well, I reckon too much of it can bloody kill you. You are not their slave, Nell.' Sylvia took a mouthful of tea. 'Look, I've got to tell you.' She

152

paused, trying to find the right words, knowing she was more than capable of sticking her dainty little foot right in it if she wasn't careful. 'Them two, the ugly twins, they came in the pub last night looking for Stephen, and I heard them saying that they thought you should be working on the stall. That you did bugger all else and they want you out there grafting instead of them.'

Nell carried on with the ironing; she finished the sheet and immediately started on another. Then, after a long moment of consideration, she said evenly, 'I was always told it wasn't right to listen to other people's conversations.'

'Don't be like that with me, Nell. I'm only trying to help you. I've been thinking about all this for weeks now. No that's not true, I've been thinking about it for months if the truth be told.'

'How do you mean?'

Sylvia put down her cup. 'I thought you and the kids could come and live with us, with me and Bernie at the pub, and you could go back to doing your old job if you wanted. It'd be just like the old times and I'd get to see you and the kids every single day. There's this smashing school just around the corner. I even made enquiries and they said that when the new term begins—'

'Sylvia.' Nell put the iron down carefully on the blanket. 'Do you really think—'

'No, you wait, Nell. You mustn't get too excited. Like I said, I've thought about it, and I'm not sure it's going to work, not the way things are. So we'll have to come up with something to sort out Stephen. Because you see it's him, he's the fly right in the middle of the pot of flipping ointment.'

Nell stared at her, horrified. 'Stephen? What

153

about him? What have you said? Have you spoken to him? Sylvia, you've got to tell me what you've done.'

'I've not said or done anything. Well, only the usual—here's your pint—that sort of thing. It's just that he's always there in the bloody pub with Bernie, sitting in the corner whispering.' Sylvia fiddled around with her hankie. 'Every sodding night he's in there, and I've seen him chatting away to women like he's a man with no responsibilities. Cheeky sod. Then him and Bernie go off upstairs with some other blokes and play cards for hours on end. Thick as thieves, them two. So if the idea's to get you away from him, for you not to have to face the horrible what's-his-name every day, what'd be the point? That's why we'll have to think of something. Come up with some sort of plan.'

Nell wasn't listening any more. Her stomach was churning and she felt physically ill. She knew Sylvia, knew that she was oblivious of the consequencces when she said exactly what was on her mind, and that she was would happily say it to men who were twice her size. She was, in fact, totally fearless. But then she didn't have two little ones to worry about, did she? What if she decided to say something to Stephen, something that upset him, and he decided to take it out on Tommy and Dolly?

Nell took a breath. 'Listen to me, Sylvia. I don't want to be rude to you, but I've got to say this straight—please, please do not, and I mean this with all my heart, do not interfere. You have no idea about my life here, and what me and the children want or need. It's our business, for us to deal with. It's nothing to do with you, or with

154

anyone else. Do you understand me?'

Nell picked up Sylvia's cup and took it over to the sink. 'And if you don't mind I'll have to be getting on now. I'll have to start thinking about the twins' tea or they'll have nothing to eat when they get in. So, like I say, if you don't mind . . .'

'Nell, don't be like this.'

'Like what? I'm fine.'

'No you're not fine, you're bloody well scared of him. Scared of that pisspot Stephen bloody Flanagan. And look at your face. He's bashed you again, hasn't he? Why would any man want to do that to a woman?'

Nell automatically shielded her face with her hand. 'Don't be so silly, course he hasn't.'

'Aw I forgot. You've got the strangest cupboard doors known to man here in this gaff, haven't you? They just wait for you to walk by and then they fly open and smack you right in the gob.'

'Sylvia, please, I'm asking you.'

Sylvia stood up and straightened her hat. 'If you won't help yourself, Nell, then someone else has to. And believe me, that idiot, who doesn't know how blessed he is, should be licking the soles of your bloody shoes, not doing that to you.'

'Sylvia, you mustn't. You don't know what he's like.'

'Trust me, he doesn't scarc mc, not one little bit.'

'I don't mean that.'

Sylvia picked up her bag and kissed Nell on the cheek. 'I'll see myself out. You just leave it to me.'

CHAPTER 24

Sylvia smiled automatically as she pushed through the crowd drinking at the counter, making her way over to her husband. He was sitting at his usual table in the corner writing figures in a leather-bound book, his face red and damp with sweat.

'Warm enough for you, Sylv?'

Sylvia ignored his pleasantry and sat down opposite him, plonking her shopping basket on her knees as if she was still on the bus. 'Bernie, I want you to do something for me.'

'What's that then, my little lovely?' He stuck his pencil behind his ear and looked at her. 'You seem a bit serious.'

Sylvia reached out and took Bernie's huge paw in her hand. 'I want you to bar Stephen Flanagan from the pub. Now. Today. For ever. Soon as he comes in. Tell him he's not welcome in here any more, and just get rid of him then and there.'

Bernie rubbed his hand over his bald head, took a deep breath and then stared down at the table. 'Don't start on about him again, Sylv,' he said quietly.

'I am not starting, I am just saying. I worked it all out on the way back from Nell's. I want you to bar him so that Nell can come back here to live and maybe work for me again. For us, I mean. And I want her to bring the kids with her and all.'

'Do what? Have you gone stark raving mad, woman?'

'What's the problem with that? We've got plenty of room.'

Bernie's face grew even redder. 'I'm not talking about whether we've got the room, girl.'

'So what is the problem then?'

He raised his head and looked at his wife. She was such a tiny little thing, he could pick her up with one hand if he wanted to, but still she always assumed that she was in charge—and most of the time she was right, but not over this, not this time. 'You want me to bar Stephen Flanagan from the Hope, eh? And when did you two come up with this little idea then?'

Sylvia studied her fingernails, and threw in casually, 'Nell doesn't know anything about it yet.'

'This just gets better and better.' Bernie wiped the sweat from his face and neck with a big white handkerchief. 'You want a woman to leave her old man and move out of her home with her kids, and she doesn't even know about it?'

'Bernie, you don't understand. Of course I mentioned moving to her, but not about Stephen being barred from the pub. I told you, I only thought about that on the way back on the bus. So how about it?'

'No, Sylv, for once I am actually going to say no to you. You know I like that girl, I like her a lot, but for one thing we are not getting involved in a married couple's business.'

'They're not married.'

'I do know, Sylv, and you know full well that they're as good as married as any other couple around here. They've got two kids and they've been together for years now.'

'But they're not married legally, are they? So it wouldn't be the same her leaving him, would it, Bern?'

157

Bernie shook his head. 'No, Sylv, I am not getting involved in this and I am not even talking about it any more, I am just not having it.'

'But—'

'No. This time, believe me, you are not getting your own way, and that's final. Stephen is a friend of mine, all right? Finished.'

*   *   *

When Stephen walked into the Hope and Anchor that evening it was just gone seven and the pub was packed. Sylvia only noticed him as she lifted her head to smile as she handed over the change from a ten-shilling note to an already slightly tipsy young dockworker, who was celebrating the fact that he'd managed to find more than just a couple of days' work that week. Sylvia's smile vanished. She was glad for the young docker, but she definitely wasn't glad to see Stephen Flanagan.

Infuriated by his presence, but resigned to the ritual, she watched as Stephen handed Bernie the cloth bag, swallowed a pint of mild and bitter, and then—as he did now on most nights of the week—followed Bernie up the stairs to the flat.

Did Bernie really think she didn't notice what they were up to? Like most men, he didn't have a very high opinion of women's ability to work things out, but surely he could give her some credit—at least for having two eyes in her bloody head.

*   *   *

The next time Sylvia saw her husband—with Stephen still firmly in tow—it was a quarter to

158

nine. They were down a bit earlier than usual. They came through the door by the side of the bar followed by four men who were as red-faced from drink as Bernie had been from the heat. The four men were speaking and laughing loudly. Stephen was neither red-faced nor speaking loudly, and he certainly wasn't laughing, in fact he looked fit to put somebody's lamps out.

Sylvia sidled casually along behind the bar, moving closer to where the men were saying their goodnights. The four strangers shook Bernie's hand, variously winked at Stephen, lifted their chins in his direction or saluted him, and then left, still talking and laughing loudly.

Sylvia caught Bernie's eye and mouthed—*tell him he's barred*—before getting back to serving.

With a raise of his hand, Bernie called another goodnight, and then turned back to Stephen, looking into his eyes as if he were trying to decode some sort of secret that Stephen was hiding behind them.

'Everything all right is it, Steve-o?'

'I've just lost ten quid, what do you think? Them bastards couldn't get away quick enough. Scared I'd win it back from them. Do you call that fair play?'

'Leave off. You'll get it back soon enough. You always do, mate. But I wasn't talking about that.'

Bernie had to be careful how he put this, but he wasn't about to let Sylvia think she was going to get away with this bloody hare-brained scheme of hers. Bringing Nell back to the pub—had she lost her marbles or something? Whatever would she come up with next? Giving away half-price beer every Saturday night? If she had her way, not only would

159

it ruin what had become a very nice arrangement between him and Stephen Flanagan, but there'd be two little cherry hogs running around the place. No thank you very much. He'd never had kids of his own, so why would he want someone else's? But, most of all, why would he want to lose a money-spinner like Flanagan? He was the most profitable runner he'd ever had, and the muscles on him meant that he never had to take any nonsense from the punters. No, it was a good set-up, one he wasn't about to ruin. He had to warn him that something was up, but without setting him off. Flanagan could go off like a rocket on Bonfire Night, and he didn't fancy being on the tail end.

'No, what I meant was is everything all right indoors? It was just something Sylv was saying earlier, after she'd been round to see your Nell. I thought you'd want to know about it, that's all. You know how women talk.'

Bernie stopped there. Had he said enough? Too much?

Shit, he had.

Stephen's face was now just as red as Bernie's. 'I've no idea what you're talking about, Bernie, or what *your wife*'—he emphasised the words with a sneer—'is talking about. In my home, Nell does as she's told. She keeps things like I want, and she doesn't spend all her time nagging and gossiping like other women. You got that?'

Bernie held up his hands, stretching his braces almost to bursting point over his big round belly. 'You know best, Steve-o.'

'As far as my own home goes, yes I do. Yes I fucking well do thank you very much.'

Bernie groaned inwardly. That went well.

'Right.'

'So long as we've got that straight.'

'Yeah, course. See you tomorrow then?'

*   *   *

At the sound of Stephen's boots in the hall coming towards the bedroom, Nell closed her eyes tight, trying to breathe calmly as if she were sleeping. Maybe it would be one of those nights when he just got into bed and went to sleep almost as soon as his head touched the pillow, leaving her alone while he snored like a pig.

But it wasn't.

Before she had a chance to protect herself, Stephen had torn the covers off her and was dragging her out of bed. He slammed her against the wall and smacked her across the face with the flat of his hand.

'I don't want to hear that that whore from the Hope has been anywhere near this place ever again, do you understand me?'

Nell's head felt as if it was spinning off her shoulders, but she knew she had to nod—she certainly couldn't speak.

'And if you make a noise and wake up them two little bastards through there and they come in and then they start screaming, and then I have people poking in their noses where they're not wanted, well then you'll be sorry. Very sorry. Got it?'

Another headjarring nod. She knew he meant Martin Lovell. She really didn't want him being involved and Stephen starting on him. She liked Martin so much. He was so kind. Or did Stephen mean Sylvia. Or . . . ? Or who did he mean?

161

But she couldn't remember any more names, because it was then that Stephen Flanagan started punching and kicking her.

CHAPTER 25

Martin Lovell stood at the window of the brewery office, looking down at the street below. The crowd was still out there, right by the gate, and, what made it worse, so was his father, right in their midst.

What was he going to do? He couldn't just go down there and ignore him, but the gate was the only way out of the building.

Martin dragged his fingers down his cheeks. This was turning out to be a royal pain in the arse. For the past couple of hours he'd been finding bits of work to occupy him, making up reasons why he had to stay in the office—papers to sort through, orders to update, accounts to be chased—all the while hoping that the crowd below would just listen to the organisers' rabble-rousing speeches, shout and holler their support back at them for a while, and then make their way home or clear off to the pub.

Unfortunately, that hadn't happened; they were still there, and if anything they were getting livelier.

But he had to leave soon; his mum would be going mad as it was. Knowing her she'd already be convinced that he'd been crushed to death under a dray in the brewery yard, knocked down by a bus on the way home, or attacked down by the dock gates by a drunken mob off the ships. What with the way his dad had started acting lately, she had enough to worry about, so he didn't want to do this to her as well.

He took his hat off the rack. Right. What he'd do was this—he'd walk across the brewery yard, all casual like, then he'd get to the gates and nod his goodnight to the watchman as though everything was normal, and then he'd just step out onto the pavement, keep his head well down, and walk right past them. Easy. Just another bloke wandering along the Mile End Road.

He looked at the clock again and then stared down at his boots.

Maybe his father wouldn't notice him.

Yeah, there'd be some chance of that. He might as well have had an arrow pointing to his head with *look this way* written on it in big red letters.

*   *   *

With his hat brim tipped down over his eyes, and his jacket collar turned up regardless of the heat, Martin reached the high metal gates with his blood drumming in his ears.

'Night then, Mr Lovell,' called the watchman. He spoke so loudly he might as well have been using a megaphone. 'Make sure you mind yourself with that lot out there. Right song and dance they've been making. Bloody trouble-makers. Could turn ugly if you ask me. They should be moved on. That's what I think. But where's a copper when you want one, eh? That's what I wanna know. You tell me that. Not like it used to be. Aw no.'

163

Martin sighed wearily. It was as if the man's words had attached some sort of a magnet to him, because without needing to look at them, he knew that the whole crowd had turned and that, as one, their gaze was now burning into him—and in that crowd was his father.

The black-shirted orator, who had been addressing the crowd from a makeshift wooden platform created from beer crates appropriated from round the back of the brewery, pointed at Martin. 'Look at him. Go on, look at him.'

As if they needed telling. Was there anyone left who wasn't looking at him?

'The likes of him think they don't have to worry. And why is that? I'll tell you why. Because he thinks he's doing just fine. Fine and dandy, because he's got work, hasn't he. And it's well-paid work from the look of his smart suit and his trilby hat. But let him wait, let him wait until the Jews and all the other foreigners step forward and offer to do his job for half his wages. You wait and see where he is then. I'll tell you where that'll be, shall I? He'll be out on the streets like the rest of you, with no job, no money and not even any pride left because he didn't act before it was too late— because he couldn't see it coming. So let's explain the facts to him, shall we?'

The crowd roared its approval.

The Blackshirt pointed at Martin again. 'Come over and join us and listen to a few home truths. Come and learn how you can protect what you've got while you've still got the chance. Stand up for your rights like a man; stand up and be heard like every decent Englishman should.'

Martin turned down his collar and ran his finger

164

between his neck and his shirt, letting the air circulate around his blood-flushed throat. 'No, thanks all the same,' he said as he edged his way past the now jeering crowd. 'I'm off home.'

'Think you're too good for us, do you, because you've got a job and this lot haven't? These men—' He looked about him like a field marshal surveying his troops. 'These men have worked hard all their lives. They've worked in the docks, and in the factories, working to build up this once great country. Abandon them to poverty, would you? Find them too embarrassing for your posh taste, do you?'

Martin's father was now only a few feet away from him, but Martin didn't meet his gaze as he replied as calmly as he could, 'No, they don't embarrass me, they don't embarrass me at all. But do you know what? You do, because me, I've never thought I'm too good for anyone. Not foreigners, not Jews, no one. So, if it's all the same to you, like I said, I'm off home.'

'Off home, eh?' shouted someone from the thick of the crowd. 'Well good for you, moosh. You with your office-wallah job, you can afford to pay the rent on a wage like yours.'

Martin guessed that it was probably the same person who shouted at him who then threw the stone that hit him on the side of his face. But Martin didn't react to the taunts or the violence, he wouldn't let them get to him, not with his dad standing there amongst them. Any other time he'd have been right in there, but he wouldn't let them set him against his own father. All he wanted was to get away from there, with, preferably, his father by his side. Joe had only been to a couple of the

165

meetings, so maybe it wasn't too late to make him realise that these people were wrong, and that the men who were putting these ideas into the heads of otherwise decent citizens were nothing more than muck-stirring yobs.

Martin raised his hand and waved at Joe. 'Dad. How about you coming home with me, eh?'

'Dad?' a voice repeated. 'Dad? Bloody hell. He's some sort of a geezer, this one. He won't even hang around to support his own old man? That's the type he is—a right two-bob merchant.'

'Ignore him, Dad. Please. We can stop off at the pub on the way home if you like. Yeah, that'd be good; let me buy you a pint.'

His mum would just have to suffer for another half-hour or so; anything would be better than this.

'Maybe get in a couple, eh? Anywhere you fancy? How about the Hope, that's only just up the road?'

'No thank you.' Joe's voice was brittle. 'A man of my age should have enough money in his pocket to buy his own pint. My place is here, with this lot, with blokes who are in the same boat as me. Blokes who've got the guts to do something about this fucking disgusting situation—a situation where a man can't even afford to put food on his own dinner table, where he can't afford to treat his own bloody wife.'

'But, Dad, can't you see what's happening here? You're a good man. Not like them.' Martin jerked his head in the direction of the speaker on the platform. 'They're just a bunch of—I don't know— bullies.'

'Bullies?' roared the Blackshirt, his eyes blazing and his finger stabbing the air. 'You just wait until

166

the day the Jews finally take over. You mark these words, and mark them well. They are going to swamp us. They are going to flood over us like a wave. They are going to take our jobs and our homes from us; steal our sisters and our daughters. That's when you'll find out what bullies really are. As for us and what we are, we are just ordinary men, men standing up for ourselves and our families. And if you were half a man you'd be doing the same by joining us. Joining us and your own father.'

Martin was about to say something more to Joe, but his father had turned his back on him.

It was time to give up—for now at least. Martin took a moment to gather himself and then threw out his chest and barged his way through the openly hostile crowd.

A voice, even louder than the baying mob, shouted over them, 'Why don't you hooligans go and do something useful, like getting yourselves some work?'

The sneering question came from a slightly tipsy, very smartly dressed passer-by, who had an equally well-dressed companion walking along unsteadily beside him.

Martin turned to see what was going on, and closed his eyes with a moan of despair. It was only one of the senior managers from the brewery. He didn't recognise the other man, but from the look of both of them they'd been making a good fist of sampling the company's products. Martin was sure as hell not going to let either of them recognise him. He started moving away again, faster this time.

'There are plenty of jobs out there for all of

you,' the senior manager went on, 'if only you'd be bothered to shift yourselves to go and look for them, instead of hanging around together on corners like a crowd of street arabs.'

'What jobs would they be then? Working in offices like you two toffee-nosed bastards? Some chance we'd have of getting cushy little numbers like that.'

'Why not go and build more cars for toffee-nosed bastards like us?' The man smirked as he opened the door of what appeared to be a brand new Austin tourer. 'I could do with a little runaround for the wife. Or how about becoming a tailor? Make me a new suit. I don't think a gentleman can ever have too many suits, do you?'

'Why don't you fuck off back where you came from?' someone called out from the back of the crowd.

'What,' the man laughed, easing himself into the car, 'Bow?' Then he added snootily, 'Tredegar Square, of course. Nothing but the best for me.'

'No, fucking Russia, you Jew bastard.'

Martin broke into a run, not wanting to hear either what he was sure would come next from the enraged mob or any more taunting from the manager and his companion, who should have known better than to flaunt their wealth in front of such desperate men. As he ran he could only hope that they wouldn't be having a meeting there again tomorrow evening. Their yelling and their abuse disgusted him, and the thought of his father being caught up in such venom was too much for him to stomach. He knew Joe wasn't a bad man, just a frightened one, but it was still no excuse. He had changed so much, it was like living with a stranger sometimes, and now having witnessed him being part of the mob, with his face contorted by hatred, he began to wonder how much more he could bear.

In the past Joe had always encouraged Martin to do the right thing, telling him to care about people and their feelings, and never to judge them because of what he thought they were, but to give them a chance to prove their mettle. In other words, he'd taught him that it was important to treat people as if they were worthwhile, unless or until he learned otherwise. And he'd persuaded Martin to read the newspapers, to listen to the wireless, to take an interest in politics—to decide what was fair and what was just. But if this was what his father had become—no matter for what reason—he wasn't that same man any more, and Martin didn't know how much longer he was prepared to stay under the same roof as him.

He heard a yell followed by a huge roar of fury from behind him.

Martin started running faster, wanting to leave the mob and their filthy ideas far behind him. And if that meant leaving his father behind too, then that was the way it would have to be.

CHAPTER 26

'Don't usually see you in here at this time of the morning, Nelly darling.'

As Sarah Meckel spoke she did her best to act light-heartedly and not to stare at the cut on Nell's lip and the swelling on her jaw, but it wasn't easy—Nell's face looked as if she'd challenged a

169

speeding, out-of-control bus to a fight and had come off exactly as you'd have expected.

'I thought you were always one to get your clearing up done of a morning before you did your errands,' Sarah smiled.

'Can I have an envelope and paper, please?'

Nell's voice was so low that Sarah struggled to hear what she was saying. Had she heard her right? Envelope and paper? It wasn't the sort of thing her customers usually requested.

She leaned across the counter, her face screwed up in concentration. 'Envelope and paper, did you say?'

Nell nodded, hardly moving her head, but still the pain ran through her, making her eyes sting with tears.

'Sorry, darling, I don't sell anything like that.' Sarah looked about herself for inspiration—how could she help the poor girl? 'I know, I could let you have a few sheets out of my receipt book, if you like. It's nice thin paper, you could write on that. But envelopes, no. I don't think I can help you there. But let's think where you could try. Here, I know, how about that big stationers up on the Commercial Road? Their windows are always full of all sorts, so I'm sure they must do packets of envelopes. And I bet if you ask nicely they'll let you have just the one if that's all you want.'

Nell said nothing, she just turned slowly, with her head bowed, and began to walk away.

Sarah wasn't leaving it at that. She dodged round the counter and rushed after her. 'Nell. Nelly. Wait, darling. Hang on. I've just remembered—I'm sure David's got some writing things up in the flat. He was a great letter-writer at one time. Used to keep in touch with his family back home as regular as clockwork, before . . . Before . . . Aw, that doesn't matter. Anyway. You come back in the shop with me and sit yourself down and I'll nip up and see what I can find.'

*   *   *

A few minutes later, Sarah was back down in the shop with two sheets of crackly lined paper and a yellowing envelope. 'Not exactly smart, as you can see. David hasn't done much writing in some time, but I think it'll do the job. And see there, look, I found a stamp in the drawer and I stuck it on for you as well, so that's something you don't need to worry yourself about.'

Nell got up from the chair, holding onto the counter to steady herself. 'Thank you, Sarah. I appreciate it. How much do I owe you?'

'Nothing. And you're not leaving quite so fast, young lady. You sit yourself back down. You're having a cup of tea with me. And you know how I like my cuppa.'

'Sorry, Sarah. I don't want to sound ungrateful, but I can't. I've got to get back.'

Yes, thought Sarah, of course you have, because you're scared that Stephen will find out you've been in here asking for paper and an envelope. Who would she be writing to? And surely even he would be ashamed for people to see her walking about looking like that. Sarah had never seen her quite so bad.

No, that beast of a man wouldn't give a damn. He was a genuine pig.

'If you can't have a cup of tea with me, then at

171

least let me give you a few biscuits. You can have them with a cuppa when you get home.'

Sarah took the glass lid off the first of the row of biscuit tins and picked out half a dozen chocolate creams.

Nell opened her bag and took out her purse.

'Don't you dare,' said Sarah, wishing she could give Stephen Flanagan something a lot more than a few biscuits, but getting involved would probably only make it worse where that man was concerned. He couldn't have any conscience if he was capable of such behaviour. 'Take them. They're a little present from me. And I'll pop in a few strawberry wafers for the little ones. I know the kids all go mad for them.'

At that moment Florrie Talbot, the prostitute who lodged in one of Sarah and David's upstairs rooms, walked into the shop. Her heavily made-up face was smudged and smeared and her hair poked out from under her hat like electrified wire wool. It looked as if she'd had a very lively night.

'Blimey, girl,' she said, pulling a disapproving face at Nell. 'I have to deal with some rough customers, but I'd never let them do that to me. You wanna look after yourself a bit more. You don't have to put up with that sort of shit, you know. No one does.'

'All right, Florrie,' said Sarah. 'That'll do.'

'Well, look at the poor kid.' She waggled a scarlet-tipped finger at Nell. 'You stand up to him. That's what you have to do with his type.'

'I don't know what you mean,' Nell gasped through her pain. 'I hit my face on the cupboard door.'

'Course you did,' Florrie called out after her, as

Nell hurried off along the street. 'We've all seen women with cupboard doors like that. Trouble is, some of them doors start hitting their kids.'

CHAPTER 27

'Get your newspaper all right then did you, Joe?' Mary Lovell didn't look at her husband as she made her usual enquiry on his return from the paper shop. Not looking at him wasn't her way of punishing him for his behaviour of the day before—storming out and upsetting her like that— she wasn't that sort of person. It was just that she was too busy fussing around her son.

She reached across the table and put her palm flat across his forehead. 'You can't hide it from me, you know, Martin, I'm your mother. I can tell something's wrong with you. You've not eaten a mouthful of breakfast and you've hardly said a word since you got out of bed.'

Martin pulled away from her.

'And I know why you overslept,' she went on. 'You couldn't drop off last night, could you? And it's no good you saying otherwise. I heard you tossing and turning in there for hours on end. Proper restless, that's what you were.'

'I told you, Mum: there is nothing wrong with me.'

'If you don't feel well, Martin, you know you shouldn't go in to work. There're some nasty things going round and you'll only be spreading it about. Ada said her granddaughter's been ever so poorly for over a week now, and if that old trout's handing out sympathy then that little love must be feeling really unwell. You're better off looking after yourself before it gets worse. You take my word for it.'

'I was a bit bilious, that's all. It's nothing, Mum, nothing at all.'

Mary stood up. 'I'm going down to the phone box and I'm going to call your manager for you. Tell him you're feeling bad.' She couldn't resist stretching across the table again and touching her son's forehead one last time. 'It won't take me two minutes. I can do it on my way in to work. You must have the office number written down somewhere.'

'For Christ's sake woman, leave him alone can't you?' Joe slammed his newspaper down on the table.

Mary reared up like a spooked horse. 'Don't you raise your voice to me, Joe Lovell.'

'Don't raise my voice?' Joe was now speaking ominously quietly. 'Don't raise my sodding voice? He's a grown man, not a bloody child.'

'And would you mind watching your language? This is not the public bar of the Turk's Head.'

Now Martin was on his feet as well. It was no good; he just couldn't take it any more. He *wouldn't* take it any more. 'I'm gonna get off, Mum. And don't worry if I'm a bit late; I'm not sure when I'm finishing again tonight.'

Mary's glower transformed into a faint twitch of a smile. 'Here, you've not got a new girl have you, Martin? Is that what's up with you? I mean, not sleeping and everything, they're all the signs, just like when I met your dad. And is that why you were late home last night?' She rolled her eyes. 'I knew something was up when you wouldn't tell me. Come on, who is she?' Mary moved around the table to stand beside her son. 'Here, do I know her?'

'Mum, I have not got a new girl.' Martin looked steadily at his father. 'It's nothing like that. And do you know what, it's something that is really so unlike that, that if I told you I wouldn't even know where to begin.'

'*So unlike that?* Martin, what the flipping heck are you talking about? You're talking in flaming riddles.'

'It's nothing, Mum.' Martin screwed up his eyes, gritted his teeth and let out a long, frustrated sigh. 'It's nothing at all. All right? I'll see you later.'

Mary put a hand on her son's shoulder. 'This is getting daft, love. You've not even said goodbye to your dad.' She sounded as if she were in pain. 'That's not like you. Now, will you please tell me what's wrong?'

'It's nothing. Nothing you can do anything about.'

Martin peeled his mother's hand away and walked out.

Mary looked at Joe—did he understand what was going on? But he just picked up his newspaper and snapped it open, turning the pages quicker than he could read them.

'Martin, at least say goodbye to us, son,' she called after him.

If Martin heard her, he never replied.

CHAPTER 28

Nell was standing at the bottom of the stone stairs that led up to the Flanagans' flat in Turnbury Buildings—she had long since stopped thinking of the flat as being hers—with her head drooping, the bag of biscuits in one hand, and her handbag hanging by her side from the other. She was trying to summon the energy to make it up to the top floor.

She wasn't doing very well.

'Nell?' Martin pulled up just short of crashing into her as he sprinted down the stairs, racing to get away from his father, his mother's questioning, and to hide in the sanctuary and neat order of the brewery office as soon as humanly possible. He stared openly at her cut and lividly bruised face. 'Anything I can do to help?'

She turned away, putting up her hand to hide her wounds. 'No, thanks, I'm fine. Fine.'

'At least let me carry your shopping upstairs for you.'

'It's nothing, only a few biscuits. No weight at all.' Nell twisted away from him, not wanting him to touch her. But she shouldn't have moved so quickly; the jolt to her ribs left her whimpering in pain.

'This is silly.' Martin took the bag and hooked his arm around her waist. 'There's no point saying no, because I won't listen to you. I am going to help you. No argument.'

*   *   *

176

It was a slow journey climbing the stairs and Nell fretted every step of the way—and not only because of the pain. What if someone saw them together and said something to Stephen or to the twins? She liked Martin so much, she'd have hated to see him being hurt.

She needn't have worried, the only one who did see them was a toddler playing on the second-floor landing, and he was far more interested in the tower he was building with his wooden blocks than in what the neighbours were up to. But Nell's hands still shook as she dug around in her handbag, searching for her key.

Please, please let me find it before Ada Tanner comes out onto the landing.

She was in luck again, and she found the key almost right away, but what happened next wasn't so fortunate. Instead of just handing over the biscuits and leaving her at the door with a polite goodbye, Martin actually followed her into the flat.

'I meant it Nell, I'm not taking no for an answer. I'm going to help you, and if George, that so-called man, is still in here I'm going to make sure he's got somebody his own size to pick on. He can't keep getting away with this.'

Martin was endeavouring to get past her, craning his neck to see along the passageway further into the flat. 'I could handle him when I was a kid, so I'm sure as hell I'll be able to handle him now. I just don't understand how Stephen lets him get away with it.'

'George isn't here, and it wasn't him anyway,' she said, tears running down her cheeks. 'So don't start on him when you see him or it'll make things even worse. And everything's bad enough as it is.'

'You're telling me it wasn't George?' Martin threw up his hands and shook his head, bewildered by what he was hearing. 'In that case, are you telling me it was Stephen who did this to you?'

'Thanks for helping me up the stairs, Martin, but would you go now?'

Martin reached out and ran a finger across her bruised mouth, making her shudder—but not with pain, his touch was so gentle. Then he wiped away her tears.

'How can you stay under the same roof as those two brutes? And if he can do this to you, what else is he capable of?'

'Martin, don't.'

'Why do you stay with him, Nell? Why? He's an old man, and he's a bully just like his no-good son. The way they treat you, it's not right. And as for him doing this to you . . . Any other man, any man with any brains, would treat you like you were a princess. Look at you, you're lovely, beautiful, and this is what he does to you. I can't believe you let this happen.'

'It's not my fault.'

'I never said it was. But you can walk out of here now, Nell. Right this minute.'

'Martin, don't do this to me. Just go.'

'How can you stand him going anywhere near you? It isn't right.' Martin tapped his knuckles on his teeth, the agitation boiling up in him. 'I don't know why you've put up with living with these monsters for so many years.' He moved closer to her. 'You're young; you can make a new life. Take the children and find somewhere else to live, somewhere miles away from him and those other two idiots.'

'Martin, you haven't the first idea about what goes on in here.'

'You're wrong. Now I know exactly what's going on here, and I'm going to take you away from it. I'm going to find somewhere for you to live. Somewhere you'll be happy, you and Tommy and Dolly.'

'What? What are you talking about?'

'And I'm going to go with you. I've got the money. And,' he took her face in his hands, forcing her to look at him, 'I could love you, Nell, you and the kids. I'd treat you like you should be treated. We'd be like a proper family. It'd be perfect. Nothing like you've had to put up with here. I'd make you so happy.'

'You're mad.'

'No, Nell, I'm not, but you are if you stay here with them.'

'Just get out, Martin, and don't let anyone see you leaving. No one can know you've been here, please.' She started crying again. 'I'm begging you. Please.'

'I'll go for now if that's what you really think you want, but you know what I've said makes sense, and you're going to think about it, I know you are. And in the meantime I'll be keeping an eye on you, Nell. I can't stand seeing bullies getting away with hurting people. And I especially can't stand seeing this happening to you. I said I could love you, Nell, but I was lying, because I already love you, I always have, ever since I first set eyes on you. You didn't even notice me that first day when you turned up here in that beautiful dress, but I noticed you.'

Nell summoned all her strength and shoved him

179

backwards along the passage towards the door. 'Go. Now. And don't ever speak to me again. Please, you mustn't. If you meant any part of what you said to me, then do this. For me.'

Martin backed away from her.

He was still looking into her eyes when she closed the door on him.

CHAPTER 29

As Nell cleaned and tidied the flat, she could only be grateful that it was Tuesday and not washing day. She'd never have been able to stand the pain of lifting and mangling piles of wet laundry.

Having at last finished her chores, she sat at the table to write the letter she had been dreading. What with having to do this and having to fend off Martin's lunatic outburst, she could only wonder why everything seemed to conspire against her.

She closed her eyes and put her hand to her mouth, remembering the touch of Martin's finger on her lips. But she mustn't let herself even think about him, she had made her life with Stephen and that was that. She knew it was wrong that they weren't married, but why did it have to be such a terrible life? And why on earth had she agreed to move in with him?

She'd said to Martin that it wasn't her fault, but maybe it was. What sort of a family had she come from that she could have done such a thing? What sort of creature had she sprung from to deserve this? Who was she that she should be so cursed?

She felt very confused. Her only memory of

where she came from was of the woman who loved and wanted to protect her. And how could she even think that she was cursed when she had her two beautiful children? Her children whom she would do anything to protect—and that was why she was going to write the letter.

She smoothed out the paper on the kitchen table and stared at it, putting off the moment when she began to write. She knew she had to, but she knew it would break her heart.

My dear Sylvia,

Stephen said that you told Bernie some things about me and him that are not true. I do not know why you said those things but they made me and Stephen very upset. You were a very good friend to me so I do not want to do this, but I must ask you not to come to see me ever again. My life here with Stephen is what is most important, and I cannot let you spoil that for me. You have also been very kind to the children and I am very sorry that you will not see them again either, but that is the way it must be. I enclose something to remember me by. Please do not ignore what I have asked of you.

I will be your friend always
Nell

She folded the paper, put it in the envelope, and then took it in to her and Stephen's bedroom.

She knew the flat was empty, but she still looked over her shoulder as if someone might have followed her—no one, not even the children, knew about what she had hidden away in her bedside cabinet. She opened the drawer and felt under

181

the pile of ironed and lavender-sprinkled handkerchiefs that she kept in there, and took out the brown paper bag that had been tucked away underneath them. She sat on the bed to shake the contents onto her lap. Two things fell out—her precious brooch and a photograph. She picked up the photograph and studied it; it showed her and Sylvia standing on the pavement outside the Hope and Anchor, arm in arm. Nell was grinning like the untroubled girl she had been on the day of her and Stephen's so-called engagement. Sylvia was smiling.

Nell touched the brooch to her lips and put it back in the bag, where it had been ever since the day of her ringless 'engagement', and hid it away back under the handkerchiefs. Next she kissed the photograph before slipping it into the envelope between the folds of the letter.

Something to remember me by.

What was it about those five little words—even more than the knowledge of what she was doing— that made her want to weep, that brought back those ghostly memories that she could never quite reach? The phrase brought back that image of the beautiful lady, like the angel from the Sunday school books, who meant her nothing but love and kindness.

Whatever the significance of the words, the letter was written. She had done it, and there would be no more Sylvia in her life, and she would make sure that there would definitely be no more Martin. Everything was going to be all right, the way it should be.

Then she sat on the bed and sobbed as if her heart would break in two.

CHAPTER 30

It was Monday morning; although Nell's ribs, mouth and cheek were beginning to heal, the evidence of her being beaten was still all too obvious—Stephen had never hurt her so badly before. But she had to go down to the laundry to do the weekly wash, or what would people say? Tommy and Dolly were in the courtyard playing with the other children from the Buildings, enjoying the freedom of what was left of the summer holidays, while she stood alone in the empty flat with a pillowcase full of dirty washing, trying to find the courage to be seen by her neighbours. What would be worse—not appearing and starting more rumours, or being seen and having previous gossip confirmed all over again? She just thanked goodness that in their innocence her children, unlike Sylvia, continued to believe her story about her clumsiness and the cupboard door. She only hoped her neighbours would be as accepting of the story—gliding along on the surface of politeness, at least—regardless of what they thought was the truth.

As she moved hesitantly along the passageway towards the front door, Nell repeated in her head the exact words she would say if anyone asked her outright about what had happened. But an unexpected knocking stopped her from moving a step further.

Her mouth went dry. She leaned close to the door. 'Who is it?' she managed to say, her imagination conjuring all sorts of possible demons.

183

'It's me, love. Mary. I wondered if you fancied a bit of company going down to the laundry.'

Nell edged towards the door, touching the handle as gingerly as if it were made from red-hot iron. She took a breath and opened it. 'Hello, Mary.'

Mary did her best to hide her shock as she looked at Nell's face; what a state. That was why she hadn't seen the poor girl in the shop all week. 'Had another accident have you, love? You're a right clumsy one, you are.'

Nell nodded.

'Here, wait a minute, I've got just the thing.' Mary dumped her own pillowcase full of dirty washing on the landing and went back into her flat, reappearing with a compact in her hand.

'You don't usually wear face powder, do you?'

'No.' Nell looked suspiciously at the shiny metal container.

'It can cover a multitude of sins, this stuff. You can take my word for it.' She grinned. 'Without this I'm as ugly as Ada Tanner. Let's go through to the kitchen where it's nice and bright and I'll show you how to put it on.'

'I don't know, Mary.'

'Look,' Mary jerked her head towards the Tanners' front door. 'Do you want her in there seeing your face all sore like that? And I'm saying this as a friend, Nell, it looks bad. And you do know what she'll say about you, don't you? And she'll say it to anyone and everyone she comes across.' Then she tacked on with a flourish of improvisation, 'Because she's never been one to let the truth go spoiling a good story, that Ada Tanner.'

'I don't want to look flashy like Florrie Talbot, Mary. Although,' Nell added hurriedly, 'I'm not saying I don't like her, because I do. She's sort of, you know, understanding. I like that in a person.'

'A lot of people like Florrie Talbot, for all sorts of reasons, especially the fellers. But I've got no intention of making you look like her. All right?'

*　　　*　　　*

'There. You look a proper picture. You're such a pretty girl, Nell. Know what, if I didn't like you so much, I'd be jealous of you.'

Nell stared at her reflection in the little shaving mirror that hung on the hook over the sink—she usually avoided looking in any kind of mirror, let alone the one used by Stephen and George every morning—and turned her head from side to side. She looked almost like she used to, sort of fresh. She ran her fingers through her hair, letting the soft curls spring back into place. It was a long time since she'd done anything more than run a comb through it, or chop off the ends when it was getting too long. When she'd lived with Sylvia she'd washed it twice a week, and had it cut at a hairdresser's in Aldgate.

'And if I had hair like yours I'd be beside myself. It's like you've had a Marcel wave. Beautiful.'

'That's a very nice thing to say, Mary, thank you. You're always so kind to me.'

Mary thought she had worries, but she could only guess what this girl's life was like. She sounded like a machine that wanted winding the way she spoke—sort of lifeless—and she was always so grateful for the smallest scraps of

185

kindness. It was as if she'd had all the stuffing dragged out of her since she'd lived with the Flanagans. Still, it was nothing to do with her; Mary could offer her friendship, but she wasn't about to poke her nose in. What went on beyond people's doorsteps was their business.

'Tell you what,' she said, slipping the compact into Nell's apron pocket. 'Now you know how to use it, you keep hold of it for a while.' She winked. 'I'll let you know if I need it to go to any dances with the Lord Mayor.'

Mary walked out of the kitchen and along the passageway to the front door.

'Come on Nell, this won't buy the baby a new bonnet, now will it?' she said, hefting the laundry up onto her hip. 'Let's be off downstairs and get this washing done.'

*   *   *

Ada Tanner, in her usual uniform of crossover apron, slippers and thick lisle stockings rolled down below her knees, stood next to Nell in the basement laundry watching her mangle her freshly rinsed washing. 'So what are you doing with all that muck on your face then? You trying to keep up with Stephen Flanagan's other fancy pieces, are you?'

Nell felt her face redden beneath the powder.

'As usual, I have no idea what you're talking about, Ada.'

'Well, you don't think you're the only one, do you, you silly mare?' Ada turned to Myrtle, her recently acquired collaborator, who was standing alongside her. 'Must have bashed her head as well

186

as her face.'

Nell carried on feeding the wet towels through the rollers, turning the handle steadily, refusing to rise to Ada's bait.

'Everyone knows he's always had a bloody harem round him, has that one. And it wouldn't surprise me if he doesn't do business with that Florrie Talbot on the side, and all.' Ada nudged Myrtle in the ribs. 'That's the tart who lives with the Jews in the corner shop. An English couple would never allow such a thing. Well, not decent ones like me and my Albert.' She paused to heighten the effect. 'Decent *married* couples.'

Mary opened her mouth to defend her friend, but the usually meek Nell surprised her.

'We'd better get this lot upstairs and out on the line, Mary, and then you can get in to work. It wouldn't be right to keep a lovely lady like Sarah waiting for you, now would it.'

'You're right, Nelly love, it wouldn't. And I could do with getting out for a breath of fresh air, cos something stinks to high heaven in here.'

Mary heaved up the big metal basin of mangled washing and followed Nell up the steps to the courtyard, throwing a look of contempt over her shoulder at Ada and her sidekick that might as well have been directed at a brick wall for all the impact it had.

CHAPTER 31

Stephen sat at the table eating his supper. He was using a hunk of bread to mop up the creamy milk, blistered with spots of golden butter, in which Nell had poached his smoked haddock. He was too interested in his food to look up from the plate when his two young children came rushing in.

'Mummy. Mummy.' Dolly hugged Nell tightly around the legs, pressing her face into her mother. 'Ouch, that feels hard. What is it?' She dipped into Nell's apron pocket. 'Is it a present for me from Auntie Sylvia?'

'No, of course not,' said Nell, casting an anxious glance at Stephen. Had he heard what Dolly had said?

He had.

He stuffed the last piece of bread into his mouth and held out his hand. 'Whatever it is, give it here.'

Nell stepped forward and put the compact on the table, and Dolly and Tommy moved closer to the door.

'Have you been spending my hard-earned money on this shit?'

'No, Stephen, really I haven't.' She hurried over to the dresser and snatched a tin tea caddy down from the top shelf. She held it out to him. 'Count it. I've not taken a penny.'

'You'd better not be lying to me.' He ignored the caddy, far more interested in the compact. He opened the catch on the lid, releasing a puff of sweetly scented, powdery air. 'And what do you want this for, anyway? Planning on going out somewhere, are you? Got yourself some bloke sniffing around after you, like you're some bitch on heat? Someone like that little arsehole from across the landing?'

Stephen tossed the compact on the floor and slowly levered himself up off his chair.

Nell put a hand on the back of each of her children. 'I want you two to go downstairs and play.' She did her best to keep her voice steady, not to sound hysterical. 'Go on. Now. Off you go the pair of you, there's good kids.'

'But Mum,' complained Tommy, as she urged them towards the kitchen door. 'We've only just come up. And everyone except that soapy kid from the bottom floor's gone in for their tea. And I'm not playing with him, he wets himself. It makes him stink. It's horrible. I hate him.' He lowered his voice so only his mother and Dolly could hear him. 'And I don't want to leave you alone here with him.'

'Then play with your sister, you little bastard.' Stephen spat the words through clenched teeth, moving nearer to the three of them.

Nell began to shake. *Just do as you're told,* she yelled at the children. *Right now.*

The unlikely sound of their mother shouting at them had Tommy and Dolly heading down the stairs before Stephen had taken another step. Something was very wrong.

*　　　*　　　*

Martin, with an evening paper tucked under his arm and a cigarette in his hand, strolled into the courtyard; he was in no hurry to go up to the flat and have yet more words with his father, and he was fed up with seeing his mother upset by their rows. Leaving work and going home to Turnbury Buildings was becoming more like an ordeal to be dreaded rather than the pleasure to be anticipated that it had once been. But at least he might bump

189

into Nell if he was lucky.

He threw his finished cigarette down onto the tarmac and ground it out with his heel; he'd have to sort something out soon or he'd wind up getting into a real fight with his dad, and one of them might do or say something that they wouldn't be able to forget or forgive.

Martin looked up from the soggy straggles of tobacco sticking to the crushed and split cigarette paper, and his frown immediately disappeared as he saw young Tommy and Dolly engrossed in a very serious game of hopscotch.

Martin caught Tommy's eye as he skipped on one leg at the top of the grid, his tongue clamped between his teeth as he concentrated on keeping his balance.

Tommy immediately put his other foot on the ground. 'I'm only playing this because Dolly's got no one else to play with.' He had to explain such shockingly effeminate behaviour—*fancy being caught playing such a soppy game, and only by Martin Lovell, the best bloke in the whole of the bloody Buildings*. 'The big girls marked it out earlier, but they've all gone in for their tea.'

'Nothing wrong with a good game,' said Martin, ruffling Tommy's hair. 'Here, lend us your slate and let's have a go.'

Tommy handed over the flat grey sliver of roofing slate that he'd picked up earlier in the courtyard. 'Mum made us come down again,' he said in the weary tone of someone far older than his years. 'And we'd only just gone up. But Dad was shouting and he called me a bastard—'

'You mustn't say that word,' said Dolly, looking around in case anyone had heard.

'*And*,' Tommy glared at his sister, 'then Mum only started shouting at us as well, didn't she. And she never shouts. I hate my dad; he's horrible to us. And them twins. I wish we could live with Auntie Sylvia.'

Martin squatted down on his haunches and looked Tommy in the eye. 'Tommy, are George and Lily up there with them in the flat now? Are they shouting as well?'

Maybe—and he could only hope—it was just one of the usual Flanagan flare-ups. There were enough of those.

'No.' Tommy shook his head. 'Them two went to the flicks ages ago. Lucky sods. Wish I could go. And they went to that new lido over Vicky Park the other day. I never go anywhere. It's not fair, they're horrible but they go everywhere.'

'Here.' Martin dug into his trouser pocket and pulled out a handful of coppers. He picked out a threepenny bit and gave it to Tommy.

'Next best thing to the flicks, I reckon. Take this round Sarah's and get you and Dolly some sweets. And who knows what might happen next week on Bank Holiday Monday, eh? There's all sorts going on then—fairs and days out and going over the park for a picnic.'

Tommy couldn't speak. Who cared about the bank holiday? A whole threepenny bit? He'd never had more than a ha'p'orth of sweets before, and that was only when Auntie Sylvia bought him and Dolly a treat. Now they'd be able to buy the whole flipping shop. He could even get one of those tuppenny Lyon's fruit pies if he liked, he'd always fancied the look of them.

Martin gave Tommy's hair a final ruffle, sprang

up from his heels and started off towards the stairs at a trot. 'And make sure you hold Dolly's hand and that you give her a fair share of the sweets.'

Tommy nodded, feeling guilty about being so happy when his dad was shouting at his mum, and—momentarily—about his fruit-pie fantasy.

Martin stopped and pointed at Tommy. 'And make sure you take a while so you choose properly. You've got plenty of time, so don't rush. I'll let your mum know where you are.'

And please don't come back before I've sorted out whatever that bullying bastard's doing to your mother this time.

CHAPTER 32

With the children on their way to the corner shop, Martin sprinted over to the stairs and took them two at a time, grabbing at the banister rail to pull himself up even faster. That tosspot would have someone more than a terrified woman to deal with once he got hold of him.

After what seemed like an age, he reached the top of the stone stairway; he skated across the landing and bashed on the front door of the Flanagans' flat.

The only reply came from Stephen. 'Whoever you are,' he shouted, 'you can fuck off.'

Nothing from Nell; not a single word.

Martin shoved the door.

Locked.

There was nothing else for it. He stepped back across the landing to the stairwell, turned sideways on and then ran at the door, barging at it with his shoulder.

The wood creaked, but didn't give way.

He snorted through his nose and tried again. The door splintered in on its hinges, creaking back against the lock.

Martin raced along the passageway to the kitchen at the back of the flat—the mirror image of his own home—from where he could hear Stephen swearing and shouting at Nell.

From the kitchen doorway he could see her cowering on the floor by the stove while Stephen laid into her with his boot.

Martin let out an enraged roar as he threw himself across the room. He grabbed Stephen by the back of his shirt and hauled him away from Nell.

'You spineless bastard. If you want a fight, try this on for size.'

Martin swung his arm back and, with all his force behind him, smashed his fist into Stephen's face, splitting the man's cheek wide open.

'How do you like that then?'

Stephen put his fingers to the cut and examined their bloodied tips. He took a few seconds to recover from the shock that Martin was not only in his kitchen—*his kitchen*—but had actually had the gall to attack him. Then anger overtook his surprise and he hurled himself at Martin, sending him flailing backwards across the kitchen, smack into the table, which flipped over onto its side. 'I'll show you fight, you little fucker.'

The men fell to the ground in a writhing mass of punches.

Nell pulled herself up from the floor, grasping

193

the stove with one hand and her ribs with the other. 'Martin, get out.'

For a brief moment Martin was distracted, and Stephen took the opportunity to land a sharp jab to his gut. Martin gasped as the wind was knocked out of him, but he wasn't going to let this arrogant arsehole get away with hurting Nell. He rolled away onto his side and grabbed the leg of one of the kitchen chairs. Lifting it shakily above his head with both hands, he brought it down across Stephen's shoulders.

Stephen, yelling in pain, curled into a ball to protect himself.

Nell staggered across to Martin and pushed away the chair before he could use it again.

'Don't, Martin, please. I'm begging you. Just go.'

Stephen took the opportunity to get to his feet. 'You've done it now, Lovell. I'm going to get you for this. I'm going to have you when you least expect it. You are going to be sorry that you ever set eyes on me.'

Then he turned to Nell. 'And you, you painted whore. You just wait. I'm going to have you and all.'

'But we're not finished here yet, Flanagan.'

'Aw no?' Stephen grabbed his coat from the hook on the back of the kitchen door. 'And that front door had better be mended before I get back or you'll be even more sorry.' He stormed out.

Nell sank to the floor and started weeping into her hands. 'What have you done? What have you done to me? To me and my children?'

Martin crawled across to her. 'Don't worry, Nell, I'll sort it all out, I promise you.'

'Don't you think you've caused enough harm

194

here already?'

'No. No I don't. I'm going to sort this out once and for all.' He touched her hair, his eyes closed. 'Even if it kills me.'

Nell pulled herself to her feet, picked up the chair and set it upright. 'If he doesn't kill me first,' she said, the tears spilling down her cheeks.

'I'd never let him do that, Nell, never.'

She covered her face with her hands. 'Just go.'

CHAPTER 33

With his breath back, Martin hared out onto the landing after Stephen, having to run the gauntlet of both his open-mouthed mother and Ada Tanner.

'Martin, whatever's going on?' Mary called after him. 'What were you doing in there? Why haven't you been in for your tea? And what's happened to Nell's front door? Has there been a fight?'

'Been in there with her, have you? What a trollop. Here, and what did happen to that front door then?' Ada Tanner demanded with spiteful glee.

He ignored them both and was now at the bottom of the stairs before the much older man had even cleared the courtyard.

Stephen was slicing his way through the gaggle of children who were now all back down playing after they had finished their evening meal. Tommy and Dolly were there too, returned from Sarah's with their mouths stuffed full of sweets.

Martin had to hold himself back from running

over to protect Tommy and Dolly as they shrank away from their father—who knew what reaction that might provoke in a lunatic like him? But he needn't have worried, Stephen ignored his children, appeared not even to notice them. He just kept walking, leaving the two little ones standing there with their paper screws full of goodies hidden behind their backs. Young as they were, they'd learned something about how to deal with Stephen Flanagan.

Martin kept Stephen in his sights, watching him as he strode along, dabbing at his cut cheek. As he passed under the archway that marked the entrance to the Buildings, Martin saw him turn to the right.

Martin nodded to himself. The Turk's Head down by the dock, that was where he'd be heading.

If Martin had it right, and that was where he was going, then Stephen Flanagan would be getting a bit of a surprise after he had filled himself with drink. And Martin couldn't wait to see how he liked being treated as if he were a punchbag.

After putting on a smile for Tommy and Dolly and a cheerful hint that their mum really wouldn't mind if they stayed downstairs and played out until it was dark and time for everyone to go indoors— he had to give Nell a chance to make herself and the flat look something like normal for the kids— Martin hurried off in pursuit of their father.

* * *

Martin had guessed Stephen's destination correctly. With a swipe of his sleeve across his bloodied cheek, Flanagan pushed open the door of

196

the Turk's Head and disappeared into the warmly lit fug.

Martin leaned back against the wall of the warehouse that stood opposite the pub and took out his cigarettes. He could wait for him for as long as it took. And it wasn't so bad standing there enjoying the last of the evening sun; in fact, at that moment, there was nowhere else he would rather have been.

*   *   *

It was almost two hours later when Stephen reappeared. Martin's eyes were used to the now late evening light, but Stephen had to squint to focus as he stepped out of the pub.

'Oi! Flanagan.' Martin straightened up to his full height.

Stephen peered into the twilight. 'Is that you, Lovell? Ain't you had enough yet, boy?'

'Do you know, Flanagan, I reckon it is me. And no, I don't reckon I have had enough. So what are you going to do about it?'

Stephen didn't even trouble to check for traffic, he just hurled himself across the street. 'This is the biggest mistake you've ever made in your whole stupid life, Lovell.'

'I don't think so. I just wanted you to know that if ever you dare touch Nell again—'

Before he could finish, Stephen swung at him, a big haymaker of a punch, but Martin was too quick for him and the blow just glanced off his shoulder. Martin, head down, raised his knee, driving it hard into the other man's crotch. Stephen doubled over, and Martin pounced on him, locking his arm around his neck.

'You have gone too far,' he puffed, dragging him into an alley that ran between the warehouses and led onto the waterman's steps that went down to the river.

Martin threw him onto the pebble-pitted, muddy foreshore.

'Come on Flanagan, let's settle this like men. Still feeling brave are you? Or are you scared, now you're drunk and it's dark, and you're not beating up a woman half your fucking size?'

Stephen, groaning from somewhere deep in his throat, scrambled across the mud and grabbed a lump of heavy driftwood. He tried to lift it above his head but he slipped on the shingle and fell hard onto his side. Fuelled by adrenalin and fury—and with his pain dampened by booze—he found the strength to roll over and somehow managed to stagger to his feet. He lifted the wood again, higher this time, but the younger, sober Martin was too sharp for him. He tugged it clean from his grip and smacked it around Stephen's head.

Stephen Flanagan went down like a felled tree.

Martin dropped the lump of wood and slumped down onto the mud beside him.

CHAPTER 34

While Mary Lovell's son had been standing across the road from the Turk's Head waiting to confront Stephen Flanagan, and Nell's children had been down in the courtyard happily eating their way through all the sweets they'd bought with Martin's money, Mary herself was tapping—somewhat nervously—on the frame that had once surrounded the front door of the Flanagans' flat. She had to help the poor kid, but Martin being involved somehow made it all a bit tricky.

'Nell, it's only me. I won't come in if you don't mind, love,' she called down the passageway, 'but I hope you don't mind, I've asked my Joe if he'll come over and sort this door out for you. Will that be OK? You wouldn't be offended or anything?'

Nell appeared from the kitchen at the back of the flat, her cheeks burning red. 'Thank you, Mary, that'd be more than OK. I really would be ever so grateful to Joe, and to you for asking him.'

As she spoke, Nell handed Mary her compact. She took it without comment as to why it was being returned so quickly; the only comments she was prepared to make were about the door.

'These flats, eh?' she said. 'What can you say? They're meant to be so good, all brand new and posh with their indoor lavs and the baths and the laundry and whatnot down in the basement, but look at this thing.'

She shook her head at the door that was now propped up against the wall, and poked at it with the toe of her slipper. 'It's fallen right off its hinges. Shoddy workmanship, that's what it is. At least that old terrace of ours had to be pulled down; it didn't just go and fall over. Disgusting, that's what it is, when there are so many skilled fellers out of work who could have done a proper job of it. Not like this flipping rubbish.'

Nell could have hugged her for her easy complicity in what they both knew to be a lie.

'So it'll be all right if Joe comes over then?'

199

'I'd appreciate that so much, Mary. Thank you. You're always being so kind to me.' Nell lowered her head, and apparently became intrigued by a loose thread dangling from her apron pocket. 'Mary, do you think Joe would think it was too much of a cheek if I asked him to do it as soon as he can?'

She wound the thread tightly around her finger until the tip went bright red, and then she tugged at it. As the thread snapped the pocket puckered into a row of tight little pleats.

'It's the kids see, Mary,' she said, continuing the lie as she fiddled around flattening out the pocket. 'If there's no door to keep them in of a night they could just wander off without me knowing, and I'd never be able to forgive myself if they got down on the road in the dark. They could get themselves knocked over—you know what the traffic's like down there—and then what would the poor driver say?'

Nell scratched her nose to distract herself. What was wrong with her? Why couldn't she just shut up?

'Of course, and I agree with you, love,' Mary colluded. 'The kiddies' safety has to come first, and I know Joe'll be only too pleased to do it just as soon as you like. Tell you what, how about if I go and ask him to do it right now? This minute. I bet he'll be over here before the cat can lick its ear.'

Mary wanted to know so badly, but didn't think it would be a very good idea to ask what Martin's part was in all of this. Some things were best left unsaid.

*   *   *

'You did a really good job there, Joe, thank you ever so much.' Nell stood next to him in the passageway admiring the repaired and now mercifully closed front door—it was as if nothing had ever happened to it. Stephen wouldn't be able to complain about it now; there was nothing to complain about. Or so she hoped.

Joe ran his hand up and down the wood of the jamb. 'It wasn't much of a job, girl. It only needed the hinges moving a bit, then a quick fill and repair with a touch of putty, and then rehanging. Easy as anything. I could have done it in my sleep. My old dad, he was a carpenter, see, and I used to help him out of an evening after school and at weekends.' He nodded at the canvas toolbag at his feet. 'They're his tools I used. And do you know what, Nell, I treasure them, I do. Better than the crown jewels to me, they are, because they're a memory of my dad. He was a good old boy. The things he made out of old bits of wood with those tools—you wouldn't believe.'

Joe chuckled grimly. 'Truth to tell though, Nell, I've been tempted once or twice to pawn them. Especially lately, but I never have. And I hope I never will. But I tell you what, I wish I'd have listened to him and done an apprenticeship, trained to be a proper carpenter like him. But no, not me, not know-it-all Joe. You know how it is when you're a kid. Would I listen to him? No, course I wouldn't. What did I do? I followed his flash brother's advice and went into the docks. I listened to all his stories all right. All about earning big money and living the high life. And he was right as well, there was good money—for a while.

201

But that was before things got hard. Mind you, times change, and let's hope them good times come back again. But even if they do, it'll be too late for me. Now I'm too old for them to even consider taking me back on, no matter what work there is about. If I'd served my time with my old dad's firm like he wanted, perhaps I wouldn't be in the state I am now. They say there's loads of work going in the house-building game these days. All over the place they're putting houses up, so it's good regular work. And making something that a feller could be proud of—homes for people to live in. That's a proper job. But muggins here, I've got no papers, have I? So who'd want me?'

He picked up the toolbag. 'I went to this meeting a little while ago and the bloke there, he told us that Stepney's got nearly twice as many people out of work as the rest of the whole of London. What do you think about that then? Shocking, eh? It's like we're not worth a light.'

Nell nodded and smiled sympathetically, but she wasn't really listening to what he was telling her. She wanted to hear what this kind, unhappy man had to say, of course she did, and she would have loved to have told him that she understood about the importance of the tools. How could she not, knowing how she felt about her brooch? And she of all people understood how it felt to wish you'd listened to someone, but had been too obstinate, and then wound up ruining everything. But she was itching to get him out of the flat before any of them came home and found him there. Especially after the business with Martin.

'I wish I had something to give you, Joe. You know, to say thank you for everything you've done for me.'

'That's all right, girl, I was glad to be of help. It's a long time since I've felt useful to anyone.'

What was she going to do? He still wasn't making any attempt to go. She'd just have to come up with some excuse to get rid of him.

The children. That was it—Tommy and Dolly.

'You'll have to excuse me, Joe, but I'm going to have to go down and bring in those kids of mine in a minute,' she said, keeping her voice light despite the rising panic that Stephen or the twins might be back at any moment. 'It'll be getting dark out there soon and they'll be needing to go to bed. The little monkey brands would stay out playing all night if they had their way.'

'Aw, yeah, course, sorry, Nell. Don't know what got into me going on like that. But it was just sort of nice, having someone else to talk to for a change.' He winked and smiled. 'Someone who hasn't heard it all a hundred times before, eh? Not like my Mary; seems like she's fed up with listening to me lately. But you're a good girl, Nell, and Stephen's a lucky man. I only wish he realised it.'

Nell looked away, not knowing how to reply.

Joe opened the door. 'Any time you've got any other jobs want doing, you promise me you'll let me know, all right? And I'll be straight over with my toolbag. It's always nice to be able to help a neighbour.'

'I will, Joe. Thank you.' She couldn't face him as she spoke.

He stepped out onto the landing, leaving Nell feeling relieved but embarrassed—not only by her behaviour, but also by what her neighbours so obviously knew about her and Stephen. 'I didn't even make you a cup of tea.'

'Next time, eh?'

'Yeah, next time. And thanks again, Joe.'

'Any job, doesn't matter how little.' He held up the bag. 'I'll bet I've got a tool in here to tackle anything you can name.' He let out a long, sad sigh. 'Except life, eh, Nell? If I had a tool to sort that out I reckon I'd be a stone rich man. I'd have everyone after me then.'

CHAPTER 35

Nell rounded up the children, helped them wash and get into their pyjamas and then put them to bed in the front room. She kissed them both on the forehead, sat down beside them and took a deep breath.

'There's something important I want to say to you two.' She hesitated, not knowing how to put her thoughts into words that wouldn't scare them. 'You do both know how much I love you, don't you? No matter what.'

Tommy and Dolly nodded gravely. This sounded as if they might be in trouble.

'Good. Because I want you to know that as long as we love each other that's all that matters, and whatever happens I'll always be here to look after you. I know your dad is an angry man, and I know he sometimes scares you, but you don't have to be scared, because I'm here. You just keep out of his way and everything will be all right. OK?'

The look on her children's faces, as they nodded silently at her, was almost enough to break her heart.

*   *   *

Even though the nights were beginning to draw in and the curtains were shut tight, Nell still couldn't sleep, she just lay there waiting and dreading the moment Stephen would eventually come home. He must have had a right skinful. She looked at the alarm clock: it was gone eleven o'clock yet there was still no sign of him, and she didn't feel in the least tired. It was a wonder she ever slept a wink with all the things that she had going around in her head. But tonight her terrors were increased. The thing that had wormed its way into her mind was nothing to do with the physical pain she was feeling, she'd grown used to that and all its horrors—for Nell, the abnormal had become the normal, as far as Stephen's treatment of her was concerned. No, what was terrifying her now was the idea that he had somehow crept into the flat without her realising it—maybe she had nodded off for a few minutes—then, just to punish her for what had happened between him and Martin, he had hurt her children, had beaten them, or, God forbid as Sarah would say, he had done something even worse to them.

What was it Florrie Talbot had said about the cupboard door maybe one day hitting the children?

It was no good, scared as she was, she had to go and look in on them and risk him losing his temper if he caught her. She had to make sure that not a single hair on her precious babies' heads had been harmed.

205

Nell eased the covers off her body, worried that they might make a sound that magically—no, wickedly—would somehow cause Stephen to appear. Then she swung her legs off the bed and stepped quietly onto the rug. If she was careful she could have a quick look in the front room, make sure the children were sleeping safely, and be back in bed before anyone noticed what she'd done.

She didn't dare turn on the light in the passageway—how could she be sure that he hadn't come in and fallen asleep in the kitchen? So she limped painfully but as lightly as she could towards the front of the flat, feeling along the wall to reach the door on the right—the door that separated her from her children. She could just make out the brass doorknob in the dark.

It was as if she was being watched: the moment she touched the handle, she heard a key being slipped into the lock of the front door.

Nell froze, knowing that she was now unable to let herself into the children's room. She couldn't give him a reason to go in there after her, definitely not when he'd been out this late. She could only imagine what state he was going to be in.

The front door opened, and, almost with relief, she heard George's voice.

'I don't know about you not liking the film, and having a rotten time, Lil,' he complained, 'cos you certainly made up for it afterwards. You were knocking back them port and lemons in the pub like there was no tomorrow. I don't know how you stay so skinny the way you eat and drink. Bloody navvy's appetite, that's what you've got. Maybe if you were a bit more ladylike, you'd be able to get

206

yourself a bloke.'

'Charming. I suppose me being skinny is nothing to do with how hard I bloody work. Well, next time I am not going to see a cowboy, I am—' Lily's words fizzled out as she turned on the light in the passageway, and saw Nell standing there flattened against the wall. 'What're you up to creeping about in the dark? You're not after nicking anything are you? Cos if you are . . .'

'No, I'm not up to anything,' said Nell, moving sideways away from them, her back still to the wall. 'I thought I heard one of the kids calling out for me, that's all. And I'd never steal anything. Never.'

George loomed over her. 'And what's Dad got to say about you messing about at all hours?'

'Nothing. He's got nothing to say. He went out. Ages ago.'

Lily looked her up and down. 'And who could blame him?'

'I thought you were him coming home.'

'Fascinating.' Lily shoved past Nell, deliberately knocking into her. 'I'm off to bed. See you tomorrow, George.' Then, without turning to look at Nell, Lily said to her, 'And you'd better make sure you've got my breakfast ready on the table before you wake me up in the morning.'

If it hadn't been for George standing there looming over her, Nell would have checked the children, but there was something about the way he was staring at her that told her she had to get away from him as soon as possible, and the only place she had to go was Stephen's bedroom.

CHAPTER 36

Martin sat there on the shore, his legs bent up and his chin resting on his knees, waiting for Stephen to move, ready to give him another clout. Stephen would learn a lesson tonight about what it felt like to be frightened if it was the last thing that Martin ever did. If the man had a single ounce of sense in him, after what had happened tonight he would never touch Nell again.

'You're a bad man, Stephen Flanagan, do you know that? A really bad man, and you don't see really bad people that often in life. Normal people might make mistakes, do or say stupid things, or even act like idiots, but normal people don't behave like you, Flanagan, and normal people don't understand why you think it's all right to do what you do to a woman. It's only a pity that more of them don't speak up about it, because that's how the likes of you get away with it. But me, I say what I think, and, do you know, I think you're worse than an animal. No man should hit a woman, especially someone like Nell. Think about it, Flanagan—she's kind, she's beautiful and she loves those kids. And from what Mum says she looks after you lot like you're all made out of gold or something. It's not right, it's just not bloody right. Any other bloke would treat her like she was the special one, not expect it to work the other way round.' He rubbed his hands over his face. 'And that's what she is—special. A little gem swamped by all the muck surrounding her. You and George and Lily should appreciate that girl, realise what

208

you've got. Not treat her like shit.'

Martin had been watching Stephen's chest rising and falling as he took slow shallow breaths, but now it was too dark to make out such small movements, and to his surprise the tide had turned and the water was lapping at his feet. He hadn't realised that they'd been down there so long. It was time for them to get moving.

Against his better judgement, he hauled himself to his feet so that he could drag Stephen off the shore and away from the surging river. Bracing himself, with his feet planted firmly apart, Martin gripped Stephen by the arms.

He immediately let go of him.

Something about Stephen Flanagan didn't feel right.

Martin squatted down and touched Stephen's face and then his neck. He was cold, and sort of clammy. Definitely not right.

Martin dragged his fingers through his hair, wondering what to do next. He lifted one of Stephen's arms and let it fall. Lifeless.

It was over. Stephen Flanagan was dead.

Slowly, Martin stood up and backed away, stumbling and slipping on the stony foreshore, his eyes fixed on the shadowy outline of the motionless form before him. When he reached the waterman's steps leading up to the alley, he took them in just three leaps.

Back on the roadway, Martin sprinted towards home as if the lost souls of every cutlass-wielding pirate who had ever sailed up the London river were all chasing after him.

CHAPTER 37

The moment the alarm went off, Nell's eyes blinked open and she was immediately thinking about her children. The ringing of the clock and the clattering of the marbles on the tin plate hadn't disturbed Stephen, but still she moved slowly as she turned to look at his side of the bed—just to make sure that he was still asleep.

She frowned, puzzled. Stephen wasn't there. And not only was he not there, there wasn't even a dent in his pillow. What was going on?

Nell pushed herself up on her elbows to look more closely, wincing at the soreness of her bruises, but distracted from the pain by the mystery of where Stephen could be. Since the twins had taken over the stalls he never got up before half past eight at the earliest.

All she could think of was that he couldn't have come home last night.

Maybe Ada Tanner was telling the truth for once in her life, and he really was going with someone else. Her first reaction was to hope that it was true, hope it was true with all her heart, as maybe that would mean he would lose interest in her once and for all and she'd be free at last from his groping hands, even when he was drunk. But she had to be sensible. Say he did decide to move another woman into the Buildings? What would it mean for her and the children? Would Stephen throw them out? He was certainly heartless enough; and if he did, where would they go? How would they live?

In moments of wild fantasising about running off and leaving him, Nell had checked in the *East London Observer* to see how much it would cost to rent a room for her and the children. The fantasy hadn't lasted very long. Because they had nowhere to go, the welfare people would be sure to start prying. Then they'd take the children away from her and put them in some terrible place like the home that she had so hated, but which had been the only home she had known throughout her childhood, and, in the end, had not wanted to leave. Say her children felt the same and they didn't want to leave the place they were sent to, even if she did eventually find somewhere for them all to live together?

Nell threw back the covers and sat on the edge of the bed, fighting to keep her panic under control. She would not let anyone take Tommy and Dolly from her, she'd make sure of that. So she would keep Stephen happy, do whatever he wanted, and that way she would keep a roof over her children's heads. And she would make sure she was nice to Lily and George. They could be so vicious, but she would get them on her side. That could make all the difference, because if they weren't kicking up a fuss, Stephen didn't pay them much attention. So she'd make sure they had nothing to make a fuss about.

Still struggling to calm herself, Nell closed her eyes. If she tried really hard, then everything would be OK—her children would have a roof over their heads and they'd have food in their stomachs, and a mother to love them. There'd be no children's home for them. Never. She would do anything to protect them. It was simple, she now had a plan,

211

and that was what she'd do. Without any fuss or upsetting anyone, she'd just make them all realise they couldn't cope without her.

Nell opened her eyes and stood up, her new resolve making her feel oddly peaceful.

*   *   *

Nell knocked gently on Lily's door. 'Breakfast in two minutes, Lil, and there's a nice clean towel in the kitchen and a basin of hot water waiting for you ready for your wash.'

Lily opened her door, her fashionable bob not looking quite so sleek after the disturbed sleep she'd had as a result of all the port and lemons she'd sunk the night before.

She eyed Nell suspiciously. 'I don't know what you're up to, Nelly girl, with all your sweet talk, but if you're taking the piss out of me or something, you do know you'll regret it, don't you?'

Nell smiled. 'Just glad to be up and about on a lovely morning like this, Lily, that's all. I'll go and wake up George now, shall I?'

Lily's only reply was to slam the bedroom door in Nell's face.

*   *   *

After the twins had moped about, moaning and complaining, and had then dragged themselves off to work—neither of them had thought to ask when or even if their father had come home—Nell left the children sleeping while she cleaned the rest of the flat with even more care than usual. Satisfied at last with her efforts, she then woke Tommy and

212

Dolly, helped them wash and dress, and gave them thick slices of toast for their breakfast, just like Sylvia used to make for her, but with marge instead of butter—that was only for Stephen and the twins. She then ushered them down the stairs to play. When he eventually came home, Stephen was going to have no reason to find fault in anything she had done—no reason at all. It would all be perfect. The place would be spotless, the children would be out of his way playing down in the courtyard and she'd have made him something special for his tea—fat pork chops with mash and gravy, he loved that. She'd go round to the butcher in Wapping Lane, he did lovely pork down there. She could juggle the money to pay for a couple of really nice ones; she didn't mind getting by on a few slices of bread.

But despite all her resolve, Nell still couldn't help fretting about what was going to happen when Stephen did come home. She only hoped that, as sometimes happened, his temper had blown itself out like the wind when it came howling up the river threatening a gale but then coming to nothing, just as if it had changed its mind.

CHAPTER 38

Red-eyed from lack of sleep, Nell opened the front door. It had been five days now since Stephen had gone missing, so she wasn't exactly surprised that it wasn't him standing there as if nothing had happened, looking like a wreck and ravenous for a meal that she would be expected to rustle up from

213

nowhere. In fact, she was so worn out, she wasn't even surprised that it was Sylvia waiting to greet her as if nothing had happened between them.

'Hello, Nell, sweetheart,' she said, speaking as if she'd been set on double speed. 'I know you sent me that letter, but I know you didn't really mean it, and as it's Bank Holiday Monday in a couple of days, I was wondering if you'd let me take the kids out for a few hours. We could have a laugh. Like me and you used to have. I could take them over to Blackheath to the fair. Or to the pictures. Or even over the lido if it's a nice day. Southend on the train, or maybe the boat. How about it? You could come and all if you like. And don't worry, it'll be my treat.'

Sylvia reached out to take Nell's hand, but Nell pulled away.

'I don't want to be rude, Sylvia, but you know you're not welcome here. Thank you for coming round but it wouldn't be right. Not after you upsetting Stephen like that.' Nell couldn't bear to look Sylvia in the eye. 'And I meant every single word that I wrote in the letter.'

Nell tried to close the door, but Sylvia, little as she was, kept it open with her shoulder.

'Nell, please don't do this. I wasn't going to mention it because I didn't want to upset you, but Bernie told me about Stephen going missing, and I've been out of my mind worrying about you. Please let me do something—anything—to help you.'

Nell didn't reply, which made Sylvia relax a little—at least she'd stopped trying to close the door on her. 'Still no news from him?'

Nell shook her head.

'So where's Laurel and Hardy?'

No reply.

'Sorry, that was unkind. I should have asked, where's Lily and George?'

'On the stall.'

'They're obviously worried sick about their father then.'

'They've got to go to work, Sylvia.'

'Yeah, sorry again. Me and my big mouth. That was below the belt. It's them twins, they . . . Aw, you know.'

'This is so hard for me, Sylv.'

The two young women stood there at the door with so much to say to one another, but with neither of them speaking and the silence beginning to build between them like a brick wall. Suddenly the silence was broken, but not by Sylvia or Nell.

'Good afternoon, ladies.'

Sylvia turned round to see who had spoken. She took a step back when she saw two uniformed police officers standing there on the landing. Nell stared at them over Sylvia's shoulder.

'Would one of you be Mrs Flanagan?' said the taller of the officers.

'This is the lady you want,' said Sylvia.

'Are you a friend?' asked the other.

Sylvia nodded. 'I like to think so.'

'Good, well then I think it would be very helpful if you came in with us while we have a word with Mrs Flanagan here, because we have some news for her.'

As Sylvia and the police officers followed a reluctant Nell along the passageway towards the kitchen, Ada Tanner opened the door of Number 56. She had seen the two men enter the courtyard through the arch when she had been nosing out of the window, and had then watched with mounting speculation as they made their way straight for her block. And now they were actually up on her landing. She was about to burst with curiosity. In Ada's book coppers only ever meant one thing: bad news, and Ada was damned sure she would be amongst the first to hear what it was.

CHAPTER 39

Sylvia busied herself making a pot of tea, doing her best to look as if she wasn't listening to the conversation that was going on across the kitchen table between Nell and the two policemen.

Nell, shoulders slumped and hands in her lap, asked softly, 'But how do they know it was Stephen?'

'When they finally managed to drag the body out from under the . . .' The officer checked himself. 'I apologise, Mrs Flanagan, excuse me, when they found your husband under the wharf in Limehouse, we had the details you supplied to the local constable about his gold teeth. They matched perfectly. And then there was the wallet inside his jacket pocket. Apart from all the money he had on him, there was what we soon realised was a stack of betting slips. We made some enquiries, talked to the lads from various stations and it wasn't long before we put two and two together. Now we just need you to come over to the mortuary in Poplar to make a positive identification, but I have to warn you it won't be pleasant.'

Nell frowned. 'I don't understand.'

The policemen exchanged looks, eyebrows raised.

'Mrs Flanagan, we think your husband had been in the water for some time, maybe up to as much as a week, and so the body's going to be—'

'No, I don't mean that, I mean about the betting slips, and you said *all the money*. Stephen wasn't as badly off as some round here, but he was far from what you'd call well off. So what money? How much are you talking about? And where did it come from?'

'Mrs Flanagan,' the other policeman said, his voice dripping with cynicism. 'Your husband was a bookie's runner, working near the markets. Are you telling us that you had no knowledge of what he was doing?'

Shit, thought Sylvia, this could lead to all sorts of trouble. 'Hang on a minute,' she interrupted. 'There's been a misunderstanding. You've got the situation here all wrong. Stephen Flanagan wasn't this girl's husband. His next of kin are his twins, Lily and George Flanagan, and they've got stalls in the markets. Down the Waste during the week, and on Sundays they're down the Lane. They must make a nice living, the pair of them. I mean, who's ever seen a poor stallholder? You want information about where Stephen Flanagan got all his dough from, or someone to identify him? They're the ones who can help you.' Sylvia paused for effect. 'Lily and George Flanagan—anyone down the markets will point them out to you.'

The policemen exchanged another look. 'Stalls on the Waste and down the Lane, but their name's Flanagan and they live in Wapping? So they're

217

hardly going to be Jews, are they? Bit unusual that, don't you think?'

'Stephen Flanagan was a well-known man. He could pull strings, because he knew all sorts of people. And a lot of them were, how can I put it? Indebted to him.'

'And you seem to know a lot about him, Mrs . . .'

'Woods. He drinks . . .' She paused again. 'I suppose I should say he used to drink in my pub. The Hope and Anchor.'

'We're with the river police, Mrs Woods. You're going to have to help me here.'

'Whitechapel. Nearly opposite the hospital.'

'There's a lot of gambling over that way. Spielers, street betting, pitch and toss.'

'I know.' Sylvia answered the officer as she took away their not quite empty tea cups. 'It's shocking the way people carry on. I don't know where they find the money to throw away like that. And that's not the half of it. You might want to ask some of the local coppers over my way about the protection rackets they have to put up with down them markets. Jack Spot might make himself out to be a local flipping hero, but if the stallholders or the street gamblers don't pay up then all hell breaks loose with him and his sidekicks wading in. Terrible violence you hear about. That's what should be interesting the law. They're right nasty men, you take my word for it. Some of the stories I hear in the pub, they're awful. It's frightening what they're capable of.'

Sylvia knew what she was talking about; she'd seen Bernie paying out enough over the years.

She hadn't even had time to dry the teacups before she'd fed the two officers with enough tasty tit-bits to have them straining to leave.

'Thank you, Mrs Woods, you've been a lot of help.'

'Good,' she said. 'Now, you stay there, Nell. I'll see these gentlemen out.'

'Wait, please. Will you be going down the market to speak to Lily and George?' Nell asked the officers.

The two men looked at one another; one of them flicked a glance towards Sylvia.

'As next of kin, we'll be asking them to identify the body and then we'll be making some general enquiries. But if you'd like to be the one to break the news to them, then that's fine by us.'

*　　　*　　　*

When Sylvia came back into the kitchen, Nell was on her feet.

Sylvia held out her arms. 'Come here, darling. I know it's hard, but at least you've still got me.'

'I'm sorry, Sylvia, nothing's changed. You'll have to leave. George and Lily wouldn't like it if they came home and found you here.'

'What's it got to do with them?'

'This is their home, that's what. Like you said, Stephen wasn't my husband, remember? If me and the kids are going to keep a roof over our heads, then it'll be down to them whether we stay or not.'

'Come on, Nell, you don't have to be beholden to that pair. They treat you like you're their bloody skivvy. It's them who should be thanking you, not the other way round.'

Nell started putting the cups and saucers back in the cupboard. 'I'll say goodbye now, Sylvia, and on

219

your way out, would you mind sending Tommy and Dolly back up here, please? I need to talk to them.'

CHAPTER 40

'Mum. Mum,' Tommy hollered as he raced along the passageway to the kitchen. 'Look what Auntie Sylvia gave me.' He held out his hand to show Nell a silver half-crown. 'I've never even seen a bloody tosheroon before, never mind had one of my own.'

'Mum,' protested Dolly, 'Auntie Sylvia gave it to both of us, she said so. Honest, Mum. It's to share.'

'That was very kind of her, give it to me and we can think about how you can spend it later.'

'But Mum,' protested Tommy.

'Just do as you're told. I want you both to sit down and have a glass of milk and a slice of bread, because we've not got time for dinner, we've got to go out.'

'Why?' asked Tommy, clambering up onto a chair.

'Because I've got something to tell you, and then we've got to go and see George and Lily.'

'Aw, Mum, I hate them two. They're right rotten spiteful.'

'Tommy, I know they're difficult, but don't you ever dare say anything like that again.'

Nell closed her eyes. This was all going to be so much harder than she had thought. 'And wash your hands, the pair of you, goodness only knows what you've been touching while you've been down there.'

Tommy sloped over to the sink where Dolly was

already working up a lather with a bar of Lifebuoy.

'I can't help it if I don't flipping well like them,' he muttered, taking the soap from his sister and shaping up to blow a few choice bubbles at her. 'They're like Dad, horrible. I hate them all.'

'You know Auntie Sylvia said that money was for both of us,' whispered Dolly, nudging him in the side.

'Grass,' hissed Tommy.

Nell smacked her hand down on the table, making them both jump. 'Just be quiet, you two. I've got something important to tell you.'

*   *   *

As the three of them left the flat, Tommy and Dolly were pale-faced and silent, and they were holding their mother's hands exactly as she had told them to. Their dad was dead, and their mum sounded scared.

Ada Tanner was standing out on the landing, her arms folded and a hairnet stretched over her metal curlers. 'You've taken your time, I've been waiting out here for over half an hour.'

'Ada, as usual, I don't know what you're talking about, but whatever it is I haven't got time for it.'

'I won't beat about the bush then. So, cough it up, what did them coppers want? Came to tell you Stephen Flanagan's been nicked, did they? Caught up with him at last?'

Nell tightened her grip on her children's hands. 'No, Ada, they came to tell me that he's dead.'

As Nell spoke, Mary Lovell had just reached the top of the stairway. 'Dead? Oh, Nell, I don't know what to say.'

221

Ada did. 'How about good riddance? That'd be a start.'

Mary shot an angry look at her neighbour. 'Even you should know to keep your mouth shut in front of little children, Ada Tanner.' She turned to Nell. 'Anything I can do for you, love?'

'I'm not really sure I know what to do myself, Mary. That's why I thought I'd best go to see Lily and George, to see what they want to happen. There's going to be a coroner's hearing but then they'll release—you know—and arrangements are going to have to be made.'

'How about if I have the kids for you?'

Nell bent down. 'What do you think? Do you want to stay with Mrs Lovell while I go down the market to see the twins?'

Tommy and Dolly were clasping Mary's hands before anyone had a chance to change their minds.

*   *   *

Nell stood on the corner of Commercial Street and Wentworth Street, plucking up her courage. Whatever would they say when they heard that their father was dead?

*   *   *

'I only hope you don't think we're paying for the funeral,' said Lily, sliding a hand of bananas into a brown paper bag.

'So who will?' asked Nell, watching Lily drop a handful of change into the already bulging money pouch that was tied around her waist. Just a little of that would have fed the children with better

222

food than they had now.

'It was you who lived with him and had his bastards.'

Nell flushed red, from both embarrassment and shock at Lily being so loud and so callous, especially in front of the queue waiting at the stall.

'What did I say just this morning, Lil?' said George, hefting a new box of apples onto the stall. 'I said I thought it was funny him not coming home all week. That he'd probably got pissed and got himself rolled by thieves. Seems I was right. Funny they didn't take his wallet, though.'

'Is that it?' asked Nell.

George shrugged. 'I suppose so, but who knows how things might have to change. I'll have to give it a bit of thought.'

'But you will go and identify him, won't you?'

'How many more times?'

She could see that George was getting close to losing his temper.

'We've said yes. When we've finished here.'

'And we don't want any pauper's do for the funeral. So make sure you don't go showing us up.' Lily lifted her chin at the next customer in line. 'Yeah?'

Considering herself dismissed, Nell walked away from the stall still not knowing what to think other than that she had—somehow—to pay for a funeral. How much would it cost? And where would the money come from? And what did George mean— *things might have to change*?

*　　　*　　　*

Nell sat at Mary Lovell's kitchen table, something

223

she had never done before, with the children sitting on either side of her. 'I don't know what to do.'

Joe, who was standing behind Mary's chair with his arms folded across his chest, said quietly, 'You have to go and see a funeral director, love. I remember when I lost my old mum and dad. They sorted it all out.'

'Does it cost a lot?'

'Depends what you want.'

Nell covered her face with her hands and began to weep.

Joe looked at the kitchen clock—nearly half past two—then at Mary, his eyes asking his wife whether it was right for him to speak.

Mary nodded.

Joe unfolded his arms and went over to the fitted dresser that ran along the back wall. 'Nell, why don't you leave the kids here with me? I'll knock us up a bit of bread and jam, and we can have a listen to the wireless or have a game of snap, while you and Mary go round to Price's, they're the ones who did my mum's and dad's for me.'

'But George and Lily have just got something to see to after they close the stall, then they're going to be back home.'

'I'll let them know where you are,' said Joe, handing Tommy a pack of cards from the drawer.

'Thanks, Joe, but I'd better leave a note for them. From me, letting them know what I'm doing. I think that's what I should do.'

'Whatever you reckon's best, sweetheart.'

'Thanks, Joe. Will you two be all right here with Mr Lovell?'

'Yeah,' said Tommy, dealing out the cards into three hands. 'Bread and jam and cards, I should think so.'

'Me too,' said Dolly, kneeling up on her chair.

Mary looked at their eager little faces. It either hadn't sunk in yet that their father was dead, or . . . No she didn't want to believe that they were glad about someone dying, even if they had been terrified of him at times. But, if she were truthful with herself, if she were a child having to live in that flat then being rid of him would have probably had her cheering from the rooftops. God forgive her for even thinking such a thing.

'Go on then, Nell,' she said. 'You go and leave your message for George and Lily, and I'll get my coat.'

*   *   *

Nell wrote three versions of her note before she was satisfied with her efforts.

Dear George and Lily,
    I have gone to Price's to make arrangements.
I will be back as soon as I can, and I will bring
in fish and chips for your tea.
    Nell

Nell propped the note against the sugar bowl on the kitchen table and then took out the money from the tin tea caddy. She counted it. Almost seven pounds. She put two pounds back, and then took them out again.

How much was the funeral going to cost? And how on earth was she going to manage without the

225

money—however mean—that Stephen gave her each week?

CHAPTER 41

Mary stood respectfully to one side of the big overstuffed armchair that the funeral director, Stanley Price, had drawn up for Nell.

'These are slightly unusual circumstances, Mrs Flanagan.'

He raised his hand to still Nell's objections.

'I think for form's sake we'll stick with Mrs Flanagan, it makes it easier all round, especially as you say there are young children involved. Now down to details, the coroner has released the body?'

'His adult children are identifying him this afternoon, and the policemen said it shouldn't be too long after that, sir,' murmured Nell.

'It's Mr Price, my dear. Now, what were you thinking of for the day?'

'I don't have a lot of money, Mr Price.'

'We'll worry about that later, but we do have a basic arrangement that is very popular. A hearse, plus two mourning carriages—all pulled by two horses each of course—and including the coffin and cemetery fee.'

He saw Nell throw a look at Mary.

Mary ducked her head. 'That pays for the burial,' she whispered, 'at the City of London and Tower Hamlets it'll be. Over in Bow.'

Nell shook her head.

'Southern Grove. Nell, I know it sounds a long

way, but—'

'No,' Nell whispered back, 'I mean all those horses and carriages.'

Mary sighed. 'It's expected, love. And you can't really get away with much less than that.'

Nell thought of the twins, and Lil saying she didn't want to be shown up. The last thing she needed was to antagonise her and George. She returned her attention to Mr Price. 'I see,' she said non-committally.

'Right, we'll look at some samples then shall we, Mrs Flanagan? You'll be wanting to choose the type of wood and so on.'

If Stanley Price's experience was anything to go by, even the misers could usually be shamed into spending just that little bit more. And rightly so, he justified his thoughts to himself, it was after all the most important day in a person's life—so surely it was only right that you were expected to put on a good show for them, and no one helped a person put on a better show than Stanley Price and Sons.

*   *   *

Five pounds, he asked for. She had been right to choose the coffin that Mr Price had suggested after all. Nell could have kissed him on his whiskery chops. She could afford that—just—and have enough left over to see her through next week, maybe a little longer if she was careful. She handed him the money.

'Thank you, Mrs Flanagan, that will cover the deposit. The office will issue a full account when I've done the final tally. Probably, let's see, another ten pounds should cover it.'

227

When Mary saw Nell's expression, she took her by the arm. 'Let's get back home, eh love? It's been a long day.'

*   *   *

'I'll just take in these fish and chips, Mary, then I'll pop over for Tommy and Dolly, if that's all right? I won't be long.'

Nell sounded so weary, Mary wanted to wrap her in a blanket and let her sleep until she wasn't tired any more, but what chance did she have with the twins wanting nursemaiding?

'You take your time, love. Tell you what, give me the kids' tea and they can eat it with me, Joe and Martin,' Mary said, holding up the newspaper-wrapped parcel of fish and chips that she'd bought for her own family.

'Thanks, Mary, but you've done enough.'

'Don't be daft. Hand them over. Joe was like his old self when he got the cards out earlier, you'll be doing me the favour.'

As Nell was rewrapping the parcel of food after taking out the children's saveloys and chips, the door of the Flanagans' flat opened. It was George. He took the food from Nell and turned round to go back in.

'You've got visitors,' he said, without stopping on his way back to the kitchen. 'I'll send them out here so's me and Lil can eat in a bit of peace. They've been driving me mad. Talking bloody non-stop.'

'But who—'

'You'll see.'

George went into the kitchen, leaving Nell to be

228

confronted by the sight of the same two police officers who had broken the news of Stephen's death walking along the passage towards her and Mary. The officers didn't look very impressed at being sent out of the kitchen, and they remained firmly inside the hall while it was made clear from their attitude that Mary and Nell could stay right where they were—outside on the landing.

As one, Mary and Nell looked over to Ada Tanner's front door. It was closed. For now.

'Would you rather have this discussion in private, Mrs Flanagan?' said the taller of the two. 'We could go to the station, if you prefer.'

'I'd rather stay here if you don't mind.' She turned to Mary, her face pale with fear. What did these men want with her? 'I've got to pick up my children soon.'

'As you wish.' He took out a notebook from his pocket. 'During the course of our enquiries we've learned from one of your neighbours that you often had facial injuries. She informed—'

'Informed?' interrupted Nell as she and Mary again both looked over their shoulders at Ada Tanner's front door.

'Informed us of the matter this afternoon. And, as I noted,' he flipped open his notebook, 'you have signs of injuries on your face now. Would you mind telling us how they happened, Mrs Flanagan?'

'I forgot I'd left the cupboard door open, and when I stood up I banged into it.' The practised lie came out like the familiar lines of a favourite song, but her voice gave away her nerves. 'Now, if you don't mind, I have to give my children their tea.'

The policeman took a while to answer. 'That'll

be all for now.'

By the time the two men had reached the landing below, Nell was shaking. What if they thought she had something to do with Stephen's death? What would happen to her children?

CHAPTER 42

Nell stood in front of the mirror that ran the full length of the inside of the wardrobe door. She was studying her reflection, considering the black two-piece costume and cloche hat. Every inch the grieving widow.

She hadn't even thought about what she'd be wearing to the funeral until the parcel had arrived from Sylvia the day before.

The funeral.

Nell was dreading it, and she was missing Sylvia so much. But, as usual, what choice did she have but to try and stop the boat from rocking? She couldn't risk upsetting George and Lily, especially not now, not in her position. She closed the wardrobe door, picked up her bag and took a deep breath. Time to drop the children round to Sarah Meckel's shop.

She knew she should count herself lucky to have so many people offering their help, but not everyone was so kind. The moment Nell stepped out of the bedroom, Lily was on her.

'Where did you get that from then?' Lily pinched the hem of Nell's jacket, feeling the quality of the barathea cloth.

'I borrowed it from a friend.'

'What friend?'

'One of the women I talk to down in the laundry.'

'If you're lying to me . . .'

Nell could feel the sweat trickling down between her shoulder blades. 'Course I'm not. Why would I?'

'Just so long as you never nicked any of Dad's money to get it, because you remember, Nelly girl, we're his family. And you are not.'

Nell would have been less worried about her and the children's future if there actually had been any money lying around for her to steal. At least she'd have known she'd have been able to feed them.

'Sorry I can't chat now, Lily, I've got to get Tommy and Dolly round to Sarah's.'

As Nell hurried away to the kitchen to collect her children she heard Lily's voice loud and clear. 'Can't even take her little bastards to the funeral. Prefers to leave them with a bloody Jew.'

*   *   *

Nell stood by the graveside. The soft drizzle had stopped and the sky was now a clear, late summer blue, and droplets of water on the trees and shrubs were sparkling in the warm sun. But Nell didn't notice anything about what in other circumstances she would have thought was a beautiful day.

She was feeling sick after the slow, jerky ride she'd had in the second mourning carriage. George and Lily hadn't thought it appropriate for her to travel in the first one following the hearse—that place held far too much importance for the likes of her. And she was still thinking about what Lily had said about her leaving the children with Sarah. Should she have brought them along to the funeral? Nell had asked Mary and Sarah what they thought she should do, and they'd both agreed that Tommy and Dolly were too young to take in what was going on, but now Nell wasn't so sure that she'd done the right thing. She could only hope she hadn't offended the twins.

The priest continued to mumble the words that she wasn't taking in, and then he began to sprinkle holy water over the coffin. She bowed her head. What had things come to when she was standing at the grave of her children's father, yet all she could think about was that she might have offended those two?

The priest finished with the water, but continued with his incantation.

Nell raised her head a little and looked about her under lowered lashes. She could see the Lovells—Mary, Joe and Martin—the three of them standing at a carefully respectful distance. Martin caught her eye and she looked away.

Next, her gaze fell on Ada and Albert Tanner; they'd shuffled their nosy way right to the front and had positioned themselves next to the twins. Over their squat shoulders Nell could see a handful of other neighbours from Turnbury Buildings, women she knew from down in the laundry with their generally uncomfortable-looking husbands, with whom she was on little more than nodding acquaintance. Much of their discomfort doubtless came from the fact that Florrie Talbot, who probably knew some of the male neighbours considerably better than Nell, was standing very close to them. She was looking surprisingly young and fresh-faced without all her usual powder and paint.

Then Nell spotted Sylvia and Bernie—Sylvia glamorous as ever, despite being grim-faced, and, unusually, not even bothering to straighten up Bernie's outfit. He was almost bursting out of the skintight black suit that looked as if he had last worn it not only a number of years ago, but also quite a few stone ago. The majority of the mourners, however, were not at all familiar to Nell; they were mostly men, some well dressed, others almost ragged. But there were two men that she had recognised and she wished sincerely that she hadn't. They were in the background, standing in the shade of a broad yew tree—the two policemen who had broken the news to her about Stephen's death. They weren't wearing their uniforms, but Nell would have recognised them anywhere.

What did they want? What were they doing here? And why didn't they just leave her alone?

*   *   *

With the final handful of soil tossed onto the coffin, the interment was over and people began stepping away, ostensibly to inspect the wreaths, but actually to light cigarettes and to break the atmosphere with a little light banter. There weren't many tears being shed for Stephen Flanagan.

Sylvia left Bernie to his mates from the pub, and went over to the twins. She said something to them and then joined Nell.

'Anything I can do, Nell, anything at all,' she said. 'You only have to say, and I'll be there. Have you got that?'

Nell cast a nervous look at the twins in case they disapproved of her talking to Sylvia, but they seemed preoccupied with accepting condolences from a huddle of the men she didn't recognise.

Sylvia carried on. 'Nell, we've put on a bit of a spread at the Hope. You know my Bernie got on well with Stephen, and it's just our way of saying so, of seeing him off. And don't worry, I've squared it with them two over there.'

'How did you do that?'

Sylvia let out a little puff of laughter. 'I was on a winner before I'd even started. They weren't going to say no to free booze and food, now were they?'

'Are you sure they don't mind? I don't want to upset them, Sylv.'

'Now let's see, Lil's exact words to George were—' She put on a whining voice. ' "At least she's taken the trouble, not like Nell, the selfish cow. So we can hardly refuse, can we George? Sad as it is for us today, we'd better at least put our face round the door. Show respect to Dad, God rest his soul." '

Nell said nothing.

Sylvia shook her head. 'Some people, eh, Nell?'

She could see that this was going to be tricky, that Nell would be reluctant to go back to the pub if the twins were going to be there. 'You know what it's like, Nelly darling, people will expect you to show up.' She shrugged. 'It's like you're obliged. Come on, you won't have to stay for very long. Let's make a move, that priest looks like he could do with sinking a couple or three whiskies.'

234

CHAPTER 43

Nell managed a sip of tea and a mouthful of ham sandwich that left her mouth as dry as if it had been swabbed with cotton wool. All around her people were drinking, eating, and now openly laughing. A release from sadness or a sign that they couldn't give a monkey's about Stephen Flanagan? Nell really didn't know. What she did know was that she had to get away from there—from the crowds and the noise. She looked around until she found Sylvia. She was busily pulling pints and pouring shorts behind the bar for all those eager to make the most of the free food and drink.

Nell struggled to get to the front of the throng. Clearly, her place in the pecking order of mourners wasn't very high.

'Sylvia, can I have a quick word?'

Sylvia indicated to one of the extra bar staff—brought in especially for the day—with a downward jab of her index finger to her place behind the bar, and then squeezed her way round to speak to Nell.

'How are you doing, darling?'

Nell pressed her lips tightly together, afraid she'd start weeping with the fear that was welling up inside her.

'Want another drink? Something a bit stronger than tea this time?'

Nell found the strength to speak. 'No thanks, Sylv. I just wanted to say thanks very much for everything. But I've got to go and pick up the children. Sarah will be getting busy with people coming home from work, and I don't want to take liberties with her. She's too good to do that to.'

She made a tiny gesture with her head to where George and Lily were getting stuck into the big enamel bowls of jellied eels from the buffet. 'And I'd like to get back home before those two notice I'm missing.' Nell dropped her chin. 'I really meant it when I said how grateful I am, Sylv.' She ran her hand down her jacket. 'The suit, it was so kind of you, and really beautiful. I'll drop it back when I've sponged and pressed it.'

'Don't be silly, Nell, you keep it.'

'But I can't—'

'Don't say another word—it's yours. What good would it be to me? It'd come down to my bloody ankles.' She touched Nell on the cheek. 'And you'll be expected to wear black for a bit, won't you?'

'Oh. I suppose I will. I hadn't really thought.'

'And don't worry, you won't have to wear that every day. I've got you a few other dark bits upstairs that I picked up for you—only from down the market—and stockings and that. I'll drop them round.'

Nell felt her heart begin to pound. She couldn't have Sylvia turning up at the flat. What if the twins saw her?

'That's so nice of you, Sylv, but would it be all right if I popped round here for them?'

'Course it would. You know how glad I am to see you, darling. Any time, any time at all.'

Nell nodded her thanks, twitched a brief smile and then pressed her way through the crowd towards the door.

Ada Tanner blocked her way. 'You're in a hurry,' she sneered, before taking a long slug of her gin and orange.

'I've got to collect the children,' said Nell, barging her way forward in a manner that was totally alien to her.

'There's something wrong here,' said one of the policemen, wiping the foam from his pint off his top lip. 'Think it might be time to have another word with Mrs Tanner.'

'You're right. Just look at them. Nobody seems upset. Nobody at all. You'd expect *someone* to be missing him. His so-called wife looked more scared than anything else. She was out of here like a rat up a drainpipe. And those twins of his, they look more like they're at a party than a funeral. Let alone the funeral of their own father. Have you been watching that daughter of his? She's been sinking the booze like she's been at sea for six months.'

'Still no word from the local station on who he was doing the running for?'

'You won't be surprised to hear that they are being a bit reluctant to be drawn on that one. You know how much money's involved in that game.'

'How about him?'

'Who?'

The taller of the two policemen inclined his head towards Bernie, who had settled himself at the corner table. 'That feller?'

The other one waggled his hand, weighing up the possibility. 'Who knows?'

'Mind you, would you risk losing your licence if you had a good little business like this? What with the hospital and the markets, and all the chimney pots round here, Mr Woods must be doing all right for himself without any need of sidelines.'

'But he does have a young wife to keep, and they don't come cheap.'

'There's definitely something more to this. They should never have released that body. Makes it all too easy to get it over with.'

'I bet the local nick can't wait to close the book.'

Sylvia had spotted the two policemen as soon as they'd turned up at the funeral, and hadn't been at all surprised when they had appeared in the pub. She only hoped that they hadn't figured out the arrangement that Bernie had with the local law, or that half the blokes in the pub did business with him. It might be best to set about charming them.

'Hello gentlemen,' she said with a rueful smile. 'Such a sad day for us all, eh? And I know how much Nell appreciates you making the time in your busy day to pay your respects, so let's get you some more drinks and a plate of food each, because I know you men never look after yourselves properly.'

'Well, I wouldn't mind.' The shorter policeman looked to his colleague. 'How about you?'

'I wouldn't say no.'

CHAPTER 44

'So does it mean he won't be coming back home ever again?' Dolly was struggling to understand what was going on.

Nell pulled the covers up to her daughter's chin and kissed her gently on the tip of her nose. 'Yes, darling. Your dad isn't with us any more.'

'Good,' said Tommy, fishing under the bed to

pull out the little tin box of lead soldiers he had hidden there. 'Now I can play with the things Auntie Sylvie got me without having to be frightened.'

'Aw Tommy.' Nell stroked the hair away from his forehead. 'I'm so sorry you've been frightened.' She sighed wearily, the day taking its toll. 'But we've still got to be careful with George and Lily until we see how things go.'

'I wish they'd die as well.' Tommy put the box back under the bed. 'And I wish that it could be just us. I hate them two.'

'I know they can be difficult, Tom, but we shouldn't be unkind.'

'Well them two are,' he pouted. 'Them two are ever so unkind. Why should I be nice to them?'

'Because we're not like them, and it would make me unhappy if you started being unkind. Do you understand?'

'Yes, Mum. I'm sorry.'

'Good boy. Now you and Dolly go to sleep, it's been a long day.'

'Sarah gave us loads of sweets,' said Dolly quietly. 'Was that naughty?'

'No, that was kind and generous of her. I hope you both said thank you nicely.'

'No, we just said thank you,' giggled Tommy.

'Cheeky thing,' smiled Nell.

'You look pretty in that hat, Mum. And when you smile.'

Nell could have burst into tears. Fancy the little one noticing that she'd smiled. Did she really smile so seldom?

'Now you two,' she said briskly. 'You really must go to sleep. Night, night.'

'Sleep tight,' yawned Dolly.

'Don't let the bedbugs bite,' Tommy finished as Nell turned off the light.

Then Tommy's voice came from out of the darkness. 'We'll have to think what to do with our half-crown soon, won't we Mum?'

*　　　*　　　*

Nell went into what had been her and Stephen's bedroom, which was now just hers—but who knew for how much longer?—and took off the black cloche hat and the two-piece costume. She draped the skirt and jacket carefully over a hanger and put it away in the wardrobe. She folded her slip and stockings neatly—they would last another day until she saw what Sylvia had for her—and then rolled up her underwear ready for laundering. She didn't know how she'd have managed without Sylvia; she had been so good to her over the years, and yet now she was too scared to have her come to visit for fear of upsetting the twins.

What was going to become of her and the children?

Nell buttoned her nightdress up to her neck and flopped down on the bed. It was barely eight o'clock but she was worn out; she felt as if she hadn't slept for weeks. Tired as she was, she could really do with a cup of tea and a wash. She would have loved to have gone down to the basement for a nice hot bath, but it wouldn't be right, leaving the children alone; things were confusing enough for them as it was, without waking up to find her gone as well. No, the kitchen and a cat's lick and a promise would have to do for now.

*   *   *

Nell stood at the sink and unbuttoned her nightdress down to her waist. She ran the flannel under the single cold tap and wrung it out. Closing her eyes with exhaustion, she peeled her nightie off her shoulders and began washing under her arms. She shivered. She should have boiled a kettle of water first and had a nice warm wash. But it wasn't just the chill of the flannel making her shudder; she had the sudden horrible feeling that someone was watching her. She opened her eyes and looked in the mirror over the sink.

George was standing behind her in the kitchen doorway.

Nell grabbed the towel off the draining board to cover herself and spun round to face him. 'What do you think you're doing?'

He moved closer.

Nell tried to step away from him, but she was trapped between him and the sink. She clamped her hand over her mouth.

'Smell of booze bothers you, does it?' His voice was slurred, and his eyes out of focus. 'Never put you off Dad, did it? I used to watch you and him sometimes. Did you know that? I used to touch myself while he was having you. In here. In the bedroom. You couldn't get enough of him, could you, you dirty little slut?'

'George, don't talk like that. We've just been to his funeral.'

'So?'

'Where's Lily?'

241

'Under the table at the Hope by now, if I know her. I thought I'd come home early and give you a little surprise.'

He grabbed hold of the opened bodice of her nightdress and ripped it apart, sending the rest of the buttons pinging across the lino.

Nell slapped him hard around his face.

'You made a mistake there, you silly bitch. You're going to pay for that.'

'George, please.' Nell felt she was going to pass out, but then she heard from the front room a murmur as Dolly stirred in her sleep, and was suddenly alert. 'Don't upset the children.'

'If you don't want them upset you'd better shut that mouth of yours.'

He dragged Nell across the room, pushed her onto the kitchen table and forced himself on her just as he'd seen his father do.

When he'd finished with her he buttoned up his trousers and stumbled out of the kitchen.

When he reached the doorway he paused. His words came out in a low growl. 'And don't think I'm going to forget what you did to me. I meant what I said—I'm going to make you pay for that slap.'

Nell stood, watching as he staggered past his own door and went into her and Stephen's bedroom. 'I'll be waiting for you,' she heard him call over the sound of the bedsprings groaning as he threw himself down onto the bed.

She washed herself quickly, pulled her torn nightgown onto her still damp body and hurried along to the front room. She slipped inside, locked the door and crept into bed with Tommy and Dolly, holding her sleeping children close to her,

her salty tears dampening their hair. She couldn't let them be part of this any longer.

CHAPTER 45

Nell woke up with a start and looked at the clock on the window ledge. She had only slept in exhausting fitful bursts—with her night haunted by visions of what George had done to her—and was traumatised to realise that she must have drifted off at last and that she'd overslept. It was half past seven and she hadn't even given the twins their breakfast. Now knowing what George was capable of, she was terrified. He'd be furious when they got back from the market.

She eased her way out of the double bed so as not to disturb the children, and put on her soft-soled slippers to muffle the sound of her footsteps. She'd wash and dress, then once the children were ready the three of them would get out of there for the day—well away from the twins when they returned this afternoon, and as far away as possible from the stench of George's sour breath in her nostrils. It would give her time to work out what to do.

Gently, she closed the door to the front room, and began to creep along the passageway to Stephen's bedroom to fetch her clothes, but as she came to the hallstand she pulled up short. Thrown across it were George's and Lily's coats. They must have been so drunk last night that they'd overslept as well. They'd never have missed a market day when their father was alive. He wouldn't have let them.

She looked at the door to Stephen's room. It was closed. She moved up to it and listened.

Snoring.

George was still in there. What was she going to do about getting dressed? And how about her brooch? Say he found it? She didn't dare risk waking him—he might do that to her again. She would just have to manage with what she had, and hope that he was too lazy to go through the drawer. Maybe he had been so drunk last night that he'd forgotten all about what he had done to her.

Maybe.

At least the children's clothes were safely in the front room.

She went into the kitchen, poured two cups of milk and then spread two slices of bread with the jam that in the past had always been only for Stephen's consumption, all the while thinking where she could take the children. Somewhere, anywhere well out of the way of the twins.

There was only one place.

*   *   *

'Sorry to disturb you, Bernie,' said Nell, standing on the front step of the Hope, with a wary-looking child holding onto each of her hands. 'I know it's early but I was wondering if I could have a word with Sylvia.'

Bernie had been about to shout at whoever was knocking on his door at this time of the morning—especially as the wake, with its free food and booze, had gone on until the early hours—but he was momentarily lost for words. He was hardly a fashion plate in his plaid dressing gown and grey ankle socks, but Nell, well she looked like a bloody scarecrow. He eyed her up and down. Why the hell was she wearing a coat over a nightdress that was dangling down past her knees? And she had bare legs and was wearing slippers. Had she gone doolally or something? You did hear about deaths in the family taking people in all sorts of funny ways. He could only hope it didn't drive her to start shooting her mouth off. How much did she know about what Stephen had been up to, and, moreover, did she know how closely he, Bernie Woods, had been involved?

'Morning, Nell,' he said, pulling himself together. 'Sorry I didn't have a chance to speak to you properly after the funeral yesterday, but I was trying to be a good host—you understand. It was a rotten old business and I tried to do my best for you both, putting on a decent show.'

Nell nodded absently. 'Can I see Sylvia?'

'Go through and sit down and I'll give her a call for you.'

At least if she was safely inside no one could see what a mess she looked and start asking awkward questions.

*   *   *

Sylvia wasn't as reticent as her husband. 'For goodness' sake, Nell, will you look at yourself? Whatever are you doing coming out like that? You look like you've just got out of bed.' She turned to Bernie as if he knew what was going on. 'It was bad enough when she showed up wearing her apron

245

and no coat, but did she really come here on the bus in her slippers and nightdress?'

Bernie shrugged. 'Search me what's she's up to. Now if no one minds I've got to go upstairs and see to something.'

Tommy looked at his mum; he'd known there was something not right about how she was dressed, but with the way she was acting, and everything being turned upside down, he'd been too frightened to ask.

'I didn't want to disturb George,' Nell said, 'or Lily. They both had a late night. After the funeral and that. And what with all the upset they've had, it would have been unkind.'

'If you say so,' said Sylvia, looking at her doubtfully. 'But for the life of me I can't see how you getting dressed would upset even that pair, but let's all go upstairs and have a cup of tea, shall we? Come on kids.'

With that, she took the children's hands and nodded for Nell to go over to the stairway.

*　　　*　　　*

Bernie was in the kitchen drinking tea and flicking through the paper; he didn't seem best pleased to see his wife, Nell and the kids standing there in front of him.

'You might as well take your tea back to bed with you, Bern.' Sylvia shot her husband a meaningful *go on, leave us alone* look. 'Me and Nell will only drive you mad with all our nattering. You know what we're like when we get going.'

Bernie thought for a moment. Why was she so keen to get rid of him? Was she making her mad

246

plans again?

'No, I'm fine here, thanks, Sylv,' he said. 'I'm awake now. I'll have a bit of breakfast in a minute, then I'll get on with the bottling up.'

'Thanks for nothing,' Sylvia mouthed at him as she picked up the teapot, weighing it to see if there was any left, and then poured a cup each for her and Nell.

'How about you, Tommy and Dolly?'

Were they being offered a cup of tea? Wasn't that for grown-ups? Bewildered by all these strange goings-on, the children looked at their mother for guidance as to how they should answer.

Nell nodded.

'Yes please,' said Tommy.

'How about a nice drop of milky tea for you and all, Dolly? With a couple of sugars?' Sylvia turned to glare at Bernie. 'And as Uncle Bernie's going to make himself a bit of breakfast before he starts work, he can make you two a nice bacon sandwich each while he's at it.'

First jam, now a cup of tea, and a bacon sandwich—all in one day? Tommy forgot about feeling confused and frightened—it looked like things were turning out all right this morning. If only his mum would cheer up a bit and the twins would drop dead, things wouldn't be half bad.

*   *   *

Reluctantly, Bernie started cooking the breakfast—at least it meant he could stay in the kitchen and keep an eye and an ear on what was going on—with Tommy and Dolly standing on either side of him like a pair of bacon-sniffing bookends. And it wasn't too bad, actually; they weren't horrible, not like some kids you came across.

'How are you doing?' Sylvia asked, taking Nell's hand.

'Not too bad, thank you,' she said in a voice that told Sylvia exactly the opposite, 'and I don't want to be forward or anything, but I was wondering about those bits you said you'd got me down the market.'

'By the look of you, Nell, I reckon you need them. You can't go walking the streets like that. You look like someone who hangs around the park even when it's raining. They see you like that, and they'll put you away in a loony bin.'

Nell started sniffling, trying not to let the tears fall, and trying to stop her hands from shaking, desperate not to worry the children, but even more desperate for some money so she could get away from Turnbury Buildings. 'And I was wondering, Sylv. Is there any chance of me having my old job back?'

Sylvia smiled broadly; she was just about to say yes, but Bernie got in first.

'To be straight with you, Nell,' he said, flipping over the eggs he was frying, 'things are not so good at the moment. Some nights it's hard to justify keeping the place open. Two old boys nursing half a pint of mild all night so they don't use their own gas or electric indoors—it's a struggle making ends meet.'

'Bernie!' Sylvia sounded as shocked as she looked.

'How about laundry or cleaning work?' he suggested, sliding the eggs onto a big blue and white striped platter. 'You were good at that when you lived here.'

'I don't believe you,' snapped Sylvia.

'Well, she was. Tell you what, you should go over and see if they've got anything in the hospital, they say they've got a massive laundry over there. All them bedsheets and uniforms and that.'

'Thanks, that's a good idea, Bernie. And I'm sorry, I shouldn't have had such a cheek asking.'

'Bernie,' Sylvia said again, her face growing redder.

Nell stood up. 'We'd better be on our way.'

'Wait, Nell.' Sylvia pulled out a couple of chairs and lifted Dolly onto one. 'The kids haven't had their sandwiches yet, and you can't go anywhere till you've got some clothes on. And they might be a bit of a squeeze but you'll have to borrow a pair of my shoes. My oxblood ones are quite roomy.'

'Yeah, she's right, Nell, no good you going asking for a job looking like that.'

'Thank you, Bernie, that's all she needs on top of everything else—advice from you on what she should wear.' Sylvia narrowed her eyes at him. 'When you've got dressed you can leave the kids with me and jolly Uncle Bernie here, while you go across and see if they've got something for you in the hospital.'

Bernie arranged four slices of bread in the bacon fat in the big black frying pan, leaning back as they sizzled and crackled. 'Here, you used to help us out with a bit of paperwork and all, didn't you?'

'Help out?' sniped Sylvia. 'She did the whole bloody lot of it.'

'That'll be a nice job for a girl like you. Office

work. But you'll need to look the part, so it's good you're not going over in your slippers, eh?'

Bernie's encouraging smile was wiped clean away by the look shot at him by his wife.

CHAPTER 46

When Nell returned, Sylvia, Bernie and the children were down in the bar. Dolly was happily helping Sylvia wipe the tables and Tommy was getting under Bernie's feet as he bottled up, asking non-stop questions of this wonderful man who made him bacon sandwiches.

'How did you do?' asked Sylvia.

'They've got a vacancy in the ironing room. I mentioned office work, and they said that if something comes up they might let me do a test to see if I'm good enough.'

'That'll be nice.' Sylvia managed a smile. She'd heard about the ironing room from one of the customers whose wife worked there, and he reckoned it was more like being inside than in a hospital, more punishment than a job. No wonder they had vacancies. How long could someone put up with that drudgery? As long as they had to, if they were desperate, she supposed.

'Are the twins helping you out with a few quid?'

Nell shook her head. 'Not really. It's like Bernie said, things are not easy for anyone nowadays. They've got themselves to think about.' She stood up. 'Anyway, mustn't complain. Bye, Sylv. Bern. Thank you both for everything. Come on, you two.'

'Wait, Nell. Just a minute.' Sylvia went to the till

and counted out five pounds. 'And don't you dare say no, it's just to see you and the kids over until you start your job.'

Nell couldn't look her in the eye, but she couldn't refuse the money either. 'Thanks, Sylv, I appreciate it.'

'You're more than welcome, love.'

Nell looked over at Bernie, who was doing his best to avoid making eye contact with either of the women.

'Thanks for the idea about the hospital, Bernie,' she said politely. 'And as soon as I can I'll pay you back. I promise.'

'No rush,' he said.

'No need,' corrected Sylvia.

'And I really don't know what I'd have done without the clothes, Sylv. You were right, I must have looked a right fool in my night things.'

'It's my pleasure, darling.'

'It's just a shame they've got no live-in work over there. That would have been ideal. But what with having the children I don't suppose anyone would offer me that.'

'Don't worry, sweetheart, things'll work out for you. Not always in the way you might expect, but they will. Now you go and buy some grub for you and the kids and make yourself a nice bit of dinner.'

'Thanks, that's exactly what I'm going to do. Sorry if I held you up. You must think I'm a right nuisance.'

'Don't be daft.' Sylvia kissed Tommy and Dolly and then hugged Nell. 'You've never been a nuisance to anyone, Nell.'

251

Bernie stood at the sink shaving, with Sylvia on guard behind him, waiting for the right moment to pounce, like a pocket-sized ginger moggy sizing up a big fat rat.

She couldn't stay quiet any longer, if Bernie cut himself then too bad.

'Bernie, that girl is at her wits' end. You must have been able to see that—her walking through the streets dressed like a tramp. So why were you so rotten to her? How could you have behaved that way? You're a much better man than that. Kinder. Nicer. More generous. We could have found her plenty to do around here, and given her somewhere to stay. There's rooms up here we never even use.'

Bernie took a long breath and let his razor drop into the bowl of soapy water. 'Sylvia, think about it—Stephen Flanagan was found dead in the river, and everyone round here knows that he—' He threw up his hands in exasperation. 'Look, I just don't want them geezers from the river police wondering why I've got his widow working here, got it? You saw the nosy bastards at the funeral yesterday. And they're hardly the approachable types, now are they? If I offer them a straightener there's every chance I'll land myself right in the shit.'

'In that case we'll take a different approach to the problem.' Sylvia shoved her finger in his face. 'You, Bernie, have got to help her by getting rid of them two idiots from out of that flat so that Nell and the kids have somewhere to live in a bit of peace and quiet. She's been through enough, Bern,

252

more than enough. In fact it's a wonder she'd not gone round the bloody bend.'

'You know how fond I am of that girl, Sylvia, but I am not getting involved in this. I can't afford to. You don't need to worry yourself about it, but it could mean trouble for both of us.'

'I have never asked anything like this of you before. And I have never interfered with you running the card school up here either. And don't bother looking at me like that, I'm not stupid, I know you've been running a spieler for bloody years. But I am asking you for this one favour. I want them two ponces kicked out on their—excuse my language—on their fucking arses.'

Bernie's eyebrows couldn't have lifted any higher. Sylvia never held back from cursing, but he had never, ever heard that word come out of his pretty little wife's mouth before.

'Sylvia.'

'I mean it, Bern, either you do something about it or I'll have to. That girl looks ill, and I am going to help her. No, *we* are going to help her. Because the only other way I reckon it can be sorted out is with the bloody poker. And you wouldn't want that, now would you, seeing your wife being put away for murder?'

Bernie took her face in his hands. 'Sylvia, you have got to calm down here, girl. You're all right shouting the odds, but you don't know the half of it. I might not be in a position to tell them what to do. It might be a bit, sort of, awkward. See . . .' He dropped his chins until they were nearly touching his chest. 'Stephen Flanagan had been, er . . . working for me for a few years, and it was, let's say a bit dodgy, what he was doing. And them twins of

253

his must have known about it, because a lot of his work took him round by the markets. And if the twins do know about it, and I start getting tough on them, then they might just decide to make things awkward for me. You know what them two are like. They'd be more than capable of grassing me up. Then what'd happen?'

'Well, since you've brought it up, Bern, I know all about Stephen Flanagan being your runner and all, cos I presume that's what you're mumbling on about.'

Bernie's face creased into a disbelieving frown. 'How? I never let on, not once.'

'Do I look like I'm stupid?'

His answer was to rub his hands over his half-shaved chin.

Sylvia took his hands in hers, drew them away from his face and looked into his eyes. 'And what if I said I might make things awkward for you? You know how hard they've been on spielers and bookies lately.'

'Do I?'

'Yes you do, you know full bloody well. I've seen you reading about it in the *East London Advertiser*.' She prodded him—not so gently. 'And I used to watch Stephen Flanagan handing over the money to you every single night, Bernie. Think about it, when have you ever been able to keep a secret from me?'

'I don't know the answer to that one, girl. But would you really gamble losing everything we've struggled to make for ourselves? We've got a good life, Sylv. You can see for yourself how a lot of other people are living round here. So why would you risk losing it?'

'If it means helping that girl then I might not mind taking a gamble on having to give up all this.' Sylvia folded her arms. 'I could handle it. I did before I met you.'

'You wouldn't.'

'Wouldn't I? Here, you're a bookie,' she said. 'So I've got a bet for you. I bet there were things went on in that flat that you and me wouldn't want to even imagine. And most of them ain't gonna stop.'

'What sort of things? Blimey, Sylv, you don't half exaggerate.' Bernie didn't know what had got into the woman. 'And anyway, the local law already know all about me,' he said, full of false bravado.

'They should bloody do, the amount of dough you put their way.'

'How do you—'

'Never mind that, all I'll say is: if someone went in the station and made a statement—and I'm talking about in full view of plenty of witnesses—what choice would they have then but to do something about it? Especially if that person threatened to go to the local papers with the whole flaming story.'

'You wouldn't.'

'Wouldn't I, Bern? Well you've got me wrong there, because what I really wouldn't do is leave her and those kids in that place with those two no-goods still living there. Now that Stephen's gone they've not even got that pig to keep them under control. You saw the state she was in, bloody terrified. So I'm telling you straight—you've got a choice, you can either get them two out of there or have Nell and the kids move in here with us. If not, you know the consequences.'

She studied her husband's face. Of course she would never do anything to hurt him, but would he really believe that she would ever grass him up? She could only hope so.

CHAPTER 47

While Nell and the children were travelling back to Wapping on the bus—with Tommy and Dolly chattering about whether they should pick butter or some more jam from Sarah's shop now that their mum had said they could spend some of their half-crown, and with Nell staring unseeingly out of the bus window—George and Lily were sitting at the kitchen table in Turnbury Buildings. They were arguing over who should put the kettle on the stove.

'Go on, Lil, I don't feel too good.'

'You, George, have got a hangover, just like I have, so why should I make a cup of tea for you? You stick the rotten thing on the gas.'

'You Lil are a lazy, rotten cow.'

She ignored the insult. 'Got any fags?'

George skidded his packet of Players across to her.

'Matches?'

'Bloody hell, Lil, what did your last servant die of, flipping overwork?' He fished a box of matches out of his dressing-gown pocket and tossed it to her.

Lily lit a cigarette, inhaled deeply, coughed for a bit, then said, 'You do realise that by next week both of her little bastards are going to be at school, don't you? So are we really going to go out to work every single morning while she sits here doing nothing? She took Dad for a right mug if you ask me, and I don't intend to be her next stooge. Just cos she had a couple of kids by him she thinks we owe her. Well she can think again.'

George took back the matches, dragged himself over to the stove and lit the gas under the kettle. 'If they were Dad's.'

'How do you mean?'

'What do you think? Do you trust him across the landing, sniffing round her like she's a bitch on heat?'

Lily perked up. 'You mean that them two have been having it away?'

'I wouldn't be surprised.'

'If you're right, George, then we don't owe her anything.'

'No, Lil, we don't, and just because we haven't found them yet, who knows whether there might be insurance policies knocking about. If there are, then the money should go to us, his proper family.

'Do you know, I think we should get ourselves washed and dressed and go and see those two from the river police. They were ever so interested in what was going on. And surely it would only be right—for Dad's sake if nothing else—to get this all sorted out. It'd be what he would have wanted.'

*   *   *

Lily dabbed at her nose with her handkerchief, eyes cast to one side like the grieving victim she wasn't. 'It broke mine and Georgie's hearts, sir, when we realised that Nell had a fancy man.'

'You're saying she was going with another man, Miss Flanagan?'

George nodded for her. 'Yeah. Embarrassing as it is to admit it, it was a bloke right under Dad's nose. Martin Lovell his name is. Lives across the landing from us at number fifty-seven.'

'It's a real disgrace to my father's memory,' chipped in Lily with a loud sniff.

'There, there, Lil,' said George, patting his sister on the back of her hankie-grasping hand. 'He's got a good job, you see, so it suits a little gold-digger like her right down to the ground. First she bled Dad dry and then she moved onto the next mug to fall for her big-eyed act.'

Unable to keep the look of self-satisfaction off her face, Lily dealt the final blow. 'This is really hard to say, sir, but neither of us would be surprised if our dad wasn't her kids' real father. I mean, who knows when you put it about like she does?'

The officers exchanged a look, and the taller of the two said, 'We appreciate you taking the trouble to come forward with this information, Miss and Mr Flanagan. We've made our notes, which we'll be considering—thank you.'

'Is that it?' asked Lily. 'Don't you need to know anything else about her?'

'We'll be in touch if there are any further questions, miss.'

*   *   *

The shorter of the two officers sat on his colleague's desk looking out at the river.

'So, what do you think? I know we've had our

suspicions about those two, but I honestly don't know what to make of them.' He curled his lip in disgust. 'They've only just buried their father.'

'You know what they say—it takes all sorts. When I lost my dad—God rest his soul—I was beside myself, but he was a good bloke. I'm not so sure what I'd have thought of this Flanagan. Sounds as if he was a right bit of work. And, think about it, there's bound to be a few bob floating about. Market stalls, gambling—there's got to be. You know what vultures people can be once they get a sniff of dough in their nostrils.'

'But it still doesn't seem very likely to me that she'd be going with someone else. She might have been Flanagan's fancy piece, but if she was as scared of him as that neighbour of hers'—he looked in his notebook—'that old girl, Ada Tanner, reckoned she was, then she'd hardly have messed around with someone on her own doorstep, now would she.'

'If she was brazen enough to live with one feller, and him old enough to be her father, what's stopping her going off with any number of others?'

'I suppose.'

'We'd better follow it up.'

'I don't reckon it would hurt to have a quick chat. And I would love to rub Leman Street and Whitechapel stations' noses in it by coming up with the goods.'

'You and me both.'

*   *   *

Standing outside the police station in the narrow Wapping street, shivering slightly in the breeze that

259

was blowing up from the river, Lily pulled her coat more tightly about her, but she wasn't complaining, in fact she was feeling rather pleased with herself. 'Fancy a drink, George?'

'Don't mind if I do, Lil. How about the Grapes, that suit you?'

'Lovely, George.'

CHAPTER 48

Nell felt the closest to what could have been described as light-hearted for a very long time as she walked across the courtyard of the Buildings. She had managed to put George and his vileness somewhere to the back of her mind where she didn't have to think about it—for now at least— she had bags full of shopping and Tommy and Dolly were each holding a hokey-pokey ice cream. Despite her worries about money, after the tensions of the past few days the stop-me-and-buy- one man on his tricycle had been too hard for Nell to resist. She hated the children always going without, and loved the idea of being able to treat them for once, especially knowing that they still had their half-crown to spend. Then they had bumped into Martin who had been on his way out somewhere, but had insisted on turning back and carrying her shopping home for her. She had hesitated for no longer than a moment—where was the harm? It was still daylight and the children were with her; she had nothing to feel ashamed about. He was only being a kind neighbour . . .

'You shouldn't be wasting your time helping me,

Martin,' she said with a soft smile, as she handed over the bags.

'It's no trouble at all, Nell. They weigh nothing for a big tough bloke like me,' he said with a grin. 'I'm a proper athlete.'

'Yeah,' joined in Tommy. 'You could have won every single race in the Olympics.'

Martin stopped on the spot. 'I wouldn't have had anything to do with these Olympics, Tom.'

'Why not?'

'They were run by people who weren't very nice. They did what this horrible bloke Hitler told them to do. You wouldn't like him. He's really bad.'

'Will he come over here?' asked Tommy.

'Course he won't. I'm so tough, I frighten the life out big old bullies like him.' Martin then deliberately lurched forward and pretended to trip over as they started up the stairway, making the children roar with laughter.

'Tough as old boots, me,' said Martin, raising the shopping bags high above his head.

'You can stay down here and play out if you like, kids,' Nell said. 'I'll call down for you over the balcony when your tea's done. How about that?'

Martin moved closer and whispered in her ear— so close she could feel his warm breath on her cheek. 'OK if I give them a few coppers to go round Sarah's?'

'No, Martin, I don't want you to waste your money on us. I mean, on them.'

'How about a penny between them then?'

'Thanks, that's ever so kind. But my friend Sylvia's treated them already, and they've had their cornets.'

Martin winked. 'But they don't get treats that

261

often, do they, Nell?'

'No, no they don't.'

'Go on, let me. I really want to.'

'OK. Thank you. But just a penny between them, all right?'

*   *   *

Martin and Nell reached the top landing, and Nell held out her hands for the bags. Why did she worry so much? Everything was fine. It had to be.

'I can't tell you, Martin, what a relief it was to be able to treat Tommy and Dolly and then to go out and buy them some decent food. You know, not just enough for a bit of tea for them, but enough to fill them up. I'm used to having an empty belly, but they're not, the poor little things. These past weeks have been so hard. But it might all be sorting itself out. That friend of mine, Sylvia, has lent me some money, and I've got a job to start next week when the children go back to school. It's only in a laundry, but I've told them I can do office work, and I think they must be interested in me because like I was telling Sylvia they said that if they get any vacancies, they might let me do a test to see if I'm good enough for the office. That would be really good, because then I'd earn enough money to get a place to live for me and the kids, somewhere all to ourselves. I know I'm lucky having somewhere for them to live now, but I don't like living here with, you know, them two.'

Nell looked hurriedly away. She hadn't thought—say they were still indoors and they saw her standing out here with Martin?

'I'm ever so sorry, Martin, I don't know what's

got into me, running off at the mouth like that, but I've—'

'You mustn't ever be sorry to me about anything, Nell. You remember what I said to you before. I still mean it. We can leave here whenever you like. We can leave here and go anywhere. Together. Me, you and the kids.'

Nell swallowed hard and took the bags from him, her hands brushing against his, making her blush and feel the way she did when he had touched his finger to her lips. 'I've got to get on now, Martin. Thanks for your help.'

'Hello, Mrs Flanagan.'

As one, Nell and Martin looked over to the stairwell. Halfway up from the landing below, moving closer by the moment, were two police officers, the ones who had come to tell Nell about finding Stephen's body—the same ones who had come back to speak to her, and who had then turned up at the funeral yesterday. Why wouldn't they leave her alone?

'We'd like to have a word with you, if you don't mind. And this gentleman, he might as well stay too.' The taller officer flipped open his notebook. 'Because I presume you're Martin Lovell from number fifty-seven.'

*　　　*　　　*

Half an hour later, Nell, still in the black mourning coat and hat that Sylvia had bought her, was sitting at the kitchen table across from Martin looking as if she'd been cast in stone. At least the twins hadn't been in to witness what had happened.

'Nell?'

263

Martin reached across to her, but she pulled her hand away.

'You heard what they were saying,' she said, wondering just how much worse things could be. 'They think Stephen was murdered, don't they? What if they think it was me? They'll take my children away. And what will the twins have to say if they find out they've been here again?' She leapt to her feet. 'You've got to leave, Martin. If they come home and find you sitting here like you own the place they'll go mad.'

'Who cares about what they think?'

'I do. Me, I care. Martin, you have no idea the trouble I would be in.' She could taste the fear in her mouth as she thought of George.

'I've got plenty of ideas, Nell, but mine are good ones. And that one we were talking about—that's the best one I've ever had.' Slowly, Martin rose to his feet and walked round the table to stand next to her. 'You, me and the kids, Nell, let's go off somewhere to live together as a family. I meant every word of it when I said I'd sort this out for you, and I did. Please, Nell, marry me. I love you so much.'

Nell shook her head. 'What do you mean, you sorted it out?'

'I sorted it out. For you. So you didn't have to be scared of him ever again.'

She backed away from him. 'What are you talking about?'

'I was there, the night he died.'

'You can't mean *you killed him*?'

'No, Nell, it was an accident. I only meant to frighten him. To give him a taste of his own medicine so he'd stop hurting you. We had a fight and we were struggling over this piece of wood, and I must have hit him harder than I thought. It could just as easily have been me who was found in the river. Think how things would have turned out then.'

'But that wasn't what happened, was it? It was him who died. And now they'll catch up with you and hang you. You've got to get away, Martin, before they come back again.'

Martin grasped her hand. 'Nell, come with me.'

'You've got to stop this, Martin. Listen to me. You have got to get away from here. You heard what those policemen were saying. How long have we known each other? Were we close friends? You know what they meant. And they mentioned Ada Tanner more than once. Who knows what rubbish she's been telling them?'

'I can't leave without you, Nell.'

'You have to. If you don't then everything will just get worse—for both of us. They'll hang you, Martin, can't you see that?'

'Nell, I love you.'

'If you won't do this for yourself, Martin, then do it for me.'

Nell didn't know why she did it, but she reached out, took him in her arms and kissed him—a long, heartbreaking kiss. Then she pushed him away from her.

She started crying.

She took her handkerchief from her pocket—a pretty, flower-embroidered linen square that Sylvia had given her—and was about to wipe her eyes, but then she changed her mind.

Nell held out the handkerchief. 'Goodbye, Martin; take this, something to remember me by.

Now go. Do this for me.'

'Nell—'

'They're onto you, Martin. I couldn't bear it if they caught you. Please, do it for both of us.'

CHAPTER 49

Martin spent the next seven hours walking around aimlessly and then drinking in a pub on the Isle of Dogs well away from anyone who knew him, only leaving the warm fug of the pub to make a call from the telephone box on the corner. He waited until it was dark and then made his way back to Turnbury Buildings.

He let himself into the flat with all the care of a cat burglar. He could hear his father's rhythmic snoring coming from the main bedroom, and his mother's soft moans as she dreamed the night away in what had once been the room that had belonged to his older sister before she had married and left home so her new husband could find work. It was the room his mother now chose to sleep in.

It made Martin so sad to see his parents like this, and none of it their fault, but, for now, he was just grateful that they were asleep.

He went into the kitchen and found a string-handled brown paper carrier bag printed with the legend *Sarah and David Meckel purveyors of fine groceries* that his mum had brought home from Sarah's shop, and then went to his bedroom.

He lifted the corner of the mattress and took out the sock that contained the money he had been saving so scrupulously. It was intended for his parents, something to give them when he eventually left home to set up in a place of his own and when he would no longer be in a position to help them quite so much. But it wasn't going to be as straightforward as that—not now.

He counted the money out into three piles—one for his parents, one for him, and one for Nell.

Then he took half of his own pile and added half of that to Nell's and half to his parents'. He took some clothes from his chest of drawers and stuffed them into the carrier bag.

Next he put his share of the money in the inside pocket of his jacket, and his parents' share on the kitchen table wrapped in a note that he had written on one of the scraps of paper that his mother kept in the kitchen drawer—as she always said, 'just in case'. The note read:

> *Dear Mum and Dad,*
> *Please don't worry about me. Things have started to get too much for me and I don't want me and Dad to fall out. I've tried to be a good son and I'm sorry if I've let you down. I'll write again as soon as I can, and will send money if possible.*
> *Your loving son*
> *Martin*

He then folded Nell's money inside another piece of the scrap paper, making it into a little packet that almost resembled an envelope, and wrote on the front:

> *To Nell. Private. From a well-wisher.*

He slipped out of the flat and onto the landing, and stood there for a long moment before finally putting the packet through Nell's letter box, praying that she would be up before Stephen Flanagan's twins.

Stephen Flanagan.

If the man hadn't been dead, Martin would have happily killed him all over again—and got rid of George for good measure. He could honestly say that he didn't have any regrets other than having to leave Nell and his family behind.

With thoughts of Nell smiling shyly, of her sitting on the steps laughing with his mother, and of her beautiful, even though battered face as she had kissed him, Martin Lovell disappeared down the stairway and into his unknown future.

CHAPTER 50

Nell had again been awake most of the night, occasionally drifting off into terrifying, fitful nightmares—visions of George and Stephen looming over her and of Martin being dragged away from her as she screamed out his name.

Martin.

She looked at her children curled up fast asleep in the double bed that took up most of the front room—the bed that she now shared with them. Tomorrow they would be back to school and she would be at work. She was grateful that her shift didn't start until after their day began, but she had to organise something for after school. She didn't want them hanging around with no one keeping an eye on them. Still, she had all day to think about that. For now she had the twins to worry about, and that was more than enough.

Nell stepped out into the passage. She looked towards the closed bedroom doors—Lily's and what had once been her and Stephen's room, but which had now been taken over by George—trying to decide which of them to wake first. Whichever one she chose, she couldn't dither around for too long, it was already half past six and they had to get to Petticoat Lane to set up for the Sunday market. She knew they intended to go because when they'd eventually come home last night she'd heard them arguing and shouting drunkenly about missing a whole day's takings when they hadn't got up for the market after the wake.

She was just glad the children had been asleep, she hated them to hear bad words and rowing—especially Tommy, who would pick up a bad word the very first time he heard it.

Nell leaned against the wall in the passageway. George or Lily? If she woke Lily she'd get a mouthful, demanding to know why she was dragging her out of bed first, but at least George might control himself if his sister was there. She closed her eyes and shuddered at the thought of him doing that to her after the funeral. It must have been because he was so drunk. Mustn't it?

As Nell eased herself away from the wall, visions of George and his disgusting body were momentarily forgotten as her attention was caught by an odd-looking packet on the doormat. She picked it up and looked at the address, dreading that it was a demand for the rest of the money for the funeral. She had a few pounds left over from the money Sylvia had given her, but that wasn't going to last long. The hospital had told her she had to work a week in hand, which as far as she could see meant that she worked the first week for nothing, as she'd been warned that when she left any damage she caused would be docked from that first week's wages. They would be bound to find a reason to do this—that was how things went. For the likes of her, anyway.

She frowned at the packet. It was actually a crudely fashioned envelope and all it said on the front was: *To Nell. Private. From a well-wisher.* There wasn't even a stamp.

She was about to open it, but changed her mind and slipped it into her apron pocket instead, feeling wary about making it into a secret, knowing how she had suffered for keeping secrets in the past. But something told her that it was the right thing to do.

Distracted by the unexpected delivery, Nell rapped on Lily's door without a second thought.

With the hollering still ringing in her ears, she woke George and then hurried into the kitchen to get breakfast ready for the twins.

*　　　*　　　*

'I've got something to tell you,' said Nell, adding more slices of toast to the plate, and then topping up the twins' teacups.

She went over to the sink and started filling the washing-up bowl from the kettle. 'I've got a job. I'm starting tomorrow.'

Lily, her mouth stuffed full of food, spluttered all over the table. 'You've got a job all right, you're

270

going to do the early mornings down the market. And we're going to take turns doing the afternoons. We've got it all organised.'

Nell stiffened. If they got her on the stalls, she knew they wouldn't pay her. So how would she get the rest of the money for the funeral? If she stayed in debt to the Prices they might call the police. Say they sent her to jail? Who would care for the children?

'You're not listening,' she said urgently, turning to face them. 'I've already got a job. I was telling you because I was hoping you wouldn't mind keeping an eye on Tommy and Dolly when they get in from school. They won't be any trouble. Just about an hour it'll be. I'll hurry home as fast as I can, and I'll get the tea ready before I leave in the morning. You won't be put out, I promise.'

'Don't be stupid,' said George, flicking toast crumbs from his big barrel chest. 'Even if we let you get a job—which might not be such a bad idea,' he said, looking pointedly at his sister. 'Because then she could start paying her way around here for her and them two bastards of hers.' He turned back to Nell. 'But why would you think that we'd keep an eye on them?'

Nell was starting to panic. She wasn't happy about her children being alone with the twins—of course she wasn't—but at least it would be a temporary solution until she came up with something better. They'd be playing down in the courtyard anyway, well away from Lily and George. She just wanted to be sure that they could get in and out of the flat if they needed to, and that there would be someone in there if there was a problem. She hadn't expected—or wanted—the twins to actually mind the children, just to be there in the flat. In fact, if she had any other choice . . .

'Because they're your half-brother and sister,' she said quietly, not really believing she could ever have any influence on them.

'They are, are they?' said Lily, raising her eyebrows at George. 'Some people might not agree.'

'What are you talking about?'

George picked up another slice of toast. 'Don't play the innocent with us. We know all about you and him across the landing.'

Nell set the kettle back on the stove.'It was you, wasn't it? You spoke to the police?'

'Now *we* don't know what *you're* talking about,' chuckled George.

'They came here yesterday and asked me all sorts of questions.'

'Did they?' said Lily. 'Well they must have their doubts about you then, mustn't they? Wonder why that is? Any idea, George?'

'No Lil, none at all. But it must be serious.'

Nell ran out of the kitchen and locked herself away in the front room with her sleeping children until she heard the twins leave the flat.

Even then she waited for the count of a hundred before she dared to leave the room. She made a dash for the front door and clicked the latch shut, and then she went into her and Stephen's old bedroom. She retrieved her brooch from its hiding place in the bedside cabinet, dropped it into her apron pocket with the mysterious envelope and then hurriedly made the bed, took her things out of the wardrobe and put George's clothes away in it as quickly as possible. The less time she had to spend in that room the better, but she had to clear it up as George had apparently decided it was his now—regardless of him having a perfectly good room of his own.

With the rest of her chores finished, the twins out, the children still sleeping and the front door firmly locked, Nell sat at the kitchen table and opened the packet.

She blinked as if someone had suddenly turned on a bright light. Seven pounds and ten shillings. She counted it out onto the table and then counted it again under her breath. That was what she'd earn from working five whole weeks at the hospital laundry. Where had it come from? She looked at the envelope again. *From a well-wisher.* That would make a real dent in the money she owed Mr Price. But it didn't seem right to spend it if she didn't know who had given it to her.

It might have come from Sylvia, but it wasn't her writing; and she wouldn't have done it like that anyway, and she'd already lent her that money yesterday. Nell gnawed on her thumbnail. Apart from the funeral money, that was another five pounds she owed already. How could she spend this as well? Her debts were getting out of hand.

The only other person she could think of with any money who would be that kind to her was Martin, but no, it couldn't be him.

She'd done everything she could not to let him back into her head, but there he was again: Martin, the man she had kissed so passionately, the man who had killed Stephen Flanagan. There was so much going on in her head, she honestly didn't know how much more she could stand.

Nell went into Stephen's bedroom and looked at

the clock. Half past eight. Was it OK to go over to see Mary this early? What would she say if Martin was there?

Worse, what would she say if Martin *wasn't* there?

*   *   *

'Sorry to bother you so early on a Sunday, Mary.' Nell was standing on the landing, hardly able to raise her head to meet her neighbour's gaze. 'But I'm going to ask you a really big favour.'

'That's all right, love. I was up anyway.' Mary stepped back and jerked her head towards the passageway. 'I've just put the kettle on; fancy a cup?'

'I don't want to be a nuisance.'

'You're not a nuisance, and I could do with some company. I'm feeling a bit off this morning.'

*   *   *

'Don't worry about the kids, Nell.' Mary poured two cups of tea. 'Me or Joe'll be here to see they're all right till you get in. We both understand what it's like to have to earn a few bob. And it might stop Joe feeling so sorry for himself if he's got something to think about.'

'It's going to be hard, but I'm going to try my best to save some money so I can get somewhere for me and the kids to live. Somewhere of our own. I'll do anything to keep us together, but I don't know how much longer I can stay in that flat with the twins. They say they want me to work on the stalls, but I know they won't pay me. And then I'll never get away. I'll be stuck here with them for ever.'

About to hand Nell her tea, Mary suddenly burst into tears and the cup fell from her hand, smashing on the lino-covered floor.

'Don't mind me, Nell,' she gulped. 'It's just that our Martin, he's gone.'

'Gone?' Nell whispered. She didn't know what to do for the best—should she clear up the broken cup or comfort Mary?

Mary made up her mind for her. She walked over to the dresser and took something out of the drawer.

Nell bent down and began collecting the broken bits of china in her apron.

Mary came over and stood beside her, and held out a folded paper packet. Nell jerked away from her, dropping the pieces of cup back on the floor— how had Mary got hold of it?

'What's that?'

'It's from our Martin. He left us a letter and some money and now he's disappeared. Fed up arguing with his dad over things, he said. Didn't want to fall out with him. We've all been at one another lately. It's the worry. And now he just took off.'

Mary started sobbing. 'Seven pound ten. Seven pound bloody rotten ten. Is that all his living here with us was worth? I'd give anything, Nell, anything, to have him back here with us. Bugger the money. Bugger everything. I just want my boy back home.'

Nell started clearing up the broken china again.

Martin. The man who had said he loved her, who had freed her from Stephen Flanagan—she

275

knew in her heart that he must have been telling the truth about it being an accident, he was too kind to hurt anyone deliberately. He had said he would take her away from the twins, and now she would never see him again, the man she now had to admit to herself that she loved.

CHAPTER 51

Mary stood behind the counter, hollow-eyed and with her shoulders drooping.

Ada sat on the customer's chair with Myrtle beside her like a skinny guard dog. 'She can look like she's just lost thruppence and found a ha'penny, but if I was her I wouldn't even be showing my face. It's all very well her worrying about that boy of hers going amongst the missing, but she'd have been better off worrying about him while he was still here. Hanging around that Nell—and her a widow and a mother of two. What a disgrace.'

'Widow?' said Myrtle. 'I always thought you had to be married to be a widow.'

Mary stepped from behind the counter, pushing away Sarah Meckel's hand as she tried to restrain her. 'And you have to have a clear conscience before you start pointing your finger at other people.'

Ada rose to her feet and Mary looked her up and down. 'If you don't mind, Sarah, I'll just take a little break.'

'Course I don't, Mary.'

Mary moved closer to Ada, pinning her to the

counter. She stuck a finger in the woman's would-be defiant, yet clearly nervous face. 'If I hear you've said a single word about my son, my family, or anyone else for that matter, you had better watch yourself Ada Tanner, because you'll have me to reckon with. I am in no mood to put up with you or with your spiteful sewer of a mouth.'

As she stepped out onto the pavement, Mary heard Ada's unmistakable whine. 'Yeah, I'd better watch myself or I'll end up in the flaming river.'

Ada should have kept quiet, or she should at least have spoken more softly, because before anyone realised what was going on Mary had burst back into the shop. She ripped Ada's hat from her head, and stamped up and down on it.

'Perhaps if you get some air to that thick brain of yours it'll start working a bit better,' she yelled into Ada's ear.

Ada reeled backwards into the row of glass-lidded biscuit tins that lined the front of the counter. 'And me with my health,' she wailed.

'Health? What are you talking about? All that's wrong with you is the poison in your tongue and the bloody lard on your arse. If you did a hand's turn once in a while, instead of having your kids running round after you like you're some sort of invalid, maybe you wouldn't look so much like a bloody beer barrel.'

Ada patted her hatless hair defensively. 'I didn't come here to be talked to like that.'

'Aw, didn't you? That's a shame. So where d'you usually go? Because people must be queuing up and it wouldn't be right to disappoint them.'

'You've got a gob on you, Mary Lovell. No better than Florrie Talbot.'

'Right, that's it. All over.' Sarah stepped between them. 'I am not having this in my shop.' Despite not wanting to spoil the entertaining spectacle of Ada Tanner getting what she deserved, Sarah would not allow Ada to run down Florrie Talbot. Florrie might do some things that most people would shudder at the thought of, but she was a kind woman who had had tragedy in her life beyond those same people's imagination.

Sarah put a hand on each of Mary's shoulders and looked steadily into her eyes. 'Why don't we all calm down?' she said. 'None of us is living what you'd exactly call a normal life at the minute, but we mustn't let it get to us, Mary. There are enough problems brewing up in the world for us to worry about without fighting amongst ourselves.'

'I'm sorry, Sarah.' Mary dropped down onto the customer's chair. 'It's just that I'm so worried about my Martin, I'm beside myself.'

'I know darling, I know.'

Ada was still standing there, lingering like a bad smell.

Sarah looked at her and jerked her thumb towards the door. 'Think it's time you were leaving, Ada. I'll get one of the children to drop your groceries round for you later on.'

With a loud sniff, Ada Tanner, followed by Myrtle, her scrawny shadow, left the shop.

'Might as well get back to the Buildings,' Ada couldn't resist tossing back at them. 'See if there's any more coppers about wanting to ask me questions about that Nell and her shenanigans. I like to do me bit. See, some of us in that place are good law-abiding people.'

When Nell had jumped at the chance of doing the ironing job at the hospital she had had no idea what she was taking on. She found herself in a high, windowless room that could easily have swallowed up two of the flats in Turnbury Buildings and still have left space for a couple of spare bedrooms. There was a continuous waist-height shelf running around three of the walls. Under that shelf were huge wicker hampers on wheels that were full of folded but unironed linen. The wall with the door in it had a run of wooden shelves from ceiling to floor, on which ironed items were stacked according to the labels glued to the wood.

The irons themselves were modern—electric, and connected to sockets in the ceiling by long, flexible leads—but the temperature controls weren't that reliable and Nell had to be careful that she didn't scorch anything. The trouble was she hadn't realised it would be piecework—her pay was dependent on the number of hampers she emptied, with money being docked for burns. She'd really thought that the one pound ten shillings was the guaranteed weekly wage, but now she realised it was nothing more than an estimate, and an apparently unrealistic one at that.

How would she ever earn enough on these wages to get her and the children somewhere to live away from the twins? Her life was slipping more out of control than ever. The memory of the stench of George's sour breath had her closing her eyes and the taste of bile rising in her throat. What if he did it again? What if that was the price she had to pay to keep a roof over their heads?

And then there were the debts.

She looked about her. Five other women were all working as hard as they could to earn what must surely be an unattainable wage for all of them— even the most experienced.

Even though Nell had learned in the home that there was no point feeling sorry for yourself, she still couldn't help thinking that sometimes life just wasn't fair. Not to her, but to her beloved little ones. They deserved more. Much more than she was able to give them.

She could only hope and pray that what George had done to her the other night didn't mean that she would be bringing another innocent child into the horrible world in which she found herself.

CHAPTER 52

'You were lucky, son,' said the stocky, gruff-looking Scot, as he stripped down to his string vest and greying underpants and climbed into the bunk below Martin's. 'One of the stokers jumped ship a few days ago when we docked here. Young Chinese lad, he was. Quiet type. Never really settled into ship's life. I'd say he's probably got pals or family down Limehouse way. There's a lot of them Chinese fellers down there. And he'll be better off with his own kind, didn't have much English see, so it was hard for the lad, he didn't know what was going on half the time. And if it wasn't for him doing a midnight flit, then there'd be nothing here for you. But you, you'll do well, you look a strong sort of a laddie, so you should fit right in here. It's not easy work, but the pay's fair. And you don't have to go worrying yourself over what to do, I'll show you which way the wind blows, explain it all to you fair and square.'

'Thanks.'

'You don't have much to say for yourself, laddie, now do you? But then I'd guess you've probably got a tale to tell, like most of us on this ship. A man's usually either running away from something or someone. Me, I've got three wives—four, I suppose, if you include the first one back home in Glasgow. But I've not seen that wee hellcat for years. She had a temper on her that one, and after a dram or two she was wild. Fight a man twice her size without a second thought, would my Maggie.'

He chuckled happily to himself, remembering. 'Then there are my—what shall we say—about a dozen or so kids dotted around this mad but beautiful world of ours. Who knows, I might try to track them all down one day. When I retire, maybe. But looking at you,' the Scotsman thumped the underside of Martin's mattress with the side of his fist, 'I'd say you're too young to have as complicated a reason as that.'

'I just want to travel.'

'You'll be doing that sure enough, young man. In a few hours' time we'll be leaving port and heading for the Bay of Biscay. That's travel all right. I'll wager you'll never have seen seas like those before.'

The man in the bunk below carried on talking about storms he had survived and sights he had seen, but Martin wasn't listening. His thoughts were back in Turnbury Buildings.

281

He opened his fist and looked at the crumpled square of embroidered linen that Nell had given him. He held it to his cheek.

At least he'd saved her from Stephen Flanagan. She was rid of him for good and she had her job. Her life could only get better from now on. But he would miss her so very much, her and her lovely face, and her clear grey eyes. If only he could kiss her just one more time.

He stared up at the ceiling.

He'd miss his mother too, and his dad. He just wished that Joe could see how wrong he was about the Blackshirts and their filthy ideas. Maybe then he'd stop feeling so bitter. It was eating away at him, and making both his parents so miserable.

Martin ran the back of his hand across his eyes. And now they didn't even have his money coming in.

What had he done?

CHAPTER 53

Sylvia stood in the street at the back of the hospital, waiting for Nell to come out after her first day at work. She watched as the great pans of dripping were wheeled out of the kitchens, and the women and children clutching their bowls jostled to get to the front of the queue ready to scoop out the fat that would provide their families with some sort of meal when it was scraped over toast. She knew Nell often made dripping on toast for breakfast, but at least she bought hers from the butcher. But even then it wasn't a meal Sylvia fancied very much, although she knew that had she not fetched up with Bernie Woods it might well have been her standing there amongst the hungry throng.

'Nell. Nelly. Over here, darling. It's me, over here.'

Nell, her fair curls sticking to her face with sweat, put the side of her hand to her forehead and screwed up her eyes against the early evening sun, trying to make out who it was who would be calling to her as she came through the big double doors.

Sylvia, of course. 'Sylv.'

'Yes, sweetheart, it's me. How did it go?'

'It was a bit disappointing.'

'No. Tell me. What went wrong?'

Nell told her about the temperature controls and the piecework.

'Aw. That's rotten, Nell. Still, it must be nice for you and the kids having the flat to yourself now the twins have gone. I'll be able to come round like I used to.'

'What?'

'Now the twins have gone.'

'They've not gone anywhere.'

Nell looked up at the clock on the church that stood in the shadows at the back of the hospital. 'I'm sorry, Sylvia, I've got to go. Mary and Joe Lovell are keeping an eye on Tommy and Dolly for me and I don't want to take advantage of them.' She paused for a moment. 'They've got enough problems of their own at the minute.'

'Yeah, OK, Nell.' Sylvia kissed her on the cheek. 'I've got to go as well, darling. There's someone I need to speak to.'

Sylvia came slamming through the doors of the Hope and Anchor—a woman with a mission. 'Bernie, I want a word.'

Bernie saw her face. Bloody hell, not again. 'Yes, Sylv?'

'I'm going to ask you one more time, because, I mean it, if you won't do this for me, then things'll never be the same between us again.'

*   *   *

George and Lily turned up at the Hope puzzled, but confident that whatever reason there had been for Bernie Woods to have sent that kid round on his bike with a note telling them that he wanted to see them right away, there had to be at least a few free sherbets involved somewhere along the line.

And they were right. The moment they sat down at the bar, Sylvia gave George a pint of mild and bitter and Lily a large port and lemon.

'If you'd like to sit yourself over in the corner, I'll nip up and get Bernie.'

George and Lily nodded expectantly at each other and settled themselves at Bernie's table.

'Perhaps it's something to do with money that Bernie owed to Dad,' said Lily.

George grinned, a foamy beer moustache lining his top lip. 'That'd be handy.'

'The different strokes he pulls, he must be worth a bloody mint. Let's hope he's feeling generous.'

*   *   *

'What do you mean, we've got to leave our flat?'

'Don't start leading off, George, I've got somewhere for you to go to. Nice and convenient it is. Much better for you than being stuck over in Wapping. A fair rent and hardly any journey to work in the mornings.'

Lily leaned across the table and pointed at Bernie. 'Is this something to do with that cow and her pair of snivelling bastards? Because if it is, she is going to be bloody sorry. Believe me. She won't know what's sodding hit her.'

Bernie didn't enjoy being treated like that by anyone, especially a woman. 'You've got no choice.'

'Who says?' demanded George, sounding but not feeling very brave. Bernie was involved with some very tough men—Jack Spot not the least of them.

'I say so.' Bernie stood up. 'But I'm not going to fall out with you over this. I'll send you over another drink and the address of where you're going. No need to rush moving out, tomorrow after you've finished work'll do.'

'No, we're not having this,' said Lily. 'Are we, George?'

'Aw yes you are,' said Bernie.

'Bernie, I think I need to have a little word with my sister.'

CHAPTER 54

Nell, tired out from her work in the laundry, had been sound asleep when the twins had come home from the pub, but she had woken up when she heard them shouting. Rather than getting involved in whatever their latest spat was about, she had stayed in bed. It would all be over soon enough—it always was.

But this time it wasn't.

The next evening Nell stood in the kitchen not knowing what was happening. She'd just come home from her second day of work at the hospital and was planning to put the supper on before calling the children up from playing to get washed, but then she'd been confronted by Lily and George, who were both acting as if she'd done something really bad. But what? What was she supposed to have done? They hadn't even spoken to her when she'd cooked their breakfast for them this morning, so it couldn't have been something she'd said.

'I hope you're satisfied,' spat Lily, rifling through the dresser and the kitchen cupboards, and piling everything she could find into any bags available.

'First Dad, now us,' said George. 'I can only hope you're pleased with yourself, now you've got what you wanted all along.' He was sitting at the table, swigging straight from the whisky bottle that hadn't been touched since his father's death. There was a cheap cardboard suitcase by his side that Stephen had used to store what he referred to as 'his papers', but which now held the whole of George's not very extensive wardrobe. The papers, after a quick look from George to see if there was anything of any value—there wasn't, just a few receipts for furniture and linen from when Stephen had married the twins' mother—were now

286

scattered over the table. 'I just hope you can live with your conscience.'

'What am I supposed to have done?'

Her pillaging of the cupboards at an end, Lily turned and hissed maliciously at Nell, bubbles of spit forming in the corners of her mouth. 'Schtupping Bernie Woods as well, are you? Because that's the only thing I can think of that's made that man behave like this. I can only wonder what his old woman will have to say about it, when I tell her. Which I fully intend to, believe me.'

'Tell her about what?'

'As if you didn't know.' George stood up and barged past a totally bewildered Nell, with Lily close behind him. 'You fucking gold-digger. You're meant to be that woman's friend. Well, people are beginning to find you out for what you really are, so I'd be careful if I was you, because you're making more and more enemies every day.'

With that, George threw two sets of keys onto the kitchen floor and he and his sister departed, leaving the front door wide open behind them.

Nell picked up the keys and put them on the table. What was all that about? And what were they going to tell Sylvia about her and Bernie? It didn't sound good whatever it was, or they wouldn't be threatening her with it. The only thing she could think to do was to go and see Sylvia before they did, but the thought of going all the way back to where she'd just come from was almost more than she could bear. She didn't know why she was so tired; she'd worked harder than this in her time, much harder. But who knew what the twins were capable of? She had to get this cleared up before they made things even worse. And she had to go out anyway, to pick up a few bits for the children's tea. For reasons she couldn't understand, Lily and George had cleared everything out of the flat, including all the food. Goodness only knew where they were taking it.

After a quick word with Joe Lovell about the children, Nell started making her weary way back to Whitechapel, paying out money for a bus fare that she could well have done with keeping in her purse.

*   *   *

Nell fought to keep her eyes open as the bus rocked rhythmically through the London streets. Mary Lovell, meanwhile, was still at work with Sarah Meckel, listening with increasing anger as Ada Tanner held forth. The woman had made the trip back to the shop especially for the purpose.

'You wouldn't recognise our landing,' Ada said to no one in particular. 'Stephen Flanagan's dead and buried. Martin Lovell's scarpered.' She flashed a sly look at Mary, who was again being held back by Sarah. 'And just now I saw the twins moving out of their own home. Fancy that, being driven from their own flat. That'll be that Nell's doing. Disgraceful. Mind you, they're doing well for themselves. I heard that they've got a set of rooms over near the market. But it still doesn't seem right does it, being driven away? You could tell they weren't very happy about it.'

'How do you know?' asked a woman from the Buildings, who was a passing acquaintance of Nell's from the basement laundry. She liked Nell, but, like a lot of the other neighbours, had been too scared of Stephen Flanagan to befriend her in any more than the most casual of ways. It made her feel bad, when she heard what the girl had been through.

'Bernie Woods, him from the Hope and Anchor over in Whitechapel, he got them a place.'

'Blimey, Ada,' said the woman, 'if we ever have another war, we'll have to have you as our secret bloody weapon. I don't know how you do it. You're like a flipping spy.'

Taking that as a compliment, Ada continued. 'Still, it wouldn't matter how nice the place was, it wouldn't suit me, working and living over there with all them Jews.'

As if on cue, Florrie Talbot appeared in the doorway at the back of the shop. 'Wouldn't it, Ada? That's a shame. Because they're my favourite people, Jews.' Florrie landed a smacker of a kiss on Sarah's cheek.

'Busy evening planned, have you?' sniggered Ada.

'Why don't you ask your old man?' suggested Florrie with a wink and a smile before disappearing out onto the street. Then she stuck her head back in the shop. 'Oops, shouldn't let on about who my customers are, now should I?'

'Tomcat,' growled Ada, and then without waiting to catch a breath she carried on. 'And you do know that all the kids are back at school now, don't you? And that that little madam across the way, that Nell—Flanagan's trollop—she's only gone and got herself a flipping job. Woman with little kids going out to work, I ask you. What's the world coming to? Anything to get out of looking after her home, that'll be the reason, because between you and me, I'll bet that that Stephen Flanagan left her a fortune.' She hauled her shopping bag up her arm. 'Wouldn't suit me, taking blood money.'

Sarah shook her head at Mary. 'Don't waste your time on her, Mary. I don't think even she knows what she's talking about half the time.'

'She knows all right,' said Mary. 'She knows exactly what she's up to.'

CHAPTER 55

Nell hefted another pile of ironed sheets onto the shelf. It was like being back in the home, but with a hundred times the amount of laundry to deal with. Then there was the noise—there was no keeping your voice to a whisper, as there had been when Matron Sully had been in charge. Her head was aching, and even though she'd only been working at the hospital for a couple of weeks it felt more like a lifetime. And she was so tired.

She should have been feeling better than this. For a start, when she'd gone to see Sylvia after Lily and George had moved out so suddenly, Sylvia had assured her that there was nothing to worry about, whatever the twins were saying was just a load of nonsense, they were being stirrers as usual. Then Nell had managed to pay off a little bit more of the funeral debt; the children loved going to school; Mary and Joe were keeping an eye on them until she got home, and the twins were becoming a distant—if still obnoxious—memory. It seemed as if even the police had given up pestering her; they either had something else to worry about, or since Martin had disappeared they didn't see any point in looking for anyone else to blame. She didn't like it, but it was the realistic explanation.

A loud bell sounded. Shift over. Nell closed her eyes. Thank goodness for that.

*　　　*　　　*

Nell knocked on Mary's door. 'I've come to collect the little ones.'

Mary stepped out onto the landing and pulled the door shut behind her. 'Nell, I'm ever so sorry love, but I've got to be straight with you, this is not working out the way I thought it would. I hate to say it but Joe's enough of a handful for me at the minute, especially since Martin went, and the atmosphere in here, it's not nice for the kids.'

Ada appeared in her doorway, and leaned against the jamb with her arms folded across her bosom.

Mary lowered her voice. 'And to be honest, Nell, even though Sarah's good enough to keep me on, without Martin's money I'm finding it really hard to make ends meet. Tommy and Dolly, well, you know what it's like, they're growing kids, so they're always hungry. Especially with the evenings drawing in so they're up here indoors more.'

Mary's voice wasn't quiet enough to foil Ada.

'I know if I was so kind as to be looking after someone's little kiddies, I'd expect to be paid for my trouble,' Ada offered from across the landing.

Nell felt herself flush bright red. 'I'm so sorry, Mary, I never thought. How much do you think would be fair, just tell me and—'

'How are you going pay anyone?' Ada piped up. 'From what I heard, all that talk about her having money was a load of old fanny.'

Ada didn't bother to mention that it was she who had started the rumour in the first place. 'No, she hasn't got a pot to piss in.' She grinned nastily at Mary. 'She's still paying off Stephen Flanagan's funeral. Did you know that? Silly daft mare thought the deposit was the whole cost of the thing. How stupid's that, eh? So pay you? No chance. Can't even afford to feed herself by the look of how pale and skinny she is.'

Mary's reaction wasn't what Ada had hoped.

'Aw, Nell, I had no idea.' Mary pushed open her door, put her arm around Nell and guided her into her flat. 'Come inside with me, love, and we'll have a cup of tea and put our heads together to see what we can do about it, shall we?'

*　　　*　　　*

Mary topped up Nell's cup for the third time, recklessly adding spoonfuls of precious sugar. She'd been so tied up with her own troubles she hadn't even noticed how ill the girl was looking.

'Right, that's what I'll do, I'll ask Sarah if she can give me a few more hours, and instead of the children coming back here on the days I'm working, I'll ask her if they can stay in the shop with us. They'll like that. And we can give them a few little jobs to do. Everything'll be fine, Nell, we'll find a way round this, love.'

'But say Sarah doesn't agree?'

'Then we'll have to think again, won't we? Cheer up and stop worrying yourself, we'll sort it

292

all out.'

*   *   *

'Told you not to worry, Nell.' Mary was leaning on the top banister, catching her breath after climbing the stairs to the top floor of Turnbury Buildings at twice her usual speed. 'I just nipped back round to Sarah's and she said it would be no trouble at all having the children there. In fact she said she's really looking forward to seeing them; said that their laughing little faces will cheer the place up.'

Mary was now grinning broadly. 'And you'll never guess what, Nell, because the shop's been getting busier, what with the workmen off those new blocks they're putting up, she only offered me extra hours. Before I even mentioned it. And you know how I do Saturdays for her—until she takes over after sunset? Well, she said she could do with staying open on Friday evenings too, now that there are going to be more customers coming in, but she goes upstairs for her special meal and prayers and that with David then. So she said I can do those hours for her as well. It's like a dream come true. Seems as if things are looking up all round, eh Nell? Who knows, Joe might even get himself some labouring work on the new buildings.'

Nell couldn't have been more grateful to Mary, but she didn't have time to thank her before someone prodded her in the back.

It was Ada.

'You know what they say?' she said. 'Don't ever go thinking that things can only get better, just because you reckon they can't get any worse.

293

Because you'd be wrong—they can always get worse and they usually do.'

'Why don't you keep your nose out of other people's business, Ada?' said Mary.

Ada let out a dismissive puff of air. 'Trouble with some people is they can't face the truth.'

Mary shook her head sadly. 'I'd rather face the truth any day than have to face myself in the mirror if I looked as sour and wicked as you, Ada.'

CHAPTER 56

It was a bright but chilly Saturday morning in December. Nell was sitting on the edge of the double bed in the front room where she and the children still slept. The twins had been gone from the flat for over three months, but she could still feel their presence and she liked the fact that the front room had its own lock. Even though the twins had left the two sets of flat keys behind—she remembered George throwing them on the floor as they went, for her to pick up as if she were their inferior—she wouldn't have been surprised if they had kept another set so that they could snoop around the place while she was out at work. They were probably the only people she could think of who were crafty enough to avoid being spotted by Ada Tanner. After the terrible thing that George had done to her after the funeral, she knew she would never feel truly safe in Number 55, despite the front room having that lock. But getting somewhere else to live would remain a dream that was unlikely ever to come true. She was just glad that the rent man's only stipulation was that he was paid each week in cash, in her case with the money she left for him with Joe. He was not concerned with who actually lived there.

At least Tommy and Dolly seemed a little more settled since the twins had moved out. They were downstairs, muffled up in the scarves and gloves that Sylvia had bought for them, playing in the courtyard with the other children, while Nell was supposedly doing the weekly clean that she gave the flat now that she was working Monday to Friday. Unfortunately, so far she hadn't even made the bed, she felt so weary. And then the letter had come by the first post.

She stared at the envelope again, comparing the writing to that on the roughly fashioned packet she had found on the doormat all those months ago, the packet with the seven pounds and ten shillings that she had still not spent. There was no denying it, the writing was the same, which could only mean one thing—it had to be from Martin.

Slowly, Nell rose to her feet and went into the kitchen. She took a knife from the dresser drawer and sat at the table, torn between wanting to know how and where Martin was, and trying desperately not to care about him. The trouble was she did care—she cared so very much.

With her hands trembling, Nell eased the point of the knife under the flap of the envelope and slit it open.

'*Mum.*' Tommy came racing into the kitchen.

Nell flushed scarlet and stuffed the envelope and the packet with the money under the breadboard.

'Whatever's wrong?'

'Mum, can I have a dog for Christmas? That kid who wets himself, he's just got a dog and he says the kids don't laugh at him any more.'

Nell frowned. 'Has someone been laughing at you?'

'Only a few of the kids at school.' Tommy pulled a face, wrinkling his nose, trying to look as if he couldn't care less. 'And some of them from downstairs.'

'What are they laughing at?'

Tommy suddenly took an interest in his shoes and started twiddling his hair. 'They said cos we haven't got a dad it means we've got no money, and so we've all got cooties. And they made Dolly cry the other day, but I said I'd bash them if they said anything more to her and they left her alone. But they might start again, Mum,' he added, remembering he was meant to be putting his case forward for getting a dog. 'Some of them are so horrible.'

'Tom, where's Dolly now?'

'She's down with some of the big girls. They're showing her how to play two balls. She's not very good at it, but she's all right playing with them. I wouldn't have left her if she was alone or with the ones who laughed at her.'

'I know you wouldn't, Tommy. You're a good boy.'

'And if we had a dog I'd be *really* good. I know it's only a couple of weeks until Christmas, but I could ask Sarah if I can do some more jobs for her and save up for a lead.' A smile of pleasure spread over Tommy's face as his attention wandered away from dogs' leads. 'You know what, Mum, Sarah's got ever such good stuff in the shop for Christmas.

She's got trees and little chocolate umbrellas that you have to hang on the branches and these shiny metal peg things for clipping candles on the trees. They're ever so nice. And Sarah was telling me all about Hanukkah. It's smashing. It's like Christmas, but you get loads of presents if you're a Jewish kid. Could we be Jewish, Mum?'

'We could, but if you were a little Jewish boy you wouldn't be able to go to Sunday school, would you? And then you wouldn't be able to be in the nativity play. And I thought you and Dolly were all excited about that.'

Tommy shrugged. 'I suppose.'

'And you sing your song ever so well, they'd proper miss you if you weren't in it.'

Nell put out her arms and, grown-up as he considered himself to be, Tommy climbed up onto her lap.

She kissed the top of his head, breathing in the sweet smell of soap from where she had washed it for him the night before. Her little boy and girl were being laughed at. She couldn't bear the thought of it. She hated so much what had happened to them and what they had put up with over the years. They hadn't asked for any of this. She hugged Tommy close and thought of the letter in the envelope, and the seven pounds ten shillings still in the paper packet, on the table right there in front of her under the breadboard. She would have loved to have bought Tommy a dog, but she knew she couldn't afford to keep it. Even if she pawned her brooch—how long would the money last? And she really didn't want to lose her brooch. Ever since she had had the children she had always told herself that she would never get rid of it. She wanted so badly to leave the keepsake for them to remember her by, just as that wonderful, loving lady had left it to her.

Tommy laid his head against her shoulder, making her feel full of love, but so helpless. She could hardly feed herself after she'd fed the children, paid the rent, had put a bit by to pay off the debts, and then there were the few things she bought now and again to give to Mary. Kind woman that she was, Mary always refused them at first. But despite the extra hours and the generosity Sarah showed to her, the Lovells were only scraping along. Joe still hadn't found anything, having received another humiliating knock-back when he'd made enquiries about labouring work on the new buildings they were putting up to replace more of the old terraces that they were knocking down. Mary couldn't manage without Nell's help, little as it might be, and both Mary and Nell knew it.

Nell cuddled Tommy even closer to her. It was all such a struggle. And the weariness was almost overwhelming her.

Despite her previous resolve, Nell knew she had to be practical—she would use some of the money that Martin had left for her, and she would make sure that the children had a proper, memorable Christmas this year. After all, with the way things were going, it might be the last opportunity she had to do that for them for a very long while. She certainly had no idea what was going to happen to them this time next year. Not after what George had done to her.

She closed her eyes, banishing the vile thoughts from her mind.

In the meantime, she would just have to work even harder at the hospital so she could put some money back in the packet each week until she had replaced every penny she had spent, ready to give to Martin when he came back—if he ever did.

She kissed her son again. 'Listen to me, Tommy. I can't get you a dog. I'm sorry, it's just not possible. I haven't got the money.'

'Mum.' Tommy dragged out the word for three full, whining syllables.

'Don't get upset, because we are going to have the best time this Christmas that we've ever had, you just wait and see.'

'Are we?'

'I promise you we are.'

'Honest?'

'Honest. I've got it all planned. It's going to be a day you'll always remember.'

'Are you pretending?'

'No. I told you: I promise. Now I've got lots to do, so will you go downstairs for me and make sure Dolly's all right?'

Tommy shrugged. 'Suppose.'

'You know I always keep my promises.'

He smiled, thinking about what such promises might mean in terms of toys and sweets and who knew what other undreamed-of delights.

Knowing she had made the right decision about the money, Nell ushered her little boy out of the kitchen and watched him as he skipped along the passageway to the front door. He started warbling the same reedy rendition of 'We Three Kings' that she had heard countless times over the past two weeks as she had helped him learn the words. He was happy. What more could she ask?

She knew exactly what—finding out what Martin had to say, finding out if he still felt the same way about her.

When she could no longer hear Tommy's singing, she shut herself in the front room, sat on the bed and read the letter.

CHAPTER 57

After reading it for a fourth time, Nell put the letter back in the envelope and tucked it away in her safe place—a handbag that Sylvia had given her—along with the packet holding the money, and her treasured brooch. She knelt on the floor and put the bag under the bed, pushing it close to the wall. She hauled herself up to her feet, hesitated for a few moments and then walked out of the flat and onto the landing.

There she stood, staring at the door of number 57, fist in the air, composing herself before she knocked. She knew she had to do this, she owed Mary so much—she wouldn't even have been able to keep her job without her—but it wasn't going to be easy.

*　　　*　　　*

'Oh, Nell, I wish my Joe was here. He's going to be so excited, so relieved to know that our Martin's all right. He only went for his morning paper, and that must have been half an hour ago. I bet he's flipping gabbing to someone.'

Mary could hardly contain herself, it had taken

300

her three attempts to fill the kettle and still she hadn't put it on the stove. She stood by the sink, staring unseeingly at the wall.

'There's one thing I don't understand though, Nell. Why was it you he wrote to? Why didn't he write to me and his dad?'

Nell licked her lips slowly and then said, 'I wondered that myself at first, Mary, and then I thought about it and I realised. You know how him and Joe were before Martin went—it was even why Martin said he went—them arguing over their politics and that. He was probably scared about how Joe would take it.'

'Take what?'

Nell found a thin smile. 'He's joined the International Brigade.'

'What the flaming hell's that when it's at home?'

'You know, that lot over in Spain.'

'What lot?'

This was the bit that Nell had been dreading. 'Look Mary, I'm not altogether sure what it's about, but Joe'll know. He'll explain it to you, because it's all to do with politics and that, and Germany.' She couldn't meet Mary's puzzled gaze. 'There's some sort of fighting going on over there. In Spain. And he said that Hitler's involved somehow. But I'm not sure how.'

Mary crashed the kettle down onto the draining board. 'What do you mean, fighting? I think I've just found out that my boy's safe and now you say there's fighting. In Spain? I don't even know where bloody Spain is.' She started pacing around the kitchen. 'I don't know or understand anything any more. What sort of world is this? Boys leaving home and going off to Spain. Fighting. I thought they said we'd had the war to end all wars.' She put her hand to her forehead. 'He could wind up like Sarah's David.'

Nell stood up. 'Mary, sit yourself down and I'll make us some tea.'

Mary didn't sit down. 'I know he used to go on about politics—like you say, rowing with Joe, carrying on alarming the pair of them—and he hated his dad going to them Blackshirt meetings. Can you imagine if he'd been here when all that business happened over in Cable Street? He'd have been right up the front stopping that Mosley. Probably would have got himself arrested, knowing my Martin.'

She dropped down onto a chair and buried her face in her hands. 'At least I'd have known where he was if he was inside. He's gonna get himself killed, Nell, and I'm never going to see him again, am I?'

'Course you are, he said he's going to try and get home, soon as he can. Now let's put this kettle on, shall we?'

'Can I see the letter?'

Nell was glad she had her back to Mary as she spun her the story she had made up. 'I'm sorry, Mary, I tore it up in little bits and put it down the chute with the rubbish. Martin asked me to. He was scared the twins would see it, cos he doesn't know that they moved out, does he? Thinks they're still living in over 55. And he didn't want them knowing what he was up to. We all know what he thought about George, and he thought them two might upset you. I know it seems silly, them not being there, but he was very firm about asking me to do it. It just seemed right. Sorry, I should have

302

shown it to you, but I was so surprised to get it and everything, I just sort of did it.'

Nell lit the gas and then came out with the words she had rehearsed in her head, the bits of Martin's long letter she could share with his mother. The bits that didn't say how much he loved Nell and how he wanted to spend the rest of his life with her—her, the mother of the children of the man he'd killed.

'He said that when he came home everything would be like it used to be and he'd be able to earn good money again. You see, Mary, on that day when he left he was clever, he telephoned the brewery, said that he had to go away on urgent family business, and asked if there was any chance that they'd hold his job open for him.'

'Did he?'

Nell turned round so she was facing her friend. 'They must really think a lot of your son in that place, because they said they'd been so pleased with his work that they were prepared to hold his job open for him for a whole six months, and they hoped his family trouble could be sorted out very soon. You should be so proud of him, Mary, you really should.'

*   *   *

When Joe returned with his paper, Nell went back to 55 and left Mary to tell her husband what Nell could only hope she had made sound like very good news.

CHAPTER 58

Nell shut herself in the front room and reread the whole letter, this time not afraid that Martin's mother would somehow to be able to hear all the words she shouldn't. Words, just little marks made on paper—how could little marks cause such fear, and longing and heartache?

*　　　*　　　*

My Sweetest Nell it began. She ran her index finger along those three words over and over again before skipping to the part with which she had tried so hard to sympathise, but had found so difficult to understand.

> *Nell, how can it be so wrong to get rid of one such very bad person, and then only by mistake, but not wrong to get rid of another? What makes one act a good cause and another a crime? There are so many brave people fighting over here, but is what they are doing, no, what we are doing, any different from what I did back in Wapping? These people decided that something was wrong and that they had to do something about it, and that they could not live with themselves if they allowed it to go on. Does that make them criminal, or, worse, make them evil? I don't think so, and I don't think you would either if you could hear them speak and hear the passion in their voices when they talk about their families and their country. Those are*

304

the things they love most of all. They might not be an official army, but what they are is a group of people doing what they know is right.

She turned to the final page.

I'm not sure when you'll get this letter, Nell. Things are not very reliable over here what with everything that is going on, but I am planning to come back to London. I do not care if I have to risk being caught, I cannot stay away from you. I have to see you again, my darling Nell. I have to be with you for however short a time. You are worth more than my life to me. No, that is not true. You are my life.

Nell touched the paper to her lips, remembering the kiss, wishing he was there with her now. But how could she ever be with Martin again? How would she ever be able to explain to him what had happened? She had no future with Martin or with anyone else.

She put the letter back in the handbag. The suede lining smelt of Sylvia, of her scent, her powder and lipstick. If only she had listened to Sylvia when she had tried to warn her against Stephen. Why hadn't she seen the Flanagans for what they were—cruel, heartless creatures who used people as if they were things. If she had listened to Sylvia then she would probably still have been living at the Hope with her and Bernie, laughing and joking, and as happy as she had been on that first day when Sylvia had taken her in, and had fed her and dried her off by the fire. And Martin would still be living here safely in Turnbury

Buildings, instead of risking his life in Spain. If anything happened to him, she would never, ever be able to forgive herself.

But then she would never have had Tommy and Dolly, her beautiful children.

Perhaps that would have been for the best. She had hardly given them much of a life. She put her hands on her stomach. And as to how she was supposed to care for them in the future, she had not a single idea.

CHAPTER 59

Nell kneaded her fists into the small of her back and turned her head from side to side, easing the ache in her neck. Thank goodness it was the dinner break at last. When she'd dragged herself out of bed that morning, she'd barely been able to stand the thought of it being Monday again—two days since she'd received Martin's letter—and that there was another week's work stretching out ahead of her. But at least she could get out of the ironing room for a while.

*   *   *

Nell squeezed through the lunchtime throng standing up at the bar, making her way over to where Sylvia was pulling a row of pints.

'Hello lovely,' grinned Sylvia over the shoulder of a customer who was leaning on the counter, eagerly waiting for his mild and bitter.

'Hope you don't mind me coming in when

you're so busy, Sylv, but I had to get away from that place for half an hour.'

'Course I don't mind. You know you're always welcome in here. Just hang on a sec while I finish this and then I'll get Bernie to take over for a bit, so me and you can go up and have a chat.'

Bernie didn't look that impressed at having to give up studying the *Daily Mirror*'s sports pages to stand behind the bar when it was so busy, but, grudgingly, he did as his wife asked him, while she and Nell went to sit upstairs.

*   *   *

'There's something I wanted to ask you, Sylvia. I've paid back all the funeral money now, but I was wondering if you wouldn't mind me waiting a few more weeks till I start paying you back the five pounds you lent me, because I want to try and give the kids a decent Christmas for once.' Nell rubbed her nose with the back of her hand, avoiding looking at her friend as she lied. 'I've managed to put a few bob by to make sure they enjoy themselves, and I'll see if I can work a bit harder to earn some extra, and then I can start paying you back.'

Sylvia tutted impatiently. 'As if I want paying back. That was never meant to be a loan, Nell, it was for you and the kids, from me. And as for you, I think you're working hard enough as it is. Look at how tired and drawn you are. I know you've got to earn your living, but that laundry's flipping doing you in.'

Nell bit her bottom lip, trying but failing to hold back the tears.

307

'Sweetheart, whatever's wrong? Is it that bad?'

'Take no notice of me. Like you said, I'm tired, that's all.'

'You have got to give up that job.'

'How can I? If I'm not working, how would I pay the rent and feed the kids? It's hard enough as it is.'

'You'll just have to come back here and work with us then, won't you? You remember what a lark we used to have together.'

Nell lifted her head. 'And I remember what Bernie said—he doesn't want me working here.'

'Rubbish.' Now it was Sylvia who was lying. 'That was when things were slow, but you saw how busy we were downstairs. He'd be glad of having an extra pair of hands, the lazy old sod. You'd be able to earn more than enough for the three of you.' Sylvia winked. 'And you know me, when I set my mind to it I can wind that man round my little finger, just like a chubby bit of string.'

'But I could only do days, because of Tommy and Dolly, and—' Nell started sobbing uncontrollably. 'No, I can't do it, Sylv. I'd only go and let you down.'

Sylvia reached out and took her hand. 'You'd never let anyone down, darling.'

'Yes I would, I'd have to. See, there's not going to be just the three of us.'

'You sly mare, you've gone and got yourself a boyfriend, haven't you? But that's no reason to cry your eyes out. It's about bloody time you got yourself a feller.'

Nell screwed up her soggy handkerchief in her fist. 'I'm not crying about that. I'm crying cos I think I'm pregnant again.'

308

'Blimey, Nell,' said Sylvia, her surprise written all over her face. 'You're a quick worker. Just so long as he's not like that idiot, Flanagan. You need someone who'll look after you for a change.'

'I haven't got a boyfriend. It was George.'

'George? George who?' Sylvia's eyes widened. 'Please tell me you don't mean you're going with George Flanagan.'

Nell bowed her head. 'No, I'm not going with him. Course I'm not. He forced himself on me.'

Sylvia's lips twitched. 'He did what?'

'After the funeral.'

'That's it; you are not staying at that flat one day longer. He could come back any time and do whatever he likes to you.'

Sylvia stood up and gripped the side of the table. 'If the lunatic's capable of that, he could even bloody do you in—kill you and the kids—if there's no one there to look after you. And I won't take no for an answer on this one, Nell. Believe me. You, Tommy and Dolly are coming here to lodge with us—no arguments. Now, you wait there a minute, and I'll go and get you a fresh hankie.'

Sylvia dashed down the stairs, went behind the bar and poured two large brandies. Bernie opened his mouth to question her, but she was having none of it, she went straight back upstairs, fetched a handkerchief from her bedroom and took it through to Nell.

'I am not going to allow this to carry on. It's not right, none of it, it never has been since you first set eyes on that Stephen bloody Flanagan, the useless excuse for a so-called man. God forgive me, but I'm glad he's dead.' She took a long swallow from her glass, while pointing to Nell's stomach. 'Right, first job for us is to sort this little lot out. Now, let's think. Do you want me to come to the police with you?'

Nell almost laughed. 'I'm not going to the police. They'd never believe me. Not after they listened to all the gossip that was going around.'

'What gossip?'

'They thought I was carrying on with Martin Lovell, Mary's son from across the landing. They'd only say it was his.' She blew her nose noisily. 'And I feel so ashamed about what happened. I don't want anyone to know.'

'Bloody hell, what a mess.' Sylvia took another gulp from her glass. 'But don't you worry yourself, Nell. There is nothing for you to be ashamed of, and there is no chance that you are going to have that baby. None. And we won't be getting it done by some back-street quack down some dirty alley, either.'

Sylvia looked away and let out a long slow sigh. 'I did that once, went to some bastard who might as well have been a butcher the way he treated me.' She drained her glass. 'It's why I could never have a baby. I've been so lucky that Bern's been so understanding over the years.'

'I'm sorry, Sylv. I had no idea.'

Sylvia smiled sadly. 'That's all right, Nell. It's all in the past; it's you we've got to worry about now.' Her face lit up. 'Here, I know. One of the young doctors from over the road owes Bernie a few quid—a good few quid, as it happens. I'd guarantee he'll be more than glad of a chance to pay off his debts.'

'No, Sylvia, I couldn't, truly I couldn't.'

'Will you stop worrying about money just for

once, Nell?'

'It's not that. I couldn't do it to the baby.'

Sylvia rolled her eyes. 'Do you really want to have that animal's child? To carry it in your belly for another what, six, seven months?'

Nell shook her head.

'No, of course you don't.'

'But I still don't think I could do it.'

'Look, Nell, we'll see about that later, shall we? For now you just go over to the hospital, get your stuff and tell them you're leaving.'

'I can't, Sylv, I'd lose my day's pay, and it wouldn't be fair to the other girls—we help each other with folding the sheets and that. I should at least work out the afternoon.'

Sylvia picked up Nell's untouched drink, took a long swig and dabbed her lips with her hankie. 'Bloody hell, you are such a good girl, Nell. You always have been. And that's half your trouble. If you'd have been a bit tougher like me . . .'

'But I have got to work the day out.'

'OK, you don't want to lose your pay and let the others down. So tell them you'll finish today's shift, but that's it. You have got to leave there or it'll flipping do you in. Tell them your husband's come back from sea or something. Tell them you're off to be that bloody Wallis Simpson's brides-flipping-maid. Tell them anything. Then come back over here and I'll go with you to the Buildings and we'll get the kids and all your stuff.'

Nell laughed mirthlessly. 'All what stuff?'

'So I gather you've not got much then?'

'Not really.' Nell looked down into her lap. 'Just the things you've bought me over the years.'

'Now why doesn't that surprise me?'

'Do you really think Bernie would let me stay here, after what he said?'

'Believe me, I can guarantee he will. Like most blokes, he reckons that what goes on between a couple is their business, private. But that? That is the one thing that no man—well, not one worth a light—can stomach lowlifes like him doing to a woman.'

*   *   *

Satisfied that Sylvia had seen Nell well off the premises, Bernie beckoned to his wife to come back behind the bar.

'Enjoy your mothers' meeting, Sylv?' he asked, without realising how accurate he was being. 'Because I have been run off my sodding feet behind here.'

'Bernie, I need to talk to you.' Sylvia led him to the quieter, far end of the bar and stood on tiptoe so she could whisper into his ear.

'I don't know how to say this nicely, darling, so I'll just have to come straight out with it.' She took a deep breath. 'Now I don't want you going off your head, Bernie, but George Flanagan . . .' She paused, taking a deep breath. 'George Flanagan raped our little Nelly. On the day of his own father's funeral. And now she's pregnant by him.'

Bernie's face screwed up in disgust. 'No.'

'On my life.'

'The dirty stinking swivel-eyed bastard.'

'I know, it makes your guts churn, don't it?' Sylvia dropped down onto her heels and poured them each a brandy. 'Here, drink that. And do you know what the worst part of it is? She was like a

312

mother to them twins. It's disgusting, that's what it is. And that's why her and the kids are coming here to stay with us.'

This time even big, bumptious, opinionated Bernie had no objections. 'He did that to young Nell, a girl who'd lived with his own father? It beggars belief, the filthy bastard.'

Sylvia stared down into her glass. 'That thing and his sister can even have that poxy flat back if they want it—they deserve it, because you know what? That place must be bloody haunted with what's gone on in there.'

Bernie knocked back his brandy and poured himself another. 'I feel right bad about this, Sylv. I just wish I could have known. I'd have never left that girl there with him if I'd had any idea that this would happen.'

'Don't blame yourself, Bern. Who would have thought that anyone—even him—would have been capable of such a thing? And what makes me sick is he's just gonna get away with it. Nell won't even think about going to the law. She reckons they'd never believe her. The poor little mare says she feels ashamed.'

'Don't you worry, Sylv, he is not getting away with anything. And if that animal's got any brains, him and his sister had better start looking at other places to park their bastard stalls. Somewhere well away from me.'

CHAPTER 60

At the end of that day—her final one in the hated ironing room—Nell left her job feeling not exactly happy, but at least a bit better. As she had worked through the afternoon she'd been aware of the jealous glances of the other women who had heard her spinning what they all decided was a tale to the superintendent about why she was leaving so suddenly. But Nell could think of nothing but the chance Sylvia was giving her and her children, and also—in a very different way—about the other child that was growing inside her. Although horrified and revolted by the memory of what George had done to her, she still didn't think she could get rid of it. She of all people knew what it meant to feel unwanted, so how could she even consider doing that to an unborn child? At least she had been given the possibility of a life when she had been put in the home.

But now, as she and Sylvia sat squashed up against one another on the bench seat of the crowded bus, with its windows steamed up and the ice-cold wind blowing in across the platform, making the young conductor rub his hands and stamp his feet to keep warm, Nell knew that Sylvia wouldn't leave it at that. Unfortunately, that wasn't her way. But Nell couldn't be angry with her, she knew her friend only wanted what was best for her. Nell would just have to be patient when she nagged at her.

'Nell, I said: are you listening to me?'

'Sorry, I was miles away.'

'I said what do you think? Shall we go to the flat first or fetch the kids from the shop?'

At least she wasn't telling her again that she should go to see that young doctor. 'If it's all right with you, Sylv, I'd rather go to the flat first. Get it over with. The sooner I'm out of there the better, and it wouldn't mean dragging Tommy and Dolly up there for nothing.'

'Good idea,' Sylvia said, catching the bus conductor taking an admiring look at Nell's legs.

She shoved Nell. 'See the way he's looking at you? If you were fancy free and not—' she nodded at Nell's middle—'you know, you could start having a life again. I'm not being hard, Nell, but a young girl like you deserves someone nice to share her life with.'

'Please, Sylvia, don't let's wind up having words over this. I really appreciate what you're trying to do, but don't keep going on about it. I've made up my mind.'

Sylvia crossed her legs and folded her arms, making herself into a tight little bundle of defiance. 'We'll see.'

*   *   *

'Why have you three all been living in this one room? It was all right for the kids, but with the lot of you crowded in here, it's more like a bloody rabbit hutch.' Sylvia looked around the front room of 55 Turnbury Buildings. 'Why didn't you use the other bedrooms?'

Nell, who was on her knees, with her head and shoulders under the bed retrieving the handbag, was only glad that Sylvia couldn't see her bright red face. 'We stayed in here because it's the only room with its own lock on the door,' she mumbled. 'And the children like me to sing them little songs and tell them stories as they go to sleep.'

'Even so, Nell . . .'

'We don't stay in here all of the time. We sometimes go in the kitchen, and we use the wash house down in the basement.'

'For goodness' sake Nell, if I'd had any idea about how the three of you have been living . . . It's like being in prison. I'd never have let you stay here like this, no matter what Bernie had to say about it.'

If George had appeared at that moment, tiny as she was, Sylvia would have punched him on the nose—or worse. 'Them Flanagans, how could they have done this to you? And how can you even think of having that arsehole's baby?'

Nell shuffled backwards on her knees out from under the bed. She stood up and her head dropped forward. 'I've just realised I haven't got anything to put our things in,' she said, her eyes immediately brimming with tears as if those were the saddest words ever uttered.

'Don't upset yourself any more, Nell.' Sylvia gulped back her own tears and touched Nell on the shoulder. 'This'll all be just a bad memory before you know it. Now, is there anything special you want to take?'

'Only this.' The tears were now pouring down her cheeks as she held out the handbag that Sylvia had given to her. 'And Tommy's lead soldiers that you got him. Dolly took her toy rabbit with her to the shop.'

'Please don't cry, Nell.' Sylvia clambered over

the double bed to the narrow wardrobe that was jammed in the corner. The door could only be opened halfway before it hit the headboard.

'I don't suppose you'll be too worried about wearing this mourning gear any more, and most of Tommy and Dolly's stuff only looks fit for the ragman.'

'I've done my best for them.' Nell's voice was flat, defeated.

Sylvia shut the wardrobe and climbed back over the bed to her friend. 'Of course you have, sweetheart. No one could have done more. You are a beautiful, loving girl, and you've been a good mum to those kids. And don't you ever go thinking otherwise.'

Sylvia handed Nell a handkerchief.

'This is getting a habit,' sniffed Nell.

'I came prepared.' Sylvia swiped the back of her hand across her eyes. 'Now, let's get out of here, shall we? Pick up them soldiers of Tommy's and just leave.'

CHAPTER 61

Nell and Sylvia walked around the corner at the top of Wapping Lane. Sylvia was doing her best to cheer them up, chattering away about her plans for going shopping for clothes, decorating bedrooms and getting the children registered at the local school. Nell tried to listen to her, but she couldn't concentrate for fretting about what on earth she thought she was doing and about what was going to happen to her and the children. What would

Bernie say when she started showing and he realised that there were going to be four of them living in his pub? And one of them a screaming baby.

'What the hell?' Nell jerked her arm away from Sylvia's and started running towards Sarah's shop on the corner of the street.

Sylvia caught up with her and grabbed her by the arm. 'Wait a minute, Nell. This looks nasty.'

Nell tried to pull away, but despite the difference in their size, Sylvia had a firm hold on her.

'Let me go. Tommy and Dolly are in there.'

'I know, darling, but just hang on while we figure out what's going on here.'

They could see that the door to the shop was closed, something Sarah never allowed even in the coldest weather—it had to look welcoming to customers, she always said. And she would rather have the wood burner going at double the rate to keep the place warm than ever shut the door. But that wasn't all. Outside the shop was a gang of men and boys—some youngsters who looked to be barely in their teens, and others far older.

While two of the crowd painted crude slogans on the walls the rest of them sang a song to the jolly tune of the one about Daisy Bell and the bicycle made for two—but with far more sinister words.

'Blackshirts,' said Nell under her breath, pulling away from Sylvia with such force that they both stumbled forward.

'Come to join in, girls?' asked one of the men, who was painting a slogan about what he thought should happen to Sarah and David and all other

318

Jews along with them.

'I've come to collect my children.' Nell stood tall, determined to control her breathing, refusing to let them intimidate her.

The man's lip curled in disgust. 'You've left your kids with the likes of them?'

The rest of the mob stopped their singing.

'What sort of woman are you?' asked another.

'It's obvious. She's a Jew-lover,' shouted a third.

Nell pushed past them and tried to open the door. It was locked. She could see Sarah and Mary cowering inside behind the counter. Nell was beside herself. Where were her children?

She felt someone grab her arm. Thinking it was Sylvia, she slapped at the hand. But the grip only grew tighter. She looked down. It wasn't Sylvia holding onto her, it was a man.

'If you know what's good for you,' he snarled, 'you'll piss off out of here right now.'

As Nell struggled with the man, a stone whistled past them. They both turned to see it hit the glass panel in the door; the window didn't break, but if it had, anyone who wanted to could have reached through and unlocked the door.

One of the men struggled to hold onto a kicking, struggling Sylvia, who had failed to get past them to help her friend. The mob laughed like fools as Nell, using all her strength, shoved the man away from her and threw herself towards the door. She couldn't let them get inside the shop. She had to protect her children.

'Aw blimey, it's not that lot again.' It was Florrie Talbot, wobbling along the cobbled street on her high heels. Her hat was tipped rakishly over one eye, and the fox-fur tippet on the collar of her coat

319

was pulled up snugly around her neck. Despite the cold and the drizzle that was now coming down, she kicked off her shoes, shoved her sleeves up her arms and sprinted over to the man who was now holding the almost defeated Sylvia about a foot off the ground. Florrie smacked him hard around the head, sending him reeling, and wrenched Sylvia out of his grasp.

'Get over there across the street till you get your breath back,' she ordered, pushing a gasping Sylvia out of the way, and then barged past the men to join Nell by the door.

'Come on you bastards,' she hissed, her fists up and her chin stuck in the air, looking for all the world like an inappropriately dressed prizefighter.

Sylvia, her chest almost bursting from the efforts of her struggle, watched with her hand over her mouth as Nell and Florrie Talbot stood determinedly by the door. What chance did the two of them have of stopping all those men? Since the humiliation the Blackshirts had faced when they'd been driven away from their march through the East End, Mosley's thugs had picked on easier targets, and their retribution had become more and more vicious.

At first the men just stood there, staring at the two women. But then, without warning, the one whom Florrie had hit around the head let out a yell. 'Did you see what she did to me?'

He threw himself at Florrie and grabbed her. Nell tried to separate them, but one of the men who had been painting slogans threw down his pot of whitewash, splattering the pavement and splashing her coat, and joined in the scuffle. It was enough to distract Nell and Florrie for an all-important few seconds. Each man grasped the opportunity. One of them took hold of Nell and dragged her away from the door. The other was less successful, getting a straight jab to his chin— Florrie had dealt with tougher men than him.

'Don't let them get to the door,' Nell yelled to Florrie.

'Don't you worry,' hollered Florrie, her eyes blazing and her blood up.

Sylvia ran back across the street and did her best to drag the man off Nell, but she was no match for his strength.

He hauled Nell across the pavement, with her slipping and skidding through the whitewash, and Sylvia hanging onto his coat. As they came to the gutter, Nell tripped and fell down into the road.

'Jew-lover,' he spat at her, kicking her in the side.

'Get off her!' screamed Sylvia, but the man was caught up in the violence and struck Nell again, not even noticing her trying to pull him away.

'Do something someone, help her,' Sylvia appealed to the men, not believing they could let this happen.

No one stepped forward, but one of them, alarmed by the man's ferocity, shouted across to him, 'All right, that's enough, what the fuck d'you think you're doing?'

Nell tried to protect herself with her arms, but her assailant wasn't ready to stop. She clutched at her stomach, moaning to herself as a pool of blood began seeping out from under her, mingling with the whitewash.

'You fucking lunatic,' shouted another one of the mob. 'Look what you've gone and done.'

The man who had been kicking Nell backed away from her, turned and ran.

'Forget about that Jew-loving cow, you can see she's only putting it on,' shouted another one, turning his attention back to painting his filth on the walls. 'Do you want these bastards out of this area or what?'

'But she's bleeding,' said one of the younger ones, clearly terrified.

'Ain't your mother told you anything yet? All women fucking bleed, you idiot.'

Florrie hurried across to Sylvia, who was folding her coat to put under Nell's head. Florrie tore off her own coat as she ran, knelt down beside Nell and draped it over her.

'Don't worry about me,' gasped Nell. 'Don't let them get to the kids. Please.'

'I'm going for the police,' said Sylvia, staring down at the puddle of blood that was growing darker and thicker around Nell.

'No. Don't leave the children. Please. You've got to stop them getting inside.'

Sylvia and Florrie looked at each other and made a rush for the door, silently praying that the others weren't as vicious as the man who had attacked Nell.

CHAPTER 62

Inside the shop, Sarah Meckel and Mary Lovell were crouching behind the counter with the children tucked in below them.

Mary had seen one of the men dragging Nell

away, and now Florrie Talbot and someone who looked like Nell's friend Sylvia were back guarding the door. The men were shouting and gesturing at them, but at least they didn't look as if they were going to hurt them. Goodness only knew what had happened to Nell. Say she needed help? Mary didn't want to do this, but what choice did she have?

'Tommy,' she murmured without looking down at him, in case the jeering, singing mob realised what she was doing. 'I know you're scared, love, but do you think you could creep out the back on your hands and knees and then climb up over the wall and run and fetch Mr Lovell? Tell him what's happening, that there's nasty men, and that we need help?'

Mary knew that Joe had been to the Blackshirt meetings—she had had to live with the trouble it had caused between them all, and watched as it had eventually driven Martin away and caused a rift between her and Joe—but she could never believe he would tolerate anything like this. He was a good man at heart. And he loved her. She knew that too.

*　　　*　　　*

Tommy had never run so fast. Within minutes he was in the Lovells' kitchen, breathlessly explaining to Joe about the bad men who were frightening them all and that Sarah and Mrs Lovell wanted him to help them.

Pausing only to instruct Tommy to stay exactly where he was, Joe ran down the stairs to the courtyard, bashing on every door as he passed each

323

landing, yelling at the top of his voice that he needed help from every available man who could use his fists or wield a lump of wood.

*   *   *

Joe and a motley group of men in various states of dress despite the now pouring rain, and with an assortment of improvised weapons, rounded the corner to see the Blackshirt mob taunting Sylvia and Florrie Talbot. The women were pressing their backs against the door of the shop. There was what looked like a body covered with a fur-trimmed coat lying in the gutter.

One of the Blackshirts broke from his cat-calling to give Joe a friendly wave. 'All right there, Joe? Come to help us have you, mate? We'd be in there if it wasn't for these silly tarts. We don't want to hurt them, but if we have to, well they're asking for it.'

Joe walked up to him. 'Let me mark your card for you, moosh, that's my old woman in there. What was I ever thinking of, listening to you and your shit?' With that, he bent low and charged full pelt at the man, winding him as his shoulder made contact with the man's belly.

Joe straightened up and stared boldly about him. 'To think I thought you yellow cowsons were ordinary, respectable people. Now let's see how clever the rest of you are at fighting men instead of frightening the life out of women.'

It was as if a dam had been breached. The group from Turnbury Buildings surged forward, and despite the mob outnumbering Joe and his neighbours, they were no match for the infuriated

324

men. They might themselves have been quite capable of bad behaviour, but there were standards, lines that weren't crossed, and these strangers coming in and frightening their own was totally unacceptable.

The battle didn't last long—fists flew, heads were butted and curses exchanged—then the remaining members of the mob who hadn't been picked off with a few choice punches, and who didn't fancy getting on the wrong end of a length of two-by-four, followed the example of Nell's attacker and ran off into the night.

Joe rattled the door handle. 'Mary, it's me, Joe. Are you and Sarah all right in there?'

Sarah threw the door open and, without a word, she rushed over to where Florrie and Sylvia were crouching down by Nell, who was still lying in the gutter.

Mary hugged Joe and kissed him. 'Thank you, Joe. Thank you. I don't know what we'd have done without you.'

'And I don't know what I'd do without you, love. And I don't know what to say about all this.'

She kissed him again. 'You're a good, kind man, Joe Lovell. One of the best. Always have been.'

'Who got hurt?' he asked, looking over her shoulder to where Florrie, Sylvia and Sarah were kneeling on the now soaking ground.

Mary looked round. 'Nell!' She ran over to the women.

'Go into the shop,' she threw over her shoulder. 'Dolly's hiding under the counter.'

'Nell?'

'Get Dolly, Joe, I'll explain later.'

When Joe came back out onto the street, with

an ashen-faced Dolly wrapped in his jacket, all the men from the Buildings seemed to have forgotten their own cuts and bruises and were looking warily at the women.

'Anything I can do?' asked Joe, sheltering Dolly from the sight of her mother stretched out in a mixture of rain, blood and whitewash.

'Sarah, can you get some towels?' Sylvia said quietly. 'And Joe, get that little one away from here, eh?'

Sarah went back into the shop, and one of the men, not wanting to hang around a moment longer while all this women's stuff was going on, muttered about having to get back to his dinner. It was the signal for the rest of them to disperse.

'Where's Tommy's tin of lead soldiers?' Nell asked, her eyes flickering in and out of focus.

Florrie looked at Sylvia and Mary. Their hair was plastered down with rain, and their clothes were soaked through. Then she stroked Nell's cheek. 'I think you've got more to worry about than toy soldiers, my little love.' She hooked her arms under Nell's shoulders.

'Come on you two, we'll have to chance moving her inside the shop or she'll wind up with pneumonia on top of everything else.'

CHAPTER 63

It was the following afternoon and George was counting out a handful of silver from the day's takings onto the fake grass that covered the stall. 'Your turn today, Lil,' he said. 'Fish and chips for me. No, wait, I'll have savs, faggots and pease pudding.'

'Make up your bleed'n' mind will you,' said Lily, snatching up the change. 'This bloody rain's getting me down.'

'Saveloys,' he said, nodding to himself as he walked off in the direction of their new home above a tailor's shop in Brick Lane, leaving a fuming Lily to put away the stall.

*   *   *

George frowned. What was going on? The narrow side door that opened onto the stairs to his and Lily's set of rooms was unlocked. They never left the place without deadbolting the door; there were too many thieving foreigners around for George and Lily to do that. Maybe Lil was home already. He had stopped off for a pint instead of banking the takings. But she'd had to take the stall back to the store, before she went for the savs, and why would she leave the door unlocked anyway?

'Lil?' he called as he pushed open the inner door that opened directly onto the living room, holding the bag of takings behind his back.

'I don't think so.' It was an enormous man— even bigger than George—whom he had never seen before. 'I don't reckon I'm pretty enough for a name like that, do you? And you know all about pretty girls, don't you?'

George caught the glint of the brass knuckles the man was wearing as he smacked one fist into the palm of his other hand. Shit, they were going to rob him. Why hadn't he gone to the bank?

'Is that him?' called a voice from behind the

floral curtain that separated the living room from a narrow little kitchen.

'Fits the description.'

The curtain was pulled back by a huge tattooed hand, revealing a man who looked like the much bigger brother of the one with the knuckleduster.

'Do you know what I hate?' he said, poking a sausage-sized finger in George's now sweating face. 'A bloke who don't respect the ladies. A bloke who takes liberties with them, in fact. No real man likes that. That's just for cowards and pisspots.'

George tried a bit of bravado. 'Don't know what you're talking about, mate.'

'One, I am not your mate, and two, I do not like liars. You have not only been very unpleasant to a young lady, but the young lady concerned is now very poorly, and a friend of hers wants you to learn a lesson, young Georgie. And we are the men who are going to teach it to you. Now listen carefully, George Flanagan, you are never again going to go anywhere near a certain young lady without her specific permission. All right?'

'On my mother's life, I truthfully do not know what you mean.'

'Sorry George, but for your own sake I think you should admit that you do.' The man stared at him. 'Because you know exactly what you did to her, you slimy little bastard. Now keep still.'

The man slipped off his brass knuckles, slipped them in his pocket and then took hold of George by the lapels to stop him from moving—not that George was brave enough to have tried. The man then threw back his head and cracked George's nose open with a sharp smack from his forehead.

George touched his face and then looked at his

blood-covered hand. 'What the hell was that for?'

'Do you really need to ask?' sneered the man, looking to his companion for support.

'Ask what?' said Lily as she stepped into the room. She was carrying a greaseproof-wrapped parcel of saveloys, faggots and pease pudding.

'Lil, help me,' moaned George, as the blood streamed down his face.

'What's going on here?' she asked.

'Nothing to do with you,' said the bigger of the two, 'now piss off.'

The one who had split George's nose open wiped the back of his hand across his mouth, remembering what Bernie had told him about this whoreson and his sister. 'Right. This is what's going to happen. You,' he pointed at Lily, 'are going to clear off for a couple of hours. Then you are going to come back here and clear up any mess. And first thing tomorrow, you will find somewhere new to stay and somewhere to pitch your stalls, because you are not—I repeat, not—going to live or work anywhere near here. And if there is ever so much as a whisper that you,' he now jabbed his finger at George, 'have come even close to upsetting a lady—any lady, ever again—then I will kill you. Got it?'

'Why have I got to clear off?' asked Lily.

'Don't act as stupid as him, love,' said the man, shoving George so hard in the chest that he staggered backwards across the room until the wall stopped him.

'Now clear off, you silly tart.'

'But—'

'Don't let me lose my temper with you and all,' said the man. 'Now do as you're told and get out.'

He snatched the parcel from her and threw it at George who was still cowering against the wall, covering him with food.

CHAPTER 64

'Think you can you manage a little drop of this soup for me, Nell?' Sylvia put the tray on the bedside cabinet in what was now Nell's new bedroom, upstairs in the Hope and Anchor. 'Before the doctor pops back to check on you.'

'Pops back? He's already been here then? When? What time is it?'

'It's Tuesday afternoon. Four o'clock. You've been out like a light since yesterday. Your body must have needed the rest.'

'Where are Tommy and Dolly?'

'They're fine. Now shall I help you sit up so you can have your soup?'

'I'm not hungry.'

'Try a few spoonfuls for me, eh? It's right tasty. Ham and pea. And there's some lovely crusty bread from the baker's next door. You know how you love their stuff. Look at it, it's all fluffy inside and spread with nice thick butter.'

'I want to see Tommy and Dolly.'

'Don't worry about them. They're in the kitchen busy gluing and drawing, making little Christmas cards and that. They know you're not feeling well.'

'They've been through too much, Sylv. It's so unfair. They're so young, and the things they've had to put up with.'

'And that's a good reason to have some of this

soup; it'll get your strength up so the little ones won't be scared when they see you all weak and pale.'

'I've lost the baby, haven't I?'

Sylvia sat on the edge of the bed and smoothed the fold of the already perfectly straight sheet down over the eiderdown. 'I'm sorry, darling, but maybe it's for the best, eh?'

'But I didn't want it to happen. I really didn't. I wanted to have it.'

'I know you did, sweetheart.'

'I would have loved it and cared for it and protected it and have been a proper mum to it, no matter what.'

'Please, don't do this to yourself, Nell.'

A single tear ran down Nell's cheek, and she closed her eyes. 'I'm ever so sorry for all this trouble I'm causing you, Sylv.'

'Don't you dare even think about saying you're sorry. After everything you've been through it's everyone else who should be sorry—sorry for letting it all happen to you. I know I can hardly forgive myself for not stepping in sooner. But I promise you, you're going to be all right from now on, Nell. You, Tommy and Dolly, the three of you, you're all going to be safe here with me and Bernie. We're not going to let anything bad happen to you ever again.' Sylvia touched her lips to Nell's forehead. 'You've got my word on that.'

'I wish I could believe you, but everything just keeps going wrong. Everything.' Nell's eyes suddenly flicked wide open. 'Sylvia, that handbag you gave me? Where is it?'

'Ssshh, Nell, don't go getting yourself excited over a rotten old second-hand bag. It got a bit knocked about yesterday, but at least I know what to get you for Christmas.'

'But it's got things in it.' Nell's voice was urgent as she struggled to sit up. 'Important things. What happened to it? Where's it gone?'

'Calm down, darling, or you'll make yourself ill. Look, it's in here.' Sylvia opened the bedside cabinet and took out the now battered, scuffed and water-stained bag. 'See?'

Nell clutched it to her. 'Thank you. I thought I'd lost it.'

'Florrie saw it lying in the road. She picked it up and gave it to me when she helped me bring you back here in the cab last night.'

'I don't remember any of that.' Nell closed her eyes again.

'No. You weren't feeling very good.' Sylvia didn't understand what could be so important to Nell about the bag's contents, but there was obviously something in there that mattered to her. Or maybe she was still in shock after what had happened. It amazed Sylvia just how much one person could take in her life. But even Nell would probably have given up years ago if it hadn't been for the little ones.

'Thank you, Sylv. Thank you so much. And I'll have to thank Florrie as well.'

'You don't have to keep thanking everyone, sweetheart.' Sylvia gently stroked the hair away from Nell's face. 'But I would like it if you'd do something for me.'

'Anything.'

'Have just a little drop of this soup, eh?'

CHAPTER 65

It was Christmas Eve, and Nell and the children were climbing the familiar stairway to the top floor of Turnbury Buildings, Nell moving slowly, still feeling fragile.

'We haven't got to see the twins have we, Mum?'

'No, Tommy, I was talking to Uncle Bernie before we came out and, guess what? He told me that they've moved away, so don't you go fretting. You're never going to have to see them again.' What Nell didn't say was that Bernie had also told her that something had happened to drive them away, but that it would be best if she didn't ask what.

'Good,' said Tommy firmly. 'Cos I hate them twins.'

'Mummy said we've got to be kind,' said Dolly.

'I can't help it, I still hate them,' said Tommy.

'That's because you're naughty.'

'Will we have to come back here to live then, Mum?'

'The flat's not ours, Tom.'

Dolly's little face darkened. 'That's good, because they could come back in the night and get us if we had to live here.'

'Come on, you two, don't start saying nasty things. We're meant to be happy, because we're bringing the presents you made for Mr and Mrs Lovell.'

'Will they like them?'

'Course they will, Dolly. You both worked really hard on them, and everyone always needs pot holders.' She bent down and gave her daughter a hug. 'And you know how often Mr Lovell puts that kettle of theirs on and off the stove. He must wear them out in no time.'

'Will you look at what the cat dragged in.' It was Ada, hanging about the top landing like the Ghost of Christmas Yet to Come. 'What are you doing here then?'

Nell smiled pleasantly. 'Hello Ada, we've come to see our friends. How are you?'

'Friends my eye.' Ada almost vomited the words.

'My dad used to say you could haunt houses for a living,' said Tommy.

Ada's eyes narrowed. 'Did he now?'

It took a moment for Nell to trust herself to speak without laughing. 'Tommy, Dolly, come along, let's take these in to Mr and Mrs Lovell.'

As Nell rapped on Mary and Joe's door, Ada stepped forward until she was standing up close behind her.

'I know what happened to Stephen Flanagan,' she taunted.

Horrified, Nell twisted around to face her. She knew that Ada had her nose in everything and everywhere, but however did she find out? Nobody knew what had happened but her and Martin.

The door to number 57 opened and Mary stood there, beaming happily and leaning forward with her arms held wide to welcome the children. 'What a lovely surprise.'

'Hello, Mary,' said Nell. 'Good to see you. Would you do me a favour and take the children inside for me? I need to have a quick word with Ada.'

Mary looked at Ada suspiciously and then back

at Nell. What was going on here? 'Will you be all right, love?'

'I'll be fine. Go on you two, you go with Mrs Lovell, I won't be long.'

Nell waited until Mary had closed the door—this definitely wasn't a conversation for Martin's mother's ears.

'You were saying, Ada?'

'You've got bold.'

'If you've got nothing to say . . .' Nell turned away from her, wanting to hear more, but scared to be told the truth about what this woman knew.

Not willing to lose her audience, Ada quickly piped up. 'Stephen must have thought that the law were onto him at last after all these years.'

That definitely wasn't what Nell had been expecting to hear.

'It'll have been all the boozing he done that would've led to it. Made him lose his marbles at last. The amount he swallowed in his time was enough to have driven a full-sized horse round the bend, let alone a man. But he was wrong; the law didn't have a single idea what he'd done.'

Nell turned back to face her. 'No idea he'd done what? What are you talking about?'

'Flanagan's wife, of course. From when we all lived down in the old terrace, before they pulled it down and moved us all up here.'

'Ada, I don't know about the law, but not for the first time since I've known you, it's me who has no idea what you're talking about.'

Ada sneered nastily, showing her wonky, stained teeth. 'Surely you don't think Violet just run off, do you? She was too scared of him to do that, although she talked about it often enough, when

335

you'd see her down the market with yet another black eye.'

Nell blinked slowly. Where was this going? 'So what did happen to her?'

'He done her in, didn't he?'

'Are you saying Stephen killed his wife?'

'Well, that's what a lot of people round here reckoned at the time. And he must have thought that someone . . .' She paused, considering her words, stretching out Nell's agony. 'That someone had gone to the law, cos they couldn't stomach keeping it to themselves no longer. And that'll be why he topped himself—rather than being caught and being hung. That man always was a coward as well as a bully. My Albert says he even saw him lifting Violet's body onto a cart. Before it was proper daylight, it was. He had one of his gippy bellies again, see. Too many dumplings the night before. He's a greedy pig of a man, my Albert; always has been.'

'Ada, you were saying about Stephen.'

'That's right. The man used to beat that woman regular. Like a gong. You of all people should know what he was like.'

'But if Albert saw that, why didn't you do something?'

'Well . . . my Albert's not got the best of eyesight.' Ada folded her arms. 'Anyway, what goes on in someone's home is their business. And me of all people, well, I'd never interfere in what goes on between a man and his wife.'

She took her handkerchief out of her apron pocket and gave her nose a good blow, then inspected the results, making Nell shudder.

She shoved it back in her pocket. 'Mary Lovell,

336

now she was a bit different about it, because she *is* an interfering cow. Reckoned we should go to the law there and then if what Albert thought he saw was true. At the time it was all you'd hear out of her mouth. Was Albert sure? Did he really see him do it? Her Joe, cheeky sod, stopped her because he reckoned my Albert was exaggerating, that he'd not seen anything of the sort. But then when Violet never came back, other people started saying that they'd seen him tip her in the Thames. Not that I ever believed any of them did, mind. You know what people are like, they just wanna be part of the poppy show. And then we were all moved up here, a lot of the men lost their jobs and Violet got forgotten.' She looked Nell up and down. 'It was then that Stephen Flanagan started moving all his fancy pieces in. Mind you, none of them lasted as long as you. None of them were silly enough.'

Nell stood there, not knowing whether to laugh or cry. Had Stephen Flanagan actually been a murderer? She had lived under the same roof as him with her children. If it was true, then he could have killed all three of them. Or was he simply a violent brute who terrified his wife so badly that she ran off and abandoned her own children? The thought made Nell want to weep.

Ada snapped her fingers in Nell's face. 'Oi! Are you listening to me?'

'I'm sorry, Ada, go on, of course I am.'

'So long as you are. Well, when the police kept coming round—after they'd dragged him out of the water—they realised from talking to me that I was the only one who could really help them.' The little barrel of a woman puffed up proudly. 'Only one with my eyes open, see.'

'You must have been a real help to them,' said Nell, nodding encouragingly, willing her to get on with it.

'It was all right at first, but in the end they got me down. To tell you the truth, they got on me nerves, them and all their questions. It was all who did what, and when and who did they do it with.'

Ada tutted loudly. 'Bleed'n' nuisances, they got. Like I had nothing better to do with my time. So I decided to get rid of them. I told them how he'd always been on the bottle, and that he'd probably just fallen in the river when he was pissed. I didn't mention nothing about Violet cos that would have started them off all over again. They seemed a bit disappointed that it was probably an accident after all. Still, now the case is closed they won't be bothering me no more.'

'The case is closed?'

'Yeah, they told me when they came round looking for the twins.' Ada's lips twisted into a nasty sneer, and again she looked Nell slowly up and down. 'Wanted to trace his next of kin see, cos that's who they tell about things like that. Not some bird he'd been living with over the brush.'

CHAPTER 66

'I think the tree looks so pretty, Auntie Sylvia.' Dolly, wearing a miniature nurse's uniform, was sitting on the floor by Sylvia's chair. She was carefully buttoning the little knitted matinee jacket on the baby doll that Father Christmas had left in the pillowcase she had hung on the end of her bed the night before. 'The candles are best. They're lovely.'

'I like the chocolate umbrellas best,' said Tommy, eyeing the tree from where he was sitting at the table, finishing a second bowl of trifle. He straightened the paper hat that he had balanced on top of his cowboy hat. 'And the chocolate money. And the sugar mice, they're good. Can I have some more of them, Mum?'

'After all that chicken and stuffing and Christmas pudding? And now the trifle? You'll go off bang like one of Uncle Bernie's crackers.'

'Them crackers were good and all,' he said, licking his spoon so as not to miss a single morsel.

'Tell you what, Tom,' said Sylvia, 'if you help me and your mum clear the table later on, I'll see what sweets are left on the tree and you and Dolly can share them out, how about that?'

'Thanks!'

There was a snorting snore from the armchair in the corner, where Bernie was sitting slumped, stuffed full of Christmas dinner.

'Auntie Sylvia, will Uncle Bernie play snakes and ladders with me again when he wakes up?' It hadn't taken long for Tommy to figure out that Sylvia was a soft touch. 'I won tuppence off him last time, and I bet I can beat him again.'

'Maybe when he's had a little rest, eh.' Sylvia reached across the table and topped up Nell's sherry glass.

'You'll have me singing,' said Nell. 'But go on then, it is a special occasion.'

Sylvia poured herself another glassful. 'This is what life's all about, eh Nell?'

'We are so blessed being here with you.' Nell

raised her glass, thinking about where Martin might be, praying silently that he was safe. 'Thank you so much for everything, Sylv. And here's to you.'

'I'm the one who's blessed. Now I've got my little family around me, it's me who should be thanking you. When that grumpy old sod woke up this morning, even he said he couldn't remember looking forward to Christmas Day so much in years.'

Sylvia pushed back her chair, and stood up. 'Do you reckon it's time for us to take Tommy downstairs to the bar for him to see his Christmas present?'

Nell grinned at her. 'Why not?'

Tommy's eyes widened. 'But I got my games compendium, and my pop gun and my cowboy outfit.' He held out his arms, showing off his fringed waistcoat.

'There was this other thing that I couldn't fit in the pillowcase,' said Nell, holding out her hand to him.

'Gonna come down with us, Dolly?' he said. 'It must be really big. Is it, Mum? Is it ever so big?'

'You wait and see.'

*   *   *

Sylvia held Dolly's hand while Nell led Tommy over to a basket in the corner of the bar.

Tommy looked into it and his mouth fell open. Inside, curled in a sleeping ball, was a pot-bellied little brown and white Jack Russell puppy.

'Whose is this?'

'He's yours, Tommy. All yours. Now what are

you going to call him?'

'Bradman,' he said without a moment's hesitation. 'After that cricket bloke that Martin Lovell told me about.'

CHAPTER 67

Sitting on the stairs that led up to their new home above the Hope and Anchor, Tommy and Dolly were sipping lemonade through straws and nibbling on the dainty little quarter sandwiches from the plate that Nell had just put down between them. Bradman the puppy was asleep in his basket by the bottom step.

Tommy brushed the crumbs off his jumper. 'Can we really stay up until midnight, Mum, like Auntie Sylvia said we could?'

'Midnight?'

'Yeah, she said we could because it's New Year's Eve, and that's what you do. And then it's next year.'

'Much as I love your Auntie Sylvia, I do wish she'd ask me before she goes making promises to you two.'

Tommy's mouth turned down. 'She was only being kind like you're always telling us to be.'

'I know, and she is kind. Very kind. I'll tell you what, we'll see shall we? If you two are good and go up after you've finished eating, have a wash and get yourselves into your pyjamas and put on your dressing gowns and slippers, you can come back down and sit on the stairs and listen to the music. Then if you get too tired I can carry you up. How about that?'

'Yeah, but I bet we won't get tired, will we Dolly?'

Dolly, looking as if she was already fit for bed, shook her head solemnly. 'No, because I want to do singing with Auntie Sylvia, when the year changes. She's taught me the words to a special song and showed me how to cross your arms with the next person, and you all stand in a circle. It's good.'

'Like I said, we'll see. Now I'm going back to help Auntie Sylvia and Uncle Bernie with all the customers out there.' Nell kissed her children on the top of their heads. 'I'll prop the door open wide so you can see what's going on. And make sure the puppy doesn't go running in the bar if he wakes up.'

Nell stood up, smoothed down the new red dress that Sylvia had given her for Christmas, and patted the N-shaped brooch that she had pinned to her chest.

*   *   *

Weaving expertly through the customers as they sang and danced with the abandon of those whose only wish was for a better and brighter new year, and who wanted to forget, just for one night, the stories about what was happening abroad, Nell carried a half of stout and a pint of bitter over to Mary and Joe. They had just come into the pub and were standing by the fire brushing the snow from their shoulders.

'Evening, you two.' Nell put the drinks down in the hearth, picked up the poker, heated it in the fire and then plunged it into Mary's stout, making the chocolate-brown liquid bubble and fizz.

'No Sarah with you?' she asked, handing Mary her glass.

Mary took a sip of the warming drink. 'No. You know what she's like. She wouldn't come out because she's looking after her David. Joe tried to persuade her though, didn't you Joe?'

'I did, but she said it wasn't like it was the Jewish new year or anything, and she's got Florrie Talbot keeping her company.'

Mary leaned closer to Joe and Nell. 'No she's not,' she said, fiddling with her beads. 'Sarah said Florrie should—you know, go out later.' She lowered her voice. '*To work*, cos tonight of all nights it'll be her harvest, won't it?'

'Sarah's right there,' said Joe, very matter-of-fact. 'It'll be a busy time for Florrie, what with all the drinking and celebrating and that. Especially down by the docks with all them jolly sailors that'll be disembarking tonight with their pockets full of money, all looking for a bit of company.'

'Joe Lovell!' Mary squeaked.

'I'm only speaking the truth, and I tell you what, I won't hear a word against either of them girls— Sarah or Florrie—not with how good they've been to people. Florrie especially. She was right brave how she stood up to them thugs outside the shop.'

Mary smiled proudly at her husband.

'Tommy and Dolly are sitting on the stairs if you want to pop through to say hello to them later,' said Nell, beginning to squeeze her way back towards the bar. 'And those drinks are on Sylvie.'

'We want to pay our way,' said Joe, suddenly very serious.

343

'First round's on her, Joe, and you know Sylvia, she won't take no for an answer.'

*   *   *

As Nell slipped behind the counter alongside Bernie and Sylvia, she looked over at Joe. If only there was something that she could do to help him. He and Mary had been such good friends to her for so many years, it only seemed right that their luck should start changing as hers had done.

*   *   *

The customers were now three and four deep at the bar, ordering drinks and helping themselves from the plates of sandwiches and cold, salty roast potatoes that Sylvia had set out for them.

'Bugger,' hissed Bernie, his face red from the exertion of serving so many people. 'This mild barrel wants changing already.'

'It is New Year's Eve, Bernie darling,' said Sylvia, nudging Nell and rolling her eyes. 'What do you want them to be drinking—cups of bloody tea? And think of all that lovely money going through the till.'

Bernie picked up a bar cloth and rubbed it over his sweaty brow and neck. 'D'you know, I think I'm getting too old for this game, Sylv.'

'Don't be daft, you silly old sod, you just need to lose a couple or three stone, and you'll be hopping around like a spring chicken.'

'How do you reckon I'm going to manage that then? And how about in the meantime?'

'Well, for a start, you'd better get a move on,

344

there's people whose bellies'll start thinking their throats have been cut if they don't get a drink down 'em soon.'

'Can I suggest something?' asked Nell, handing another tray of brown and light ales, port and lemons and stouts across the counter.

'What, how to get a figure like yours? Don't think it'd suit me, girl.'

'Not quite,' laughed Nell, hoping above hope that this was going to work. 'Wait there, I won't be two minutes.'

She was back quicker than that, with Joe following closely behind.

'Nelly here said you needed a hand with something, Bern. What can I do for you?'

'Joe, you can save me from passing out, mate, that's what you can do.'

*   *   *

As Bernie tightened the fixings on the pipes that led from the barrels up to the bar above them, he chatted away to Joe. 'Like I said, thanks for that, changing these things don't get any easier.' He stood up straight, groaning from the strain. 'And my bones don't get any younger.'

'No trouble at all, Bern, my pleasure.'

'You ever thought about doing a bit of cellar or bar work, Joe?'

Joe shook his head. 'Can't say I have, but I'd be more than happy to give it a go if there was ever any going.'

'Well, how about giving me a hand again sometime?'

'So long as you show me the ropes, Bern, I'll

345

turn my hand to anything you want doing around the place. Always glad to help someone out.'

Bernie shook him by the hand. 'Good man, Joe. I just don't seem to find the time for everything that wants doing round here. I've got other business interests, see.'

'Have you?' said Joe non-committally, knowing full well what sort of business interests he meant.

Bernie patted his belly. 'And I'm hardly up to the heavy work like changing barrels these days. Then there's the deliveries and the bottling up of a morning, and Sylvie's started going on about how the flat upstairs needs a coat of paint now that Nell and the kids are living here with us. And there's always something around the place that wants fixing or mending. But you seem a handy sort of a chap. Work like that would be ideal for you.'

Joe laughed. 'You're right there, Bernie, I've even got my own tools.'

'Well, the job's here, when can you start then?'

'What, you mean it'd be like a proper job? Not just helping you out now and again?'

'If you're interested, you can start tomorrow, mate.'

Joe could hardly believe his luck: he was so used to disappointment, and now this had been put in his lap, right out of the blue. 'Why me?'

'Look, Joe, when there's money around the place, you have to be able to trust someone. I've heard what good friends you and your missus have been to our young Nelly, so that's why you, because you must be a good 'un to have done that. So if you want the job, it's yours, mate.'

*　　*　　*

Joe emerged from the cellar grinning like a lovesick schoolboy after a first date.

Mary was still standing by the fire.

'Mary, excuse my language, but I've got some bloody good news to start the new year, love.'

'And so have I, Joe.'

The man standing next to her turned round to face him.

'Hello, Dad, I had to get back to say happy new year to you and Mum, didn't I?'

'*Martin?*' Joe felt his eyes begin to prickle.

'Yeah, it's me, Dad.'

'But how did you know we'd be here?'

'I didn't. So I looked everywhere for you. Must have gone in and out of every pub in Wapping. Then as a last resort I went round to see Sarah. Lucky I did, eh? It was her who told me you'd come here.'

'Son, I can't tell you how pleased I am to see you.'

'Me too, Dad. And like I said to Mum, I've been thinking a lot while I've been away, and what with everything that's going on over in Europe, I just wanted to be at home with my family. After what I've seen, I've realised what's important in life, and who's important to me. The world's a dangerous place and it's getting worse, and we've got to value what we've got. Treasure it. Even fight for it if necessary.'

Joe swallowed hard as he took his son by the shoulders. 'I've come to realise that too, boy. I've had my eyes opened to what's what, and I can't say I'm proud of some of the things I thought and said in the past. But I've come to my senses now.'

'We've all said a lot of things, Dad.' Now Martin's eyes had misted over with tears, and he took his father in his arms and hugged him. 'Let's forget all that, eh?'

'Yeah, let's do that.'

Joe held his son at arm's length and looked at him.

'Some of the things that were said in the past weren't so bad,' sniffed Mary. 'Remember, Joe, how Martin always used to say: *I'll take you to the seaside one day, Mum?*'

Joe shook his head, remembering. 'It was all we heard out of you when you were little, son.'

'Well, I reckon it's about time I kept that promise then, don't you? So as soon as the weather looks up let's go down the coast.'

Joe took out his cigarettes, and made a fuss of fumbling with his matches, avoiding looking at his son or his wife. 'Maybe we could all go.' He spoke quietly, almost shyly.

'I'd like that a lot, Dad, because we should make the most of every opportunity, never take anything for granted. Who knows how much time we've got together, eh?' Martin scratched the side of his neck. 'I was thinking it'd be nice if Nell and the kids came with us and all. Be a good day out for all of us.'

'You'll have to ask her then, won't you?'

Martin nodded. 'I will, Mum. Shame she's not here or I'd have asked her right now.'

'But she is here.' Mary looked over at Nell, who was busily serving behind the bar, completely unaware that Martin had come home and that he was standing there in the Hope, just yards away from her.

'Look.' Mary nodded towards her. 'So you can. You can go over and ask her right this very minute.'

Martin put his hand in his jacket pocket, his finger outlining the familiar shapes of the embroidered edge of the handkerchief that Nell had given to him, and made his way over to speak to her.